*"This novel is one of the warmest and most understanding of all those dealing with the Indian.*

"The sacred articles and lore, the deep conviction of the Indian's closeness to the country, the rigid effort of the military to carry out rigid and hampering orders, all of these seem freshly realized. There is a fine naturalness about the novel which keeps it free of the usual stereotypes of the Western story.

"For a while the reader is immersed in that wild, sad life. And for a while after he has finished the book, its doom-touched glow is on him."
—Paul Engle, *Chicago Tribune*

"Moving...absorbing...compassionate."
—*New York Herald Tribune*

*Dance Back the Buffalo* was originally published by Houghton Mifflin Company

# Dance
# Back the
# Buffalo

by Milton Lott

PUBLISHED BY POCKET BOOKS NEW YORK

**DANCE BACK THE BUFFALO**

Houghton Mifflin edition published October, 1959
A *Pocket Book* edition
1st printing ............................... January, 1968

This *Pocket Book* edition includes every word
contained in the original, higher-priced edition. It is printed
from brand-new plates made from completely reset, clear, easy-to-read
type. *Pocket Book* editions are published by Pocket Books, a division
of Simon & Schuster, Inc., 630 Fifth Avenue, New York, N.Y. 10020.
Trademarks registered in the United States and other countries.

# ACKNOWLEDGMENTS

I would like to thank the authors and publishers of the following works for permission to make use of brief quotations:

*Wovoka, the Indian Messiah* by Paul Bailey. Westernlore Publishers, Los Angeles.

*Patterns of Culture* by Ruth Benedict. Houghton Mifflin Company, Boston.

*When the Tree Flowered* by John G. Neihardt. The Macmillan Company, New York.

*Indian Cavalcade* by Clark Wissler. Sheridan House, New York.

TO VIVIAN

# CONTENTS

## Book I

## AUGUST
## 1889

### I

FIRST IT WAS a circle of light below him, as small and far away as a star but growing as he came nearer, as he fell toward it in darkness, turning like a wheel without spokes, nearer and faster and with yet more light. There was a rushing in his ears as of prairie wind or fire and in his eyes a vivid sense of distance. Even in darkness he saw the far blue-black roll and sweep of the earth and the rivers curving and shining under a night sky.

Then he was at the center of the ring and the light was still; it faded slowly, changing to shadowy figures that moved outward into darkness, breaking the circle, and he could not tell if they were animals or men. He tried to cry out to them but he was dumb. The figures were gone and he was alone in darkness and silence, held rigid, immovable.

And Turning Hawk awakened, struggling up in the chair, sweeping outward with his hand, pushing aside thick blankets of darkness. There was a movement at his side and he came fully awake. The noises of the train broke against his ears like a wave from great waters. He dropped his hand and leaned back, shaking in all his body.

Little Wound was pressing against him under the robe,

his wide, sightless eyes fixed toward the front, his nostrils flared and searching.

Across the aisle the white man with the fine cloth coat and stiff white collar was standing to stretch; a blue-coated soldier walked cautiously along the aisle, staring down at the boy as he passed.

Turning Hawk caught the small tense shoulder of his grandson and pressed gently. The muscles relaxed and Little Wound leaned back, releasing his breath.

It was breaking dawn. In the half-light Turning Hawk saw the grey landscape rushing by at fearful speed. He jerked his head for a better look and saw with relief that the train was running beside a bluff. Great rocks at the bottom flashed by seeming almost to strike the windows, causing him to flinch in spite of the tension in which he held himself.

As he watched, the light increased and he saw again the grey-brown hills stretching into blue distances that were still and changeless. When he looked ahead, it seemed that the land rushed up and toward him, flashed by, dropping down and away; and as his eyes moved out, turned slowly like a shield revolving.

All night he had watched the familiar stars shifting in the sky with the imperceptible bendings of the iron road; under the night glow had seen tall, long-remembered hills slide past and down in the east. He knew where he was, and watching could almost forget the strange noises and uncertain swaying of the train that carried him tirelessly and headlong into the night. In darkness not much spoke of change. He could imagine the hills black with buffalo, moving slow and ponderous, with the solidity and weight of sliding earth, or antelope, as light and gliding as the shadow of a summer cloud.

He could imagine this and feel a welling, a springing in his blood. He felt his hands moving in the sign for death; the noise assailed his ears, and with the sinking of his heart came a vivid image of iron rails glistening into distance, straight, spear-like, knife-like. He was an old man now. He was tired in the very bones; his power was gone. He looked forward even to the little island of the reservation, where he might rest after a time.

The trip was almost done. White doctors had no medicine for Little Wound. There was no more hope. His road would

2

be dark and soundless, with only memories of the green hills of summer, the shining snows of winter, and all the voices of earth to strengthen him on his way.

Turning Hawk became aware that the white man across the aisle was watching him curiously, and he restrained the movement of his hands, drawing them under the robe. Little Wound also drew back and Turning Hawk knew that the boy had been following his thinking signs. He tried to shake off his troubled thoughts, turning again to watch the land whirl steadily by.

It was autumn. The year had been dry and harsh. The grass, burned dry in early summer, now scarcely colored the land. When strong winds traveled the hills, the sky swirled grey with dust, and on warm, quiet days the whirlwinds rose up tall in shapes of dust dancing and twisting against the sky.

He was restless. The restraint of his hands under the white man's eyes galled him. When he forgot himself they moved unconsciously with his thoughts in signs, and Little Wound's delicate hands caught every movement, hovering light as butterflies. He clasped his hands to keep them still; the small ones followed, scarcely touching, then withdrew.

His thoughts came back to the dream that had awakened him, troubling him with their insistence. He did not want to think of the dream until he could be alone and properly strengthened. It was Wakan, he knew; of mystery and yet of meaning. But he did not trust himself to understand it yet.

☙ 2 ❧

Across the aisle the old Indian was again staring out of the window, sitting bolt upright as he had sat all the way from Chicago—almost a day and a night—except for brief intervals of caring for the boy or talking with him in signs.

Westland Roberts opened his portfolio and took out a notebook, glancing around surreptitiously before opening it. On the outside he had printed in large letters: Notes on the

Ghost Dance or Messianic Craze. This he had crossed out and writtten underneath: Two Indians.

Inside he had begun a systematic catalogue: Tribe—Lakota; Lingual stock—Siouan; Culture—stone age, nomadic hunters modified by white influence. He began a summary of what he knew about the tribe, then gave it up and with irritation crossed out all he had written. Somehow it did not apply.

He turned again to regard the two, fascinated. He sensed that the old Indian resented his curiosity, and felt ashamed; but he could not help looking and speculating. The boy might have stepped out of a museum showcase, so perfectly native were his dress and appearance. His shirt, leggings, and moccasins were of whitened buckskin, quilled—not beaded—in circular designs of red and yellow. His hair was parted in the middle and carefully braided, the ends of the braids decorated with white fur, the part traced with red. His face was symmetrically decorated with light, curved strokes of red paint, smeared a little now from a night of dozing.

He was a strong, square-shouldered boy of maybe six years with clear, sensitive features, mobile and expressive in spite of the slightly bulging, sightless eyes. His hands, seeming always in motion, were delicately shaped and unbelievably quick and supple.

It was hard to guess the age of the old man—perhaps sixty, perhaps eighty. About him was a timeless, enduring quality as of statuary or old, long-used leather. His face was bony, high-bridged, intricately wrinkled; nose thin and straight, eyes deep-set and almost black. His expression was unchanging, neither harsh nor pleasant. Westland could read nothing in the face, and yet he perceived—without knowing how—a fierce bitterness and pride.

The old Indian wore a black, high-crowned hat with a stiff brim—the only part of his clothing that was new— black coat, and trousers that fit loosely and shapelessly, shining with grease on the knees and legs. His moccasins were old and undecorated, molded roughly to the bones of his feet. His hair in two long strands, one wrapped with cloth, the other with fur, hung down in front. His robe was old and worn and probably, Westland thought, lousy.

As he watched, the old man turned suddenly from the window and extended his hands to the boy. Pausing till the boy touched him, he made a quick series of signs. He seemed

4

to restrict his movements for the small hands to follow; yet the gestures were sweeping, each curving into the next with few angular or abrupt motions. When he finished, he turned again to the window, not waiting for a reply. The boy sat up straighter in the seat, his face turned expectantly toward the front.

Westland put away his notebook and stood up to reach for his coat before he realized that he had understood the old man's meaning—that the station was near. He was amazed. He tried to remember the signs and their sequence but he could not, though his hands moved awkwardly forming a sign or two. He found himself remembering similar deaf-mute signs he had known as a child. An uncle had been deaf; but it was long ago and almost forgotten.

He was strangely affected by this discovery; not elated as he should have been at finding a means of communication, but vaguely irritated and somehow involved. The feeling persisted in him, even after the train had stopped and he carried his luggage into the station at Valentine.

The stage for the Rosebud Agency would be ready soon, the agent assured him. There would be a smaller one leaving Rosebud for Arrow Creek the next day. In the meantime there was a hotel across the way where he could have breakfast.

He stepped out into the street and the early sunlight. August heat was already in the air; sudden gusts of wind swept the street, each with its gleaning of dust. Across the street a newspaper skittered with the wind, catching on the raised platform in front of each building, then sailing on with the next gust. In front of the general store a dog hopped onto the platform just in time to meet the newspaper. There must have been a hole in it, because when the dog turned with a surprised yelp, the paper was around his neck like a clown's collar. He tumbled off the platform and rolled around in the street biting and pawing at the paper.

Westland, surprised by the shout of laughter at his side, turned to see the old Indian with his head thrown back, shaking with glee. It was the first time he had heard an Indian laugh, and somehow it bothered him. The boy, holding the old man's hand, was also smiling, his face, bright with color, turned toward the dog.

When the dog broke free of the paper, he retreated to the front of the store, growling and raising the hair on his back.

He barked indignantly when the wind again lifted the tattered paper and floated it on down the street.

The Indians went across and into the store. Westland went into the hotel next to the store and had breakfast. When he came out the two were sitting on the platform against the store front, eating. There were two women at the other end of the platform talking but also watching the Indians curiously.

As Westland watched, the boy finished and stood up to explore the store front. His hands moved on the boards, nimble and swift as little animals, hardly seeming to touch the surface. There was a rocking chair near the door with carved lion heads at the ends of the arms. He found these and explored them, following the surfaces now slowly and carefully, now quickly and lightly touching. His face, at first curious and interested, suffused suddenly with pleasure. He turned toward the old man, smiling, and put his right thumb to his nose, pushing it flat—the sign (Westland knew instantly) for cat. The old man reached out and patted his shoulder and he turned back to his exploring.

The dog Westland had seen before was lying at the other side of the platform near the women. He rose now and went over to the boy, sniffing cautiously, growling deep in his throat. The boy sensed his approach, turned, and also sniffed. When the dog's nose touched his leg, he stood quite still; even his hands paused. The old man stopped eating for a moment.

The women had been watching the boy with a veiled tenderness in their faces. One of them moved toward him now, with concern in her voice.

"The dog is mean. It might hurt him."

The dog turned toward her, showing his teeth. The boy also faced her, his nostrils flared. She stopped irresolutely and put out her hand to him, but he shrank back toward the old man, fear visible on his face. The woman stood there holding her hand out, embarrassed. When she spoke to the old man her voice was sharp.

"You should watch him. He might get hurt."

The old man only shook his head and went on eating.

She turned away, and Westland heard her say, "The poor thing should be in a home for the blind."

He went into the store. When he came out again the dog was lying down. The boy was sitting beside him playing

6

with his front feet. He would raise one paw and spread the toes, then the other. He did it again and again with untiring patience. It occurred to Westland then that he was trying to teach the dog signs.

He left abruptly and returned to the station to wait for the stage to Rosebud. Waiting, he tried once more to organize his knowledge of the Indians he was to study, but the image of the boy and the dog kept recurring, touching him with sadness and dismay.

🐉 3 🐉

The stage left Rosebud at dawn and late in the afternoon climbed the last hill beyond Bear-in-the-Lodge Creek and paused at the top. Far below, shrunken and shimmering in dry, yellow heat, the valley of Arrow Creek sloped off to the north. The day was clear, though clouds towered white in the west; but only a breath of haze softened the valley and blued the badlands wall far off beyond White River, merging above with blue-white sky.

Below, where the land sloped out from the hill, Turning Hawk could see the agency in the small pointed flat where the forks of Arrow Creek joined, could see the grey buildings of the square, their dirt roofs hardly visible against the earth, and across the straight knife edge of the road, the lodges of his people, set in a circle, seeming almost white from the distance.

On down the grey and yellow valley, Arrow Creek wound a green path of willow and cottonwood and little meadows of grass, was turned in long curves by the low hills, joined here and there by smaller creeks. Far off he could see the line of Leaf Creek curving from the west and at its mouth the little flat where the white men had built him a house and measured off a little plot of ground they called an allotment where they hoped he would stay.

He sat absorbed in the scene, describing what he saw in

7

sign for Little Wound's inquisitive hands. He was relieved to be so near the end of the journey, but shaken, seeing the shrunken valley—the last of the wide land his people would know—a small island in a rising sea of white men. And even this might go . . .

Half the great reservation had gone in this same season, when General Crook had called the Lakota together and, with threats of war and promises of payment, persuaded them to sign, relinquishing the land. No promises had yet been kept. The beef ration—payment for Paha Sapa, the Black Hills—had again been cut. There would be no payment, but the land was gone. And no one knew yet where the new boundaries would be. Perhaps this little island too would sink. He did not know; the future was dark.

The coach moved, swinging forward on heavy straps as the road dropped; wooden blocks squealed on the iron rims; dust rose inside. He settled himself to wait, unable as ever to trust himself to the care of the driver, aware irritably of the eyes of the young white man watching him always. It was not a dislike of the man, white though he was, but a need to be alone and be strengthened. But sitting opposite in the small coach, there was nothing they could do but look at each other and, with no words to communicate, it was hard to bear.

The road dropped steeply for a while, then flattened out among sagebrush hills; on one of these, Four Guns, a policeman from the agency, was waiting. He rode alongside, shouting, and the coach stopped. He tried to speak with the driver but the man could understand neither sign nor the Lakota tongue. After trying for a long time, Four Guns gave up in disgust, but seeing Turning Hawk, dismounted and put his head in the window.

"I have found a lost child," he explained, "the small daughter of the White Robe at the agency, who ran away from her parents and became lost here in the hills. I tried to take her back but she is so afraid of me that I haven't the heart to approach her. I thought that the driver, being white, might take her back. But there is no way I can tell him. This one," he indicated the young white man, "seems to have open eyes; perhaps you could make him understand."

"It is not likely," Turning Hawk said doubtfully, but with his eyes caught the white man's attention. He made the signs for female child and, though the man was puzzled

8

by the parturition sign, Turning Hawk saw with surprise that he understood.

He continued, moving his hands slowly, repeating and restating as if conversing with a child, reading easily in the man's face his comprehension or doubt. And though he made no answer, Turning Hawk could see his hands moving unconsciously as if in sleep. He finished; the white man called to the driver and in a moment the coach moved off the road following Four Guns.

Having spoken with the white man, he found himself more at ease; and where he had seen nothing but an alien face before, he saw now a man, a person with whom he could speak.

The coach pulled over a hill and came to a stop at the edge of a small flat where the sage was scant. And in the middle of the flat he saw the child, walking away. She was small, no taller than the sage, frail and flower-like. Her dress was thin, of a pale, frothy blue, blowing in the slight breeze; her hair white, hanging in long curls down to her shoulders.

Four Guns had ridden beyond her, and when she saw him, she turned and ran back toward the coach; but seeing it, she turned again and ran off to the right. She passed a clump of sage and fell, disappearing. And for an instant Turning Hawk had the feeling that she had never been except in vision—a figure of lostness and loneliness out of his own dreaming. She was out of place, impossible in this land.

But as he watched, she appeared again, running, and even from a distance he could hear her crying as she darted here and there as if seeking a place to hide. The white man was already out of the coach walking toward her, and again Four Guns turned her, this time toward the white man, but she dodged by him and was again in the open.

Turning Hawk stepped out to wait and, watching, described the action to Little Wound, bringing smiles to the boy's lips. Yet he himself did not find it funny; the feeling persisted that the child was not real but a figure of dream.

The two men caught her finally, trying awkwardly to be gentle, but she screamed in such anger and terror that Turning Hawk had a quick impulse to interfere, to save her. Yet he knew he would only frighten her more.

The white man held her for a moment and Four Guns rode quickly away toward the agency. And watching him go, e child quieted. She let herself be led toward the coach, though she kept her face buried in the man's coat as she walked. But close to the coach she looked up and, seeing Turning Hawk, jerked away and again ran.

The white man caught her again and carried her screaming and struggling to the coach. As he put his foot to the step, she burrowed her face against his shoulder and bit his neck. He almost fell but caught himself and, holding her out at arm's length, got into the coach and sat down. He held her gingerly on his knees, keeping her head away from him. She was crying now, trying to put her head on his shoulder.

Turning Hawk got into the coach then and the child screamed wildly. For an instant the man held her away, then let her burrow against his neck as she had done before. And Turning Hawk could see that he expected her to bite again. But she did not. The coach moved on, and the child's panic subsided. She lay shivering as if with cold, catching her breath in sobs at lengthening intervals. And in a little while she was asleep, though she still kept shifting and burrowing as if trying to hide.

Turning Hawk settled back to wait, in his mind recurring the image of the child running frightened and lost on the alien land.

It was nearly dark when the coach reached the agency and pulled up in front of the square.

### 4

At first it was her mother covering her for the night, spreading the covers gently, the green, the blue, the patchwork quilt with the satin binding. She felt the cool breeze of them on her face as they fell and the cradle rocking with a light squeak and snap. The satin was smooth and cool in her fingers.

Then the rocking stopped, and the stillness was at once

terrifying. The blankets had smothered the sounds and now kept falling on her steadily, black and colorless, the wind of them blowing her face. She felt the weight building, pressing her body tightly. They had a strange, oppressive smell—and suddenly they were Indian blankets, black and falling in darkness, smothering her . . .

Christine awakened hearing the sound of her own screaming. She was in someone's arms and he was rocking her, singing softly, a lullaby she had never heard. She pulled away from him, remembering now where she was. She slipped to the floor; then seeing the two Indians, shrank back against him, and he lifted her again to his knees. She clung to him fiercely, pressing her face against the pleasant whiteness of his shirt front, her breath chattering in her throat as she tried to keep from crying.

The coach stopped. Outside a single dog barked, then another, and in an instant there was a howling, yelping clamor of dogs from the sides and behind and underneath the coach. Then above the barking came the sound of someone pounding an iron kettle and an Indian woman's shrill voice scolding the dogs into silence.

Someone called from far off; the driver answered, but she did not understand his words. The dogs barked once more and were again silenced.

The man holding her said, "We're waiting for your mother."

She looked around then. Across from her the two Indians sat in silence, their faces glowing darkly in a red sunset light. The old one was facing the window, but the boy was looking straight at her. Yet instantly she knew he was not seeing her. His face was bright with joy, as if he were seeing something she could not see. She glanced around and behind her, seeing only the wall of the coach; then sat staring hard at him, waiting for him to see her. She felt a sudden rush of loneliness, of strangeness, when his expression did not change.

The man holding her opened the door and stepped to the ground. He tried to put her down, but she clung tight to him, searching the while for her mother.

It seemed darker outside. Clouds were solid in the sky and low, moving ponderously in the wind, swallowing the hilltops. Only to the west was there an opening like gates, or doors, and the red light burning through with radiant, staining color.

A crowd of Indians stood silently between the road and the Indian camp, black and motionless, touched with red light. Their blankets were wrapped tightly to their necks, their dark hats straight and square on their heads. They stared openly, only their eyes moving, and she shrank from the darkness of their faces.

The last of the light died; there was a rain smell in the air that made the night seem darker still. Beyond the Indians, at the edge of the camp, a ragged canvas tepee flapped in the wind with popping, swishing sounds. Beside it a small fire glowed; someone stirred the fire and the wind sent the sparks swirling upward into the darkening sky. In the flare of light she saw an old man sitting with a drum between his knees.

In an instant came the muffled beating of the drum, a quick changing throb. A quavering voice rose up, taking the rhythm of the drum, rising and falling with a crying, moaning song that gripped and chilled her. The voice stopped suddenly and she was clinging, pressing against the man's shoulder, her heart beating wildly.

The man turned with her, asking, "Is that your mother?"

Her mother was coming quickly through the crowd dressed in her white tea-party dress. In the wind her cape fluttered out from her shoulders like wings. Christine slipped out of the man's arms and ran, throwing herself against the smooth white skirts. Hands were stroking her hair and she could hear her mother's weeping.

She did not see her father till he knelt down and pulled her away from her mother's skirts. Turning, she saw that his face was stern. He was dressed in his black preaching suit, the one her mother called his Indian suit. Red light from the sunset colored his glasses, and she was afraid. When he tried to lift her, she drew back and clung to her mother.

There was some talking that she did not listen to. The stage pulled away into the square and her father tried once more to carry her, but she would not let him. She knew her mother was not strong enough. So she walked along close beside, tripping and stumbling. Behind her the drum had started up again. She shuddered and clung tightly to her mother's hand.

## 5

Smells of the white man's buildings: burnt iron, ashes, harness, the pungent odor of new-cut wood, dust, horses, axle grease, all in quick changing whiffs—the uncertain wind dipping and curling, its flow broken—told Little Wound of the square. Stepping from the coach he could feel the enclosure, as if he might reach out and touch the buildings that moved about him in four straight sides, feel the dry logs, the lifeless lines.

There were clouds pressing down, he knew, though the air was clear of rain; but it carried the rain smell even with the dryness of dust—the living earth smell and, faintly, the sharp odor of the thunder. He had felt the thunder in the air, the beat of great wings, the shaking of the earth as from stones falling. He imagined the jointed, jagged blades of fire as he had seen them far back and down the darkness, almost beyond his heart's holding. There had been the sound, too, but this he could not hear again as he could see the light; he remembered it as not different from the vibrations now against his skin. But the fire flashed dream-like across the darkness after the beating wings, the stones falling. It was not real, he knew; only the flickering of other fires long past.

He walked beside his grandfather, Turning Hawk, knowing the sun was gone by the uncertainty and care of the old man's steps. He felt strengthened then and not so helpless.

He had not been often in the square, had no way of judging the distances; yet he knew when he was leaving, felt the closeness of the buildings on either side of the entrance and the lifting, widening sense of space beyond. The wind came steady, rising toward him, the breath of the wide land, bringing the earth smell and the smell of the village, his people. And after the dust and roughness of the square, his feet found the short springy stubble of the grass; he knew again, as if he walked it, the prairie dipping and climbing high and far, the path of the wind.

Beyond the entrance, they were waiting, his father and

mother and the small sisters. He caught the smell of them from straight into the wind, the odors all mixed together. Then his mother was separate, and he sensed her nearness before she touched him.

Her hands were firm and lightly moving on his face and down his arms: tears on her cheeks were warm, then cool, to the tips of his fingers, her lips soft and slightly trembling. She was bending above him, strong and sheltering against the wind, and in the little hollow of quiet air, warm with the smell of sweet grass and wood smoke, he was home again.

Other hands touched his head and he turned and found with his fingers the hard tenseness of his father's hands; reached to his face and stood so, sensing the tears held back, the quick violent love and sadness in the changing muscles. Strong hands lifted him and returned him quickly to the earth.

He felt the shift of attention and knew that Turning Hawk was speaking of the journey on the iron road, of the failure of the white man's medicine. His father's hand closed on his convulsively and was gone; he felt suddenly like weeping, for his father's hurt, for the lost light and sound.

He turned quickly to the two small sisters, pulled their braids and smiled, and, as with a rush of water, was enveloped in their arms, was pushed and pulled and buffeted and finally led, a small hand in each of his, toward the wind-blown presence of the lodges.

### ⚜ 6 ⚜

"I still don't understand your motives," the agent told Westland. "What in God's name can a man with a strong body and good education have to gain listening to a lot of Indians? If there's anything you want to know, ask me. I've been here almost ten years now." He paused to regard Westland severely. "As for your Ghost Dance, I never heard of it. Whatever it is, there's none of it here."

"It may be that it hasn't spread this far," Westland said. "But there are dances among the Arapaho and Shoshone at Wind River. In any case, I'd like to study the Indians here."

"Well, it still doesn't make sense. You know, of course, I could send you on. But I won't. Not, at least, till I find out what your real game is. In the meantime we'll do it this way. If old Turning Hawk will take you into his camp and look out for you, you can get on with your study—if that's what it is. If he won't—well, I guess you'll have to leave. Can't antagonize my red charges, you know."

"How can I find him?"

"He's the one you came in with on the stage."

He stood up behind his desk with a stiff, military bearing and handed Westland his letters, indicating that the interview was finished.

Westland turned and, with as much dignity as he could muster, left. His letters from the Institute had not impressed the agent. Probably nothing would, short of a congressional appointment. He thought of the missionary, Martin Hall, who perhaps might help, but, remembering the little girl and her mother, rejected the idea. There was something in his sudden, unasked involvement with the strange, frantic little girl that made him react deeply to her parents in the brief moment he had seen them—the mother, disquieting, familiar, like someone he might have known at home; the father, stern yet with a remote, dedicated air. He could not ask help from the man; he would not ask himself why.

It was dark outside. Above the quadrangle, which was lighted in patches by yellow lamplight, the sky was densely black, as if the clouds had solidified and dropped to rest like the lid of a box on the little square of buildings.

The night was alive with the noises of the Indian camp to the north: dogs barking, drums, children shouting. The sound rose and fell in long rhythms with now and then a louder pulse, a long running swell. In the lulls he could hear voices from the buildings around the square: words he could understand, a scrap of a familiar song. But these seemed plaintive, boxed up in the darkness of a strange land. He shivered, remembering the little girl, and walked back toward the hotel.

His room was in the attic at the back of the building with a single window overlooking the Indian camp. The rest of the attic was unfinished and hung with rows of skins that

15

gave off a musky, slightly putrid smell. Flies buzzed in the light of the little hand lamp the host had given him to light his way to his room. He closed the door tightly and opened the window to let out the oppressive odor of the furs.

He went to bed immediately, determined to ignore the noises, his interest dampened by the possibility of having to leave. But he could not sleep. Finally he got up, dressed, and sat by the open window.

The camp was on lower ground than the square and, though close, it seemed far down in the darkness. He could not see the ground except in round patches revealed by campfires outside. A few of the lodges were clean cones of light illumined by fires within, all arranged in a circle. Shadows moved on the walls, distorted, depthless images. On some of the lodges were painted figures that might have been shadows cast by living animals inside.

One of the fires outside lighted a single figure, seated cross-legged, an old man with a drum, shapeless and still as a lump of earth. At intervals he tapped the drum and briefly sang and fell again into silence. His quavering song, scarcely audible among the other sounds, seemed to approach, then recede, as if blown by the wind. Short bird-like phrases of a flageolet arose somewhere outside the circle, curious, disembodied flutings like wings in the darkness. From the far side of camp came the low, wild sound of a group singing and dancing. A single dog howled, a lonesome, keening wail that raised a harsh hullabaloo of dog noises all out of proportion.

As he listened, watching the strange figures moving on the cones of light, the whole scene seemed to float and recede; he was looking down from far off through a distortion of darkness that swirled between himself and the scene he watched till he could no longer think of the figures as people, could not correlate them with his own familiar world and species. He was detached, raised up to a point of vantage, but his vision was obscured. The sounds floating up through the moving darkness were wild, incomprehensible, isolating. His vantage point was a lonesome hill, himself alone at its peak.

After a long time the darkness lessened. The ground rose in a filter of moonlight as clouds thinned; the lodges arranged themselves solidly in the circle. Wagons appeared, and pole tripods, drying racks, sun shelters. The clouds broke and patches of moonlight came on the low hills and moved and dissolved. A patch brightened at the edge of camp and moved across, revealing it sharply in black and silver. Beyond the camp, where the forks of the creek joined, he could see dimly the squat cabins of the winter camp, dark and lifeless, still in shadow. The light passed, leaving the camp again in dimness.

The noises were fewer. From the nearest lodge he could hear a man's voice alternately rising loud and fierce then subsiding to a sorrowful chant that was like singing. The voice had the blurred, fumbling quality of drunkenness. Now and then a woman's voice answered briefly and firmly or, with a sudden change of tone, sang to a querulous baby.

The man's voice at last rose to a frenzy, a hysterical yell. The wild sound in the night made Westland catch his breath and raised the hair on his neck. It rang in his ears, feral as the cry of a hunting animal.

There was a sudden movement of shadows on the lodge and a figure appeared at the entrance, bent low like an animal running. A short distance from the lodge it rose up and continued, staggering, out of the circle into the darkness east, beyond the creek, where the horse herd grazed.

There was an interval while a baby cried lustily, then the woman singing a crooning, repetitive lullaby that was yet sad and foreboding. After a little time the singing stopped and the child was silent. The clouds were thinning, the light increasing. Instead of light patches, shadows of clouds moved on the mottled hills.

There was a lull, a hush in all the sounds till he thought he could hear the low, intimate murmurings of the blanketed couples around the edge of the circle, though he knew it was too far. The wind moved with a hushing, whispering past the buildings and among the lodges. Beyond the white tatterings of cloud, the moon sailed sharp and polished in a thin foam of stars. From the pine hills, faintly, came a crying, wildly modulated chorus of coyotes. Then from the east began a faint pattering that resolved itself quickly to the sound of a horse running. A figure emerged from the willows along the creek, a horse and rider; the hoofbeats grew loud, explosive. There was a sudden barking of dogs that stopped as suddenly, a scurrying of shadows on the lodges, a few figures appearing at entrances.

The rider pulled up at the edge of the circle, dismounted and ran unsteadily to the nearest lodge and disappeared. The horse, marked black and white, stood quietly, scarcely visible in the dappled light.

From the lodge came a chilling crescendo of dispute, the same two voices he had heard before—the loud resonant voice with the depth of grief under its frenzy; the woman's voice, low and controlled and somehow resigned.

The voices stopped; a tangle of shadows moved on the lodge, and the man again emerged, running bent over as before, but this time with something in his hand. Reaching the horse, he disappeared in a flurry of movement, appearing again astride the horse, his hand extended over his head.

Westland saw the flash of orange as the gun fired. The sound crashed flat and echoless in the night. Over his head a windowpane shattered and rained down on him.

He ducked instinctively, not afraid but shocked at this sudden involvement. The flat, moving picture had suddenly become real. But he could not stop watching. He crouched at the window, just high enough to see over the ledge, wincing each time the gun fired.

A woman had emerged from the lodge, a coil of rope in her hand. She walked toward the horseman, talking quietly between shots.

Westland realized then that the man was shooting close, trying to frighten her, and she was making no attempt to dodge. He saw a puff of dust at her feet; the side of the lodge jumped explosively where a bullet struck.

Then the woman threw the rope. He did not see the loop, but the horse lunged and the rider fell heavily to the ground, his arms pinned to his sides. He lay there motionless, and in a moment the woman was kneeling over him, crooning in the same voice that had sung to the baby.

A boy had come out of the lodge followed by an old man, and Westland recognized them instantly as the two Indians on the stage, Turning Hawk and the blind boy. The boy walked forward uncertainly till the other caught up. Then, with the old man just touching his side, he walked quickly to the woman and knelt beside her.

Turning Hawk stood above, motionless, his head bowed, and the little group paused for a moment, solidified; there was

18

no sound or movement. The whole camp seemed to cease breathing, to wait. Then movement again began; a few figures came from other lodges to join the group. From the back of the quadrangle he saw two men running toward the camp; policemen, he knew.

The group stirred and the man rose and stood beside the woman. He bent over, touched the boy's shoulder, and made a few signs which the boy followed with his hands. When the policemen arrived, there was a little talk and the man walked between them toward the entrance to the quadrangle.

The group dispersed slowly. The sky cleared. The blanketed couples around the circle disappeared one by one, till there was no sign of life—not even shadows on the now darkened lodges. Only Turning Hawk remained, staring into the darkness the way the police had gone.

### ❦ 7 ❦

Turning Hawk stood with his daughter and grandson. Crazy Walking had gone with the metal breasts, the police, walking between them straight and upright as a runner, not drunk now but proud and defiant. In moonlight the white men's clothes he wore seemed to change, and Turning Hawk, watching, was stricken with a vision of young warriors he had known, of himself also when young. Darkness, like time, killed the details, leaving only the moving image, as if the spirit of the young man shone in dim form and dance-like movement—light feet (in spite of heavy shoes) swung neatly in a curve with every step, placed quietly and precisely and again raised, each motion part of a circle drawn on the darkness. In the other days he would have been a chief; in sorrow like this would have gone to war and died fighting for the people. Now—a rebellious Indian, a contemptuous white man, both and neither. The old road was broken; he could not make a new one. There was none that did not offend him. He was a strong man, a father with two sons, one away in the white man's school, the other blind and deaf for all his life's road. The drunkenness was a crying, the grief of a man without tears.

The metal breasts made a sharp turn at the entrance of the quadrangle and disappeared into the square little world of the white man's buildings—unmoving, angular with the lines of stone, of death, scars forever on the earth mother.

The camp was again quiet. Tall Bear, old beyond knowing, sang of a dream and was silent. Coyotes, still many in spite of the white man, chattered on the hills.

The fires were out. In the night's dimness the canvas lodges were white as the old bleached leather. Looking up and over, above the clutter of wagons and buggies, Turning Hawk could see the low hills where the horses grazed and where cloud shadows moved and gathered and broke, like spirit herds of the lost buffalo.

He caught his breath and turned to look for his daughter and Little Wound. But they were gone. With a start he realized that he must have lingered a long time. He had slept fitfully before the shooting, the darkness under his eyelids broken by vivid, changing images—light flashes, the earth moving, turning and turning like a broad shield; and recurring over and over, the circle of light, himself above it and falling, the ring of dancers, revolving and breaking. Now sleep would not come again, he knew.

There was a fear, a strangeness in the night. Before him a line was stretched between the high wheels of two wagons hung with squares of white cloth that fluttered and flapped in the wind with a ghostly sound. Wagons and buggies, harness, pack saddles, cluttered the spaces between the lodges, and in the air the foreign smells of axle grease, coffee grounds, bacon.

He was a stranger in his own camp, looking with eyes of the past at the changed ways, fear and unbelief in his heart. The whole world was shaken. A proud people fallen: waiting for food at the white man's agency, the buffalo gone and the land gone, fenced, scarred by the plow, the old trails wiped out.

He entered the lodge, where his daughter and her children slept, and with shaking hands kindled a small fire. He forced himself to sit, pressing his hands on his knees to still them, holding his vision dark to the images, his heart closed to the past. With time the blood quieted, the shaking stilled. He eased the tension of his muscles and leaned back on the willow back rest, closing his eyes, pressing his hands to the grass-less earth.

And immediately before him was a wide, grassed plain stretching far to the red-stained hills; and in the distance a stream flowed, fringed with darker grass, crested with shining cottonwoods. Wakinyan-oi, country of the Thunder's track —he knew it instantly—country of his boyhood, of his first vision. For an instant only, he saw fences appear, squares of black, violated earth and the grey houses . . . He jerked erect, opening his eyes, and the scene was gone.

And again the blood quieted. He was on a hill in the same country and around him the land was dark with buffalo, moving, flowing like a great river, and he among them moving also, but looking backward fearfully. And far off he saw the pursuers, numberless, faceless, implacable.

The speed increased, the buffalo flowing above the grass, their noise the sound of wings beating. The pursuers came on soundless, motionless, but gaining, streaming solidly over the horizon. At the back of the herd, then, with no shock, no surprise, he saw buffalo become men and make stand and fight. He tried to stay but could not, was borne onward by the buffalo. The fighters went under and were gone, but still, undiminished, the pursuers came on.

And suddenly it ended. He was alone on the hill, lying on a bed of sage, weak and shaken. Below he saw the camp— white lodges beaded on a circle on a green flat by the stream. He arose and walked toward the lodges, carrying a smooth and polished stone which he turned over and over in his hands. And suddenly—without looking and with a strange, sharp, thrill—he recognized the emergent form of a buffalo, the head and hump rising clean and smooth out of unshaped rock.

He stopped, deeply moved, vividly aware of his life, all his senses drinking the world: the sun warm on his back, wind touching coolly the sweat dampness; the warm grassed earth intimate to his feet, and in his nose the green, salt smell; water clear bright in sunlight; trees leaf-shining, bird-flickered; and nearer the lodges, clean and light, among them like a singing, the sound of his people.

The time was Wakan, sacred, as clear and living now as then. Reluctantly he let it go, opening his eyes to the low burning fire.

He stood up and took his medicine bundle from its tripod, resuming his seat holding the bundle across his knees, the softness of otter skin cool and alive in his hands. Opening it, he drew out the tobacco and the pipe, filled it and with a small coal gave it fire. Holding the bowl in his palm, the stem extended, he made offering to the four winds—the messengers—and to Wakinyan with the sky, praying for the life of his people.

He took the buffalo stone from its wrapping, closing his eyes and with his hands knowing again, even with the uncounted snows blown between, the thrill of wonder, of discovery: the buffalo still emerging from formless rock as all life might have come from earth in the beginning, one horn formed perfectly, the other only begun, a bud only; the head and body with upward streaming lines arising; earth's promise of renewal, of rebirth.

The stone curved and bulged under his fingers with a furry smoothness, a hardness that was yet the hardness of muscle, the strength of flesh. It was Wakan, a sign, he was sure with all his heart's knowing.

He sat for a long time, the living stone under his hands, arising only when the fire burned down and died. He could sleep then.

### ⚜ 8 ⚜

The cell door slammed, the key turned in the lock, the light went out. Another door, another key, and Crazy Walking stood alone in the dark silence of the jail, the smoke of the lampwick pervading the air with suffocating odor.

He stood in the center of the cell hearing the rushing sound of his own breathing: hollow, whistling, like a winded horse. He could not get enough air. He sat down against a wall and leaned back but jerked erect again, struggling to his feet as if under a weight. His chest labored outward with violent effort, collapsed, and labored again. He found himself rising on his toes, stroking with his arms, straining upward as to the surface of dark water. His heart beat wildly; yet his mind was clear, apart, watching with wonder. There was nothing to fear, nothing he was afraid of, no one.

He tried to remember what had happened, why he was here, but the frenzy began again and he was lost in the darkness . . . As he stood the darkness thinned. On the floor of the cell opposite, a spot of moonlight brightened, separating into the lights of the small square panes, lined vertically by the iron bars. A shadowy moth climbed and fluttered against the blued light.

Through the blurred, wavy glass he could see the buildings across the square, squatting low and shapeless against the oval hills beyond. Above them a shadowed cloud moiled and turned. There was a groaning, faraway screaming in the night that finally came to him as the sound of the windmill in the square. He held his breath to listen and realized that his breathing had quieted.

He found the cell bed against a wall and sat down, weak and shaken but wide awake. All his senses were keyed up, in wait. His eyes traveled the darkness, returning constantly to the spot of moonlight, the barred window, the blurred night scene beyond. He listened for all the small night sounds, sorting them, naming them with an intentness, a sense of urgency that puzzled him. He could think of no reason; his mind was quiet but curiously blank.

He sat thus, drawn up, with no sense of time, hearing at length a new sound from the square, a low, hoarse squealing that seemed to grow louder, to approach. It was a mechanical, yet faintly human sound he could not quite name.

The sound stopped abruptly, and after a time a key rattled in the lock and the door of the jail swung open. Two men entered, carrying something between them which they took into the cell opposite. They lowered their burden into the spot of moonlight on the floor and Crazy Walking saw a man, small, pale, rigid as a corpse.

One of the men went out of the cell to light the lamp, and in the blaze of the match he saw the two policemen, Tall Bull and Four Guns.

His eyes went back to the still figure on the floor, searching the frozen, bony features for some sign of life, but finding none. The body under the black clothing was slight— hardly bigger than a child—fleshless; the face was thin, sunken and shadowed in the cheeks and around the glittering, open eyes. At one corner of the mouth a zigzag trickle of blood shone.

The two policemen stood bent over, intent, only their shadows moving in the flickering light. After a long time Four Guns exhaled loudly; his right hand moved quickly under his left in the sign for death. Tall Bull nodded and the two retreated from the cell, closing the door.

"If he's dead," Crazy Walking said loudly, "take him out of here. You don't need any bars to hold him now."

"No," Four Guns said emphatically. "Our orders were to put him in jail. We've brought him here. Now we'll report it."

"Take him out," he repeated tensely. "This is no grave."

The two had paused outside the cell door, looking back, watching the body with fascination, paying no heed to Crazy Walking.

"Who killed him?" Crazy Walking shouted angrily, "what brave man?"

The two men looked at each other, shaking their heads vigorously.

"He died all at once," Four Guns said. "No one hurt him. He was fighting to get away, then he was dead. Stiff, like one dead a long time, all at once."

"A strange one," Tall Bull said, "Wakan. He told us he had died before and come back. It is true all white men are liars, but this one was strange. I think his medicine was strong."

"You're afraid to touch him again," Crazy Walking said with sudden insight. "So you'll leave me buried with him. Your hearts are strong."

"I'll stay," Four Guns promised uneasily. "He can go."

Tall Bull started quickly for the door but Four Guns held up his hand.

"Wait," was all he said.

Tall Bull came back and stood as before, looking down at the dead man through the bars of the cell. They stood silently, all three, a presence in the room holding them tensely. Crazy Walking gripped the bars, waiting.

An intricate grillwork of light and shade lay on the still figure, shadows of the cell bars enlarged by the yellow light overlaying the blue crisscrossing of the moonlit window. There was no movement, nothing save the concerted breathing of the three watchers, curiously in unison with the sad metallic screaming of the windmill in the square.

Then low, rising as if from the earth, began a hollow eerie humming, scarcely audible at first, but growing louder, taking the same rhythm as the windmill, becoming finally a wavering melody.

Crazy Walking drew back, with shock knowing that the man on the floor was not dead. He had seen no movement, not a breath—the lips were immobile as stone, the eyes unblinking. The humming came from nowhere—everywhere in the room, unearthly, bodiless. Yet in that instant, with no preparation, no gradual awakening, the man sat up. For a moment the humming stopped, then went on, becoming a singing, the words elided, unrecognizable. But the lips were moving, the eyes blinking rapidly in the moonlight.

Four Guns stepped quickly to the cell door and locked it, his hand still held to his mouth in amazement, but the man did not heed, did not even turn his face from the window. In the same moment Tall Bull blew out the light and the two left, hurriedly but silently, locking the door behind them.

The singing stopped and the man stood up. He turned completely around, gazing blankly into the darkness, then staggered forward, seized by a violent fit of coughing. He groped blindly till he caught hold of the bars, hanging limply between spasms, fighting for breath with gurgling, liquid sounds.

As he watched helplessly, Crazy Walking became aware that his own breath was coming hard again, his chest heaving under the strange pressure; the walls, the darkness seemed to fall toward him, enclosing, crushing. He yelled suddenly, without volition, the sound shrill and frightening to his own ears. The darkness closed around him, solid . . .

He was standing at the door of the cell, shaking it with all his strength. But above the rattle of the steel he could hear a voice speaking. Waiting till he could understand the words, he turned reluctantly toward the other cell and saw the strange white man standing against the light of the window.

"You don't need to be afraid. I'm not dying. I'm no morsel, even for death."

"I'm not afraid," Crazy Walking denied. "I'm locked up, that's all."

"I'm locked up too. Why are you here?"

Crazy Walking drew back tensely, his mind curiously blank.

"I can't remember," he said slowly. He reached forward and gripped the bars, hearing the man's voice but not catching the words. There was silence again, and again the far-off screaming of the windmill.

"What are you in for?" His own voice surprised him with its harshness.

"Trapped, like Christ, for bringing the light."

"Your light don't shine much here in the dark."

The man started to answer but was seized by another fit of coughing.

When he stopped, Crazy Walking said, "You must be some kind of a preacher."

"No. More. I bring a new life, the estate of natural man and the light of a life beyond death. I bring the rebirth of the Indian nations, a new culture rising from the ashes of the old."

"A white Messiah with a new religion for the heathen. They won't swallow it. They like the one they've got." He was suddenly irritated by the preacher, yet fascinated.

"Are you an Indian?"

"No," Crazy Walking said, "not exactly."

"Then you couldn't know," the preacher said with open hostility. He walked to the cell bed, lay down on his back, and began singing. In a little while he was asleep, but he breathed in irregular, gurgling snores, like a lung-shot animal.

Crazy Walking found his own bed and lay down, but sat up again immediately. He would never sleep. He sat on the edge of the bed clenching and unclenching hands in an agony of self-control, trying desperately to close his ears to the drowning sounds from the other cell, to the sound of the windmill in the square.

Inside the carpenter shop Westland waited for the old man to cut a windowpane to replace the one the Indian had shot out in the night. It was early morning but already the floor of the shop was littered with sawdust and shavings. The back wall was lined with stacks of new-cut boards of various lengths.

"Coffins," the carpenter explained as he worked. "Come winter there's always a run on 'em so I like to have a few ahead. But I daresn't nail 'em together."

"Why not?"

"Damn superstition, that's all. If I make a few of different sizes and one of 'em happens to fit a dead Injun, then I must have known he was gonna die; and if I knew he was gonna die, I must have killed him. So I just cut the lengths and nail 'em together on order."

He handed Westland the pane and continued, "These Injuns are damn careless with guns. He wasn't shootin' at you, was he?"

"No, I think he was shooting at the whole world."

"It's likely. It's a wonder he didn't kill somebody. When an Injun feels bad, look out."

"I guess everyone's like that."

"No, this is different. Sometimes they just go berserk and kill anyone they see. Back before the reservations, they'd go to war and fight till they died. Now they just go crazy. This one surprises me, though. He's the most civilized Injun I ever saw. I didn't think he'd do anything like that."

"You know him?"

"Yeah, his name's Crazy Walking. He married Turning Hawk's daughter. Went to school back east; punched cows all over the west. He could pass for white if he wanted to, but he don't give a damn. I can't figger him out. But he ain't bad, for an Injun."

They had stepped out onto the wooden platform while they talked and stood looking out across the square. A gusty wind was up, lifting dust and whirling it sporadically around the buildings. At the middle of the square a windmill squeaked and rattled, pumping water into a wooden tank which in turn overflowed into a horse trough below. Gusts of wind flared little sheets of water off the end of the pipe, dissolving them in thin flashes in the morning sun. At the west end of the square in front of the agent's house a flagstaff rose, bearing a tattered flag and, at its tip, a weather vane in the shape of a rifle, its muzzle swinging menacingly with the changing wind.

Directly across the square was the jail, a log building with dirt roof, no different from the other buildings except for the barred window. No one was in sight; but as they talked, Turning Hawk and the blind boy came into the square and stopped in front of the jail. The old Indian stared in at the window for a long time, the boy beside him catching every movement of his hands.

Through the barred, dusty window beyond them, Westland could see movement, the faint outline of a man waving his arms. And blown in gusts by the wind, a voice, shouting or crying, he could not tell which.

The two Indians turned away and sat cross-legged on the ground under the window, moving in unison like puppets drawn by the same wires. But the movement beyond the window went on.

"He's here to get Crazy Walking out," the carpenter remarked. "But unless I miss my guess, he'll have a fine to pay. The Major's strict."

"The Major?"

"The agent—they're all called Major, for no reason I know of. This is him coming now."

The Major and two Indian policemen came along the other side of the square, unlocked the jail, and went inside; Turning Hawk and the boy followed. Westland hesitated a moment, then walked quickly across.

The Major was sitting back to the door behind a desk, talking to Turning Hawk, with one of the policemen interpreting. Westland stopped just inside the door and waited.

There were three cells in the jail, the two along the east side occupied, the third, at the back, empty. The remaining quarter of the room was the office. In the front cell a cadaverous little white man clung to the bars with thin, fleshless fingers, complaining constantly to the Major, who appeared not to hear him. His eyes glittered in deep, shadowy sockets; from one corner of his mouth a streak of dried blood zigzagged downward through frosty whiskers. From his black clothing and high-collared shirt, Westland guessed him to be a preacher.

The man in the other cell had to be Crazy Walking, he knew. And yet in spite of the carpenter's description, Westland was surprised. He had expected an Indian, but this man might have been white. He was about thirty, dressed in well-fitted cowboy clothes, oddly all black, even to the high-heeled boots. The only color in his outfit was a red bandanna wrapped closely and tucked into the front of his shirt. The black seemed out of place with the cowboy outfit, yet somehow it was right for the man. His face was lean, clear-cut, the nose slightly aquiline, the eyes a startling yellow in his dark face. He stood erect, moveless as stone, yet emanating a restless energy. From the middle of the cell, he watched the Major, a faintly sardonic twist to his expression.

"He'll have to pay the fine or stay in jail," the Major said with finality. "Can't have that kind of conduct, you know. It's not civilized."

The policeman interpreted to Turning Hawk. When he finished, the Major turned and spoke to Crazy Walking.

"Can you pay it?"

Crazy Walking continued to look at the Major without moving his eyes or in any way indicating that he had heard. Yet Westland saw that the answer was negative.

He walked around the desk and the Major noticed him for the first time.

"I'll pay the fine, if it's all right with you," Westland told him.

The Major looked at him doubtfully. "Well, it's agreeable with me if he wants to accept your help." He turned again to Crazy Walking questioningly and again the man answered in silence.

Westland paid the money and one of the policemen unlocked the cell, but Crazy Walking did not immediately come out.

In the other cell, the preacher had continued to protest; but when the Major turned to look at him, he was hanging on the bars coughing liquidly and spitting. The Major watched in alarm, motioning to one of the policemen to open the door.

29

The Indian hesitated, making a circular motion beside his forehead.

"Maybe," the Major said impatiently, "but I can't let him die in here."

The Indian shrugged, then spoke in halting but clear English, his hands moving deftly in an accompaniment of signs: "We won't touch him. He died and came back."

The Major laughed. "But not all the way. There's sign of the grave on him yet. Anyway, a little bone bag like that won't be hard to handle. Let him out."

The policeman opened the door and stepped back quickly.

The preacher stopped coughing but did not notice the open door. "You can't keep me in here," he told the Major. "I've got a mission and I haven't got much time."

"I can see you haven't got much time," the Major said ambiguously. "Besides that, you're leaving. You can't stay here without a pass. What church do you preach, anyway?"

"No church. A new religion, of life beyond death. I am its only leader."

"You'll do for the first part of the trip." He glanced suspiciously at Westland. "Does this have any connection with your Ghost Dance?"

Westland shook his head. "No. That's an Indian movement. This one . . ." His hand unconsciously moved upward tracing circles beside his head as the Indian had done. He stopped in embarrassment.

The preacher stared at them all impartially, poisonously. Then he saw the open cell door and scurried through it, making for the door to the outside.

Turning Hawk drew back and the boy followed, his nostrils dilating as the man approached.

The Major stepped into the doorway just ahead of the preacher. "Hold on, now. As long as I'm leaving you free till the stage comes, you'll have to behave. No preaching, understand? It's beef issue today," he said to the others. "That usually brings trouble enough."

"Let me out," the preacher said, a tautness in his voice. "I've got no time to treat with white men. They're long doomed. It's the Indians I have to save."

He tried to walk past, but the Major, a short stout man, brushed him back as he would a child, smiling with composure. But the smile did not last. The preacher charged him with cat-like swiftness. He almost climbed over the Major and out the door before he was thrust back.

The Major held the door, chagrined. His hat was gone and there were claw marks on his pink, smooth-shaven face.

"Put him back in," he shouted angrily to the policemen.

Both shook their heads, drawing farther back toward the door of Crazy Walking's cell. The Major made a rush for the preacher then, but the man eluded him, spinning away, dodging toward the two policemen. Instead of grabbing him, they scurried into the cell with Crazy Walking and slammed the door.

The preacher again darted for the door, but again the Major beat him to it. He was panting and white-faced with anger.

"You can help me," he said grimly to Westland, "if you ever want any help from me."

Westland stepped forward reluctantly.

The old man had retreated to the back of the office and stood there gazing wildly around, coughing shallowly. They cornered him and approached. The Major was just reaching out to grab him when explosively, without warning, the preacher spat—twice in quick succession. Both men jumped backward, hands to their faces. The preacher darted between them and was gone. The Major ran to the door and stood looking out, but he did not go on. He stood there swearing, rubbing his face with his handkerchief.

Westland wiped the spit from his face, feeling slightly ill; and when he had rubbed till his face hurt, put the handkerchief in the wood stove.

Turning Hawk and the two policemen were serious, gloomy-eyed. Only Crazy Walking laughed. He stood in the middle of the cell roaring, holding his sides, gasping for breath; but his eyes held a look of pain, his laughter a note of hysteria.

The two policemen came sheepishly out of the cell, avoiding the Major's eyes. Crazy Walking stopped laughing but made no move to come out. There was a brightness in his eyes as of tears.

"You're free to leave," the Major told him. "This man has paid your fine—for reasons of his own, I suppose. I'm sorry you landed here. You're the only civilized Indian I've got and I'd like you to set a better example."

"There's not any civilized Indians," Crazy Walking said

bitterly, "or white men either." He came out of the cell and stopped in front of Westland. "If you did this as a favor, thanks. But as a white man, what did you expect to gain?"

"I didn't do it for you," Westland said honestly. "I don't even know you, except for a close acquaintance with one of your shots last night. But I'm interested in Indian culture. I'd like to be your friend." He extended his hand.

But Crazy Walking did not take it immediately. His expression was of shock, of unbelief. "One of my shots?" He shook Westland's hand absently, then left, walking carefully, his eyes fixed straight ahead.

Little Wound stepped forward eagerly as he passed, but Turning Hawk restrained him. Waiting for the boy to touch his outstretched hand, he pushed down twice in the sign for wait. The small, delicate hand remained briefly on the old one as if for reassurance.

They all left then, the Major walking quickly toward his house, followed by one of the policemen. The other paused beside Turning Hawk.

Crazy Walking was just leaving the square, still with the strange, somnolent movement. Turning Hawk watched him go, his wrinkled face impassive, but in his eyes a visible sadness. Then he turned to stare at Westland, openly, unabashed, till Westland felt himself flushing clear to the brim of his hat and shifting back and forth from one foot to the other.

"Will you interpret for me?" he asked the policeman.

The man nodded.

"Tell him," he said, "that I'd like to talk with him, to learn the wisdom of his race; to understand it and write it down so that other men may read and also understand."

Turning Hawk did not answer immediately but went on staring at Westland. Finally he spoke, accompanying himself with signs: "The road of the white man is the track of death for the Indian. The small one with the bloody spit breathes the air of death but lives. From this same breath the Indian dies. The Indian who walks in the white man's track too far is doomed." He paused for the translation, his eyes moving briefly in the direction Crazy Walking had gone, and continued, "Who knows where the road of the Indian might lead the white man?" He looked at Westland with a touch of laughter in his eyes and finished with a rush, "But that road is broken, rubbed out; there is no danger. I will talk with you; you are welcome to my lodge." He turned and left, the boy following as if drawn by a magnet.

Westland thanked the policeman and walked back to the hotel. He was relieved at having accomplished his purpose, and yet he had a contradictory sense of being drawn unwillingly onto unknown ground.

## 🐾 10 🐾

With the lid off, smoke rose in the kitchen in dense puffs with each gust of the wind. Leah hastily thrust a stick of cottonwood into the dark flames, burned the back of her hand, and slammed the lid back on. In her haste she always burned her hand, she reflected with annoyance; but she could not bear the smoke in the closeness of the room. And she was hours late now with breakfast, having let Christine sleep late after the ordeal of the day before.

She turned away, tears (partly from the smoke) welling in her eyes, and saw Christine standing in the doorway, her slight body lost in the voluminous nightgown. Tenderly in the crook of her arm she held the rag doll, wrapped in her own satin-edged blanket. A curl hung over her face, shining white against the deep blue of her eyes, the unnatural red of her sunburned cheek. She stood quietly in the doorway, and there was something different about her. She did not meet Leah's eyes but stared straight ahead, her face calm and expressionless. For an instant Leah thought she might be sleepwalking.

She dropped to her knees, brushing back the curl, and kissed the small red nose, smiling.

But Christine still did not meet her eyes or smile. "I can't see, Mother," she said calmly.

Chill gripped Leah, an instant of terror; then she saw the doll's face and, with a wave of relief, understood. Both button eyes had been pulled off, leaving only the broken threads in the white blankness of the face. She remembered

33

another face—the blind Indian boy in the coach that had brought Christine home.

"Buttons is blind, too." She had followed Leah's eyes, betraying her pretense.

"She's unbuttoned," Leah smiled—but her voice was shaking—"undone. And so are you; you just looked."

"No." Christine hesitated. "I looked but I didn't see."

"After breakfast we'll go to the store and buy Buttons some more eyes; then you can both see. Now, dress yourself."

"You'll have to find my clothes, Mother."

Leah almost scolded her, but refrained. There was a fragility about the child, a tenderness as of moth wings. She could not punish her for this make-believe, this imagined living in another, darker world. Other games of make-believe they played together in the terrible loneliness of the reservation. They had tea parties and birthdays with imaginary friends for Christine, children from Leah's own childhood, even herself when young. For there were no white children of Christine's age. And her father could not bear the sight of her playing with the brown little Indian children.

"My mission," he said, "is to destroy paganism. I cannot risk its infection of my own child."

So Leah played with her daughter, aware dimly that she too lived too much in the world of make-believe—or of the past.

She glanced apprehensively toward the dining room, hoping Martin would not arrive to witness this new pretense. He was annoyed already because of the late breakfast, she knew. She could hear him now, intoning his daily Bible reading. From the kitchen, she could not understand the words. But they always sounded the same: a regular, inflectionless chanting, the sounds of exorcism rather than prayer. She brushed the thought aside with a quick feeling of disloyalty. Yet the truth of it remained.

Coming onto the reservation, Martin had seemed like a man coming suddenly out of sunlight into shadow; he had assumed the hue of darkness. He came to think of all Indian ways as a fabric of evil, a dark blanket smothering the good. And, though he made defense with his preaching, his congregation was small. It did not increase. So he remained in shadow.

Christine dressed herself in a curiously awkward fashion.

34

She had a flair for acting; her expression was rapt, inward; her fingers exploratory. And most curious of all, she turned her head from side to side, her nostrils flared and searching. She lived in a world of darkness without closing her eyes. So complete was her immersion that Leah, watching, felt a pang of loneliness; for an instant her daughter was a stranger.

She set the table and, before calling Martin, helped Christine to her place. She still clung to her game, walking carefully with outstretched hand, still holding the doll solicitously.

"I'll have to hold her," she protested when Leah tried to put the doll aside. "She's afraid of the dark."

She sat at the table, rocking gently, not looking at the doll but stroking its face with one hand, pausing often to feel the broken threads where the eyes had been. Her other hand fingered the satin edge of the blanket.

Martin's hand touched briefly on Christine's head as he passed to sit down, but he did not pause to look at her. Not till after he had said grace did he notice the doll and blanket. He pointed to the doll, then to the bedroom. But Christine pretended not to see.

Leah caught his eye, in appeal, but he shook his head.

"The doll is bad enough, but the blanket is disobedience. I've told her not to bring it to the table—often enough."

"It's for Buttons," Christine said. "She's cold."

"No," he said with exaggerated patience, "we have to be truthful. The doll doesn't get cold. It's just a piece of cloth. Put it away."

"I'm afraid—" she corrected herself hastily—"I mean Buttons is afraid."

"Nonsense. Afraid of what?"

"Of the dark."

"But it isn't dark."

"For her it is because she's blind." She held up the doll for him to see, keeping her eyes averted in the same constant stare.

"For the last time," he said, visibly controlling himself, "put it away."

Christine stood up slowly, turning her head from side to side with a bewildered, pained expression. And again Leah was struck with the terrifying thought that maybe she was really blind. Christine turned and walked slowly toward the

35

bedroom, feeling her way with outstretched hand. In the doorway she stopped, leaned her head against the jamb—just an instant—then went on. But the image of her in the doorway, small, burdened, and shadowed, stayed vividly in Leah's mind. With intense effort she kept from following.

In a little while Christine was back. She bumped the table lightly and felt her way to the chair with her hands. Her face was more intensely calm, her eyes far-fixed. She was alone in darkness, lost.

Leah rose quickly to put more wood on the fire. With the smoke in the air, Martin did not comment on her tears—or even notice them. He was eating, with concentration. When he left for the church a little later, he still had not noticed his daughter's make-believe of blindness.

There was a crowd of Indians outside the trader's store, young men and boys standing quietly and stiffly, their dark eyes unblinking under their black, broad-brimmed hats. She had not thought of that—had not remembered that it was beef issue day. Whenever there were Indians, Christine would shrink close to her, terrified, trying to hide in the folds of her skirt. But when Leah glanced at her now, she saw with surprise that the child's face was calm and unconcerned; her hand in Leah's was relaxed.

They climbed the platform and went in, finding the store also crowded. Along the front of the wooden counter sat a line of middle-aged Indian men passing a stone pipe back and forth. She sensed that they had been talking but had stopped as she entered. They stared at her curiously, unabashed; yet today she did not resent it.

There were several families waiting. And at the back of the store she noticed immediately the man Westland who had brought Christine home the day before. She knew him at once. Yet he was not the same as her memory of him. He was taller; his face bony, not even; his hair dark, not light. Only the eyes were the same, long and deep-set, light brown and wrinkled at the corners. It was his gentleness with Christine, she decided, that had softened his features and lightened his hair.

He was talking to a man in cowboy clothes whom she took to be white; yet, as she regarded him further, she became sure he was Indian. His complexion was dark, and his hair, but his eyes were amber, almost yellow. His clothes were all black save a red bandanna, like a splash of blood at his throat. It was this that marked him as Indian.

Near her she saw an Indian woman of about her own age also watching the two men. She wore a beautifully beaded white buckskin dress and carried a baby in a cradleboard on her back. Two shy little girls with long braids and dresses exactly like her own crowded her on one side. At the other was Little Wound, the blind boy she had seen in the coach.

Leah stepped back against the wall to watch as she waited, immensely relieved by Christine's unwonted behavior; her embarrassing fear of Indians was gone completely—or she was so completely immersed in her make-believe that she did not notice them, or even see them. The recurring thought shocked Leah and turned her attention again to her child.

Christine had withdrawn her hand and was standing alone, just her shoulder touching Leah's skirt. There was a change in her attitude, her expression, the way she stood. Leah could not quite define it. But glancing at the blind boy, she saw that Christine must have been watching him. Her mimicry had caught a subtle dignity and quiet from the boy's manner.

His mother was watching Christine now, a certain recognition in her face. Her eyes touched Leah's briefly and moved away. But in the brief look was an eloquence of sympathy that moved Leah, and embarrassed her too. She wanted to explain Christine's deception but was afraid to approach.

Instead she turned partly away, hiding her feelings but glancing covertly at the woman, trying to fathom her strange attractiveness.

It was her clothing, Leah decided, that had caught her attention. It had none of the somber darkness of the reservation but was openly bright and colorful. The beaded patterns were stylized bird forms and curiously stepped triangles whose meanings she could not guess.

The man in cowboy clothes came over to the woman, and Leah knew immediately they were man and wife and, connecting him with the blind boy, knew his name as Crazy Walking. She had heard of him.

He stepped to the counter and bought some groceries, ammunition, and, after long consideration, a choker necklace of shiny dentalium shells, which he put around his wife's neck. He had some difficulty because of the cradleboard, but he worked with serious expression till the effect pleased him. Then he stepped back to look at her. A slight smile passed between them; the two little girls laughed up at them in sudden radiance; the blind boy raised his head, his eyes expressionless but joy alive in the lines of his face.

They gathered up their groceries and left, Crazy Walking in the lead, his family following. As the woman passed on the way to the door, she bent over and pressed something into Christine's hand and went on without looking at Leah. Christine did not look at the gift but stood turning it over and over in her hands with a half-fearful expression in her eyes. Then her face glowed with pleasure as she recognized the features of a small wooden doll.

The door closed, but Leah stood looking after the Indian family in a confusion of feeling. It was her first direct experience with Indians—not in the presence of her husband —and she was amazed and somehow chagrined. Christine held the two dolls uncertainly, the one of polished brown wood, the other of cloth, her eyes nervous, seeming to waver between her make-believe and the temptation of the reality.

Leah became aware then that the man Westland was standing before her, waiting for her glance. She hesitated an instant, collecting her feelings, before looking up at him. Yet when she did she became instantly herself again and calm. Something in his attitude—his eyes, the way he held his hat —made her conscious, with sudden, almost forgotten warmth, of her own beauty.

He met her eyes for a moment and looked down at Christine.

"Is she all right?" he asked. "No ill effects from her adventure?"

Leah shook her head. "No. She's lonesome. She has no one to play with except Buttons—the doll. And now the doll is blind. So we've come to find buttons for eyes. Or eyes for Buttons," she added, trying to elicit a smile from Christine.

Christine did not smile. But impulsively she thrust the rag doll toward Westland without looking up.

He took the doll reluctantly and with evident embarrassment. But when he saw the missing eyes, he became immediately concerned. He put the doll under his arm and pulled a pearled blue button off the cuff of his coat. He bent over and held the button against the doll's face for Christine to see.

"It's blue, like your own," he said, "but not as nice. Do you like it?"

She nodded—still without looking. And before Leah could stop him he had pulled off another button. He knelt beside Christine and held them in place with two fingers.

"When they're sewed on with dark thread she'll look much better. See much better, that is."

Christine took the doll and the buttons, at last finding her voice. "Thank you," she said, her voice just audible. But when he stood up her eyes followed him in recognition and shy pleasure. "I'm sorry I bit you," she said. "I like you now."

Leah looked at him, startled.

"It's all right," he smiled, rubbing his neck. "I can spare another bite if it'll make you go on liking me."

Christine did not take her eyes off him.

"When you go away," she asked, "will you write to me and maybe send me pictures of the world out there?"

The earnestness in her voice brought tears to Leah's eyes. She looked down quickly, knowing he had noticed.

"I'm not going away," he said. "Not soon. But maybe you'll let me walk home with you and we can talk about what it's like out there?"

Christine nodded. She held both dolls in one arm, gave him her hand, and turned toward the door.

He glanced at Leah. She nodded.

## ❧ II ❧

The people were already gathering at the issue ground when Turning Hawk crossed the creek and stopped at the top of the hill. Below on the dusty, grassless flat was the release corral that he himself and his young men had built, bare poles set in a circle, tied together with rawhide. At one side, across the release gate, was a smaller division, above it the raised platform where the white man would sit with his book calling the ration for each hungry family.

The circle of poles, the gathering people, stirred a faint and far-off memory; he stopped at the top of the hill to wait for it to rise, to shine clear of the darkness of the past.

Little Wound, coming abreast, stopped his pony and turned his face questioningly, for an instant, then ahead toward the flat as if he were seeing. He sat the horse with ease, making himself one with its line and movement, his face confident, eager—a terrible bravery shining from silence and darkness.

Turning Hawk looked again at the flat, the image of the boy vivid in his heart. Wagons, buggies, horses were clustered on the near side of the corral; the people were gathering near the gate, forming slowly into two lines that extended out from the gate like horns. Beyond he saw the dust of a band of cattle moving in slowly.

It was then that the memory he was awaiting rose up before him to merge somehow with the image of the boy: far below, a great circular enclosure at the foot of a bluff; above, two lines of stones spreading back from the bluff's edge like wings, like horns over the yellow, undulating hills. The picture spread vividly before him, overlaying the tiny ring on the grey flat below till it was gone and he became the boy on the painted horse, looking down from a high hill. The yellow color of fall on the far-turning hills shimmered under the sun, far to the red and blue distance of the mountains. White clouds bloomed and grew towering against the sky edge of the world, casting shadows below, dark islands in the yellow sea. A band of antelope, a moving cloud shadow, circled, flashing as white as foam on each turn, a prayer to the sun of movement and color.

From a white circle of lodges in a green valley, a line of people and horses moved toward the enclosure, behind the four councilors, buckskin, beadwork, and paint bright on the earth. They gathered at the base of the bluff, paused, and went on up, separating into files that moved out along the wings. Beyond the last stones a herd of buffalo grazed, dark brown on the yellow grass, among them clouds of birds that rose and circled and dropped. He saw the caller of buffalo with his brown robe dancing near the animals to catch their attention; saw the herd move toward him, gathering to a brown stream, flowing between the converging wings toward the bluff. The leaders plunged wildly over and the stream was solid, flesh of the earth sliding, a fall of meat and robes —life for his people. Dust rose in the enclosure and the vision was gone, fading to the grey land before him, the yellow to the color of dust.

The cattle were nearing the corral, trailing a grey plume; in the distance the dust rose shadowy against the sky. The two lines of people formed an arrowhead, its point against the circle of the corral at the gate; far out between them, at the point where the shaft would join, a man stood, moving his arms and body in a strange dance.

Turning Hawk rode down slowly, with the shadowy, unclear feeling of a dream begun, not ended; he would awaken. He arrived at the corral before the cattle. The man was still out between the wings, waving his arms and shouting—the small white man with the coughing sickness who had been at the jail.

The people watched him curiously, though few of them could understand his words. His voice was loud, with the hoarseness of the crow, but compelling with intense, controlled rage. The movements of his hands were jerky, angular; yet through the blur of unknown speech and gesture, Turning Hawk could sense a strange and tortured meaning. He spoke of the road of the living with bitterness and anger, but of the road of the spirits with a curious tenderness, his wrinkled face softening, his eyes bright with a rapt, inward shining.

The riders were bringing the cattle in with much show and shouting. But they came slowly, rebelliously, though the herd was small. It was the last of the agency herd, the old, the wild ones, cattle from the south, culled from the white men's herds, tough and wiry from the long trail north. There would be scant rations, hunger in the lodges, before the arrival of a new herd. And he knew now that it too would be short. The drought had taken the crops. He shook his head, closing his heart to the darkness of the future.

The cattle came on, more slowly now, sensing a trap in the waiting lines of people. The preacher heard the riders and looked toward them, not ceasing to shout and gesture. And for an instant Turning Hawk was on the hill again, the richness of the sun-bright grass, the buffalo vision, filling his heart. Then it was gone and the scene before him struck again, shaking his heart with its mockery: the small corral, the shrunken numbers of the people; and the pale death-

41

ridden white man gesturing between the wings, strange caller to the bony, white man's buffalo.

The cattle were close now. A tall buckskin steer in the lead shook his head and bawled at the preacher, lifted to a trot and, close up, lowered his head and broke into a gallop. But on the first jump his knees buckled and he fell forward, nose plowing the dust.

The preacher only glanced at the steer and went on talking even after the shout of warning rose clamorously above his voice. The steer came to his feet again, straightening his knees carefully as he rose. The knee cords had been cut, Turning Hawk knew, a trick of the white man for taming the wild ones.

Crazy Walking, one of the riders, rode up then, putting his horse between the steer and the preacher. He shouted something, but the man did not heed or even look at him. The steer lowered its head, close to the horse now, and Crazy Walking grabbed the preacher by an arm and carried him struggling over to the line of people. The cattle moved in and the people closed behind, hiding the man from sight. They moved around the corral, peering at the cattle between the posts, the animation of hunger on their faces. A few young men on gaunt, listless ponies rode around the corral, awaiting impatiently the short excitement of the beef killing. The clerk had not arrived. The riders, who would handle the cattle at the gate, waited awhile in the corral, then came out and dismounted.

Turning Hawk saw the preacher again, climbing the gate. He clambered down inside, walked through the release pen to the center of the main corral. The cattle were crowded against the side of the corral opposite the gate, milling restlessly and bawling. The buckskin steer came to the edge of the bunch and stood watching the man suspiciously. When he raised his hands again and began shouting, the steer shook his head and trotted forward, head up, his long neck slightly arched. A murmur rose among the people, subsiding as the steer came to a halt, not five steps from the man.

The preacher did not turn, but he seemed to sense the animal's nearness. He stopped talking and stood motionless, arms upraised, seeming to balance on his toes. For an instant there was complete stillness, even the sounds of the children ceasing.

The man dropped his arms and the steer charged, head

down, but slowly as if knowing that his knees might buckle. At the last possible instant the preacher stepped backward, turning the steer slightly, then ahead again, and it looked as if the steer had missed him. Then he was lifted up and jerked violently backward, and for an instant he seemed to be impaled on the great length of the steer's horn.

The steer tossed his head and the man dropped free and rolled on the ground, stripped clean of clothing from the waist up. But the horn had missed him.

The steer went wild with the coat and shirt flapping across his eyes. A sleeve had wrapped around the other horn, preventing him from shaking it loose. He bawled in terror and tried to run, but his knees buckled and he went down. He struggled for what seemed like a long time before he regained his feet, then he tried to run again and again fell.

The preacher stood up slowly, dazedly. He was wrapped with dust as with a robe, only a spot of skin showing under one arm, shining bloodlessly white. He stood for a while motionless, a figure of clay; then, with dreamy slowness, he drew a white cloth from his pocket and began brushing the dust from his arms and chest. The dust came off in little puffs as from the surface of dry rawhide, leaving his body spotted grey-white, like sun-bleached bone. He stopped brushing and stood motionless again, exposed in a bright light.

A gasp of wonder escaped the people; and Turning Hawk knew that they, also, were seeing the bones under the skin. The bones moved. The preacher put the cloth back in his pocket, still with the same dream-like motion, and turned slowly, gazing around with fixed, glassy eyes.

He stopped and raised one arm toward someone among the people, one finger extended, and drew it toward himself, beckoning. For an instant in Turning Hawk's vision the figure seemed to burn with inner fire, a dreamed figure of fearful, unrecognized significance.

He looked away and saw the steer coming finally to his feet. He trotted toward the other cattle, still tossing his head, trying to shake loose the clothing. The cattle watched him approach, and Turning Hawk knew they would run.

Then, as if drawn by the beckoning figure, Crazy Walking stepped into the corral. And in that instant Turning Hawk had a vision of him gone under the hoofs of the cattle. He moved his horse forward to interfere, but a mass of people

43

was pressed between. He could do nothing but watch with foreboding. Crazy Walking reached the preacher just as the herd stampeded ahead of the steer. They came toward the two men, following the curve of the corral. Crazy Walking caught the man up under one arm as he would a child and stepped back toward the center of the corral, just beyond the sweep of a passing horn. As the last one passed he hurried through the gate into the release pen. He set the pale white man carefully on his feet and Turning Hawk drew a breath of relief. But it was short. Crazy Walking returned to the main corral, closing the gate behind him.

The space was alive now with racing, bawling animals, blurred with swirling, eddying dust that rose and swept outward, a grey banner in the wind. The cattle were no longer in a bunch but crisscrossing, dodging, twisting, colliding, trying to climb the fence; and at the center the buckskin steer whirled and bawled.

Crazy Walking paused at the edge of the corral, balanced like a diver, then moved in cleanly, threading the maze of motion with the sure skill of a dancer, always just out of the path of the hurtling bodies, beyond the curve of the sweeping horns. He gained the clear circle where the steer whirled and, in a few quick passes, unwound the sleeve and pulled the torn clothing free.

Eyes clear, the steer charged as Crazy Walking moved away, but he turned off sharply, a horn just brushing his side. He regained the gate, emerging from the dust as from turbulent water, and gave the white man his clothes.

A shout of approval went up from the people. The sound startled Turning Hawk; his vision cleared; around him the light seemed to brighten. And as the small, dusty white man emerged from the corral still buttoning the tattered coat, he found himself smiling.

Though the horse was lagging, Martin put the buggy whip back into the socket, determined not to use it. By some perverse animal instinct, the horse seemed to know when he would use it and when not. Fortunately the issue grounds were just over the rise beyond the creek.

He glanced at Westland self-consciously, but the young man's eyes, alight with interest, were scanning the scene around. He had an open sketchbook on his knees on which he had drawn the agency and the camp below; and even with the buggy in motion he was filling in the details.

They crossed the west fork of Arrow Creek, and at the top of the rise Martin stopped and watched curiously while Westland continued his sketching. The plan he had drawn was too symmetrical, Martin thought, the figures too neat; yet when he looked back from the rise, he saw that it was accurate: the square of agency buildings was at the base of a triangular flat that sloped downward, north, for half a mile to the point where the two forks of Arrow Creek joined. The road they had just traveled ran straight east and west between the two crossings dividing the square from the circle of Indian lodges—perhaps fifty of them, though not so many were on the sketch. On down and shaped to the point of the triangle was a cluster of cabins, the winter camp. Almost the only asymmetry in the sketch, he noticed, was the chapel east of the square on the north side of the road, and his own small house across from it; both seemed oddly out of place.

He spoke to the horse and drove on toward the issue grounds, and seeing the flurry of activity was sorry he had offered to make this trip—though he felt indebted because of Christine. But he hated the custom of the live beef issue, had worked hard to have it abolished. It was depressing, heathenish. It seemed to revive, as nothing else, the latent savagery of the Indians. It was this he hated. He had tried to explain it to Westland, but to no effect. The man was consumed, eaten up by an unholy interest in the old ways of the

Indians. It was almost indecent, Martin thought—though he had not said so.

Below, he saw a swirl of dust rising from the corral, within it a scramble of milling cattle. A wild shout rose suddenly from the Indians, sending a chill through him. The sound was savage, the voices of the men distinct from the high fluttering cry of the women. It was not a Christian sound—not even human, he thought. He found the whip in his hand and again thrust it back into the socket.

When he reached the grounds, he pulled in among the wagons and buggies next to the corral and unhitched, declining Westland's help. He tied the horse to a wheel and, reaching his walking stick from under the seat, led the way toward the corral.

A vicious, hungry-looking band of dogs had gathered among the wagons. He tried to go around them, but they had caught his scent and came at him now, full cry. He gripped his walking stick grimly and, waiting till the first dog was almost on him, struck. The leaded end of the cane connected solidly with skull; the dog dropped, his roar changed to high yelping timed to the rhythm of his still-galloping legs. The others scattered, and Martin went on, glancing back nervously till he saw the dog rise and crawl dizzily under a wagon.

He found himself smiling then, feeling again the swing of the stick, the solid impact. In his long battle with the Indian dogs, it was the first time he had used the stick since filling the end of it with lead. It was better than he had hoped. He saw Westland, who was abreast of him now, glancing at him curiously.

"They're vicious," he explained. "The very symbol of savagery, these Indian dogs."

"They've found an able antagonist."

"The Lord strengthens me. A mission among the Indians is not for the timid or the weak. As you shall see."

There was a circle of Indians at one side of the corral. Coming nearer, he saw a small, disheveled man within the circle, speaking. He knew the man instantly as a preacher in spite of the dirt and rags. He crowded up close, unmindful of Westland, listening, amazed at the words of the preacher.

". . . the Indian nations rising, reborn to the old ways, a new culture rising like the Phoenix from the ashes of the

46

old. Civilization is doomed, the white man is doomed to burn everlastingly in the hell of his own making, the unending fire with no ashes and no rebirth."

It was incredible. For the moment he was too amazed even to be angry. The preacher went on, but at that moment someone touched Martin on the shoulder and he turned to face the Major and his two clerks.

"Reverend, are you a convert already," the Major asked, "or will you help me put a stop to this nonsense? My police won't touch him."

Martin nodded. Westland also agreed to help, though reluctantly, it seemed.

"Spread around the circle then, and move in," the Major said decisively.

Martin pushed to the front of the crowd, filled all at once with anger at the little preacher.

It was a perfect surround. They were in close on all sides before the man even noticed them. When he did, he crouched like a frightened animal, immobile for an instant. Then, without even looking for an opening, he rushed directly at Martin, with a wild, ferocious look.

Instinctively, Martin stepped backward; and in the instant of his unbalance, the man hit him, fingers, curved to claws, reaching for his face. He fell, striking out with the cane and missing; and the man fell on him, face against Martin's, eyes fierce, breath foul.

Then the preacher was on his feet, free; but at the last instant, just as he started to run, Martin rolled over and reaching out with the cane caught his ankle in the crook. He came down hard, splashing a puff of dust outward, his breath exploding in a cry. He lay still, stunned.

Martin stood up, brushing self-consciously at his clothes. He felt week-kneed and shaky and a little sick. Looking at the little man crumpled there in the dust, he was amazed and puzzled by his own fierce anger and sudden fear. The clerks stood over the preacher, waiting for him to move.

"Thanks, Reverend," the Major said. "We might have missed him except for your shepherd's crook."

"It's a versatile instrument," Westland said.

Martin turned away, embarrassed. The little preacher stood up slowly and the clerks seized both his arms, forcing them together behind his back. The Major stepped forward and snapped on a pair of handcuffs and, after thanking Martin and Westland, led the way through the crowd, the clerks following with their captive.

The Indians parted ahead of them and closed in again, shifting their gaze now from the preacher to Martin himself, their faces, as always, impassive, dark.

Unconsciously Martin began brushing his clothes again, but stopped, aware that he was the center of the circle. He was oppressed by it, constricted; he could think of nothing to say, had not even a desire to talk. He wanted to run, to escape; but he did not move.

There were members of his congregation among the Indians, but they gazed at him as impassively as the others. They were not unfriendly or hostile, he knew. They only seemed more alien than usual, more uncivilized.

It was the clothing, he thought. Many of the young men were stripped to leggings and breechclouts, chests and faces painted with wild designs, in preparation for the beef killing. Nearly all carried guns. In front of him an ancient medicine man stood, leaning on an old Sharp's rifle. He was wearing a striped flannel nightshirt, unspeakably dirty, that hung almost to his knees, cinched in at the waist by a cartridge belt. His braids, wrapped in fur, hung far down in front; his head was lost in a huge, black hat. The clothing, combined with the indescribable pride and dignity of the old man, was explosively funny . . . The urge to laugh was sudden, hysterical; but he suppressed it. He turned to Westland, but he had moved into the crowd. Martin saw him at last, talking to Crazy Walking.

The circle seemed to dissolve then of itself, and Martin was alone in the crowd, no longer surrounded. One of the clerks came by, carrying the ration roll book under his arm. He climbed to the release platform, opened the book, and called the name of an Indian. The Indians were moving in lines forming a V with the point at the gate. Martin found himself alone between the lines and hurried to join Westland at one side.

A middle-aged Indian rode up then with half a dozen savage-looking young men and boys following. The clerk made a mark in the roll book and shouted, "Release." The gate of the chute below swung open and a long-horned steer burst free. The waiting Indians charged in behind him, yelling and whooping fearfully, and the steer bolted for the open, tail in the air.

48

Dust rose up behind and moved off in the same direction as the steer and riders, obscuring them; the yelling came as from a cloud, wild and eerie. The figures faded to moving outlines, scarcely visible.

Martin held his ears against the expected shots, yet he heard them. And in the same instant Westland nudged him. He turned to find himself directly in the path of a bunch of mounted Indians coming full tilt around the corral. They were laughing and yelling, riding toward him deliberately. Instinctively, he stepped behind Westland, gripping his cane, holding his arm up before his eyes. The riders swept by, just grazing him on either side. The smell of Indians, horses, paint was strong in the air.

He lowered his arm to find Westland smiling at him unperturbed and was swept by a violent resentment.

"Are they always so playful?" Westland asked.

Martin nodded and turned quickly away, not trusting himself to speak. He started for home then, leaving Westland to get back by himself. Thinking of the blood and smell of the butchering to come, he knew he could not stay longer. He did not look back. Skirting the clutter of Indian wagons to avoid the dogs, he came at last to his own buggy. He hitched the horse and, climbing into the seat, took the whip from the socket. But the horse stepped out fast with no urging.

## ❧ 13 ❧

Little Wound sat his pony on the dusty side of the corral, absorbed in the beef issue. One hand resting on a post told him of the opening and closing of the gate—the harsh, tickling vibration of the hinges, the sudden smash of wood on wood as it closed. He caught a whiff of cattle smell each time a steer left the chute, then the swirl of dust it raised. He felt the chatter of its feet on the earth and the sudden thunder of horses drumming off in pursuit, fading, ended after a little by the sharp smack of rifle fire against his face.

The pony moved restlessly under him, crouching, trembling each time a group of riders left the gate. In himself was an answering excitement, a pulsing need to follow. Instead he held the pony sternly against the fence, gathering eagerly with his hands all the grating, scraping, pounding vibrations.

Within the circle of the corral he could feel the presence of the cattle—the movement of the fence when they pressed against it, the pounding of their feet as they moved away from the riders; the pause, then the sharp, solid footfalls of the horses and the frenzied beat of the single steer separated and forced into the release pen.

The sense of the movement came to him through his fingers. Their presence, the knowledge of their placement in space, was a reaching out, a touching, as if his hand moved out and held them, separate, knowing the curve of horn, the furry, sharp-boned, tightly muscled bodies. But as the steer moved off after the release, with its pursuers drumming into distance, the feeling changed. Dark figures entered a field of yellow light that hung always far and dim at the edge of his memory, moving blurred, brown on a yellow circle till the smack of shots battered the air and the hoofbeats grew still. He was drawn backward, then, out of the past and the light. Almost with pain he felt the now of darkness close and his perception once again became a hand moving in space.

The dream was like this, the dream he had had on the iron road: he was held in the white man's moving house, drawn backward into a tunnel of darkness, its mouth the circle of light, growing smaller, dimmer, till he awakened fearfully, opening eyes on darkness, with his body feeling the motion, the din, with his hands finding his grandfather's and knowing—only then—it was a dream.

Yet now, with each release of a steer, he seemed to move with the riders toward the light, and each time felt the tense excitement of the people rise, as if they moved beside him, then pause and fall away in darkness.

Another steer was ready for release—he felt it straining the sides of the chute trying to turn. Horns clattered on the wood, poles of the chute twisted, grating in their rawhide bindings. His hands knew the twist of neck and spine, the reaching muzzle, as if they held the animal. Currents of wind brought him the green, dusty smell of its excitement.

In the pause a rider approached; Little Wound caught the

well-known odor of his father and reached out, touching hands, knowing instantly with near-bursting excitement that he could ride after this one.

He moved his pony up beside his father's, facing the gate, felt the muscles under him tighten, the head turn, felt through the horse the faint impact of the steer's feet as it left the chute. He gripped with his knees and the pony shot forward, leaning into the turn, straightening full speed, muscles bunching, flattening under him in waves, and he riding only the crests, lightly, hardly feeling his own weight.

There were riders beside him, he knew, but none ahead. Dirt and sand from the steer's feet stung his face and hands. He could smell the animal clearly, the cattle smell and the sharp, indefinable odor of its terror.

He rode easily, with no thought of fear, seeming to float, to soar bird-like, encompassed in warmth, even with the cool wind pushing against him, curling and catching at his back.

Shots crashed flat as thunder on the air, the pony swerved, jarred to a stop, and danced, trembling and tossing his head. His father's hand touched his leg and he dismounted, downwind from the steer, catching the hot, steamy smell of its blood, feeling through his feet the loose-muscled, galloping spasm: hoofs striking and scraping, a rubbing of furred liquid muscle on the dry stubble of the grass.

He stood beside his father, holding his hand, the vision of the animals and the light returning. His mother arrived with the pack horses and also came to stand beside him, her hand in his. He was enclosed, enfolded in a sphere of warmth, of strength, before him bright and strong the circle of the yellow light, the blurred, moving figures.

Yet even as he stood, the dream recurred: he was drawn backward into a tunnel of darkness. He held tightly to the two strong hands, trying to stop, to stay, to hold the vision. But he could not.

He let go then and, turning, found his pony. On his cheeks he felt a wetness, a coolness, and found with surprise that his eyes were streaming tears.

Westland worked at his notes and sketching, leaning against the corral, at the same time keeping an eye on the progress of the beef issue. He had drawn the corral itself, the circular structure and its divisions, giving just an indication of the lines of Indians spreading out from the gate. It was only a rough sketch, the jogging of his pencil a graph of the times the cattle had crowded the fence or the gate slammed. Yet it was not just a diagram; there was feeling in it too, a mood, an elusive meaning.

He had drawn in detail the raised platform and the clerk who called the Indian names from the roll book. Looking at the sketch now, he wondered why he had given so much prominence to the one white man when his main interest was Indians. Yet he did not change it. The man was a focal point, important beyond his function as keeper of the roll. He was a representative of the victorious, a symbol of dominance; yet for the moment, surrounded by the defeated, he seemed nervous. Westland had seen him in the Major's office and later in the hotel, an assured, even arrogant young man. He hardly seemed the same person now.

It was the beef issue, he decided, remembering also the anxiety, the thinly veiled fear of the missionary, Martin. It was a part of the old ways, a heathenish custom, as Martin had said, an unexpected, surprising manifestation of cultural strength, yet also a blindness, a backward turning. But it accounted for the elation he had sensed in the Indians since his arrival at the issue grounds, as it also accounted for the nervousness of the two white men.

He himself was not nervous but was also filled with elation, partly, he hoped, as an identification with the Indians—he felt their excitement intimately—but mostly, he knew, from the success of his own plans. He was free now to get on with his study; he was full of impressions, eager to get them all down, to understand.

He was too much involved, he thought, his impressions too

personal. Yet for all that, he felt a meaning, a continuity in all the impressions, if he could disentangle it. Even the shadowy figure of the little preacher seemed of a piece with the rest. But it was all strange, unreal; the reservation a curious twilight land between two worlds. To explore it, he would need the light of both.

Out some distance from the gate, behind the near line of people, Turning Hawk sat his horse, impassive, gloomy, taking no part. Little Wound, the blind deaf boy, sat a pinto pony near Westland, his hand resting on a post of the corral. What he could know of the action Westland could not imagine, but he seemed as alert and curious as a colt. His face was flushed after his ride, alight with what seemed joy. Yet on his cheeks were stains of tears.

Westland had been amazed by the ride, the skill of the child, the strength and courage; he tried to imagine riding in a dark, soundless void but could not. The very thought was fearful. The scene was fixed in his mind as if by shock: the boy in clean, quilled leggings and breechclout, naked from the waist up, riding the pinto pony with unbelievable balance and grace; beside him Crazy Walking, dressed in cowboy clothes, horse saddled and bridled, resembling his son only in the skill and the joy of doing.

Watching them, Westland had an intimation of time reversed, the strange riders moving downwind into a cloud of dust as into the past. Only the figure of Crazy Walking had seemed out of place, but in the dust, the wild riding, he became one of the group.

After the kill, he had watched the boy ride back alone to the corral, circling till he was directly downwind, then coming straight in, as if by scent. Another group of riders swept out on the tail of a steer, passing close to the boy. His pony reared and tried to turn but he turned it back easily and rode on in.

The boy found Turning Hawk and sat beside him briefly, then rode back to the same spot he had left, on the dusty side, near Westland, putting his hand again on the post.

The pony was keyed up after the run. Sweat roughened the sorrel hair of the shoulder and flank, darkened the white of the neck. He danced in one spot, tossing his head, trying to go, but the boy held him calmly, never taking his hand from the post.

Westland moved closer along the fence. The pony, catching his scent, snorted and reared, white-eyed. He stepped back and sketched the boy and horse quickly, thinking that if he were painting he would try to catch the living glow of color against the dead grey of the fence and the dust that swept over from the corral.

Westland heard the gate swing open and, glancing up through the line of people, saw a buckskin steer step out of the chute and stop. He stood facing the riders, tossing his horns and blowing. When they crowded in, yelling, he turned and trotted away along the edge of the corral, scattering the far line of people, disappearing around the curve of the fence toward the spot where the wagons and buggies clustered.

Westland returned to his sketching, hearing the yelling and whooping of the Indians trying to stampede the steer. There was a single rifle shot and, a moment later, a clamor of voices near the gate. He looked up to see the people scattering away from the gate and, beyond, just appearing around the curve of the fence, a runaway team and wagon, stampeded, he supposed, by the riders. The off line was flapping loose, but the near one, still tied to the seat, was drawing the team in toward the corral, directly at him.

It was too late to cross in front; the fence was too high to climb. He turned to run, looking back at the team that was almost on him, not afraid but gauging the distance he would have to go beyond the point where the team's path would touch the corral. He heard a horse snort ahead of him and only then remembered Little Wound. Looking ahead, he saw the pony, eyes and nostrils wide, shying away from him into the path of the runaway. He turned in close to the fence, went on by, and stopped, paralyzed, almost afraid to look.

He saw the pony try to bolt away from the corral, saw the boy rein him back toward the fence. But it was too late. In the last instant the pony tried to go between the two horses. There was a sickening impact of flesh and leather and breaking wood. The pony reared and came over backward screaming, impaled on the tongue.

Little Wound jumped clear of the pony, striking the ground on his back, hard, almost at Westland's feet, and lay unmoving. The team paused, plunging to clear the pony, and in that instant Westland caught the boy by the arm and jerked him back against the fence, just as the near horse plunged by, brushing him with outflung rump. The hub of a wheel sent him spinning along the fence and he fell, twisting to light on his shoulder with the boy on top. His head struck the bottom of a post and for an instant he was in darkness.

He sat up, with odd patches of light and darkness shifting around him, and lifted the boy and laid him on the ground, though he still could not see, aware vividly of the heavy limpness of the sturdy young body.

He looked up, vision clearing, to see the team still running, the wagon zigzagging wildly behind them, the tongue broken. Some distance out, where it had been dragged by the wagon, the pony was struggling to rise, lifting its head and dropping it and lifting it again, making odd snuffling noises. The neck and shoulder were smeared with blood; a splintered piece of the wagon tongue showed in the chest.

Westland turned back, his hand shaking as he touched the boy's forehead. Red paint smeared in his hand, almost the color of blood, but not wet; being near he caught the Indian smell of tallow, wood smoke, leather, an earthen, musk odor. The boy's eyelids fluttered open and Westland let out his breath in a long sigh.

Little Wound sat up then, just as Turning Hawk reached his side, a wildness in his eyes. Westland, glancing up, saw the look mirrored in the old man's face; saw the relief, the return of calmness settling on the lined old face like a mask.

He heard a shot near and saw the pony drop its head and lie still. He touched the boy's shoulder in reassurance, trying to communicate some measure of his concern. For an instant the boy seemed to respond, then he stiffened suddenly. Westland saw the blind eyes widen, the nostrils dilate. Little Wound rolled backward, twisting cat-like, and was on his feet, backing away in terror. Turning Hawk stepped to him quickly, grasping his arm, and the small, drawn face relinquished its terror, the brow smoothed.

Westland was shocked; he had an affinity for children, a spontaneous affection that had never before been rejected. He was perplexed and, seeing the smile in Turning Hawk's eyes, realized that it showed on his face.

The old man moved two fingers up past his nose in a sign that Westland guessed meant smell, then drew an index finger across his brow, a graphic sign for hat—hat people, he remembered, white men. He nodded, understanding, remembering that the horse also had shied from the smell of him.

There was a circle of Indians around him now. Turning Hawk was making more signs, but Westland could not grasp the meaning, in his confusion did not even try. He felt alone, a stranger; for an instant even saw himself as strange, an alien with an alien odor, an odor that could frighten an animal, a child. It was a humbling, belittling thought.

In his fall he had dropped his sketchbook. An Indian stepped forward, holding it out. Pages blowing open gave him glimpses of his notes and drawings—the oddities only, he realized suddenly, the points of difference from the white man. A white man's view, no more. He was ashamed of his presumption.

The Indian pointed, smiling with appreciation, to his drawing of the corral. He felt encouraged then; there was common ground.

Crazy Walking and his woman rode up at a gallop, both bloody and sweating from the butchering. They reined up barely in time to avoid hitting the circle of people, dismounting in the opening they had made while the horses were still moving. They lifted the boy up and held him between them, chattering nervously with Turning Hawk, relief and affection shining in their faces. They turned at last to Westland with gratitude and no reproach.

Crazy Walking held out his hand. "It was a brave thing to do," he said. "A runaway wagon is a dangerous contraption. Now I owe you more than money."

Westland took his hand with some ambiguity of feeling. "I did only what anyone would do, or try to do. It was my fault in the first place, since the pony shied from the smell of me."

"You can't help the way you smell. You were born white as he was born Indian. More Indian than most, I think. But it's too late now to shy away from the smell of the white man."

The clerk called another name then from the platform. The crowd dispersed. Little Wound seemed quite recovered, though he was still pale. When Crazy Walking set him back on the ground, he drew his grandfather's attention, made the question sign, and straddled the edge of his left hand with two fingers of his right—horse, Westland knew.

The old man passed his right hand under his left, out and down. Gone under, dead—it was almost the same as the deaf-mute sign.

Little Wound looked puzzled and moved away downwind, searching. He passed the dead pony, stopped, catching its

56

scent, and walked directly to it. He touched the neck first with his feet and, stooping, ran his hand along the mane and down the muzzle. His hand paused briefly on the nose, then moved back up to the glazed, open eye. He touched the pupil lightly with his finger tips, over and over, his face intent, doubting. He caught the forelock and pulled tentatively, trying to lift the head, but he could not. Westland had expected him to be shocked; but there was only doubt in his face, and a tense curiosity.

He ran his hand back down the nose and, finding the braided rope that was looped around the lower jaw, drew the whole length of it through his hands, recognition clear on his face. He pulled on the rope for what seemed a long time before he gave up and walked further downwind, wandering, seeking.

"It's something he doesn't understand," Crazy Walking said. "Death. He knows the carcass is not the horse and he's right. But he still thinks he'll find it alive—it's lost, not dead. Like the buffalo," he added with irony, indicating the group of riders just leaving the gate in pursuit of a steer.

"But you rode too," Westland said, questioning.

"It's a custom. But it was a steer I chased, not a buffalo. I know the horse is dead, and the buffalo. For an Indian, the future is dead, only the past alive."

There was nothing Westland could say. He stood silently while Crazy Walking mounted again and, riding up alongside, took the boy up behind him. His woman and Turning Hawk rode after him. Westland went back to his place by the corral, but he had no more heart for the sketching.

$\approx$ 15 $\gg$

Crazy Walking sat at the back of his lodge smoking in the quiet coolness of evening. The wind had gone down. The lodge cover was rolled up at the bottom and the air flowed around him, bringing the smell of cooking, of green hides and smoke and fresh meat from the beef issue of the day before.

At one side of the lodge his woman, Blue Fawn, was pegging a hide out for fleshing, moving with sureness and vigor. Her hands were strong and she used them with skill and visible pleasure. Her face was shining and all her movements rhythmical, as if she moved to a drumming and singing inaudible to him.

Near her, cradleboard propped against a wheel of the wagon, his youngest son babbled and cooed, squealing shrilly each time she looked his way, glowing in her affection as in the light of a fire. He was laced tightly in beaded buckskin, against the stiffness of the two boards, yet he was happy and unconstrained.

In front of the lodge Crazy Walking's two small daughters, Pretty Shield and Her Eagle Robe, played with much chatter and running to and fro. They were lacing a small white pup into a miniature cradleboard their mother had made for them, gleeful in anticipation.

The pup was enduring, yelping when he was dropped or squeezed too hard, licking their hands with conciliatory meekness.

When they had him fast, they dragged him hither and thither, hanging him up, taking him down, feeding him, brushing him with endless persistence. They tried to make him babble as the baby was doing, but he only licked their faces anxiously and whined.

They were tireless, his daughters, small replicas of their mother, secure in her imparted sureness, moving to the same music. They were patient and solicitous with the pup, but they would not let him go. They petted him and talked to him with affection. But the pup was not comforted. He became more and more fearful, turning his head from side to side, the whites of his eyes showing in a growing wildness. But the girls did not notice this. When he wet and the water trickled out at the bottom of the cradleboard, they shrieked with glee.

Crazy Walking stirred uneasily, curiously moved and irritated by the pup's predicament. But he expected the little girls to realize that the pup was only a pup and not a baby. They would release him soon. He sank back trying to ignore the play, to recapture the feeling of peace. But he could not. He was not much concerned about the pup; he supposed it would live for another kind of death. Being an Indian baby for a while would not kill it. But there was something about

58

the rising fear and wildness in the animal's movements that made him lean forward unconsciously, chills moving on his skin in little gusts.

Blue Fawn glanced at the girls now and then with amusement, but she did not interfere with their play. She was absorbed in her work with the hide.

The pup began yelping wildly then. He bit the younger girl on the hand and she cried for a moment. But her smiles soon returned, and her solicitude for the pup. They rocked him and sang to him—careful to stay out of the reach of his teeth. Still they made no move to release him. He was twisting his head from side to side, crying continually, snapping his teeth crazily on the air.

Crazy Walking stood up then, a gathering nervousness jerking at his muscles. He stooped through the doorway of the lodge, holding himself tense and quiet, and jerked the cradleboard roughly away from the girls. He cut the lacing with the point of his knife, with intense effort controlling the shaking of his hand so as not to cut too deep.

The pup had not ceased to struggle. He came clear of the binding and, without any apparent change in his movements, gained his feet and began to run, still snapping, teeth clicking audibly. After a few jumps he fell, but again came up running. He was moving in a circle, gradually spiraling in. When his path tightened at the center, he fell again, his legs still galloping, though less rapidly. In a moment the movement stopped, the yelping died down to a rattling in the throat. The small body relaxed, then stiffened and lay still.

Crazy Walking was amazed. The pup was dead, for no apparent reason. He nudged it incredulously with his toe and was certain.

The two little girls were looking up at him in breathless wonder and fear. He sensed an accusation in their faces, too, as if he himself were responsible for what had happened. He knelt beside them and stroked their hair, and in a moment they were smiling again.

But he could not stay. He was nervous, possessed by a need to move, to act. He left abruptly, walking distractedly through the camp, hearing faintly above its busy humming the approach of the stagecoach. He saw it in the south, moving fast, dragging a plume of sunset-colored dust.

He was greeted often, with friendliness, but did not stop to talk. He went on, making a complete circuit of the camp by the time he saw the stage pull into the quadrangle. A moment later he heard his name, moving toward him on many lips.

Without knowing why, he broke into a run and did not stop until he reached the ring of people around the stagecoach in the square. The ring opened for him, leaving a small road to the open door of the coach. But having stopped moving, he could not start again, was strangely paralyzed. The stage driver stood by the coach, talking, swiftly and hysterically, his voice rising in pitch from the beginning to the end of each sentence and dropping again, a weird, musical singsong that he could not understand. Crazy Walking started along the road, his legs heavy and reluctant, held back by an invisible force, his ears full of the singsong of the driver's voice.

What he saw in the coach did not surprise him: a boy of perhaps twelve years lay face up on the floor between the seats, eyes open staring fixidly upward. His face was painted in smeared designs of red, his hair cut short. There was a dream-like familiarity in what Crazy Walking saw, as if he had seen it before, as if he himself had lain there staring upward.

The stage driver poked him with the butt of his whip and suddenly his words became intelligible.

"Is he yours? If he is, get him out. I'm late now. But I won't touch him. Get him out. You got to clean it up, too." His voice ended on a high flute-like note.

Crazy Walking saw the blood on the floor and the seat and the boy's clothing. The designs on the face were not painted but the marks of frantic fingers. The boy was his own Coming Sun; dead.

He let the realization touch him like baring flesh to knife. He saw the boy dying in the dusty coach on the white man's lonely road, drowning in his own blood.

He gathered the body up, vaguely aware of the continued singsong of the driver, and laid it on the earth. He took the rag the driver thrust at him, walked to the windmill, and wet it in the horse trough. Coming back to the coach, he scrubbed slowly at the blood on the floor and the seat, watching himself wonderingly as from a distance. He was lethargic, numb, yet deep down he felt a stirring, like the return of blood to frosted limbs, painful, stinging. The driver was hurrying him in his crazy voice, frantic to get rid of the blood.

Crazy Walking stopped scrubbing then, relieved as he had felt relief in the past on making offering to his medicine. But under the relief, the stirring became irritation. He decided with finality to silence the driver; he could stand the crazy singsong no longer.

But when he turned, knife in hand, the driver was on the coach, looking down at him silently and in terror. He sheathed the knife and turned back to the boy, kneeling, trying to see again the one who had gone away to the white man's school; but he could not. With the short-cropped hair, light-colored eyes, and the cloth suit, this boy might pass for white. A small cardboard folder showed in one of the pockets. He took it out and found two pictures, one of a boy in fringed, beaded buckskin, hair braided and wrapped, face painted, holding a fine stone pipe. The face was smiling and brave. The other, the same boy, was dressed as white, the hair short, the brave smile gone. The face was thin and serious and somehow frantic—the Indian boy looking out of a white boy's eyes. He remembered irrelevantly, but with a queer sinking feeling, the frightened pup bound in the cradleboard. He had sent the boy away to be made white as he himself had been—but as a man, a warrior, not a child. He had no defense against the thought. He threw the pictures down.

A piece of white tape was sewed to the boy's coat, a name, John Crazy Walking, printed on it. He pulled it off and tore it in strips. Then with sudden purpose, he took off all the clothes, leaving the thin body naked on the earth, only the burned bowl of a stone pipe tied by a leather thong around the neck. The clothing he took piece by piece and tore apart, the ripping sound a painful, bitter satisfaction in all his body. He worked at it long, even after Blue Fawn came and knelt over the body, beginning the terrible keening of her grief.

He saw dimly the ragged, pale preacher come out of the jail between two clerks and toward the stage. They put him into the coach on the far side; but instantly he was out of the door opposite, running. He disappeared into the warehouse, the clerks in pursuit.

Crazy Walking went on tearing the clothes till there was no piece big enough to hold with his two hands . . . He stood then, motionless among the shreds, sweating, in his heart rising a vision of flight, of soaring, circling, lifting in a high blue distance. A wind stirred in the square. The wind-

61

mill turned slowly, gathering speed, with each stroke of the jack its tinny scream rising hysterically.

He saw the clerks coming from the warehouse, a bundle between them wrapped tightly in a winding of red cloth. They brushed by him and he saw at one end of the bundle the grey, bony head of the pale preacher. The stage driver began shouting again in his singsong complaining voice, but the clerks paid him no heed. They lifted the red bundle to the railed top of the coach as to a burial platform.

Crazy Walking started then, with gathering terror. He caught up the thin, naked body of his son and fled from the square, the labored sound of his own breathing a screaming in his ears.

## 16

The night was quiet to Little Wound's listening touch, almost without vibration—only the rubbing of the breeze on the lodge cover against which he leaned and the almost imperceptible waves of his mother's muffled keening. He sat in the fireless lodge, tracing its circle with a finger in the palm of his hand, placing with light or heavy pressures the quiet persons of his family: at the back of the lodge (near his thumb) sitting upright, tense, a fireless pipe in hand, his father, perceived as a presence by little curls and wisps of odors in the moving air, the strong masculine person odor, the sharp tingling of cold, burned-out tobacco; nearer (deeper in his palm) his mother, her odor subtle, warm, earth-like, changed slightly in grief. His finger tips still held the sharp, contracting spasms of her throat when she had entered the lodge, bringing, with his father, the curious, cold image they called his brother. Beside his mother, the baby slept, his faint scent feathery and sweet as grass. The two small sisters slept uneasily beneath their robe, their odors babyish still and indeterminate, hardly differing from each other or from the baby.

These living he held in his hand; but not the cold, doll-image of his brother, Coming Sun, to his touch not even a particular image—he could tell that it was like a boy, but only as a doll was like. Yet about the still, hard form hung a faint persistent person odor that brought to him a memory of warmth, of flames flickering from a lodge fire, warm tongues licking his face lightly.

He shivered as if touched by a cold wind, the chill a presence in the lodge, odorless yet tainted. Something fearful hung just at the faint far edge of his odor perception. He flexed his legs to stand but settled back, subtly restrained, a weakness growing in his limbs, a nausea pressing with growing insistency at the pit of his stomach. His fingers numbed; the solid world of touch seemed to recede, to hang just out of reach, flat, unrelieved, leaving him alone, isolated with the tainted fearful presence. He sank backward on the robe, his limbs of terrible weight . . . But the nausea left him; he moved upward, outward, to float in a dark pool of air-thin water, in the distance a faint shining that grew brighter, yellower, till he could see dim figures against it. He strained to distinguish the blurred forms, but he could not. Yet in his touch perception he knew them: a child with a wooden doll under a tall dark-leaved tree, and beyond, against the light, his pony running away. He strove toward them but was drawn backward. Darkness fell on the bright circle like a tree falling, and with the same leaf-rustling movement . . .

He sat upright violently, with a sense of foreboding. Something was approaching, drawing nearer, not footsteps but a humming, whirling, faint vibration that he felt with his whole body. The air in the lodge seemed to stop, to freeze for an instant. Then the whirlwind came. With his head he felt the lodge quiver and strain upward; the entrance cover lifted and snapped with a report he felt like a blow against his face. Ashes and dust whirled up and eddied thickly in the air. Under his hand the furry robe arose, gathered itself like an animal crouching to spring, then dropped back flat and lifeless. The wind moved on, but he could feel it still, receding. His hand moved, bent at the wrist, the fingers drooping, tips whirling spirally upward, describing for his vision the wind person walking the darkness like a dancer. The dust and ashes settled.

He rose, released, and moved toward the entrance of the lodge. Passing, he paused to touch his mother's face, finding her distracted, withdrawn.

Beyond the entrance, he stood in the still night, knowing its quiet by the few, infrequent earth vibrations: a far, single drumbeat, light as the touch of a feather to his feet; a horse stamping, sharp and solid. Now, in the night, the world widened, became less tangible and solid. Distance was in the far earth scents that the wind carried; he knew vividly its freedom and loneliness.

He left the camp circle, walking slowly with a sense of seeking. His feet caught the sound of horses and he moved toward them, coming finally among them and standing, the sweet scent of chewed grass, the musky horse smell warm and comforting. But in a moment the band took fright and drummed away, leaving him alone in a drift of dust.

In his vision the dream rose again: the pony running away against the yellow light; the child that was himself under a dark tall-tilted shadow falling.

He turned quickly to another direction, as if to flee the dream. A dog nosed his hand; he paused to stroke it, then moved on restlessly, in his very hands a need, a reaching out toward flames. He turned again, keeping direction by the steady, dry flow of air, from the east, he knew, that brought the sacred burning smell of sage and cedar. He crossed the road and paused, reached out and touched a building, knowing its presence by the deflection of the air, the dry sun-baked smell of the logs. He turned along it, coming finally to the entrance of the square and going through.

He found the windmill, guided by the measured lift and fall of the pump. He drank at the horse trough and let his fingers swim in the cool water, the strange tingling need for a moment eased. Through the trough came insistently the rhythmic thin vibration of metal sliding on metal, a crying like an animal in fright or pain.

He moved on, wandering aimlessly in the square, placing the buildings in a solid pattern in his mind. Passing opposite the windmill again, his feet caught in a tangle of soft stringy stuff; he stooped and with his fingers found a mass of tangled, shredded cloth.

Again his nostrils caught the faint familiar person odor of his brother and, with a shock again, the tainted presence he had known in the lodge, more fearful now among the white-man smells. He ran then, following with his feet the wheel tracks that led from the square, slowing again to a walk only when he felt the constriction of the breeze between the buildings at the entrance.

Still he did not go back to camp. Following the road he moved east, past the trader's buildings, toward the place of the white man's sacred house, catching a whiff of smoke, of grass and sage burning like an offering of incense.

As he walked the smell grew stronger, smoke crossing his face in little gusts and swirls. He walked quickly along the road toward the fire, drawn by the odor of sage, by the memory of light leaping flames. Near the fire he left the road, finding a wooden fence which he followed till he came to a gate in the direct path of the smoke's flowing. He entered, already feeling the heat of the fire, the licking flames comforting as the touch of a friend, the odor of sage strong, mysterious, and sacred.

He touched the wheel of a buggy near the fire and stopped, aware suddenly that he did not know where he was. The buggy had a foreign smell of paint, cut pine, and metal. He ran his hands along the smooth side of the body toward the front, finding a thin, upright stick that came loose in his hand. He was trying to put it back in its hole when someone seized him fiercely by the shoulder. Above the hot smoke of the fire he caught a scent of white man, a strong, male person odor.

He jerked free, dropping the stick, and ran in terror, forgetting in his flight the wooden fence. He struck it shockingly and fell back, the world of his fingers spinning away beyond reach . . .

❧ 17 ❧

Leah sat quietly in the darkness of the bedroom, waiting for Christine to sleep. But the child was nervous and afraid, watching the leaping shadows cast on the wall by the fire outside. She held the rag doll protectively under the covers, asking often for the small brown Indian doll and as often thrusting it away.

Sitting by her, stroking her hair, Leah could see Martin moving around the fire, gathering trash to burn—trimmings from cedar fence posts, a pile of sagebrush grubbed out of the yard for the planting of poplars. Sagebrush and the low-growing wild roses he hated fiercely.

He moved vigorously now at the burning, crossing and recrossing between the fire and the window. Parts of his body, distorted and magnified, flashed constantly on the wall of the room. It was this, she discovered, that frightened Christine.

She rose and hung a quilt over the window and again waited, almost in complete darkness now, herself a little afraid without the light. She found herself holding the doll as she would a child. Through the fabric of the quilt she could still see dim flickering shadows, a clouded orange color. But as her eyes grew used to the darkness, the light increased and she was comforted and strengthened.

In a little while Christine's breathing evened. She was deep in sleep when Leah left the room, still carrying the doll, hearing Martin shouting for her excitedly from the yard . . . She put the doll on the kitchen table as she passed and ran out, driven by the urgency in her husband's voice.

In the jumble of shadows around the fire she could not immediately tell what Martin watched. He was bent over something dark beside the fence, gingerly, as if it were dangerous or repulsive. She thought he had killed an animal, a stray dog perhaps. Then she saw the color of buckskin, the black shining hair and, close now, kneeling, the pale face of the boy, the slightly bulging, open eyes, and caught her breath in recognition.

"He was trying to steal something," Martin was saying excitedly, "my buggy whip. But I caught him. He jerked away and ran, but he hit the fence and stunned himself. Is he hurt badly?" He paused, awaiting her answer anxiously, fearfully, she thought.

She did not answer. She was breathing hard, aware deeply of an intimate beauty in the child on the ground. She lifted him against her shoulder and knelt, rocking him, crooning in a disturbing outflow of emotion.

Martin waited for a while, silently, then burst out, "He hurt himself, I didn't hurt him. It was his conscience. He was trying to steal and his conscience struck him."

"He's blind and deaf," Leah said and rose and went into

the house, feeling the child begin to stir against her breast as she walked.

She sat on a chair in the kitchen and rocked again, knowing only with her body that the boy was awake now, though immobile. His eyes were dull, face blank, still pale. But his hands moved, smoothly supple, long-fingered, delicately shaped. The left ran along her arm, fingers lightly touching, over her shoulder, finding her hair finally with a fluttery movement as of a bird alighting. Color came to his cheeks. He sat up, nostrils flaring, a look of alarm but not fear in his face.

His hands moved in a swift bird flight of signs she did not understand, then came again to her hair and face in wonder and seeking. She drew him toward her and, surprisingly, he did not resist but lay against her—tentatively, though, and with reserve. His hands moved constantly, as if they felt the very air, still seeking, seeming to live apart and of themselves.

She remembered the doll on the table then and reached it. His hands found it immediately and claimed it. His body relaxed. A smile trembled at his lips. She smiled at him, forgetting for the moment his blindness, and, as if he could see, his smile widened in answer. She laughed aloud, hardly noticing the moth-wing touch of his fingers at her lips.

For the first time she became aware of his odor—like that she had noticed about the doll—leather, wood smoke, horses, a child smell, familiar, too delicate to hold. She sat rocking, gently, curiously content. When he became restless, she stood up and, holding his hand, found her coat and led him out into the night.

It was completely dark—only the red embers of the burned-down fire giving the yard substance. She did not see Martin and was relieved, realizing now that she had decided to take Little Wound back to the camp. She was afraid in the dark; yet her husband's presence would not help her, would even deepen the darkness. Of all places, he would be angriest with her for going to the Indian camp. But that was something she could face. She had to go. And yet, having made the decision, she found herself shivering as if from cold.

She found the gate and reluctantly left the warm circle of red light cast by the embers. Her feet found the road and carried her along it, though her mind was hesitant. It would be moonrise; she could wait. In the east she seemed to see a paling, a thinning of darkness among the sharp bright stars. She could wait. Yet she went on. And the light increased.

Little Wound walked beside her, even a little ahead, leading her, she realized, his step firm, his hand in hers strong and (the recognition sudden and unaccountably moving) masculine. For an instant she seemed to move inside him, knowing intimately his quiet world of darkness, feeling no shock or terror.

Around her the darkness lessened, light brightening in the east. She forgot the hesitation, becoming aware slowly of the world that lay about her unseen but palpable in darkness as in light. The dust of the road, the individual wheel tracks were familiar, her feet knowing what her eyes had never noticed. The breeze at her back still carried from the yard the smoke smell, the faint incense of sage and cedar. She heard horses grazing near the road and, from the camp ahead, still not in sight, a steady drumbeat, muffled, more felt than heard, like the beating of her heart. Her step had taken the rhythm of the drum, though whether directly or through the boy—who also moved with it—she did not know. She had a sense of singing, but in her ears was only the drumbeat.

The traders' buildings took faint shape beside her, then, to the right, the camp, a few lodges alight, strange lantern flowers in the darkness. The buildings of the square were dark except for one window, a lonesome square of yellow lamplight glowing. She passed the entrance and turned right, or was turned, then paused, aware of a presence though she could see no one, warned, she realized, by the tightening of the boy's hand.

She was alarmed, caught up by the boy's imparted fear, yet surmising from his very fear that this was someone white, therefore most probably familiar. She heard footsteps and spoke, disturbed but voice calm. She was startled by the reply, recognizing in the voice the man Westland.

"You surprise me," he said, "being out in this darkness. But naturally a minister's wife would have a strong sense of the light."

"I can't see either. But I know who you are."

68

She would have known him, she thought with embarrassment, even without the voice. He had approached from the right, the windward side, and she could smell him now, standing close to her, not an odor she could name but a perception that lighted his face in her memory.

Little Wound had moved around to the other side of her and was standing immobile, tense, reminding her of a young animal frozen to escape detection.

"I'm taking Little Wound home. I think he was lost."

"I thought you were alone. How did you find him—or persuade him to come? He's afraid of white people. Of me, anyway," he ended with audible chagrin.

"I know. He's afraid of you now. He came to the fire and hurt himself running away from my husband."

"But not from you. I envy you."

"No. I think he learned to like me while he was unconscious. Out of his head, I guess I should say." She laughed. "But then it's only fair, since I like him."

"Then I envy him too. I'll come with you, if you don't mind."

"All right. But it'll be light now and I can see—if you're worried about that."

"No. I'd like to come."

As they stood, the darkness over the eastern hills turned blue. A bright edge of moon showed in a cleft, clear silver beyond the black of trees, and rose with perceptible motion, forming, clearing, rinsing the wide land in liquid light. Westland stood before her, his back to the light but his eyes bright with an intentness, an intensity.

She turned quickly toward the camp in an instant of panic, with a fleeting vision of herself as another woman, a stranger. A pack of dogs came toward them from the camp, moving silently, shadowy as fish. They barked briefly but, catching the scent of Little Wound, moved on. The lodges had risen from darkness since she had last looked, white cones in a circle, washed clean in moonlight, canvas shining as if risen from water. And strange, with a fugitive beauty like fox fire in the night.

The drum was near now, a strong-beating pulse; somewhere a flageolet warbled thinly, bird-like. Near them, revealed now in the new light, a blanketed couple, wrapped close, murmured. She was immersed yet afloat in strangeness; a part of it, yet apart.

Then startlingly, from a lodge at the edge of the circle, a wail arose, a woman's voice in grief or pain, a strange, sad singing. Leah was shocked. Her heart filled with grief.

Little Wound was again leading her, guided by some inner knowing. From the shadow of the lodge of the crying, a man stepped to meet them and she recognized Crazy Walking. Little Wound let go of her hand and met his father. She watched in wonder their exchange of signs, an intimate language of touch and pattern—pictures drawn invisibly on darkness, perceived by a following hand.

"I think he was lost," she said simply. "I brought him home."

Crazy Walking nodded. "I'm obliged."

At that moment the strange wailing began again.

Seeing the question in her eyes, Crazy Walking said briefly, "My woman. Crying for a dead son." His voice was dry, noncommittal.

"Not the baby?" Westland exclaimed.

"No. One you never saw. Been away at school being made white. He was almost white when he died—of the coughing sickness."

He turned to the lodge, lifted the entrance cover, and spoke briefly to someone within.

"I'm sorry," Leah said quietly, but he did not hear.

A woman stooped through the entrance; Little Wound stepped to her side and her hand explored his face, coming to rest gently on his forehead, where the bruise was.

Leah recognized her from the encounter in the store and knew also that she was recognized. There was nothing to say. Yet she felt a bond of sympathy with this woman, a stranger, deeper than she had ever felt for any other. She seemed to move outward, to stand outside herself, to speak silently and with emotion.

Impulsively she slipped the bracelet from her wrist and pressed it into the woman's hand, thinking of it not as a possession, a gift, but as a word, a phrase of beauty spoken across a barrier of language. The meaning was clear and understood. For the moment there were only the two of them with the child between, an awareness of each other, a communication felt as palpably as a touch of the hand.

The woman turned and entered the lodge, returning in a moment with a folded, beaded blanket which she held out silently. When Leah accepted, she smiled briefly and was gone. Leah left then, hearing Westland at her side, aware of his feeling toward her yet still excluding him with fear not of the man but of something hovering, a part of the night, a shadow of wings.

Behind them the wailing began again, startling yet expected, attuned to her own feeling. Ahead, at the edge of camp, she saw the shadowy movement of the dogs. They gathered to one dark spot, pointing toward a figure that moved obscurely in the distance, and broke into raucous, chilling cry. The spot flowed forward, split like water around the dark figure, and broke scattering. The united barking died, uncovering a single high-pitched yelp of a dog, hurt.

The figure came on and she knew it was Martin. She was seized by a quick panic, a desire to flee, but she did not hesitate and the fear left her as quickly. Still she could not face Martin; she would not. She stopped, and with sudden decision turned to Westland and held out the blanket, giving no indication of her meaning, making no appeal.

He took the blanket and without hesitation unfolded it, put one end over his shoulders and threw the other around her, catching it on the other side and drawing her toward him. She was enveloped breathlessly in the strange-familiar odor of Indian, encircled, the blanket tight in the small of her back yet unconstraining.

They did not touch; yet she was enfolded, covered, at one with him. She clenched her hands tightly to still her breathing, quell the beating of her heart, her eyes on the darkness of the blanket between them.

A shadow passed them, near. Startled, she saw Martin, almost within touching distance, pass, face averted as if from evil. She could not help smiling; yet she shivered, suddenly cold for all the warmth of the blanket.

Westland withdrew the blanket, flaring it in the air, catching the middle to fold it. He handed it back and walked beside her, making no comment. She left him at the square, with decision and strength, and hurried home, worry for Christine nagging at her insistently. She had had enough of strangeness and disquieting emotions. Yet even at home in sleep she moved in the fox-fire light of the camp, felt the pressure of the blanket against her back; and recurring darkly, the flaring of the blanket on the air like wings.

It was early when Martin came in sight of the square, but the wind was up already, wearing away at his nerves, a constant reminder of the raw savagery of the land around him. It gathered dust lifted by the wheels and carried it forward and up, keeping him in a state of breathless discomfort, rustled curious fingers among the sacks of food and clothing on the seat beside him and, in gusts, rained audible showers of sand on the brim of his hat and the leather back of the seat.

He turned into the square with a feeling of harborage, of escape from the wind. But the wind was here too, only its directness abated. Overhead it moved with a rushing in the sails of the windmill, held the vane wind-taut and, atop the tattered, whipping flag, aimed the rifle steadily east. In the lea of the buildings, flow broken, it eddied restlessly, as visible as water, formed by its floatage of dust and paper— of a startling drift of raveled bits of cloth.

He stopped to study the cloth, curious and somehow irritated, perhaps by the waste, he thought, or by the savagery that had reduced good cloth almost to lint. Near him on the ground was a scattering of heavier pieces, held down by buttons or buckles. Among them a cardboard folder lay open revealing two pictures partly covered in a drift of dust.

He stepped out of the buggy and picked it up, shaking it free of dust, and saw two boys, an Indian and a white, contrasted in clothing, looks, all. Yet they bore a strong irritating resemblance. With relief it came to him that they were of the same boy, only the clothing, the hair different. Yet the one was pure heathen, with long wrapped braids of hair and trappings of feathers, fringes, fur, even a pipe. In mind's eye, he could see the glaring colors of the quilled designs, excrescences of the pagan mind. The face seemed to smile at him derisively. The other was quiet, subdued, with a certain meekness in the face and no derision. The hair was cut neatly, the clothing of sober, civilized design. One could go far, he thought, and not find so clear a case of the transforming power of Christianity. Perhaps it was intended he should find it: a small manifestation of grace to give him strength.

He put the folder in his pocket, smiling, and led his horse to the door of the carpenter shop. The coffin was not ready as he had expected, was not even begun, though he had spoken to the carpenter about it the evening before when he heard about the dead child.

"Are you sure they want it?" the carpenter asked. "Most of these Injuns still favor tree burial. No use makin' it if they don't want it."

"Whether they want it is beside the point. They have to be taught to want it. It's a Christian precept. The government is supposed to furnish coffins. You should have some made ahead to save delay."

"You don't know Injuns, Parson. I tried that once at another place and almost lost my hair. They saw it as a kind of partnership with death. Oh, no, I don't want 'em to get the idea I'm tryin' to nail a lid on 'em. The government or the church is another thing. The Injuns expect it of 'em. But not of a lone carpenter."

"I'll be responsible," Martin said with irritation. "They'll always take food and clothing, so I'll make it part of the gift."

"All right. On your say-so. And since there's already a dead Injun." He set to work reluctantly, but Martin saw with satisfaction that he already had boards cut to length.

"Food and a coffin. You have a sense of fitness, Reverend."

Martin looked up to see the post doctor smiling at him from the doorway. Perplexed, he did not answer immediately. The man's smile seemed pleasant, genuine, yet for all that he sensed hostility lurking. "Is that a riddle?"

"No. Only a metaphor. The taker of the white man's gifts must also take the coffin—a short history of the Indian."

"That wasn't my meaning. I meant only that Christ's teachings go also with charity—the greater value of the gift."

"Exactly. A traveler's guide to the inside of a coffin. In exchange for this time and this place."

"These Indians can be Christians and live. I know it," Martin replied angrily.

"It's what I doubt," the doctor said, turning from the door.

"Nevertheless, I think you should still take the food. And don't forget the coffin." He stepped from the platform and went on along the square.

Martin gripped his cane, twisting it hard against the floor, the carved crook soothing to his hand. He stepped through the doorway and stood on the platform in front to wait for the coffin, fighting his impatience. A memory of the Indian camp in the night flooded his mind: the dogs, black shadows under the stream of darkness surging toward him, shark-like. He was engulfed by their savagery, striking out . . . He shook his head and paced the platform, imprinting the dust in the warped hollows of the planks with the tread of his cane.

The carpenter helped him load the coffin. It had to go on the seat beside him, one end on the floor against the dashboard, the other against the back of the seat. So there was no room for the sacks of food and clothing.

The carpenter, smiling, unscrewed the lid of the coffin and piled the sacks inside. Martin climbed into the seat, restraining his anger while the carpenter put the lid back on and replaced the screws loosely with his fingers. "I won't tighten 'em," he said. "There's nothing in it yet that might want out."

Martin left and drove rapidly out toward the camp, resolving to be less volatile of temper in the future. He was in no fit mood to be on an errand of charity. He had to slow down when he left the square. The coffin was unstable on the seat, sliding from side to side, jostling him when the springs swayed. Its bulk prevented him from reaching the whip—which the horse seemed to know, somehow.

He drove into the camp with a reluctance he did not understand—the insecurity of the coffin, perhaps, or the thought of the dogs. (They were there to meet him, the whole ragged, vicious pack, running beside the buggy, jumping at the horse's nose, snapping at heel.)

He did not know exactly the location of Crazy Walking's lodge, but he expected he could find it by the wailing of the women if the dogs would stop their racket. Meanwhile he drove along the inside of the circle, merely looking.

There was no windbreak in the village. The grass was dry and trampled, no longer holding the dust which snaked with the wind among the lodges, rasping, slithering. He felt exposed, unprotected, as in an uninhabited desert.

A few men sat in the sun beside the lodges smoking stolidly, oblivious to the wind. Women worked with the fresh steer hides, fleshing, scraping endlessly, the only sign of industry in the entire camp. Behind the buggy a pack of dark, ragged children ranged with the dogs, encouraging them, he knew, with their shouts and laughter.

He stopped by a lodge, recognizing the man in front, Yellow Bird, as one of his congregation who spoke English. He was just beginning to ask directions when the man's wife stooped through the lodge opening carrying sticks and a fringed, cylindrical bag. She set up the sticks—a tripod— and hung the bag on it in the sun. With a shock he recognized the pagan symbol, the medicine bundle. And these were two of his most devoted members.

He stopped speaking abruptly and drew his horse around left toward another lodge, saddened, and incensed, too. The buggy swayed the coffin against him; he pushed it with his right arm, loosening the line on that side. A dog jumped at the horse's nose from the right and he shied, cramping the left front wheel back under the buggy. The side lifted, the coffin tumbled out, striking right side up, rolling, lid off, contents spilling out.

The sound of the coffin falling threw the horse into a plunging panic; he almost upset the buggy before Martin jerked him back around to the right. He heard the dogs converge, growling and fighting on the spillage of the coffin. A shout of laughter, not only of children, rose above the dog noise and the wind. By the time he fought the horse to a standstill and looked back, Indians thick as ants were hurrying toward the coffin.

A white billow of flour erupted on the wind and blew toward him, submerging him. A dog passed him in the haze, carrying a flitch of bacon; a shirt billowed on the wind, flapping its arms as it left the ground, and came toward him, a fearful bodiless assailant in another cloud of flour dust.

A new shout of laughter rose up and spread as another dog fled the moiling mass by the coffin, its jaws somehow entangled in a strip of cloth Martin recognized as the winding sheet. It unrolled and rose up, flying kite-like behind the dog. The dog came toward him under the white cloud and the bright serpentine sheet with a sad, demonic wailing, blinded by the cloth but running straight and fast.

Martin sat holding the horse distractedly, watching the

75

dog come at him from the side and back, not thinking to move till too late.

The dog, running low to the ground, just grazed the front wheel and went under the horse, miraculously missing his legs. The long sheet, sailing free on the wind, enveloped Martin, enclosing him with terror. In the same moment the horse snorted and plunged, almost pulling Martin out of the seat with the lines. The sheet jerked with the sudden movement, but it still clung fluttering to his head and shoulders. He could not let go of the lines or shake himself free. The sheet, like a live thing under the wind's force, pressed to his face, strangling, suffocating.

Then it jerked free with a ripping sound, the horse stopped plunging. He straightened his glasses, relieved that they were not broken and, looking up, saw the man he knew to be Crazy Walking holding the horse's bridle, grinning up at him. The dog was gone, freed, he supposed, when the sheet caught on the buggy. The sheet was wrapped around the dash, one end under a front wheel, the other fluttering across his knees. He thrust it down distastefully, stepping on it as he climbed out of the buggy. His knees were watery and he felt a queasiness in his stomach.

"Thanks," he said, in his nervousness not trusting himself to shake hands. "I heard of your bereavement and, as pastor of the church, brought a small token of condolence. But as you see, it's gone now."

"What's the coffin for, just to haul the food in?"

"No, for a decent burial for your child. I've heard that you've not yet come to the light but, being educated, you should be willing to assist in the advancement of your people."

"Advance them by locking them underground?" He shook his head. "The reservation is grave enough for an Indian without covering him with dirt."

"I'm sorry it appears that way to you. It's only Christian and decent. However, perhaps you'd let me say a few words over the child for the good of his soul?"

The man hesitated visibly, then shrugged. "He's safe now from your help. You can pray if you like." He turned and led the way into the lodge, looking at the dead child on the pallet with tearless, indifferent eyes.

In the lodge Martin felt his queasiness returning. The man's wife sat with a baby and two small girls inside on

76

the left. Her face was streaked from weeping, her buckskin leggings and moccasins stained with blood from gashes (he supposed) on her legs.

The dead boy was wrapped tightly in a red blanket, his face painted weirdly—red patterns on the cheeks, a blue crescent on the forehead. But strangely the hair was cut short. He had the strong feeling of having seen the face before; but he could not place it.

Before he began praying he was afraid he might faint. The slanting, conical walls without windows oppressed him; the smells of incense, leather, smoke—all the trappings of savagery—and above all, the disquieting presence of death seemed to constrict his breathing, to weigh on his heart and lungs.

But as he prayed, his strength renewed. A sense of power lifted him up, sustained him. Even as he said and heard his own words of prayer, he saw himself standing dauntless in the seething mass of dogs by the coffin, scattering them with irresistible sweeps of his cane, exulting, exalted in his advocacy of the right. He saw the child inside the coffin, dressed decently in Christian clothing like the boy in the photograph.

His voice stopped in the earnestness of the vision. He forced it on again, hardly restraining himself from bending over to rub off the painted symbols marring the dead child's face. Yet he dared not. A power and a revulsion withheld his hand. Finishing his prayer, he felt the faintness returning and left quickly, without ceremony, his feeling a confusion of nameless fear and defeat, changed suddenly from the brief moment of power.

He climbed into the buggy and drove rapidly out of the village, not stopping to retrieve the coffin. Looking back, he saw three ragged urchins playing in it and for an uncontrolled instant imagined the lid clapped on them.

He brushed the thought away in shame and saw again the dead child in a strange, evil beauty: he was fascinated, enthralled before it as a bird by jeweled serpent eyes. He shook his head to clear it and drove on, thinking that he had seen the face before.

## ☙ 19 ❧

Christine sat staring out of the window toward the road, knowing the broad dusty pair of lines on the earth as she had always known them, yet feeling within herself the curious certainty that if something passed along them she would not see it; knowing also that if she thought about this, her sight would return, the power be gone.

It was not darkness but a blank unseeing; she wondered if it were like this with the blind Indian boy, if his blindness were only a lack of seeing or a palpable darkness like the night. She shivered at the thought, aware momentarily of the light beyond the window. For an instant her eyes focused on the road and she saw her father directly in front of the house, revealed suddenly, driving fast.

She had not seen him coming, though the road was visible as far as the Indian camp, yet she felt like crying, having failed in the last instant to hold the blankness of vision. She turned from the window, disturbed now by an odor that had troubled her vaguely all morning; she could not place it. Glancing through the open door of the bedroom, she saw her mother standing before the mirror wrapped in a dark, brightly marked robe. With a shock she recognized it as an Indian blanket; she knew the odor at once. She caught her breath in fear. For an instant the figure in the robe became a stranger blurred and far away. Christine was small and alone within herself at the center of lost, empty distances.

She turned back quickly toward the window, afraid her mother might notice her agitation and come toward her, forgetting the blanket. She imagined herself enfolded in it in darkness and suffocation. She shut the vision from her mind, capturing again briefly the blankness of the road—broad lines retreating, merging in the distance.

But she could not hold the feeling, could not shut out the sound of her father in the yard. She heard a gate close and waited as he crossed the yard and entered the house. She grew tense with foreboding as he hung up his coat and came into the kitchen, closing the door soundlessly. He would not notice her if she sat still, she knew; she did not have her blanket or doll, so there was nothing definite to fear. Yet she had a sharp feeling of lines crossing, of forces converging.

She sat tensely, staring hard at the roadway. She thought again of the Indian boy, seeing him safe, protected in a silent, sightless world—was it like that, she wondered?

Her father had stopped in the middle of the kitchen; she could feel him there behind her, could see in vision the darkness of his face, the lines drawn tight around his eyes, hands stroking restlessly the shepherd's crook. He was watching her mother, she knew.

The blanket—the memory struck her sharply—he would not like the blanket. She closed her eyes and tried to close her ears as well, but she could not. She heard her mother's startled *oh;* something of glass fell to the floor and shattered.

Her father's voice was cold, controlled. "What kind of mockery is this? Where did you get it?"

"It was given me."

"By whom?"

"By the mother of the boy you hurt."

Some of the steadiness was gone from her father's voice. "I didn't hurt him. I told you before, he ran into the fence."

"Running from you."

Christine stared hard at the road in growing panic. She had never heard her mother so defiant. Frantically, she willed her to be silent, to retreat.

"He was guilty; the punishment was just and not of my doing. He tried to steal the whip."

"Why would he steal your whip—to hurt you? How could he know you prize it so highly? That would need malice and vision; he has neither."

Christine heard him draw breath to speak, then check himself. When he went on his voice had returned to a strained quietness.

"What does that have to do with bringing an evil, filthy blanket into my house?"

"Does it bother you so much? A gift given in gratitude and kindness because I tried to undo what you had done? It doesn't seem evil or dirty to me. There's something about it I like, that makes me feel clean; maybe the fact that it was

79

given me by a stranger. I don't know. But it's a new feeling not to suspect or be afraid. I like it."

"I'm not suspicious or afraid; I'm only facing the facts. You know as well as I how fast their young are dying. They're dirty and diseased; can the blanket be otherwise? Get rid of it."

"No."

"Then I'll burn it myself. It's a threat and a danger to have in the house."

"If you burn it I'll leave you."

"No. You can't. It's impossible." His voice rose almost to a scream. Christine heard the cane twist in his hands with tortured vibration and closed her eyes and pressed her hands to her ears till, in darkness, she could hear only the drumming of her heart and a low, far-off rustling like wind or fire.

She remembered the fire of the night before, the burning; shadows of her father stalking the walls like giant animals. She shivered at the nearness of the vision, the shadows solid living rock in the red firelight, the flames' sound a roaring . . . She fled the vision and was again before the window staring out.

There were sounds of struggle from the bedroom. A chair crashed to the floor, then a long-held sound of tearing cloth. She whirled and saw her mother and father standing apart, each holding a piece of the blanket, staring at each other. The cane was on the floor between them.

Her father lowered his eyes first, picked up the cane, and left the house, appearing in a moment outside the window, the piece of blanket caught in the crook of the cane, held out and away as he might hold a snake.

She turned to her mother, finding her standing, still rigid, the blanket clutched tightly in her hands, her eyes distant, fixed. There was a bruise on her cheek, a thin smear of blood at the corner of her mouth. There was something different and frightening about her, a terrifying strength and stubbornness; for a moment Christine herself stood thus in vision, unshrinking in the face of danger. But she could not stay.

In fear and loneliness she cried out and ran to her mother, unmindful of the strangeness or of the robe. Her mother seemed to soften then. She lifted Christine up and rocked her softly, singing. And for a little in the brightness of the room there was no loneliness or any shadows.

Wind, raised upward by the slope, unfurled above the hills brown banners of dust. The air was thick, hazy, dimming the sun with smoky color.

Below, Crazy Walking saw the camp, reduced by distance, obscured by feathery forms of dust waving above it, unreal: a circle of pointed stones in a stream bed, swept by swift currents of roily water.

He climbed rapidly with a shadowy, breathless feeling of swimming upward through muddy water toward clear, sunlit air. His breathing, shallow, labored, seemed to hurry him yet hold him back like the reaching, bodiless hands he had seen in dreams. He looked backward often with an insistent expectation that the scene below would change somehow, or disappear. But it did not, and above him the dust still thickened. There was no clear air.

At the top of the hill he stopped, breathless, and stood restraining himself now from looking back. There were no trees on all the hill, only a scant growth of sage by an outcropping of rock: grey-green, black, cut sharply out of the brown-earth color of the hot hilltop.

He stood looking at the rock a long time, becoming finally aware of a movement at its base. In the shadow he saw a snake, and in the same instant was startled by the dry whir of its rattles. He stepped backward instinctively, then forward again, bending to watch the snake with fascination. It was coiled in the shadow of the rock, dully grey, the pattern of its skin barely visible against the earth. The eyes were dull with the same dead, dusty look of the skin, but above the coil the head moved constantly, irritably, bright tongue tasting the air, flickering. It had caught his scent, he knew; but it was blind.

He moved aside so that his scent would be blown away and settled down to watch, a curious sympathy in his heart. The snake quieted, its tongue stopped flashing, but still it was restless. It moved farther into the shadow and, raising its head against the rock, struck blindly but with a dogged, terrible insistence.

He watched, chilled; waiting. Then—as if torn by the rock—a scaled flap of skin appeared on the nose, peeled backward slowly as the head continued to strike the rock. The eyes glittered suddenly clear, stripped of the blinding sheath, and the head appeared, complete, renewed above a necklace of wrinkled, lacy skin. Ripples moved in the muscles along the body, the snake writhed against the rock, and slowly the sheath rolled back revealing the body clean, shining, reborn, patterned in bright, startling colors. In a little while the skin came free, reversed, a ghost snake now behind the other, itself not dusty grey but dappled white, almost transparent.

The snake lay quietly against the rock, uncoiled now, no longer nervous; shining, alive in a quiet radiance of color. Crazy Walking moved closer; the head turned, eyes caught the movement, and the snake slid silently around the rock and was gone. He stayed staring at the wrinkled, papery casting, struck by sudden, breaking emotion. He felt a gathering, a drawing up within him; muscles tightened like iron across his chest; all his body was knotted till it seemed he would be crushed. Then he relaxed; sweat drenched him, soaking his clothes. Wind cooled him. He leaned against the rock breathing deep and long as after huge effort . . .

After a long time he turned toward the camp and, unmindful of the wind and dust, walked downward to it, seeing it clear, undistorted, changed. He crossed the creek and was running when he reached the outer circle, eagerly, heading directly toward his own lodge. But seeing old High Bear sitting in the sun, he suddenly changed his course and stopped and spoke briefly.

"Grandfather, my son is dead. I want to give what little I have to the poor. Will you tell this to the people?"

He laid his tobacco pouch on the ground, a gift.

The old man nodded and with difficulty gained his feet. He peered earnestly into Crazy Walking's face, with visible surprise, and turning, hobbled painfully away. Going toward his own lodge, Crazy Walking heard the old man's voice creaking hoarsely above the wind.

He said nothing to Blue Fawn but began immediately piling all his possessions in front of the lodge, knowing she would understand but reluctant to face her, to admit even to himself the meaning of what he was doing. But he worked rapidly,

82

with a feeling of purpose that was stronger than any reticence. He withheld nothing; all went into the pile: the silver-mounted saddle, bridles, ropes, packsaddles, rifle, and revolver; all.

When he had brought his horses in from the herd, the people were gathering. He stood by the lodge giving, hardly aware of what he gave, racked, held in a feeling of emergence, of breaking free. He seemed to grow lighter, taller, move from darkness into the light. His perceptions sharpened to an awareness that was vivid and painful. All had changed: the persons he had known all his life were strangers to him, moving in an aura, an emanation of feeling, a shining out like moon rings. Each encounter was an entering and a looking out again through other eyes back toward himself. He stood revealed in his own sight, chagrined, vulnerable, yet somehow more, not less, than he had been.

Blue Fawn was also giving, things of beauty she had made with her hands; and he saw that with her the giving was as natural as breathing—not a shedding, a sloughing off. Yet he had never felt so much at one with her.

His things were gone. He gave his hat and boots and finally his clothing and stood naked beside the lodge, conscious of the whiteness of his skin but clothed in the warmth of the sun, the pressure of sand-laden wind against his body. Someone gave him leggings, moccasins, and the people left. He sat all afternoon in the sun by the lodge in a curious suspension between waking and sleep.

In the evening friends came with a horse and drag to carry the body of his son. He walked behind the drag in a long procession that led out of the camp and west toward the low hills. The wind had slackened. A few clouds over the mountains, west, turned slowly against the sky, gathering a thin dust of red. North along the valley, the hills browned in the slanting light, dry and hot, fingered by spires of cottonwood along the creek, green, burnished color of shining leaves. On the earth nothing moved, no rabbit, antelope, or prairie dog, nothing; but in the sky a single eagle curved and swung, wings flashing, turning in the sun.

He was drawn up for an instant, looking down from curving, bodiless height, seeing the people, the procession wind slowly, serpentine, along the trail, alive, joined, vivid under the sun; saw the drag, the body of his son, himself among the people, alone and yet invisibly sustained; saw himself a part of a living, many-footed animal moving sinuously among mother hills.

They left the valley, climbing a hill toward the lowering sun, and came to a scaffold of peeled, cottonwood poles standing high and white at the summit. Someone lifted the bundled figure to the scaffold and tied it; and the people departed, leaving only himself and his family.

The day was almost gone. The sky was red. A final slanting ray, thin as a knife, lay over the hilltop, striking the legs of the scaffold sharply. In that last instant of sun the figure seemed to glow, shine as red as cloud; to float released above the hilltop. Then the sun died. In the west a ring of clouds, like dancers, whirled high in a red dust, burning.

He stood on the darkening hill in the red light and wept.

*Book II*

# SEPTEMBER-DECEMBER 1889

⚜ 21 ⚜

IN THE EVENING Turning Hawk hunted the side of a small valley in the badlands, hoping to find an elk, or a deer perhaps, or even a rabbit. He was hungry; there was no meat in the lodge; yet there was a deep, unthinking peace within him, a receptive clarity of perception. Only the thought of the little ones hungry in the lodge kept him moving. Except for this he would have climbed the hill to pray, feeling the moment sacred.

Many days now they had wandered in mourning, the family alone away from the people, subsisting on roots and berries and the little game they could kill. And though they were hungry often, he himself had found renewal and release from strife.

Across the valley and part way up the hill he saw Crazy Walking and hoped that the game, if any, would be on that side. His own strength was adequate: he could not die before he was ready. It was the young man who needed strength and reassurance, some sign, some intimation that the earth was not hostile or indifferent. He prayed that Wakan Tanka might vouchsafe this necessary thing: a deer, a rabbit—some gift of the earth.

The manner of Crazy Walking in the giving away and the burial of the child had been an act of courage; it was a coming home, a return in a sacred way to the road of the people. There was pride in the act and hope; but also a foreboding, as if, once having found the road, he were lost forever.

Darkness was near. In the distance, nightward, the red color of evening joined with blue and red of hill, rose up, a colored dust: dust of the dancers beyond death, they who had traveled the black road west that all men walk. Turning Hawk stood as the colors darkened, holding his hands outstretched as if to warm them at the lowering fires, feeling the change of color within his heart like a change in his blood. North a humped band of clouds blued slowly till only one at the center glowed alone, brightly, then drowned, red fire in the blue waters.

He brought his mind again to the hunting, but with little heart; he felt that he would see nothing, that there was no game near. Toward the head of the valley he saw an eagle flap heavily upward from a spire of rock and sail free. He stopped hunting and walked slowly onward, knowing that someone was there ahead of him.

The valley was small, sloping upward west toward a high butte, ending at its base in a jumble of boulders and a little flat peopled with strange figures of clay his people called the Silent Ones. Between himself and the flat a gully curved right and upward toward the north end of the butte.

Approaching the gully, he heard singing and in the gathering darkness saw white smoke of a fire and finally the fire itself, small, not flaming but glowing. The odor of the fire set his heart leaping till he realized it was cow chip, not buffalo. On the wind shift that brought the smoke, the singing was clearer: a sacred song in the soft rhythmic tongue of the Blue Cloud people, the Arapaho.

Beside a pool of water in the bottom of the gully he saw the fire and a large man sitting close before it, bent forward in prayer song, stripped as if for battle, body painted, a bird form perched in his hair. Near him, nose drooped almost to the ground, was a bony, yellow horse, standing still as rock, not even switching at the swarms of feeding insects. He was painted in clean stripes and dots of red: arrows of the thunderbird, red hail. Braided in his mane were sheeny blue-green feathers of crow or magpie. By the slit ears Turning Hawk knew the horse as a Cheyenne buffalo runner—old now, to have known the hunting.

He entered the gully and stopped at a distance, waiting for the man to finish his ceremony; and Crazy Walking, coming off the hillside, joined him.

Finished with the singing, the man emptied his pipe, wrapped it, and replaced it in his medicine bag, then with visible reverence took up a shining, dark-colored stone—a buffalo stone, Turning Hawk knew—wrapped it carefully, and replaced it also. The ceremony over, he began moving fast and with visible excitement. He hung the medicine bundle on an improvised tripod, beside which his clothes were piled, took an old cap-and-ball rifle from where it leaned against a bush, checked the load, and turned toward the old yellow horse.

It was then he saw the two men watching him. Without ceasing his hurried motion he seized the lead rope and rushed toward them, dragging the reluctant horse with the hand that held the gun. He raised the curved index finger of his free hand over his head in half the sign for buffalo, and turned and led them to the point where the gully curved upward. In the smooth sandy bottom near the water were the tracks of a single animal. They were round and clean-cut, and for a moment Turning Hawk almost believed.

The Blue Cloud leaned his gun against the unmoving horse and curved his index fingers above his head, holding them there insistently. Turning Hawk stepped closer and gently straightened the fingers to the sign for cattle.

Anger flashed for a moment in the man's face, and he stepped backward as if offended at being touched. But the anger died as suddenly and a vivid excitement again suffused his face. He made the signs for wait and shoot, seized the gun, and mounted. The horse staggered sidewise under the weight, recovered, and moved slowly up the gully.

Crazy Walking's face was contorted with laughter, though he was making no sound. He stood watching the man ride away, shaking his head as if he could not believe his eyes. Turning Hawk moved away from him in a moment of resentment. The situation was funny, he knew, yet he could not laugh. He climbed out of the gully and stood on the bank at the edge of the little flat of the Silent Ones, still watching the rider. The Blue Cloud followed the tracks along the gully to a point where they climbed the bank and tried to follow, but the trail was too steep. In a moment he returned, splashing through the shallow puddles and, where the bank was lower, climbed out and rode past Turning Hawk through the little flat toward the slope of the butte.

He rode with short stirrups, leaning forward, the gun held high like a spear, his heels beating wildly on the horse's ribs. He was large, heavily muscled, and from the way he rode, the exaltation on his face, he might have been riding headlong into battle. But the horse moved reluctantly, galloping now but slow, no faster than a man could walk. In the dim light the yellow color blended with the figure of clay, so that the horse seemed to fade, to disappear, and Turning Hawk's last image as he passed from sight was of the vivid, painted warrior borne onward by an unseen force, the power of his desire.

Beyond the flat a rocky slope rose steeply toward the butte, the top of which seemed to burn in the last red light of the sunset. He saw the horse and rider again at the base of the slope, just beginning to climb, and halfway up, weaving back and forth across its face, a white animal. In the black shadow of the fire-rimmed butte, it moved upward like a light, sure, unhurried, unrecognizable.

Turning Hawk started to run, then checked himself, stopped, gripping his gun, resisting with all his power the hope, the sudden winging of his heart.

The rider gained the slope and moved upward also, but with terrible, dream-like slowness, the yellow horse appearing and disappearing against the rock-strewn yellow slope, striving visibly, each step an agony of effort. The rider stood high over the saddle, stretched upward toward the moving light, gun at arm's length still, like an offering, a gift proffered in a strange dance.

The animal was near the top; it paused at the last steep edge and stood, looking downward. The horse stopped also, braced, leaning against the slope. And in that instant the rider aimed and fired.

Turning Hawk saw the smoke at the gun's tip, heard the sound crashing with unexpected violence along the valley.

The animal did not move but remained in the same attitude as if turned to stone. The rider raised up again in the stirrups, extending the rifle, straining upward, seeming to shout, yet no sound came. The horse swayed, moved upward one more step, and dropped to his knees. He stayed kneeling, balanced an impossible interval, then dropped, and horse and rider in a blur slid downward, stopping at the foot of the slope in a cloud of yellow dust.

The white animal moved at the top of the slope, rose up on its hind legs at the last bright edge, and gained the top. It stood briefly, black now, not white against the sky, outlined with fire, and then was gone.

Beside him Crazy Walking laughed harshly. "Somebody's cow," he said. "A white heifer, not a buffalo." He was laughing, yet with pain in his eyes as if he too had hoped.

There was a drift of dust at the foot of the slope but no movement of horse and rider. Turning Hawk hurried forward and found them lying quiet. The rider stirred drowsily as he approached, but the horse did not move.

When Turning Hawk touched him, the Blue Cloud sat up suddenly, facing the slope and, standing, tried to climb. But one leg buckled under him and he sat down again. Seeing Turning Hawk he made the signs for sun and buffalo, pointing to the top of the butte—dark now, a black sharp edge against the sky. He was bleeding and scratched from his fall, the painted designs on his body smeared, altered with the different red of blood, the yellow of clay. But he showed no sign of pain. His eyes were shining and he talked volubly for a moment, forgetting the signs.

Suddenly he became silent; his eyes clouded as he turned toward the hill, and he seemed to be gazing into the earth. In a moment he began humming a song. He repeated the melody several times, then sang it with words that Turning Hawk could not understand. Finished, he looked at Turning Hawk, surprise in his eyes, as if seeing him for the first time. Then he saw the horse, walked to it limping, and prodded it with his toe; but there was no movement. He stared down at it for a while and, indicating the slit ears, made the signs for brave and buffalo runner.

Crazy Walking signed, "Gone under with the buffalo."

The Blue Cloud signed, "No," and went on, "We can bring back the buffalo, by means of the new Spirit Dance. The earth is old and worn-out, destroyed by the white man. She will be young, and all the dead Indians live again. The white man will be no more. All by means of the Spirit Dance."

It was dark now, the only light a faint sky glow, a liquid, blurring light that seemed to shine not on the earth but from it. There were no colors below the sky save black and grey and a water-bright silver shining out of the rocks and all the shapes of clay in the little flat.

In the dimness the Blue Cloud's hand talk blurred, but he would not stop. To make his meaning clear he enlarged the gestures, moving his whole body in a slow, eloquent dance, silently against the shining images.

He told of a journey west to a rocky, rainless land of sage under snowy mountains; of a sacred person who had died and come back, bringing from the spirit world a sacred dance, the Spirit Dance, which he gave to his people; of the dance, the people turning in a circle, the visions, the singing.

He stopped moving then and sang again in his own tongue the song he had made, standing still as the clay and with the same inner shining, a spirit light that made him one with the earth. The song, strange, haunting, seemed to come from far off in the night. When the singing stopped, no one moved or spoke. The silence was complete, but tense, expectant, a pause between breaths.

In Turning Hawk was a trembling, a shaking he could not control. He had seemed to awaken after the song as after a dream. He could not believe about the dance; it was a false dream, a turning back: it was death. Yet he had been disturbed and deeply moved.

The shaking stopped. He was suddenly weary and without strength. Except for the other men he would have stretched out face down on the bare earth and slept gratefully. He turned away and, turning, wondered how it was with Crazy Walking. He touched the young man's arm and found him tense, withdrawn; and yet in the touch he felt the strange laughter and a wild agitation of the heart.

The Blue Cloud moved to the body of the horse. He found the lead rope and pulled on it hard, as if he expected the horse to rise and follow him. Then he turned suddenly and, almost running, left the flat.

Turning Hawk followed slowly. It was a long road back to the lonely camp—White Flat—and they were empty-handed.

He had been roused, Westland thought, by singing, a far-off joyous music, but there was no sound now, not even a breeze to rustle the tent canvas, only a far murmurous sound of water, a sea-shell whisper. Yet he lay half awake in child-like anticipation, holding the freshness, the delight, willing his mind to be quiet, unquestioning.

The sound came again, piercing his drowsiness with faint shock—no human voices but animal, in curious, high-pitched clamor. Coyotes: he had heard them before but never with the sense of joy, of singing. He lay listening, prolonging the moment, coming fully awake at a perfect phrase from a familiar choral.

The light was grey, filtered through white canvas, unfamiliar, till he remembered where he was—in his own tent at the Indian camp near the junction of Leaf and Arrow Creeks, awaiting the return of Turning Hawk and Crazy Walking from the mourning. Three weeks had passed since he had seen them, time spent mostly at the agency, and he was anxious for their return.

He dressed quickly, eager to begin the day, though he heard no sound of stirring in the camp. Quietly he left the tent—which was outside the camp circle—crossed the creek on a fallen log, and climbed the bluff west, moved by a desire to see the camp from a distance. He climbed slowly in the half-light, feeling his way among the round, abrasive surfaces of sandstone, pausing often to run his hand along some oddly curving, bending, fluted shape, knowing the stone with awareness his eyes had never known.

Chokecherry and service berry lived in the crevices, leaves night-black, fruit touched with dew and faintly odorous. Higher, a silvered spray of buffalo berry shone. And at the top, thrust out of solid rock, roots clutching the surfaces, gnarled fingers tapping the cracks for moisture, were shadowed jack pines.

Above the stream terrace, a hill rose, spotted with rock and sage, and he climbed on till he reached the peak. There was a small shelter of stone and brush at the top, facing east, lined with sage—a prayer shelter, he knew, though he had never before seen one. The sage was recently cut, exuding still a sweetly camphorous smell, an atmosphere in which his own presence was an intrusion. He moved away a few steps and turned toward the east to watch the growing light, and for an instant knew the power that could bring a man to this spot to pray.

Coyotes still clamored in the hills, awaiting the sun. Over the far, shadowed mountains, a single star shone brightly in the paling sky. The camp was beginning to stir. Below, from the circle of tepees, a man emerged shadowy and stood facing the star with arms upraised. Someone called and was answered. A woman chopped wood for the morning fire, swinging the axe with sure overhand strokes, each one completed and the next begun before the sound of the last reached him. Smoke rose white, threading itself straight up through the quiet air.

Dawn came in a mirroring of light, a springing wash of color. Trees—cottonwood and aspen—flared from the mist and darkness along the creek, leaves brilliant green against pale trunks. From green along the creek, grass faded as the land rose east to brown, yellow, tawny, to the grey-green of sagebrush on the low hills. Beyond, the pine hills rose, dark green against the brightening sky.

With the first sun the whole camp was astir: children swirled among the lodges, shouting, waving their arms; dogs barked; women worked by the fires or brought wood or water from the stream. Tripods appeared before the lodges, bearing medicine bundles; the men lounged in the sun.

Near camp he saw the horse herd: red, yellow, black, white —pinto, piebald, spotted—bright flares against the monotones of the land's color. All stood heads up, ears pointing east.

And far out, on the line their ears pointed, he saw movement against the sage hills, a small procession moving slowly down a white trail. He waited while the air filled with light and with more and more sound and the smell of food from the camp below.

The small procession came slowly on, out of the grey of the hills onto the tawny, yellow flats, coming finally to the edge of the green where the horses grazed—an old man leading a horse with a drag of long poles on which was a kind of wicker cage; a young man, a woman, and last a boy, all moving with a slow, ceremonial pace. He recognized them as Turning Hawk and the family of Crazy Walking.

The horse herd approached the procession, ears forward, then raced away with a small sound of thunder. The camp ceased its bustle, stood still at attention, aware finally of the newcomers. An old white horse, apart from the rest, threw up his head and circled them single-footing, tail in the air, mane streaming, stepping high and light as a colt. The voices of the Indians below rose, as clamorous as the sound of the coyotes, louder, but with the same joyousness and with a wildness that made Westland shiver. Then the sound became singing, beginning low with a single voice and spreading and growing, a welcoming song.

The procession entered the camp circle and turned to the left, circling it, clockwise, with visible ceremony, as he knew returning warriors circled after a victory, faces upturned, shining, having withstood death. The circle complete, they stopped and were lost in a surrounding surge of people, a closing ring.

The scene impressed itself vividly on his mind: the ring of smoke-topped lodges on the green, the circling; the change in the faces of the mourners returned, the shining, the color, a suffusion that was more than morning light, that changed them as the clear water of the stream gave shine to the jeweled pebbles beneath.

The mourners unloaded their few possessions and set up a patched canvas tepee in the camp circle. By the time they were settled, people from the whole camp were converging on them bringing gifts.

Westland descended then. From his own tent he brought presents—hawks' bells for the little ones, beads and vermilion for Blue Fawn, a carved stone pipe for Crazy Walking, tobacco for Turning Hawk. With these in his arm, he untied the spotted pony he had picketed by the stream and led it into the circle of lodges.

The air was a hive of sound, rich, blurred as bees humming: laughter and shouting and, withal, like music, the sound of joy and welcoming. But as he approached, the sound changed. Children still shouted, there was still talk; yet in the tone was an alteration perceptible as a change of light that for a moment touched him with despair.

A crowd clustered around a newly erected leather lodge near the old canvas one—a honey-colored buckskin painted with a succession of bright blue, red, and black figures in profile, conspicuous at once for its newness and its quality of age, of a time past.

The people moved aside to let him pass and he found Turning Hawk and Little Wound standing together near the new lodge; but for a long moment he did not recognize Crazy Walking. The man standing beside the door of the lodge seemed another person. The short hair (longer now after the period of wandering) was that of an Indian in mourning. Only the amber eyes with their look of tension brought back the Crazy Walking he had known. He had been at the giving away, had had a brief glimpse of Crazy Walking leaving the agency with the dead child, but even that change had not prepared him for this.

The man was naked to the waist, sunburned a deep brick red, the old skin peeling off in patches on shoulders and upper arms. On both lower arms was a regular design of freshly healed, round scars—visible evidence, Westland guessed, of some personal, religious reaction to death.

The laughing, cynical expression was gone, sloughed off with the sunburned skin. He was surrounded by gifts, none the same as, nor even similar to, the things he had given away. There was an archaic quality about them: quilled, buckskin clothing—moccasins, shirts, leggings—an old sinew-wrapped cap-and-ball rifle; and most curious of all, an old but well-kept buffalo robe. There was much more, but it was not the quantity, Westland thought, but the quality of the gifts that affected the man Crazy Walking, things transmuted, become feeling, a gift of strength from the people to the man.

With sudden perception he saw his own gifts in that light and was ashamed of his presumption. But he could not turn and go now. He put the presents on the grass a little apart from the others, and tied the pony to a tepee pin—Little Wound had already caught his scent and was drawing back. He turned to hurry away, anxious to avoid thanks for an ambiguous generosity. But he was caught. As if they divined a sincerity beyond his intentions, they closed round him, cutting off his retreat.

He returned then and, picking up the gifts, presented them. He gave the bells to the little girls, who accepted with downcast eyes and a veiled smiling; the paints to Blue Fawn, who answered with a short monologue meaning, as Crazy Walking explained, that she had been honored much by her own people, but now in the course of one moon she had been honored twice by white people; her heart was lifted up by the unexpected generosity.

The pipe he presented to Crazy Walking, knowing as he did so that the act would have meaning beyond his own knowledge or experience; he hoped it would not offend.

Crazy Walking hesitated, his face for a moment assuming a familiar tenseness; a slight derisive smile came and went fleetingly. But when he spoke his voice was low, with a forced, halting movement that was almost a stutter. "I know the pipe is one from the trader's store, that it has no meaning for you beyond itself. I know this. But it means nothing. It is a pipe—given now—meaning more than you know. I am honored."

He handed it to Blue Fawn, who held it carefully before her, addressed it in a low voice, then wrapped it in a piece of cloth and took it inside the lodge.

Westland watched with fascination, perceiving in Crazy Walking a depth of response he could not have anticipated, sensing a flow of emotion beneath the event that he could not fathom. And yet he was moved, lifted up, involved.

He gave the tobacco to Turning Hawk, the pony to Little Wound, who stood his ground manfully, accepting the lead rope. His hands moved swiftly in a series of signs Westland could not follow, then reached out fearfully, found Westland's hands, paused briefly for a response, and withdrew. Westland stepped back in a torture of elation and inadequacy.

Little Wound approached the pony, ran his hand lightly over its neck and head; and for a moment the two touched noses, as two horses getting acquainted. And in a moment the boy was astride, moving away confidently through the crowd and among the lodges in warm yellow sunlight.

The whole camp had gathered around the new lodge. In front of it several pots boiled vigorously over an open fire, filling the air with the odors of meat and sharp wood smoke. The men formed a circle and sat on the grass in dignified silence, passing a large pipe around. Westland joined them, at Turning Hawk's invitation, becoming composed and suddenly hungry. He smoked the pipe in his turn calmly, thinking of the feast that all awaited with an eagerness that was more than hunger.

❧ 23 ☙

Martin delivered his sermon with more than usual feeling, observing with some pride the impression he seemed to make on the Indian side of the congregation; yet at the same time he felt a curious apartness, was struck sharply by a duality of the situation, an ambiguity of feeling.

Beside him, outside the pulpit, with powerful presence and dignity, stood his Indian interpreter, Eagle Voice, dressed in immaculate Prince Albert, black as the shining braids that hung down his shoulders. He spoke in a strong, baritone voice, resonant and musical, giving the sermon a ceremonial, faintly pagan quality. With each translation he spoke at greater length than Martin, as if delivering the sermon while Martin supplied only the text. And sometimes, observing a faint ripple of amusement on the white side of the church (among those who understood the Indian tongue), he was sure of a discrepancy in the translations. Though in the past when he had asked someone, as a check on Eagle Voice, he had been put off gently or evaded. At such times he was furious with his inability to learn the language. So he felt as if only half the audience were really his, and it the white half where his words had little visible effect.

Standing in the pulpit on the exact median line of the building, he sometimes had the impression that the one lens of his glasses was darker than the other, that the very air on the Indian side was shaded slightly, tinged with emotion of a strange, darkened hue. The source of the subtle difference he recognized as Eagle Voice—and suppressed with a twinge of guilt his resentment and suspicion. For without this unusual man, he knew he would have small force among the Indians.

He was overly sensitive, he was sure, unable to forget that

before his conversion, Eagle Voice had been a practicing, influential medicine man; and that even afterwards, in childlike ignorance, had suggested that he and other Indians be invited to bring their medicine bundles—the very source and symbol of paganism—to hang on the walls of the church. Martin had scotched the idea with shock and indignation, and no more was said. Since then Eagle Voice had made remarkable progress in the knowledge and outward practice of Christianity, and Martin was sorry for his own distrust, recognizing, with shame, an envy of the man's style and power.

Yet this day he had taken as a text, "Thou shalt have no other God before me," thinking subtly to test the man's loyalty—if his effect on the Indians were less than usual, it would be a kind of key. But at the end of the sermon he was no more certain than before. He despaired of ever penetrating the man's darkness.

After the services the usual people met him with congratulations, the white ones first, the Indians waiting till later. But he was surprised to see some shaking hands with Eagle Voice also. And with a shock he realized that Leah was among them. He watched her take the Indian's hand, smile at him in too friendly fashion, and say something inaudible from where he stood. Sudden anger and revulsion rose into his throat with bitter taste.

He excused himself as quickly as possible, and at the gate waited for her in anger. But when she came, smiling and talking with Christine, he could not bring himself to speak. He walked home in silence, still resentful of her but ashamed of the reason.

In the afternoon he hitched his horse to the buggy, intending to take his wife and daughter for a drive; but at the last minute he drove away without them. As he left the yard he saw Christine's small white face at the window staring out, as he had seen her so often before. But he could not stop.

He crossed the east fork of the creek and turned north, away from the agency, keeping his eyes set straight ahead, jerking the horse impatiently when he turned his head aside. He was not angry; yet he felt driven, compelled. He had to keep moving. He drove for a long time in numbness, relaxing gradually into weariness as the road lengthened behind him.

The sky greyed, low clouds moving gloomy under the high.

The hills were grey, touched with brown mist, the green in the hollows showing a trace of autumn yellow. In the distance over the badlands the air distilled red-purple from colorless hills, was darkened by it, yet remained clear. A wide lonesome land; he was moved by it, yet repelled. There was a pagan quality as perceptible as the color in the air, distilled.

He remembered the atmosphere of the church with haunting dissatisfaction. Yet the sermon had been good, had made a deep impression. Attendance had been poor, but there was reason: the Indians were busy on their allotments finishing their haying, preparing for winter. They would be in for rations again the next week and the church would be full again. Nevertheless, he decided to stop at as many allotment and haying camps as time allowed, to urge attendance.

By coincidence, the first place he reached after his decision was that of Eagle Voice. He saw it in the distance, an unusually neat frame house of several rooms—the only painted house on the reservation belonging to an Indian. There was no tepee pitched by it, no sweat lodge or sunshade; nothing to mark it as Indian. He had passed it several times before but had never been inside.

He stopped in the road in front, thinking that if Eagle Voice would come with him as interpreter, it would ease his task. But there was no one home. No smoke came from the chimney, no children played in the yard, there was not even a dog to yap at him and spoil his temper. In a meadow below the house were a few horses, one apparently picketed, but they were not fenced in.

He drove on, realizing with disappointment and annoyance that he had counted on Eagle Voice for help. His resolution weakened, but he kept on; and in the end made several calls. Coming back in the evening his spirits were up again. In spite of the language difficulty, he had exacted several promises of attendance, some from Indians who had never been inside the church. It was almost sunset when he came again in sight of the house of Eagle Voice. In the west above the hills was a long rift of sky under the clouds, and from it a last brilliant light colored the land. In it the neat white house glowed warmly with sudden, nostalgic charm. In the distance it was like his father's house.

He stopped again when he reached the house, though he still saw no sign of life. Nothing had changed, though the horses were gone from the meadow leaving only the one on the picket. Still he got down from the buggy and walked to the door—there might yet be someone inside. He knocked and waited and knocked again; but there was no answer.

Finally he opened the door quietly and looked in. He was surprised and pleased by what he saw: a well-ordered kitchen that would have done credit to a white woman. The furniture was simple but good—a few chairs, a table, stove, a small cupboard of dishes, bright curtains at the window. He stepped inside and called but got no answer.

Feeling guilty and slightly nervous, he walked through the kitchen into the parlor and was again surprised: there was a rug, a good settee of maple with matching chairs, a mahogany dish cupboard with china. A large tinted photograph of Eagle Voice was hung on the wall. This and a peculiar odor, an atmosphere, were all that marked the room as Indian.

The door to the next room was closed. He hesitated a moment, then opened it quickly, intending only to glance through and leave. The room was dark, without windows, and at first he saw nothing. But from the darkness a strong odor of incense assailed him, and a smell of leather and sage. His heart leaped suddenly and he almost closed the door and fled without having seen the room. But again he stayed, held by hypnotic fascination. A recurring image of a serpent with jeweled glittering eyes rose up in vision.

His sight cleared to the darkness and he stepped into the room, oppressed and constricted, as he had felt in the lodge of Crazy Walking. And except for the shape, the room might have been a lodge: the walls were covered with buckskin, hung with pagan trappings—bows, arrows, beaded bags, painted rawhide containers, herbs, roots. Near the door a tripod stood bearing a medicine bundle.

There was no floor in the room, only a hard-packed, clean-swept clay. At the center was a small raised square of stone, painted with strange figures in red: a Maltese cross, a crescent (such as he had seen on the forehead of the dead child), a thunderbird, and others he did not know. At the center of this strange altar was a tiny fireplace, white with new ashes, remains of some heathen offering. Around it were pallets of blankets, each bearing rattles and a drum.

He tried to imagine the strange rites; for a moment saw Eagle Voice among naked, painted savages crouched on the pallets, heard the beat of drums, dry rattles, and the weird

99

singing. He turned to go, touched by a chill, sudden breath of fear. But again he stayed, drawn up in a tension of guilt and fascination.

Beside him, within reach, hung the medicine bundle, decorated, painted, mysterious; he could not leave without one look. He had the feeling that in it he would find the deepest secret of Eagle Voice. He reached out to touch it, thought he heard a sound in the yard, and in terror hurried out through the kitchen. But there was nothing. He walked clear around the house and in the brilliant red light of sunset saw nothing, no sign of life, only the picketed animal, nearer now in the meadow. His own horse stood quietly in the road, waiting.

He re-entered the house, breathing thickly, hurried back to the room and quickly opened the bundle, spilling its contents out on the floor. He stared for a moment at the strange spillage; broke into quick laughter that changed as suddenly to an inexplicable anger. He had a fierce desire to grind the objects under his feet, to destroy: a bedraggled bluebird skin; a worn redstone pipe, stem wrapped with fur and feathered; a tobacco pouch; some kind of fossil shells, painted red; something wrapped in bright red cloth.

He checked his anger and picked up the cloth-wrapped object and opened it. A smooth, shining stone rolled into his hand, shapeless, unrecognizable. Yet, as he turned it, he caught an image of buffalo: the hump, the neck, a suggestion of curved horn. He started to wrap it, and in that instant was assailed by a weird, terrible sound—a long-drawn pulsing animal cry. His heart stopped for an instant; he almost screamed. The stone dropped from his numbed hands and struck the stone altar with glassy brittle crash.

He ran out in horror and fear; and as he reached the door, the sound began again. Still running, he glanced fearfully toward the sound and saw the picketed animal close to the house now, nose in the air, mouth open—a mule.

He stopped and almost fell. He was breathing hard, sick in his stomach; his knees trembled. He tried to laugh but his voice was nearer a sob, the voice of a stranger. With courage he had not known he possessed, he returned to the house. He wrapped the pieces of the buffalo stone—broken now beyond recognition—in the bright cloth, replaced all the objects, hung the bag again on the tripod, and left. He ran the few steps to the buggy, unhooked the lines, and was whipping the horse up before he was in the seat.

Behind him the mule brayed again, a wild, metaphysical laughter. Looking back, he saw it pass the corner of the house, trailing a long rope attached to a drag of wood. It struck the road and trotted after him, head held to the side.

He forced his horse to a gallop, supposing that if he gained enough on the mule, it would stop following. But it did not. The farther ahead he pulled, the more it brayed—never forgetting to trot. He tried to ignore the animal, to close his ears to its wild importunity. But the sound seemed to grow as darkness fell, to roll over him in paroxysms, to rack him like laughter or grief.

His horse slowed to a trot, winded, and he did not urge it any more, though the mule drew near again. Strangely, though, as it caught up it stopped braying, and trotted contentedly behind. He could hear the wooden drag chattering and sliding at the end of the rope. But it was better than the terrible braying.

It occurred to him then that the mule might follow him clear to his home and stand at the gate before the church trumpeting his guilt—the very thought threw him into a sweat. Frantically he whipped the horse again to a gallop, standing up in the buggy, shaking out the lines, straining his eyes at the darkness ahead.

And again the braying began, more fearful than before. He fled in darkness, drawing away once more but still pursued. The sound had begun to recede when he saw the fires of a haying camp ahead. But his heart sank. He could not pass by like this with the mule proclaiming his flight. He stopped to wait and again the mule quieted, following at a distance.

Once past, he gave way once more to frenzy, and this time he did not stop till he gained his own yard and closed the gate. He stabled his trembling, lathered animal and, without unharnessing, stepped out into the darkness to listen for the mule.

He had left it far behind; yet he still seemed to hear it, far off, faint, not a sound of laughter now but of dole and pain. He left the yard and entered the church and, sweating, prayed.

After a long time his heart quieted and he stepped out from the shelter into the starless dark. There was no sound now, nor any light.

Crazy Walking stopped the team and, still holding the lines, got off the mower to oil the smoking pitman bearing, holding his breath against the hot oil stench and the tobacco-sweet smell of grass burning against the heated metal.

The day was warm. A crow sailed over him and lighted on the new-mown swath and, with neck outstretched, feathers ruffled, cawed at him in a hoarse, accusing voice. He raised his arm as if to throw the oil can and the bird flapped off, voice rising shrilly.

He finished oiling and climbed back on the mower, ears still ringing from the beat of the knife, the clatter of the chain. The horses did not move when he slackened the lines, so he let them stand. They were dead-tired now, beyond fighting, broke well enough to go on the rake. A pair of old pack horses they were, the gentlest of the bunch that had been given him on his return from mourning a few days before. They had never been touched before by a harness. They took it hard; but in the end they would accept the work. He remembered the ones he had given away, the well-broke teams, with a growing desire to quit and go hunting. But he had to have hay, or the few cattle he had left would die in the winter.

There was nothing on the hills, not even pasture. Drought had burned it off early in the year so that even the short, curly buffalo grass had not matured. He looked west toward the hills and saw the grain he had planted above the flat, not four inches tall, headless and papery, in spots buried completely in drifting sand.

There was grass here in the little flats along Leaf Creek, swamp grass mostly, poor feed, light as feathers when it dried, and hard to mow—full of mudholes, old buffalo wallows, and occasionally bones that stuck the knife or sometimes broke a section.

A sudden memory of buffalo lighted in his mind, this same

flat alive with brown and muddy bodies, the air thick with green, musty odor. So vivid was the image that he could see the individual animals, their places in the flat, the bird flights numerous as gnats, could feel the rifle in his sweating hands. The time between seemed hours, not years.

He finished the round and, unhooking the team from the mower, changed them to the rake. He made one round without incident and Turning Hawk came unexpectedly out of the shade by the river and took over the raking.

It was the first time the old man had worked with the machines—he hated them fiercely—but he offered no explanation. He took the rake and went to work, first saying a quiet prayer to Maka, the earth mother, and addressing the rake in a low shaking voice as if it were a living thing. He was forcing himself to do the work he hated, Crazy Walking could see. And he sensed that something, some change, perhaps within himself, was the reason.

Watching him drive away, operating the dump, back and arms flashing in the sun, he noticed for the first time that Turning Hawk was stripped to moccasins and breechclout, his medicine quirt hanging down his back. He might have been going to his death. Crazy Walking remembered suddenly the Blue Cloud and the old yellow horse, that strange comedy of the white cow, but he could not laugh. Something had changed the memory; it was bitter now and sad.

The next team he harnessed up was a pack horse—the last one—and an old spotted Nez Percé war horse, both gentle but both afraid of the mower. He had to put on blindfolds to make them stand while he fastened the neckyoke and hooked the tugs.

When he was in the seat and ready, Blue Fawn pulled the blindfolds and the horses stampeded. But he was in the grass with the mower in gear and the cutter bar down. The drag was too much for the horses to run with. They moved in long jumps for a while, seesawing the doubletrees, terrified by the clatter of the machine. Finally the pack horse settled down to a trot, but the spotted one went crazy as he was forced to slow down. He jumped straddled of the tongue and threw himself and lay there bellowing and kicking, too wild even to get up again.

Crazy Walking was startled. He had ridden horses that bellowed in fear and anger; but he had never seen the wild uncoordinated terror of the spotted one. He sat fascinated, affected sharply by the animal's fear. The bawling went on in a weird rising pitch that raised the hair along his neck. The other horse stood straining away against the neckyoke, trembling so hard that Crazy Walking could feel it through the machine.

When he saw that the horse would not get up, he stepped down, holding the lines carefully, and unhooked the tugs. He dropped the lines then, ran around to the front, and worked the breast strap loose from the neckyoke and unsnapped the lines.

As he raised up, he saw two cowboys sitting their horses watching him. He recognized one as a rider he had worked with in Montana, a man named Rosser; but the man was looking at him critically with no sign of recognition. He turned back to the horse, puzzled. Rosser had been not merely an acquaintance but a friend.

The horse had stopped bawling and lay there trembling and kicking spasmodically. But when Crazy Walking pulled on the lead rope he came up with a bawl and, walking on his hind feet, came at him viciously. He jumped aside and, with luck, threw a half hitch on the animal's forefeet and threw him, grabbing his head to hold him. When the horse stopped trying to get up, he began unbuckling the harness, hearing the riders talking—but as if from a long way off.

"He's gonna turn him loose. I thought he'd kill him. Loco, sure as hell."

"Naw," Rosser answered, "just scared. It's funny too—an old war horse like him. That crease on his hip ain't any brand. He's smelled powder and felt lead. Now look at him."

"By God, it's a sorry way to treat a good old horse."

"What about the Injun? He don't like it any better than the hoss, or I miss my guess."

The other did not answer.

"Looks like a boy I knew, but he was white; Walker, his name was."

Crazy Walking finished undoing the harness, spread it back on the ground, and unbuckled the collar, hearing the talk clearly but feeling numb and unaffected by it. The horse, sensing freedom, stood up, not fighting now but shaking as if from cold. He tied the other horse to the mower and, leading the spotted one, turned his attention to the two men.

They were riders with a herd for the agency, asking about the trail to the range where the cattle were to be held. Rosser did the talking with meager but understandable signs. Crazy Walking answered in signs, but with ambiguous feelings. He wanted to speak to this man he had called friend; yet he did not. He was seeing himself as in a mirror, but changed: the image he saw through Rosser's eyes was another person not yet familiar. He was perplexed and bewildered.

It came to him then that he could no longer call this man friend. He was, in reality, the stranger the other saw. He breathed easier, as if some burden of the past had dropped away. He pointed the way to the range near the mouth of Arrow Creek, where the herd would be held a few days. The riders left, jogging westward toward a low-hanging cloud of dust he knew was the herd. He watched them go, still with the sense of wonder and of relief; but of hurt too that he could not explain. He turned away, rubbing his arm across his eyes to clear them of dizziness, and looked at the half-mown flat, hot and green in the morning sun but suddenly unfamiliar.

He was astonished at the condition of his life; how he had come here he could not imagine. He had a sudden desire to escape, to mount the spotted horse and ride into the hills, never turning or looking back. His eyes traveled the purple distance far and long. But returned to the flat. Turning Hawk passed him, operating the rake with strained concentration, as if he feared some violent retaliation.

Little Wound rode toward him on the pinto horse, bringing water, sitting straight and solid in the clean light, vividly alive in a world of sound and shadow he would never know. Crazy Walking's heart filled with affection for this strange child; he was, himself, for a moment blind and deaf in an alien, uprooted land. The feeling was fearful, yet familiar. It was the atmosphere of his own life, of the life of his people. He became rigid with the sudden, terrible truth of the insight . . . He wanted to stop, to lie down.

Little Wound came toward him slowly, judging carefully his whereabouts. Blue Fawn, nearby piling hay, stopped and looked at him; the two small daughters burst from the willows—and all came toward him, exuding the strong power of living. His strength returned slowly. In a little while he would bring another horse and begin again.

## ❧ 25 ❧

The wind came in the afternoon, suddenly. Riding across the flat among the drying, odorous piles of hay, Little Wound was touched with quick foreboding—a subtle sense of change in the air as if the earth had paused for a moment in her breathing. There was no movement of air yet—there had been no wind all day—only an increased calm, a waiting.

He paused a moment, then, ignoring an inner prompting to return to camp, rode on toward the log house, avoiding the piles of hay he had helped to make the day before with growing sureness, as if in the increased calm his skin sense had sharpened, or the delicate extensions of the piles had strengthened.

He crossed a swale near the edge of the flat, knowing his distance from the river by the dryness of the air, the different odors of the grasses. He felt the approach of the trees near the house, secure in his sense of location, depending not at all on the new horse he was riding.

But when the wind struck, he was lost, enveloped suddenly in tumult. Odors of the hay were gone, lost in the smother of dust from the dry hills, the delicate tactile sense destroyed by buffeting air and stinging sand. The pony swung rump to the wind and tried to run, but he forced it sideways, toward the house, knowing its placement now only by memory. Yet he felt the trees again, even in the confusion—a shifting, hissing movement in the air, coming to him across the wind's flow. He was afraid to enter the grove, knowing the danger of falling limbs among the brittle cottonwoods.

He turned back, feeling the direction only by the wind's angle—he had to travel across and a little down the wind. But it was hard to judge with the horse swinging rump to the wind and wanting to drift with it. He was dependent on the horse now for all his perception of the ground ahead. While still retaining control, he had to give the animal freedom to avoid obstacles.

The horse was new, given him by the white man, and he did not trust it yet. It was steadier than the one he had lost, but also less alert, and its unusual movements were harder to understand. Remembering the other now in his fight with dust and wind, he felt the loss so sharply he almost wept. In memory the pony was an animal of light, white and red, though he had never seen it. The image merged somehow with another, farther back in the past.

Of the pony he rode he had no visual image, but in his hands he knew its bulk and shape already as he had never known a horse before. If he could mold rock with his hands, he could make this pony.

The wind grew stronger as he crossed the flat. Hay was mixed with sand in the wind, stinging his neck and shoulder, catching in his hair. The horse dodged and shifted as if traveling through a running band of animals: hay piles rolled by the wind, he knew.

A heavy flake hit the side of his face and clung under the wind's pressure—he clawed at it with one hand, the other holding the horse from running. But before he was free of it he was enveloped with the horse in a tremendous rolling mass of hay and dirt.

The horse bolted, buck-jumping to get free of the hay, and he had to cling to the mane with both hands to stay on. He still knew about where he was but he was afraid now, infected by the horse's panic. He let the rein free and lay close to withers, thinking of the willows along the creek.

In a moment he was among them, leaves and stems whipping his face and legs. The horse stopped of its own accord, trembling and shaking its head, and he dismounted and stood for a moment with his head against the animal's heaving side till his fear subsided.

The air was turbulent among the willows, the wind's current broken and swirling; against his face he felt innumerable, feathery explosions of popping, fluttering leaves. He left the horse and made his way along the creek through the whipping brush till he found the trail to the watering place and, leaning against the wind, followed the trail up into the open.

The wind was like a hand, thrusting him backward, stopping his breath; he tried crawling to ease the pressure, but next to the ground the air was so thick with dust and sand that it was like swimming underwater. He could not breathe.

He rose again and stayed with the trail, feeling for it with his feet through a drift of dust like snow, till he thought he was opposite the lodge, and turned off.

There was a point of willows he had to pass, and the white man's tent, which he usually avoided. But now he went directly toward it, intending to touch it as a bearing point in the confusion of the wind. He passed it, downwind, forced off his path, but when he came opposite he knew by the sharp explosions of the straining canvas where it was. He paused for a moment to steady himself—and was suddenly enveloped in canvas, thrown violently to the ground. He struggled in terror but could not rise; the white-man-smelling canvas held him like a covering of earth. He went on struggling, smothered, buried in confusion.

The canvas came alive then, pulling, jerking, heaving; and abruptly he was free. He rose and tried to run but struck someone's legs—the white man, he knew instantly—and fell. A hand caught his arm and raised him to his feet, gently, but holding firm when he tried to pull away. He stopped struggling and the fear died slowly, even with the white-man smell close in his nostrils.

Another hand caught his free arm, turned him slightly, and let him go. He hesitated briefly, then, with quick trust in the man's direction, walked straight ahead, and in a moment stumbled into the lee of the lodge, released by the streaming wind. Inside the lodge, the air was quieter but laden heavily with dust, agitated by the shuddering lodge cover. His mother greeted him with relief, touching his hair and face with warm hand; but in her touch he could feel tension and fear. The whole air of the lodge was heavy with fear as with dust.

After a moment, the white man entered—he had expected it, since the tent was gone—the strange odor startling him as it always did. But after a while he accepted it, even coming to detect an individual person odor under the white-man smell and an assurance, a lack of the fear that clung to the other adults. In the evening there was no fire or cooking of food. They ate only dried meat and some fruit the white man had brought.

He slept early but fitfully, awakening often in uneasiness and tension, feeling the straining of the poles, the drumming flutter of the leather under the battering wind. Near him the little ones slept untroubled, but in the attitudes of the unsleeping adults he could feel an intentness, a waiting for the end of the wind. Once, waking from a disquieting dream, he rose quietly and found his grandfather, knowing somehow that he was awake; but touching the wrinkled lips with his fingers, he was startled to find him singing in a low tense voice. He could tell nothing of the meaning of the moving lips or changing tones, but it frightened him more than the wind.

He slept again, but the wind did not stop. He knew it was morning, but his mother still sat by the pallet of the baby, awake, enduring. He waited for her to begin her morning work but she did not move. His two small sisters awakened and sat up near him; he touched the one nearest, Pretty Shield, and she was coughing. When she stopped she fumbled curiously at his hand, followed his arm with her small fingers, and touched his face. He realized then that it was still dark, but he was sure the sun was up. Dust, he remembered then, dust darkening the air.

He stayed where he was a long time, waiting for someone to move. The little girls came to his pallet and sat beside him restlessly. Sensing their discomfort, he took them outside, then found them pieces of dried meat. Sitting beside them he talked with them while they chewed, following with delight the quick, small bird flights of their hands.

Finally the grownups bestirred themselves and he knew there was light, but they moved slowly, indecisively, with a disturbing helplessness, and in a little while relapsed again to a tortured waiting.

The wind lasted steadily the day. He slept again, to be awakened in the night by a peculiar jarring of the earth like animals running. Something struck the lodge on the wind side, breaking the poles and tearing loose the pegs. In an instant the wind swept under the loosened side and toppled the lodge, tearing the rest of the pegs from the ground.

He was seized breathless in the dusty anger of the wind, terrified; yet instantly he remembered the little girls and groped for them through the tumult. He found both and held their hands, waiting till his mother should find them. But when she did she seemed helpless and ineffective. His father found them next and then his grandfather and finally the white man. They stood huddled together and, standing beside his grandfather, touching his hands, he understood that they were talking about the log house and how to get there. His father and grandfather carried the little girls, and staying close together they moved off in the direction of the house, fighting the dust and wind.

All was confusion: his nose was of no use to him—there was only the raw, smothering odor of dust; the delicate skin sense was destroyed by the turbulence. He could only know direction by the angle of the wind, the land through his feet. And the land had changed. The grassy meadow he remembered after the haying was gone. There was no grass stubble now or hay, only a layer of dust and sand like snow, drifted in little hollows and ridges, muffling the earth.

And yet for all this he knew where he was and, in the country within his mind, where the house lay. When they stepped into a depression not yet drifted full, he recognized it as the largest buffalo wallow, too near the creek to be in the line of travel to the house. They were being forced off by the wind and would pass, downwind, the cabin and the trees beside it.

He pushed ahead between his father and grandfather and, finding their hands, pulled them to the left, trusting his own sense of direction, knowing that they were more helpless than himself in the darkness and dusty, furious air.

Fear left him. He moved ahead, leaning on the wind, knowing under the muffling sand drifts the contour of the meadow as he had learned it crossing and recrossing on his horse. From the change in the current of the wind he knew the approach of the trees and near them turned left, skirting them till he felt the solidity of the house.

He found the door and opened it, and inside in the sudden calm and safety was seized by dizziness and shivering weakness. The thunderous wind seemed to surge still within him, the earth itself to rock and sway under its power.

He clung to his grandfather for support till the dizziness passed. Hands were stroking his head and he was strong again and happy. He stepped back and stood alone but touched, enclosed by a richness in the air, a warmth like the warmth of the sun.

## 26

Turning Hawk awakened sweating from the turmoil of the dream into still darkness that was thick with dust, the cloth over his face wet and in his mouth the gritty taste of mud. In the dream the wind had howled, tearing at him with hooked, invisible fingers, choking him with dust. He had never known such fury or such fear: the wind was a raging animal seeking his life. The lodge had gone, flown like a great bird, and he was seized suddenly by wind, a mysterious, cosmic rage. He was helpless, impotent, in the blinding, scarring rush, the suffocating darkness, clinging to the hand of a child for support, staggering into unseen, unheard dangers. Nothing in all his past could help him then. And in the dream the realization came late and with horror: the child was Little Wound and he was deaf and blind.

Now, awakening from tumult into the eerie silences of night, he was not relieved. Memory brought the dream and the reality before him and they were not different: the dream was memory, the memory dream.

He arose and found the door of the house and stepped outside into the perfect silence, a death's darkness thick with dust, full of the memory of earth's anger—and a strange waiting. He was lost, bewildered. He could only stand remembering, searching his heart for meaning. But it was too soon. The terror of the dark wind still shook him.

He walked away from the house until he found a tree and stood beside it, running his hand over the rough bark with a kind of hunger, finding in the familiar surface a certain solace. Calm returned. He drew his blanket tight and sat down, back and head against the tree, to wait for the sun. It was a long time coming, the first light slanting dimly through the dust, more like a sunset than a dawn. The sun rose red as ember, shrunken, old, but growing as it cleared the hills.

He stood and prayed, facing the sun with outstretched arms, finding slowly a lost strength and courage. He was able at last to turn from the trees and look at the earth, knowing beforehand—with despair—what he would see. Yet seeing, he was filled with wonder.

The flat was a wrinkled, earthen lake, sand rippling in static waves: far out, pure water forms where the earth was flat; rounded or scooped out in the hollow places; and next to obstacles, long tapered points like spears. Against the willows and among them were ragged drifts of hay and sand. The ponds near the creek lay still and grey, filmed with dust. He could tell them only by the flatness of the surfaces: the waves were on the land.

Beyond the ponds, a cottonwood, blown down and drifted under, raised still some green and yellow leaves above the sand, like flowers. Near him in a swale was the hayrake, half buried, wheels and teeth looping from the earth in burnished curves and in its lee a complex, rippled pattern of drifts. He stared at it a long time, fascinated and repelled.

He heard the door of the house open and, turning, saw Little Wound emerge, pause, and feel the sand with his feet, then come unerringly toward him following the tracks in the sand. His face was bright as if with expectation.

Turning Hawk stepped to meet him and touched the dusty upturned face, remembering the dream and his own helplessness; yet even now finding himself reassured by the boy's presence, by his touch. Strangely, it was not pity the young face brought him now but a lifting of the heart.

Little Wound made the question sign and pointed to the flat.

"Everything is dust. The flat is a lake with waves of sand. The ponds are flats, floating a dusty surface. The hay is gone, the grass buried."

Blue Fawn came out of the house and went across the flat toward where the lodge had been, to salvage, he knew, what she could from the sand. If she was downhearted she did not show it but moved dauntlessly, leaving a clear, unwavering track in the sand.

Little Wound's hands still rested lightly on his own, waiting for him to go on. When he did not, the boy moved away among the trees, stooping often to run his hands over the transformed, sandy surfaces. He moved methodically, with purpose, as if he were building within his darkness a touch-image of the changed land.

Turning Hawk watched him go with a sense of lostness in

his heart, bereavement of a sharpness he had not felt since childhood. Alone, he felt again the silent brooding that hung in the air like the dust that colored the sun, a red darkness pervading his heart.

He turned and saw the young white man standing by the house with an open notebook, sketching the flat. He wore an interested, absorbed expression; he was not depressed. The storm, Turning Hawk guessed with a trace of bitterness, had no meaning for the man, no terrors. He was detached from the earth, apart. Near him the little girls played quietly in the sand, subdued, their voices muffled by the dust in the air as by snow or fog.

Crazy Walking stood beside them looking at the flat. After a long time he walked out to the rake and tried to find the tongue by reaching down through the sand. Failing, he walked over to a wheel and kicked it. From each of the shining teeth, a ribbon of dust stretched downward to the ground, dissolved and floated in the air. He turned away, shoulders drooping perceptibly, and came toward Turning Hawk, weaving a little like one tired or drunk.

Turning Hawk was disturbed by his approach; he wanted to turn away and hide. There was no strength, no courage now he could give the young man. With relief he saw the white man also approaching—to speak with him would be a diversion; and Turning Hawk had come to trust this man, so different yet so honestly respectful of the Indian way.

The two men reached him at the same time and spoke briefly in the white tongue.

In halting yet expressive signs the white man commented on the storm, the loss of the hay. It was bad, but he hoped another year would be better.

"This is the end of farming," Crazy Walking signed with his bitter laughter. "Finished."

The white man shook his head, sympathetically, but in protest. "Not the end—only for this season. In the spring the grass will come up greener through the dust. It was likely a small storm; the earth is large. This dust is only a small part."

"The earth is large," Turning Hawk agreed, "but only for the white man. This," he pointed to the flat, "is the earth of the Indian, changed: in place of the buffalo, bones; in place of the grass, dust. The machines have offended the earth. The dust is anger."

"No. White men farm with machines on much of the earth and do well."

"The Indian is not a white man; he is born of the earth. The white man—I do not know; his medicine is strong to destroy. Perhaps he is born of rock."

The white man turned away toward the flat, but not in anger. He shook his head and signed, "It looks bad now; but only now. It will be past and forgotten, behind us."

"No," Turning Hawk denied. "Can any man see the future? No. But before the eyes the past still lights—it is ahead. The future lies unseen in the darkness behind."

Across the flat Blue Fawn still worked, hardly visible in the unreal twilight of dust. She had salvaged much from the sand and, having found the lodge cover, was pulling it loose from a bank of sand and willows.

Nearby, Little Wound was still exploring the flat. He was approaching a single, lonely bush, behind which a tapered spear of sand pointed toward the creek. Just before reaching it he stopped, seeming to test the air with his nose. He bent far over and, with hands almost touching the ground, moved forward softly. Near the bush he pitched forward suddenly; something exploded into the air in a spout of dust that resolved instantly into three flying grouse. Then, out of the dust they left, the boy emerged holding in his hands a fluttering bird.

Gradually the bird quieted and he held it against his chest, close to his face, with one hand stroking the bright feathers. His face was shining, suffused with warmth. For a long time he stroked the bird quietly, then impulsively held it up at arm's length and let it go.

The bird dropped toward the ground, leaving his hands, then rose, curved overhead, and was gone in the trees. The boy stood for a moment, risen on his toes, face bright, as if waiting for the bird to return.

Turning Hawk laughed aloud, involved in the child's joy; and with a start returned to himself and found the others also watching and smiling.

The day was brightening; overhead the sky was a powdery blue. With sudden purpose he started across the flat to help with the lodge.

## 27

The Indian, Yellow Bird, met them at the gate, seeming
pleased by the visit, Leah thought, even though he knew beforehand what Martin had in mind. In English (he was a
Carlisle graduate, she knew) he invited them in, including
Leah with his glance. And she accepted, knowing that Martin preferred to have her stay outside but knowing also that
he would say nothing now.

She was surprised at herself, realizing that she had already
decided: she would not sit waiting in the buggy any more.
She carried Christine, hoping that she would not scream at
the sight of the Indians in the house, feeling an exhilaration,
though she did not like the thought of what was coming.

It was a small log cabin with a sun shelter in front, at the
side a cone of lodge poles, and beyond, a small, leather tepee,
patched and weathered, smoke-blackened at the top, yel-
lowed below, and covered with shadowy, painted figures,
the colors almost gone. The patches were of Indian cloth,
bright red and green. Near it in the sun, an old man sat, bent
far over under a red blanket, only the lower part of his face
visible below a broad-brimmed hat. He was as motionless as
stone. Beside him, on its tripod, swinging a little in the breeze,
hung his medicine bundle.

Yellow Bird's wife met them at the door with two small
children clinging to her skirts. She greeted them shyly, in
good English, and brought chairs, then sat down near her
husband and did not speak again.

The cabin was neat and clean, the walls and ceiling lined
with new white tepee canvas decorated with hand-painted
designs. The floor was clay, hard packed, swept clean. Along
one wall were bundles of roots and grasses, a parfleche full
of little tubers Leah did not recognize, all filling the air with
rich harvest incense. She was glad she had come. But listening
to Martin, she was suddenly embarrassed.

"You understand," he was saying, "I want nothing valuable in itself, only the fetishes, the charms—medicine, I think you call them. I'd like to make some show—a small ceremony, perhaps—of destroying them."

"Do you mean as a sacrifice?" Yellow Bird asked.

"No, no, that would be offensive to the Lord. Only as a demonstration of the worthlessness of these things. And as a symbolic renunciation of paganism by those who participate."

"Do you think anyone would—except white people?"

"Why not? The members of my congregation should be glad to do it. After all, there are many precedents in the Bible."

The Indian only shook his head. He stood up and walked across the room, then returned and sat down again in visible agitation.

"You promised some yourself," Martin went on. "Just some small thing to begin with. Once begun, it will be easier for others."

Yellow Bird said nothing but stood again, a look of blankness in his eyes, lips moving silently. Finally he left the room and came back carrying a dusty, cylindrical bag made of brown fur, fringed with the black and white tails of some small animal. He handed it to Martin with averted eyes. But when Martin laid it down beside his chair, the Indian sprang forward and picked it up, handing it again to Martin. He stepped back with a weak smile and again turned his eyes away.

Martin seemed a bit nonplused; he sat holding the bag awkwardly away from him, not wanting it to touch his clothes. But he smiled at Yellow Bird.

"You realize, of course, as a Christian, that these things are worthless; but evil also in the eyes of the Lord. You will not regret their destruction."

Yellow Bird nodded violently in agreement, but he kept his eyes averted. "It is true," he said, "the old ways have failed."

"Is this all?" Martin persisted.

"I could teach you the songs, but you could not burn them."

"It's not what I meant. Perhaps the old man, your wife's father?"

"He is old," Yellow Bird said, "not a Christian. But he might give something; he will not need his medicine much longer."

He led the way out of the house, avoiding everyone's eyes,

116

Leah thought, but especially his wife's. The woman followed them to the door but did not come farther.

The old man still sat unmoving before his tepee, not looking up even when Yellow Bird stood in front of him. And Leah sensed at once that he was blind. When the young man touched him he raised clouded eyes and tried to stand but could not.

Yellow Bird spoke at length in Sioux, shouting into the old man's ear. Leah, watching the shrunken, bony face, saw it change from suspicion to a kind of warmth and benevolence. He answered in a hoarse, rattling whisper, pausing often while Yellow Bird interpreted.

"He says that to a Wicasa Wakan—a sacred person—he will give his eagle-bone whistle; that he is old, of few remaining days; the light is gone; he will fight no more. The whistle is for protection in war, to be sounded only then, only in time of danger. Made from the wing bone of an eagle caught in the sacred way, painted in designs shown by spirit power, its song is strong prayer in the fighting."

Yellow Bird translated the quavering speech in tones of derision; but he could not detract from the power and dignity of the old man who could neither see nor understand him.

When he finished speaking, the old man reached up to touch the bundle swinging on the tripod. Yellow Bird handed it down to him. He opened the bundle with ceremony and, reaching in, drew forth a piece of brightly painted bone. Holding it before him, he addressed it in whispers, the tones rising and falling in a pattern of song. Finished, he extended the whistle with shaking, withered hand, in his face the look of one who has given much.

Martin stepped forward and took the whistle, putting it hurriedly in his pocket. His face was a mask; Leah could not tell what he felt.

"You should thank him," she said softly, "as for a benediction."

Martin looked at her fiercely and, turning, walked toward the buggy.

Leah paused, regretting that she had nothing to give—she knew from the waiting, upturned face that the old man expected a gift in return. She resolved to send him tobacco in spite of what Martin might say. She returned to the buggy, hearing in memory the whispered tones of the old man's singing.

With brief leave-taking, Martin drove on, waiting till he was out of earshot before speaking.

"What did you mean, benediction?" he asked angrily. "You know as well as I these things are evil."

"It was his intent. Couldn't you see in his face? It was a thing he loved and gave only because he was about to die; and because Yellow Bird told him you were a 'sacred person'— that means medicine man, doesn't it?" She smiled to herself in spite of the anger she was provoking.

"It was only a way of saying priest."

She knew she should be quiet, but she could not. "No, they call you a White Robe, don't they? I think Yellow Bird said you were a sacred person, knowing the old man could not tell the difference. As a medicine man, you should have given something in return."

Martin did not answer but lashed the horse to a trot, his face set angrily against the road ahead.

She had to hold tight to Christine—the road was crossed with long, diagonal drifts of sand from the dust storm that kept the buggy lurching and jerking. Christine clung to her in terror, her breath shuddering with each sidewise movement of the buggy. And suddenly Leah herself was afraid. It was not fear of falling, but a vague, undefined terror as of a shadow descending. She tried to speak to Martin, to tell him in some way of her terror. But she could not; her voice was no more than a whisper. She did not try again, fearing that she might scream. Instead she held tight to Christine, trying not to communicate her fear. But in a moment the child was sobbing hysterically against her shoulder, thin arms clutching with surprising strength. Leah forgot her own fear then in her concern for Christine, and gradually the sobbing quieted. She looked at Martin and saw his face still set stonily ahead and knew with relief that he had not noticed the crisis.

For a time they rode in silence, Martin still trying to keep the horse at a trot and the horse trying to slow down. She could see that Martin was trying not to use the whip: he would hit the horse once, then place the whip firmly in the socket; but in a moment the horse would slow down to a walk —for all the flapping of the lines and shouting—and Martin would seize the whip again. Leah was sorry she had crossed him, seeing the horse suffer.

They followed the road down the east side of Arrow Creek, stopping at several haying camps on the way, finding all of them disrupted by the recent dust storm. In all the open places, hay was scattered, drifted in tangles against trees and bushes. Stacks already up were tipped over or their tops blown off. Indians stood disconsolately among wind-torn lodges or around dusty cabins. A surprising number of them gave Martin the things he wanted.

It was past noon when they approached the lower crossing and she knew they had to turn back to reach home by dark. But Martin would not. There were a few allotments on the west side of the creek near White River that he was determined to visit.

The day was quiet and, except for a yellowish haze in the distance, clear. But when they turned west toward the crossing, she saw beyond the creek a low cloud of dust and heard faintly a low, brassy sound of cattle bawling.

They came down to a wide, rocky creek bed, smooth bars of gravel broken by scattered, odd-shaped boulders lined on either side with willows. Martin set the brake and threaded a narrow passage down through the rocks, coming out on a gravel bar that led down to a wide, shallow ford. The creek, usually clear, was muddy now from the storm. The horse stopped at the water's edge and, after a struggle, Martin let him drink.

Across the creek, beyond the willows, the cloud of dust raised by the cattle was near now: she had visions of meeting them in the water and the fear rose again. But she could not mention it to Martin. Instead, she suggested that they stop and have the lunch she had packed. But Martin shook his head and, when the horse finished drinking, drove on.

The wheels jolted and clattered on the stones of the creek bed; muddy water swirled noisily through the spokes. She was fascinated by the earthen sweep of the water; and as she watched, the buggy instead of the water seemed to move, to sail swiftly sidewise. She looked up quickly at the bank ahead to break the illusion, and saw the first cattle emerge from the willows at a gallop and plunge downward among the rocks.

The horse threw up his head and snorted wildly; she heard Martin catch his breath and saw him reach for the whip. A widening stream of cattle poured over the bank with a drumming, vibrating sound; the leaders crossed the bar and struck the water, throwing up a wall of spray.

The horse reared and turned left in spite of the whip lashing his rump. There was a crack of breaking wood; the front wheel cramped under the buggy, lifting it sidewise. She felt herself falling and jumped clear, holding Christine, twisting herself in the air to fall backward holding the child up, and struck the water with chilling shock. She went completely under, head upstream, but the current's force helped her sit up. Without pausing, she stood with Christine clinging to her neck, screaming, and struggled through the water toward a boulder she remembered from the instant of her fall. Her eyes were blurred with water; she could hear nothing but the screaming child; but she smelled the cattle near and was on the point of screaming herself when her outstretched hand touched rock. Instinctively she swung behind and began to climb, feeling rather than seeing the cattle going by on either side. Not till she was on top of the boulder did she allow herself to look at them.

They were still coming over the bank but not running now, covering the bar and the water around her, those in the lead trying to drink and being forced on by those behind. She saw the buggy lying on its side among the cattle; the horse was gone. She found Martin then, near the buggy, balanced on a thin spire of rock, his feet just above the level of the cattle's backs. The thrown-up heads of the cattle made him seem knee-deep in horns. For a moment of terror she looked out through his eyes, involved in his loneliness above the terrible sea of horns. There was a shadow in the air, an enshrouding darkness, even in the sunlight, that seemed to rise among the animals like mist.

She shut her eyes and bit her lip, drawing away from him with an effort that was almost physical, and the terror faded. She opened her eyes on brilliant sunlight. Noise assailed her ears as if only beginning: Christine crying; the bawling and splashing of the cattle; the sucking, blowing noises of their drinking; and a rattle of clicking horns.

There was another sound she could not locate, an intermittent, high-pitched whistle. Searching for it, she looked again at Martin and saw him drawn up stiffly on the rock, on tiptoe now, encircled by a ring of curious cattle, shaking their heads at him and blowing through their noses. When one came close, he raised something to his lips and she heard again the high-pitched whistle. She began shivering violently, feeling the cold of the wet clothing suddenly. Christine stopped crying and, drawing back a little, looked at her curiously.

She noticed then that Christine's dress was almost dry except in front where it had been against her own. She could not imagine how she had held the child clear of the water when she herself had gone under; but it gave her a quick feeling of strength and pride.

She looked at the cattle again, really seeing them for the first time: the many colors—roans, buckskins, reds, whites, blacks, and all combinations of spots—the long, gracefully curving horns; the way they drank, sucking the very surface, noses snubbing with each swallow; the glint of sun on their hides. With their grassy, earthen smell, they seemed to exhale, to emanate a warmth and vitality that made them no longer strange or fearful.

Then she heard a shout and saw a rider come down the far bank and among the cattle and rocks, an Indian riding bareback, naked to the waist, with long braids shining black against his leather-colored skin. He crowded a lane through the cattle and put his horse in close to the rock, grinning up at her. With signs he offered to take her to shore.

She hesitated an instant, looking at Martin, and saw that he had stopped blowing the whistle and was watching her. He shouted at her, but she did not understand him over the noise of the cattle. She turned back to the Indian resolutely and, holding Christine, slid down the rock till she was on a level with the horse's back, then stopped, uncertain as to what to do. The horse, seeing her for the first time, shied violently, but the rider forced him back against the rock, where he stood quiet but snorting. Christine was clinging tightly to her neck with both arms, trembling but not crying.

Seeing her uncertainty, the Indian touched her left foot, then the horse's back, behind him. She had never ridden except with a sidesaddle; but with quick decision, she lifted her wet skirts high with one hand and stepped astride the horse, in the same movement dropping the skirts and seizing the Indian around the waist.

The horse plunged and reared and she clung desperately, pressing the side of her face between the man's shoulder blades, all her attention on Christine. In a moment the horse quieted and she relaxed her hold, shifting suddenly from fear to amusement at her predicament. She had a brief glimpse of Martin watching her with scowling eyes and partly open mouth and felt a quick twinge of guilt for her unladylike behavior. But only a twinge. When they reached the bank and went up among the rocks away from the cattle, she was laughing aloud.

The horse stopped and the Indian made a stirrup for her with his foot. Looking up at him from the ground, she thanked him, though she knew he could not understand her words. He only grinned at her and, wheeling the horse, rode back toward Martin.

She stood Christine on the ground and sat down on a rock, feeling weak and shaken. But suddenly, remembering Martin, drawn up on the pinnacle, blowing the medicine whistle, she was laughing again. The image did not seem funny, but she could not help it. She succeeded in controlling her laughter only when Christine began to cry.

❧ 28 ❧

Awakening, the first thing Crazy Walking saw was the bright flame of the match, half burned, its black end curling down, above it the whiskered face, familiar yet strange, bent close, looking at him intently. Something had been said, he knew, but he could not remember the words or the meaning. He could not recall yet where he was; but he was tense, on edge —if the man touched him he would fight.

The match burned close to fingers, guttering, and fell to the ground. He saw the stars, the bright moonlight, and heard cattle bawling in the distance. He sat up automatically, thinking night guard, still only half awake, and reached for his boots and hat. But he could not find them, only a flat, worn pair of moccasins. He swore; and the sound jerked him fully awake and out of the past, remembering suddenly—this was the agency herd he was helping to hold till the animals were used to the new range. It was almost a week now and he was not used to it yet himself.

122

He rolled out of the blankets, chagrined, and put on his moccasins, aware of Rosser's intent gaze on his face.

"For an Injun that can't talk white, you can sure cuss," Rosser said softly.

He stood up, avoiding the man's eyes, possessed by an uncanny feeling that this had happened to him before. In the intensity of the illusion, he almost spoke in English, catching the words in his throat, using his hands instead to make the question sign and the one for horse, moving them up clearly in the moonlight.

Rosser led him silently into the darkness, past the sleeping forms of the other Indians, to a blaze-faced horse standing at the edge of camp with reins dropped. There was another night horse saddled and picketed close in and, strangely, the nighthawk had the whole remuda corralled. Crazy Walking looked at him questioningly.

"They're wild as hell," Rosser said, speaking English, making a meager translation with signs. "I got a hunch they're gonna bust loose and we'll need some help."

He handed Crazy Walking a belt and revolver, still watching him curiously. "You might need it."

Crazy Walking took the gun silently and mounted the blaze-face, making a little show of approaching on the right, then going around to the left. He rode off, trying to understand why he kept up the pretense with Rosser, but he could not.

He approached the cattle obliquely, whistling, and found them quiet except for a few old steers standing here and there around the edges. Too quiet. The bawling had stopped and the grunting and groaning sounds that easy cattle made when they were bedded down. They seemed to be waiting, listening. He made a round slowly, singing in a high-pitched voice a white man's song from his punching days, "Ride round little dogies, ride round them slow, For the fiery and snuffy are a rarin' to go," grinning to himself at its fitness.

It was a wild bunch—as he had known at a glance, approaching it a few days before, nearly all longhorns, Texas cattle mostly, Rosser had told him, with a heavy sprinkling of outlaws, old mossy-horn snuffers jobbed in a variety of ways to tame them down: horns partly ripped off or slits of hide cut to dangle before their eyes; flaps of rawhide tied to their horns for the same purpose; a few with knee cords cut to drop them when they ran. But they were still wild, and the worst ones seemed to stay in little bunches as if waiting to take the lead in case of trouble.

They had run once the day they were brought across the river to the north range, and Crazy Walking had seen what started it: a big red steer with a rawhide flapper over his eyes had caught it on another's horn. He had pulled loose and run in circles, tossing the flapper and blowing through his nose. The whole bunch had lit out, running a mile or so before they were turned and brought into a mill. They were still jumpy from that run.

The moonlight was brilliant; he had the impression that he could see better than in the daylight. The contrast of light and shadow gave shapes a solidity as of carven stone and, without colors, a kind of second reality. The horse was spooky, shying at every shadow, moving with short jogging steps to keep his feet well under him. His nostrils were distended, ears forward, as if the land were dangerous by moonlight. Again Crazy Walking had the eerie feeling that he had been here before with these same thoughts and feelings.

He turned his mind to the cattle, wondering idly which way they would go if they spooked again. They were well spread out on the bed ground; they would run together first, then probably take out after one of the little clots of renegades. But there was no telling which way they would go.

He was surprised that he was not more worried, remembering the times in the past when he had suffered agonies with a nervous herd, sweating under the lonesome responsibility of night guard. But he was detached now, more curious than anxious.

He was still singing, but he had changed the music unconsciously as he rode. It was a lullaby in his own language that he sang now; and at its end another came unbidden, a medicine song of his own making, long forgotten, coming to him out of his youth. He remembered the thunderstorm, the wood knockers clinging to the quaking trees in blinding rain. It was a song to bring protection in storms, he had believed. He smiled, remembering. The words came slowly, tentatively; he almost stopped, then gave in suddenly and sang.

He was still singing when he completed another round. In the distance at camp he saw the bright flare of a newly made fire and, by its occasional flicker, knew there were men moving around it. Part way around again, a white steer came

124

out of the herd and followed him, half belligerently. He turned and bluffed it back into the bunch.

An owl slanted by, a silent shadow, moving low above the cattle, hovering here and there over the open spaces. At the edge of the herd he saw it plunge downward suddenly and heard the quick death squeal of a rabbit.

There was a drumming like many stones falling as the herd came up. They ran together, a darkening, shrinking spot. He heard horns clicking, the impact of bodies, the breathy grunts of squeezed animals. The spot expanded then like a hand opening, fingers of cattle extending toward the badlands beyond camp.

His horse was running as soon as the cattle, moving up on the flank of the nearest bunch, crowding in without guidance. But Crazy Walking had to ease him off—the bunch was moving on a line just to the left of camp. If he turned them now they would hit the horse herd. Across the backs of the cattle he could see other bunches splitting off.

There was no bawling, only the rattle of horns and dewclaws, the pound of hoofs, the windy breathing, and another sound, hardly audible, like rain, from the flying dirt. Dust rose in the moonlight, white as mist, to hang quietly in the still air, marking the many streams of cattle.

The horse strained under him, beating a fast rhythm to the cowboy song that had returned to his mind. He found himself smiling in exhilaration. He was almost up with the leaders when he passed camp. There was a tangle of horses and riders around the fire; he saw the loose horses break out of the rope corral and stream away parallel to the cattle.

He crowded the leaders over, intending to join them with the next bunch, but even as they responded, the riders burst from camp—Indians shouting a high wild cry, "Hoka hey, hoka hey," coming up on the other side of the cattle, spreading out, lost suddenly in the dust. He thought he heard Rosser shouting above the noise, but he was not sure. He continued to crowd the leaders, yelling now, and they moved in a curve to the right toward the dark stream of the other bunch.

He could still hear yelling behind him, but looking back he could see no riders, only the separate streams of dust, ascending, white hills in the moonlight, radiating like the spokes of a wheel. Voices of the riders following the far bunches were hardly audible now, receding.

The ground was rougher toward the hills, rocks and sagebrush and little gullies cutting the down slope. The shadowed bushes and rocks dappled the earth in the blue light, blurring dizzily as he passed over. The two bunches were nearly together, separated by only a shallow gully; but the leaders would not cross. They swung parallel, with just a few on the far edge being crowded over, hitting the bottom in little spurts of dust and running there.

He moved farther ahead and, drawing the pistol, fired once in front of the leaders. They shied and went over the bank with the sound and solidity of a landslide, curved up across the bottom and climbed, the herd taking the shape of the gully like a blanket thrown.

He slowed his horse to cross and saw two riders appear in the dust on the other side of the cattle and, yelling, plunge into the gully and up again, reappearing in the narrowing V between the two bunches. They were shooting, leaning low on their horses to aim; and suddenly he heard the wild, almost forgotten cry of the buffalo kill, "Owee—yuhoo." He saw them reach the point of the V and collide with cattle, horses rearing and fighting to keep their feet, the riders never ceasing to yell and shoot.

The gully was steeper now where he had to cross, a vertical bank on the near side, dark rocks in the bottom, and a brushy, rocky slope beyond. But without hesitation the horse went over, landed hard, and sank to his knees, thrusting his nose far out ahead as he flopped. Crazy Walking jumped clear, still holding the reins in one hand, the pistol in the other. He fell and was up and in the saddle before the horse had gained his feet. He kicked the animal to a run again, buck-jumping over the rocks and brush, the medicine song loud in his ears.

Beyond the gully he emerged into the sudden light of an alkali flat and was yelling with overpowering excitement, "Hoka hey, hoka hey," leaning over to shoot, seeing the animal fall and roll darkly on the white earth and disappear in blinding dust. He went on shooting till he was out of bullets.

The flat ended in cutbanks and gullies; he was trying to reload when the horse went down again, sending him crashing into darkness . . .

He came awake, still holding the reins, finding the horse standing quietly over him. He stretched his legs and arms cautiously and stood up unhurt. Feeling the lightness of the holster, he searched the sandy bottom of the wash where he had fallen till he found the pistol. Then, leading the horse, he climbed up out of the shadows into the moonlight. In the distance he could hear cattle bawling and guessed that Rosser had rounded up some of them. Of the cattle he had followed, there was no sign; he could not even hear them in in the maze of badlands, north.

He mounted and rode back across the white flat with no thought of the steers he had killed until he saw them. He paused, the memory coming vividly, racing in his blood. He laughed aloud as at a stranger; but he was puzzled and full of wonder. He stopped to bleed the animals before he started out again to help Rosser.

৶ 29 ৶

Westland sat cross-legged, back to the counter, in the trader's store, smoking the pipe as it passed back and forth along the line of Indians. He was at ease but absorbed, attentive, following the conversation only sketchily with his meager knowledge of the language—though in the six weeks of his stay he had learned with a rapidity that surprised him.

A pleasant, broad-faced Indian named Wolf Head was telling a story of a white man he called Dogs-Are-Afraid-of-Him, supplementing his words with signs when he saw that Westland was lost. The white man, it seemed, had met a herd of cattle at the lower crossing and had been dumped out of his buggy into the water. Wolf Head spoke of the accident with evident relish, intimating that it was the inevitable result of the man's having offended the spirit of a medicine bundle.

Wolf Head gave an amusing picture of the man marooned on a rock in the river, blowing frantically on a medicine whistle to keep from being knocked off by the cattle. The story was interrupted here by the laughter of the other Indians. They lingered over the image, adding their own touches, building it in their minds, savoring the irony—the white man,

127

according to Wolf Head, despised all Indian medicine and was collecting bundles to destroy.

He himself, Wolf Head continued, had carried the man's wife and child ashore on his horse—a woman of courage and humor, he added thoughtfully, though white. It came to Westland then with a shock that the man must have been Martin, the woman Leah.

There was silence for a while, the pipe passing back and forth, the Indians relishing the story, chuckling softly. Westland had been amused by the image of the man whistling on the rock among the cattle, but the thought of Leah and Christine in the same danger disturbed him deeply. He could not imagine it. Taking the pipe as it passed, he found that his hand was shaking. He forced himself to smoke and pass the pipe, suppressing the emotion, concentrating on Wolf Head's monologue.

He had a gift himself for this white man, Wolf Head went on, and was only awaiting the proper time to present it. A medicine bundle—he held it up, rather gingerly, Westland thought, and put it down quickly against the counter.

Westland could not tell what there was about the bundle that so amused the Indians, but he was sure from the way Wolf Head handled it that there was a catch. It was some little joke he was making, and the others were enjoying it immensely.

Westland had not known that Martin was a collector of artifacts; he made a mental note to ask about it. Perhaps he could see the collection. He heard horses then outside and through the open door saw two riders, one Indian, one white, dismount and tie to the rack. As they walked toward the store, he recognized the Indian as Crazy Walking, though his face was skinned up almost beyond recognition.

A ripple of amusement passed along the line of Indians.

Wolf Head spoke loudly, "Have you heard of the Indian who lives on Leaf Creek and who has become a true farmer? They say he has no plow and tills the soil with his face."

Crazy Walking entered, having heard what was said, Westland knew, but his face showed no change of expression. No more was said. He waited till the amusement died down and asked if the Major had not just come to the store.

Wolf Head pointed to a back room; and a moment later the Major appeared. The white man, evidently a cowboy, did the talking.

"We lost a lot of cattle last night," he said abruptly. "Stampede. And those damn fools you gave me for help only scattered 'em worse. We rounded up part of them this morning but there's still some that'll have to be drug out of those badlands one at a time. That's a hell of a job, even for good cowhands, which these Injuns ain't—except this one," he indicated Crazy Walking, "and he's about half crazy. We'll never get 'em all."

"Damn," the Major exploded, "we're way short now. We can't afford to lose them. Have you got any other ideas?"

"Yeah. Let these Injuns hunt 'em, like buffalo. The meat'll pack out a damn sight easier than those steers'll lead. They can do that—and enjoy it. I got a hunch that's what part of 'em were doin' in the run last night. Anyhow, there's meat to bring in."

"It might work, but the Indian office won't like it. You're sure you can't get them any other way?"

"Sure I can—if you hire me some good hands. But even then it'll take time. And where you gonna get hands? The ones that helped bring 'em in are long gone now. Hell, you got the best bunch of hunters in the world. And the cattle have to be killed for issue anyhow. It's the only sensible thing to do."

"All right," the Major said. "We'll do it. Let's talk it over in my office. I'll send for the headmen."

The three men left. Glancing at the Indians beside him, Westland realized that none of them had understood the talk. He was just trying to arrange the words to tell them when Martin and Leah came in and he forgot all his composition. He had the pipe in his hand when he saw her and almost dropped it, then passed it on without smoking. He recovered himself to find Wolf Head grinning at him, delighted at his confusion. The Indian made a remark about blankets and women that Westland did not catch, and for that moment he was glad of the language difficulty.

Martin stood near the door, ignoring him. (He resolved not to break away from the group by getting up.) Leah smiled at him in surprised recognition but did not speak.

Wolf Head seized his opportunity. He stood up, beckoned Westland to interpret and, with comical deference, presented the bundle. Westland joined him with some embarrassment; he knew a joke was being played and, because of Leah, wanted no part in it. Yet he could not refuse and separate himself from the Indians after winning their confidence. He could see Wolf Head—and the others too—enjoying his discomfiture and resolved to be less transparent in the future.

"Tell him," Wolf Head said, "that the bundle is sacred, its powers many and lively. If he offends the spirits, he will feel their displeasure."

After the translation, Wolf Head returned to his place before the counter, and though the Indians preserved a dignified silence, Westland could see they were full of laughter. He still did not divine the joke.

"Do you have much of a collection?" he asked Martin.

"Collection of what?"

"Indian artifacts. I understand you collect them."

"God forbid! I only want to get them out of circulation."

"Would you be interested in placing them in the museum?"

"No." Martin broke off and went to the back of the store where a clerk waited.

"I'm sorry he's so abrupt," Leah said. "But it's a sore spot with him. I try to make amends, not very successfully. Do you think I should pay the Indian for the bundle?"

"I'd give him tobacco," Westland suggested, smiling at the thought that perhaps Wolf Head's joke might boomerang.

"Will you buy it for me?" she asked, then added quickly, "No, I'll do it myself."

He watched her buy two plugs of pipe tobacco, appreciating her courage and aplomb—he could see Martin was both confounded and furious. Asking the clerk to wrap one, she brought the other back along the counter and presented it to Wolf Head.

"Will you thank him for the bundle on my husband's behalf?"

Westland translated, partly with signs, laughing aloud at Wolf Head's confusion, knowing he had not expected a return for his dubious gift.

Leah looked at him questioningly, but he could not explain. She went back to stand beside Martin, ignoring his angry glances.

Westland remembered then about the cattle hunt and, with signs and the few words he knew, explained to the Indians what he had heard. They were transformed, suddenly excited as children. For the first time he saw them lose their dignity and reserve. They gathered around him chattering and gesticulating, but he could understand nothing. And all at once, there was not an Indian left in the store. He joined Martin and Leah at the counter.

"What the devil did you tell 'em?" the clerk asked.

He explained about the cattle. "I didn't expect to produce such an explosion."

The clerk shrugged. "Injuns!" was all he said.

But the effect on Martin was as startling as on the Indians. "It's the worst thing that could happen," he stormed. "Just as they begin to be civilized, to revive all the old savage patterns. The worst thing possible, all the effort wasted." He turned abruptly and rushed out, leaving his purchases on the counter but still carrying the medicine bundle.

There was something fearful in the man's rage, Westland thought, and something comical also. But he did not laugh.

Leah finished with her purchases, leaving all but the tobacco on the counter. He walked with her outside to the platform and stopped, sensing that she would not want him to go farther.

She smiled up at him with an openness, a directness he could not have anticipated; he was thrown off balance, knowing by the slight crinkling of her smile that she read his feelings. She held out the tobacco, covering his awkwardness but not retreating. "Will you give this to old Walking Bear? It's another return gift. I'm not likely to get the chance— I've gone too far now." She paused, then went on, rushing the words, but with the same directness. "You've changed. Or maybe it's me. I envy your work."

"I guess I've changed," he admitted, recovering his voice, "and it's you certainly. I'll deliver your present. May I see you home?"

She shook her head. "Come for dinner, though, if you like. Christine would be delighted."

He was standing in front of her; she moved to leave and he stepped aside to let her pass. She stepped in the same direction at the same instant, then back again; and again he found himself in her way.

"Dance?" she asked, laughing.

He stepped back against the building and she was gone, leaving him with a faint odor of perfume and a turbulence of emotion he did not have the courage to examine. He turned reluctantly toward the Indian camp.

Martin walked on toward the square, already out of breath though not tired. But he had the sensation of moving against an unseen resistance, of climbing, though the ground was level. To the right the Indian camp was already alive with activity, Indians gathering, streaming in toward the quadrangle. He could sense their excitement, realizing anew the perniciousness of the Major's plan.

He increased his pace, and for the first time noticed that he was still carrying the medicine bundle. It flapped awkwardly against his leg as he walked, seeming more bulky now, heavier than he remembered, and annoyingly conspicuous. He would have liked to leave it, to hide it, but he could not. He would have to carry it and face the gibes of the Major and the curious stares of the Indians already gathered in the square.

He had to go on. The idea of a cattle hunt now was monstrous—the very enthusiasm the Indians were showing was proof enough of its unwisdom. He crossed the square and found the Major busy. With the help of two Indian policemen he was moving all the furniture out of his office into another room. He motioned Martin in but did not stop to speak.

Martin waited impatiently, sitting on a bench by the window till it was the only piece of furniture left. On a final trip the two Indians approached him, looking at the bench. He stood up quickly and stepped aside, and they picked up the bench with not a glance at him, as if they had not even seen him. He was sure they would have carried him out with the bench if he had not moved.

The Major came in, smiling inevitably at the sight of the bundle. "Well, Reverend, I take it you've come to make medicine against the hunt."

"I'd like to talk with you about it," Martin said, ignoring the feeble humor. "I think perhaps you don't quite realize the evil of such things, Major. It will call up all the old savage patterns—"

The Major held up his hand imperatively. "Hold on now, we're having a council here in a little while and that'll be the time for you to talk. I think the Indians should have some say in this, too. Don't you?"

Martin shook his head and started to speak again, but the Major walked away abruptly, leaving him alone in the empty room. After a moment he stepped into the hallway and found the room where the furniture had been moved, supposing it to be the place of the meeting. But it was smaller than the office, completely filled with furniture. He was puzzled and uncertain.

The Indians were arriving, standing outside the building, not only the headmen but the whole band, filling the square. The sound of their voices grew in volume, steady and un-modulated as the sound of bees. The dominant tone, he knew, was of joy, and yet it was oppressive—as the sound of bees was also.

The Major returned, carrying a bucket of water in which two cups were suspended on wire hooks. He entered his office and, as at a signal, a number of Indians and a white man filed in from the outside. Martin followed and found himself standing in a circle which the Indians had formed instantly on entering. They dropped down lightly to a cross-legged position on the floor, hitched their blankets in a roll over their knees to hold them, and were at ease.

The Major and the white man, a cowboy he had seen before, had taken their places in the circle almost as soon as the Indians. Martin was conscious suddenly that he was the only one left standing and dropped down awkwardly in the space left for him between two Indians. He recognized some of them: Turning Hawk, Eagle Voice, Wolf Head, and a young man with a skinned-up face he could not name at once.

An Indian he did not know produced a large stone pipe, filled it, and passed it to Turning Hawk. Seeing the pipe, Martin became acutely uncomfortable; he could not understand how he had let himself into such a situation. He would have to sit in respectful silence now while the old medicine man went through his heathen ceremony, blowing smoke to the four winds and whatever else it was they worshiped. He did not know whether he could do it.

Turning Hawk lighted the pipe, drew a few wheezing puffs,

then held it up, stem outward toward the west, intoning in a controlled ceremonial voice a prayer which Eagle Voice repeated in English at each movement of the pipe, conveying perfectly the tone.

"Friend of Wakinyan, I pass the pipe to you, and
  Circling (to the north) pass the pipe to you who dwell with the Grandfather,
  Circling (to the east) pass to the beginning day,
  Circling (to the south) pass to the beautiful one, and
  Circling (west again) complete the four quarters and the time.
I pass the pipe to the father with the sky and to the earth, mother of all.
Give us a blue day and the power to see beyond the things that are."

Turning Hawk passed the pipe then to the left, each Indian making a few abbreviated motions and smoking. Martin, waiting his turn, was in a torture of indecision: would it be sin to smoke? He had not imagined such reverence among savages; he did not know the gods invoked, but a prayer to "the father with the sky" he could not object to. And he was sure that if he refused to smoke he could not hope to speak with effect against the hunt. He resolved to draw lightly at least once, trusting for forgiveness, since it was in the service of the Lord.

But when he held the pipe in his hand his resolution almost failed him: The pipe was of finely carved redstone, stem wrapped with brightly colored quills; but the mouthpiece was covered with green skin, like the skin of a chicken. It took all his power to put it between his lips. And when he drew, he inhaled some of the smoke and, in embarrassment, coughed. He was sweating, impatient, ill at ease, beset by sudden itching along his arms. But in all the quiet and solemnity, he could not scratch. He was constrained by a strong, incongruous feeling that he was in church.

The smoking finished, the Major took a drink from the bucket and passed it around. Each drank, the Indians with the same solemnity with which they had smoked.

There were two cups, one of china, the other of unglazed pottery and, with relief, he saw that the Major had used the china cup while all the Indians, by choice, used the other. He himself without hesitation chose the white one and, drinking, was shocked to find there was whiskey in the water. But he had to finish—he could not pour it back.

By the time all the ceremony was over, he was calm but numb—the effect of the whiskey, he supposed. But thinking of what he would say when he came to speak, he was confused and indefinite; the reasoning that a moment since had seemed so clear and irrefutable was now distasteful.

The Major spoke first, explaining the situation. "As you know, we've lost some cattle in the badlands, wild ones at that, old renegades dragged out of the brush in Texas, one or two at a time. We can't afford to lose them. With the new cut in beef, we face hard times at best. The question is, how can we get them out with the least amount of loss? Shall we try to round them up and drive them out or shoot them and pack out the meat?"

Eagle Voice interpreted. After a while Turning Hawk spoke. "It is well known that the spotted buffalo and the Indian do not speak the same tongue. The white man," he indicated the cowboy, "seems to know how they think, what they will do. For him it might be best to round them up, to kill at close range, without hard work. This is his way.

"The Indian, on the other hand, has always hunted his meat, killing in the open, testing skill and courage in the chase. For this his medicine is good; he has a skill beyond the white man.

"So, because we are Indians who will do the work, let us hunt the spotted buffalo in the old way, killing them where we find them. The women can dress the meat where it falls, bringing it into camp, as is their right. This is the Indian way. For a little while we can walk the old road, harming no one."

There were murmurs of approval from the other Indians, something like "washtay, washtay."

When Martin spoke, he addressed the Major, knowing he could never influence the Indians. "I think you agree, Major, that we are here to lead these people upward toward a better, a civilized life; any regression is itself a loss just as the cattle might be. The handling of cattle is part of the new way which they must learn. We should look on this as an opportunity to teach, not merely as a problem to be solved in the simplest fashion. Granted that the hunt might be the simplest solution, at the same time it will call up all the old patterns of bar-

barism: the recklessness, the needless danger—men will be hurt; the blood lust itself—it is perhaps not such a long step from the killing of cattle to the killing of men; the debasement of the women who will be forced to do the butchering in the old unsanitary way; the haphazard apportionment of the meat; and finally, perhaps worst of all, the return to the old rituals of the hunt, to the invocation of the heathen gods, to the practice of magic, to the personal fetishes and charms. These are practices that must be forgotten, not revived, if the Indian is to proceed on the way to civilization."

With the pauses for interpretation, it took a long time to finish the speech. And at the end there was silence, no approval or agreement, not even from the Major.

It was again Turning Hawk who, after a long pause, answered. "In the beginning Wakan Tanka gave to each people a cup," he indicated the cups in the water bucket, "a cup of clay from which to drink their lives. All dipped into the water, yet their cups were different, of different shape and color and size, each according to the nature of its people.

"The Indian prefers his own cup, the white man his. Yet the Indian would not force the white man to drink from the Indian cup, knowing that while the water of life is everywhere the same, yet it is subtly changed within the cup.

"The white man," he glanced at Martin, "would destroy the Indian cup. But when the cup is broken, the life runs out. It is death."

Again the Indians voiced their approval. There was no point in answering, Martin knew. He could not hope to refute a figure of speech with logic. His only hope now was to convince the Major.

But in the pause, waiting, he realized he had been moved by the old Indian's eloquence. He sat staring down at the medicine bundle on his knees, puzzled by his own reaction. He was not really looking at the bundle at first, but suddenly his eyes focused, drawn by an almost imperceptible movement on the fur; and to his horror he saw that it was alive with lice. They were hardly visible against the fur, but against the dark cloth of his suit they were clear and unmistakable. He brushed frantically at his knees and almost stood up before he got control of himself.

He settled back, glancing around the circle of faces, seeing no hint that they had noticed him. Yet he could sense a silent and repressed amusement. He was suddenly furious, hardly able to contain his rage. But the anger passed quickly, leaving him with a curious sinking feeling that almost lowered him into darkness before he could catch himself. He rubbed his wrists and with great effort recalled his mind to what was going on.

The cowboy was speaking. "All this is way past me, except the cattle part. And as to that, if you want 'em, you better hunt 'em. If you want to teach these Injuns cowpunchin', this ain't the place to start; you got to begin with what's easy, not what's impossible."

"You made a good try, Reverend," the Major smiled, "but it looks like you're outnumbered."

After the translation, there was a ripple of laughter among the Indians. The Major looked perplexed and Martin saw that he knew nothing of the lice; but he was certain then that the Indians did. He could not bring himself to speak again; he was defeated, he knew. He did not even listen to what was said after that, but sat withdrawn, contending with the lice, trying not to show his discomfiture. They were all over him now; his whole body was crawling.

The time seemed hours before the meeting was done and he was able to rise and leave the building. He still had much to do before returning home. He set out across the square, walking fast. He was still carrying the bundle.

## 🪶 31 🪶

When the tea things were all washed and dried, Christine held the last gleaming, golden-figured cup in her hands, reluctant to have done. Closing her eyes, she traced the delicate patterns with her finger tips, seeing them in the darkness as clearly as with open eyes. The cup was light, shell-thin; she could break it with even a little squeeze of the hand. But she was very careful.

It seemed to her that her mother lingered too with a faraway dreaming, a remembering, in her eyes, a little half smile on her lips. She had been gay and talkative during the party, taking the parts of the imaginary guests with such art that they were almost visible. It had been a sweet but nearly unbearable joy; she had wanted it to last, yet had herself hurried to end it. Now in the silence the joy was gone and she was suddenly alone. She pressed the cup between her hands, restraining an impulse to squeeze or drop it, to shatter it with a crash and recall her mother's presence.

Before the extra chairs around the table, the untouched cups and saucers of the imaginary guests still shone on the embroidered cloth, bringing tears to her eyes. She thought of her father then and hurried to the window to see if he were coming. But he was not. Still, she ran back to the table and began putting things away, knowing he would disapprove if he should see. But her mother stopped her.

"I'd rather you didn't, Christine. The cupboard's much too high for you. But if it worries you, I'll hurry."

Christine waited anxiously, seeing that Leah was still abstracted. She was puzzled and a little frightened; usually it was Leah who hurried to conceal the evidence of their make-believe. But she was unconcerned now, somehow changed; the realization struck Christine with terror. In panic she tried to help again and was again prevented. But, as if reading her fears, Leah began to work more quickly.

In a little while, relieved, Christine turned her attention to her doll, but she could not find her immediately, though she remembered leaving her in the dollhouse. Then, through the doorway, she saw the house beside the stove in the kitchen, obscured by the ovenrack her mother had leaned against it. Through the dark grating of the rack, she could see the doll, wrapped in her own patchwork blanket, propped up beside a window in the tiny room, blue eyes staring out.

Something in what she saw made her catch her breath; without cause, she was suddenly crying. She ran through the kitchen, threw the rack down with a clatter, and caught the doll up in her arms. Still sobbing, she went into the bedroom, avoiding Leah, and sat down by the latticed window. Wrapping the doll tightly in the blanket, she rocked quietly, fingering the smooth binding, remembering vividly the doll behind the grating in the square little room of the dollhouse.

It was evening; not dark, but the air was turning red. The lattice her father had put over the window after she ran away divided the sky into squares of blue, touched lightly now with purple. She moved closer and saw the grey road glow with a light of fire, above it a tower of smoky cloud, flame edged. She saw her father then, a dense black shadow hurrying toward her on the fiery road, bent forward under a large sack, a dark bundle flopping at his side. Small puffs of glowing dust exploded at his feet with every step.

She got up quickly and put the doll and blanket away, and hurried back into the parlor to see if Leah had finished. The dishes were in the cupboard, but the chairs were still placed around the table. Leah was busy with dinner in the kitchen. Christine moved the chairs hurriedly to their proper places, finishing just as her father burst into the kitchen and dropped the sack.

"Heat me some water, lots of it," he ordered Leah, and without further words was gone out the door.

Leah brought in a tub and, removing the front lids of the stove, slid the tub over the flames. She emptied the water bucket into the tub and went out again and Christine heard her at the pump getting more water.

She went back to the window in her room and in the yard saw her father bringing wood to build a fire. On the ground in the middle of the yard she saw the dark bundle he had carried. He piled the wood beside it and without a pause went back for more, hurrying. Something in the way he handled the wood—as if each stick were a weapon—caused her to move over behind the curtain and watch covertly from an opening at the edge.

When he had brought enough wood, he knelt and cut little fans of shavings with his knife. These he arranged carefully in a little pile; then, selecting the smaller sticks, made a square around the shavings. He built the square up in layers, the sticks in each athwart the ones below, continuing to build till all the sticks were used. When he finished, it was as high as his chest as he knelt before it, reminding her clearly of the pulpit in the church. His glasses, reflecting the light of sunset, were for an instant glowing points of fire. She jerked the curtain in front of her face, closing her eyes as if the fire could touch her.

When she looked again he was still kneeling, but the reflection was gone. He rose, picked up the dark bundle gingerly, and laid it on top of the pile. Then, instead of lighting it as she expected, he turned and came toward the house.

In the kitchen the tub of water was beginning to steam. Thin tongues of flame curved from the fire underneath up the

139

side of the tub, painting delicate, jet-black spires of soot. The kitchen was full of the sharp odors of smoke and the acrid, metallic smell of the tub.

Her father came in, and without speaking, tested the water.

"What is it for?" Leah asked.

"Lice," he said with shaking voice, "from that filthy bundle the Indian gave me in the store. I'm crawling with them. Bring me soap and a change of clothes to the barn. And you gave him tobacco!"

He seized the tub and carried it out, steam floating back over his shoulder like a white scarf as he went through the door. Leah replaced the lids on the stove, then brought clothing from the bedroom. With amazement Christine saw that she was smiling.

Christine went back to the window of the bedroom. It was dusk now. The red had gone from the air and there was only black and grey on the earth; but the sky was deep blue, filled with a receding, far-off light. Touching the curtain, she stared through a square of the lattice till she became a part of the sky, floating upward, till there was nothing in all the world save the light, the color . . .

She was drawn back by a spot of white moving in darkness below and, looking down, saw her father, wearing a white shirt, approach the fire pile. He knelt before it, bending low so that he almost disappeared. She saw the flare of the struck match and a feathery curl of white smoke rising. He straightened up, still on his knees, face veiled by the spreading smoke. She saw the orange light of flame through the spaces of the pile, saw the glow creep upward on his body, illumining the whiteness of the shirt, shining redly on the jutting darkness of his face. He leaned backward and his glasses, catching the light, flashed fire, and in the same instant he seemed to smile. He stayed kneeling while the flames climbed high on the pile, curling blue and yellow fingers over the top to flick lightly at the bundle. A bright yellow blaze enveloped the bundle and went out, leaving a shadow of smoke rising darkly above the flames.

The whole pile was solid fire now, casting living, fleshy shadows outward on the yard. Her father's shadow flickered beyond him, extending into the night a gigantic, headless bulk. The column of flame began shifting with unsteady, life-like movements as the lower sticks burned. The bundle was flaming again but still smoking darkly.

There was a white flash suddenly, a report like a gunshot, and the fire for an instant was a huge, many-petaled flower that, opening, was gone. The whole yard was spangled with brilliant red embers, blinking quickly into darkness.

She saw her father on hands and knees, crawling away among waving white stalks of smoke that grew from the darkening embers, moving with a galloping motion like an animal. Her laughter was changed suddenly to screaming. She turned from the window and was caught up quickly in her mother's arms.

≋ 32 ≋

Leah was lighting a lamp for the parlor when she heard the explosion and, through the open door of the bedroom, saw a fountain of red curve up and out, covering the window. She dropped the chimney into place and ran into the bedroom, heart leaping at the wildness of Christine's screaming.

With the child in her arms, she paused to look out at the yard and saw it dimming as with the smoke of many fires, down low thin trunks that issued from the ground, spreading white branches up and out to touch and join. At the center of the yard a scattered bed of coals glowed; and through the smoke and darkness she saw a figure like an animal, moving away. She ran to the door and out, still carrying Christine, not certain yet what had happened but hearing her husband calling her name with compelling urgency.

The smoke was dispersing upward whitely. In the middle of the yard a small fire was beginning to blaze and in its light she saw the ground littered with charred sticks, some still smoking. There was a strong, acrid smell of gunpowder in the air with the odors of burning wood.

She crossed the yard and found Martin leaning against the fence, wiping his eyes with a handkerchief, still calling her name. The white shirt she had given him was blackened with

141

soot and there were small holes burned in it. One of them was still smoking, showing a thin circle of red, and she reached out with her hand and struck it to put it out.

He started violently, almost falling backward over the fence, and she realized he had not seen or heard her coming. She thought he might have been blinded by the explosion, but he looked at her and stopped rubbing his eyes.

"I lost my spectacles," he said, as if explaining all that had happened.

Christine stopped crying long enough to turn in Leah's arms and look at Martin, then buried her face and went on crying. Martin began rubbing his eyes again, turning slightly away from the light. His face was blackened except around his eyes, darker on the jutting bones, shading lighter in the hollows, exaggerating its stony gauntness. In the red firelight there was no texture of skin: he might have been wearing a mask. And yet the dark visage had a vivid familiarity, a reality that blotted out all memory of his living face. As if feeling her scrutiny, he turned away from her, face twisting, out of the light, and with amazement she saw his shoulders move spasmodically; he was weeping.

Someone approached the fence from the roadway and she turned to see Westland coming toward her into the firelight.

"Is someone hurt?" he asked. "I saw an explosion; what happened?"

"I don't know yet."

Christine stopped crying and peeked surreptitiously at Westland. Martin turned toward Leah, his shadowed face immobile now.

"I lost my spectacles," he repeated petulantly. "See if you can find them."

She tried to give him Christine to hold; he reached out his arms, but Christine only looked at his face and began screaming. He turned his face away again from the light.

Leah felt suddenly burdened and helpless; he would not move, she knew, till he had his glasses. But she could do nothing with Christine clinging to her so rigorously. She backed away from Martin and leaned against the fence, unable to resolve the conflict. Christine stopped crying, and Leah saw that she was watching Westland again. With certain intuition, she turned and passed Christine across the fence to him. She went rather shyly but without resistance, pressing her face against his shoulder, sobbing a little still. He held

142

her awkwardly, his expression changing quickly from embarrassment to tenderness.

Leah turned to look for the spectacles, puzzled by her own lack of surprise: she could not have predicted her child's reaction. Yet something within her had known. The fire was burning down, giving small light to search by. Going toward it, she gathered some of the charred, scattered sticks and placed them on the coals. Then she began a methodical search on the ground between Martin and the fire.

The first thing she found was the cane, glittering glass-like in the darkness. For an instant she thought she had found the spectacles, then reaching down felt the silken, polished stick. With annoyance she tossed it away from her, not following with her eyes but knowing by the burst of sparks from the fire where it had fallen. She had not intended that. She turned toward the fire, drawn up in alarm, yet immobilized. It was her intention to retrieve the cane, but she could not move. She saw it lying directly across the fire, shining brilliantly, oozing oil, beginning to smoke. It burst into flame and she turned back to the search, exhaling a long breath, released.

She found the spectacles unbroken near the fire and returned them to Martin, not meeting his eyes till he had the spectacles on and was himself again.

"What happened?" she asked. "What were you doing?"

"Getting rid of the lice."

"My God," Westland exclaimed, "with gunpowder? You're tougher than I thought. But do you think it hurt the lice as much as you?"

Leah watched him carefully, intending to resent any derision. But his face was serious.

"No, no," Martin said, "they were in the bundle, the medicine bundle Wolf Head gave me." He paused, then turned on Westland fiercely, "You must have known about that—it was a filthy, savage trick."

Westland shook his head. "I didn't know. I suspected something, but I didn't know what it was. You could have put it in an anthill, though. They say ants will clean out the lice. You didn't have to use gunpowder."

"I didn't use gunpowder," Martin said, almost crying with exasperation. "I was only burning the bundle. Something exploded, I don't know what."

"Didn't you look inside before you burned it?"

"No, God forbid. It was full of lice."

"Probably a powder horn. Some of these Indians still use the old muzzle loaders. I wish you had given it to me instead of burning it, though."

While he was speaking, some Indians rode up from the camp and stopped their horses silently in the roadway just at the edge of the firelight. They were stripped to the waist and painted, hair feathered and wrapped, wearing beaded, fringed leggings and moccasins, resplendent as Leah had never before seen them. Shadows of the fence pickets played darkly on the painted horses and on the shining bodies of the Indians. Among them she recognized Wolf Head, who had helped her at the ford and had given the bundle to Martin. His face was solemn, impassive; and yet she sensed a smile somewhere behind his eyes.

Westland spoke to them haltingly in the Indian tongue, using signs to supplement his words, and Wolf Head answered, at first with a hint of laughter, turning quickly serious again.

"I asked him what was in the bundle," Westland said. "He asked me if I meant how many—then added that he couldn't say exactly since it wasn't his. He says it was strong medicine for the buffalo hunt and that its owner would like to have it back for the cattle hunt. He had thought he wouldn't need it again. Do you want me to tell them what happened?"

"No!" Martin said vehemently. "Just tell them it's gone."

"It would be better to tell them the whole story—they're likely to find out anyway."

"From you, I take it."

"No," Westland said patiently. "But I have a hunch they've guessed it anyway. You'll stand better with them if you just laugh it off and admit that it was powerful medicine."

"No, no. There was no spiritual power—or medicine, as you call it—involved. It was gunpowder."

"Very likely. But it's not what they'll think. You offended a spirit power and were punished. If you see it their way this time you'll gain respect and influence."

"No. I can't compromise with superstition. Just tell them I burned it to get rid of the lice, that's all."

Westland spoke briefly to the Indians, and Leah expected an outburst of laughter. Instead they talked seriously among themselves, for a moment, then Wolf Head spoke briefly and Westland translated.

"He says it seems you have blackened your face in victory over the lice; but that the spirit of the bundle has also counted coup. There is strong medicine on both sides; they are willing to call a truce."

"I've no quarrel with anyone," Martin said stiffly. "But there can be no truce in the work of the Lord."

"That's hard to translate. I'll just tell them your heart is good. Maybe they'll believe me," he said doubtfully.

He spoke briefly to Wolf Head, and the Indians turned and galloped off toward camp, leaving a dust that rose gently as mist along the road. For a little while the air seemed to hold the vitality of their presence, a strong masculine odor compounded of horse and leather, paint and tobacco. When they were a solid shadow in the distance, Leah could still see the living shine of their bodies in the blue moonlight.

She remembered her cooking then and, without a word, ran for the house, feeling buoyant and free. Nothing had burned. For the moment she lost herself in cooking, singing softly, not stopping even when Martin entered, looking morose and rather fierce under his make-up of soot. He went immediately to the washstand and began soaping his face.

Christine came in with Westland, chattering to him in a feverish, excited voice, holding his hand. Leah walked with them into the parlor, bringing the lamp. But she did not stop to talk. Back in the kitchen, she went on with her work abstracted, absorbed in a new feeling of freedom and release.

Martin started toward the bedroom to change clothes, then turned abruptly and went back outside. She knew he had missed the cane and she was suddenly tense and afraid.

She went quietly into the bedroom, closing the door behind her, and from the darkness looked out at the yard. It was rinsed clean with moonlight, the litter of sticks were shadows on the whitened earth. The fire was a bed of pinkish embers wreathed with an eerie blue light. Beside it, just visible, the shepherd's crook handle of the cane curved lustrous as a serpent, the stub end sprouting a thin blade of smoke.

She saw her husband approach the fire, stoop quickly, and retrieve the crook, uttering a low cry. He stood rigidly in the darkness, face touched faintly by the mingled light of moon and embers, softened. In his hand the shepherd's crook turned harmlessly, smoking still, its power lost.

She turned from the window, all fear and tension gone, in her heart, expanding like a breath, a wordless, joyful singing.

A joy was in the air of the camp that Little Wound had never known before, coming to him as if he touched the hands of many people. He worked with his mother in front of the lodge, braiding rope, sharpening knives in preparation for the hunt, feeling on his face the feathery, changing touch of the flames of a small fire.

It was night. His father and grandfather were in council, the little ones asleep. The air was still, but alive with odors and vibrations long past the usual hour of quiet, even after a day of travel from the agency. A group of riders passed trailing a scent of paint and a faintly musty odor of ceremonial clothing long unused. He recognized one of the horses by its odd single-footed gait; there was a lame one also.

He was sharpening a knife, moving the long blade in little circular motions against the stone, keeping time to an unheard drumming, a beating that seemed inside him as the beating of his heart. When he finished, he stood up, unable to stay quiet longer and, touching his mother lightly to let her know, turned away to walk through the camp.

There were many fires to guide him, all around the wide circle of the lodges, casting heat shadows as he approached that told him of objects near them. By the odors around the fires he knew many of the families. Now and then, as he passed close to a fire, a hand would stop him and proffer a tidbit from a feast. There were many he did not know.

The drumming was nearer. Through his feet came clearly now a lively drumbeat and, softer, a shuffle of dancing feet. It was this that had drawn him. The fire in the circle was strong. From a distance he could count the shadows of the dancers cast in its clear heat, could feel the movement of the flames and the figures.

He approached slowly, keeping the beat, picking it from the earth with moccasined foot as he might gather clean round stones with his hands. Near the drummers he sat on the ground, close to the fire, seeing in memory a moving yellow light that licked his face and danced before his eyes. But only for a moment. His hands knew more of the scene—the fire, the dancer—than he could remember from the world of light; and on his face, more clearly now than any time before, he could feel the size and shape of presences, the moving tracery of feathery fingers.

He sat entranced, keeping the beat lightly with his hand, catching the bouncing toe-heel step of the dancers through the earth, moving his body slightly with the sinuous, flying movement of the shadows. He was drawn out, involved beyond all previous experience.

Then someone touched him lightly on the shoulder. He rose and a firm hand caught his arm, drawing him in among the drummers, and made him sit; placed a drum between his knees and gave him a stick. For a moment he sat running his hand over the tight rawhide, afraid to touch it with the stick. But the fear passed. He was caught again in the rhythm and, scarcely noticing, began to pound softly, finding the leader's beat, feeling again the heat shadows on his face and the clear perception of shape and space. His free hand rested on the side of the drum and, against the palm for a little while, he seemed to feel the dancers, the whole circle, turning, and in the center the fire a burning coal.

Then the beat quickened. He picked up the new rhythm hungrily, leaning forward, himself a dancer, his free hand moving now above the drum—it was himself, living wholly within the hand, dancing, his fingers feet. He was one with the dancers, not one apart: the circle was the shape of his consciousness, at its center the living fire. He seemed lifted, with all the dancers and drummers, in the palm of a great warm hand, held yet free, strengthened with a power beyond himself.

The dancing stopped, and the drums. He sat motionless, still part of the vision, till a hand again touched him, taking the drum and stick and at last lifting him gently to his feet. Large hands found his, held them with gentle pressure for a moment, moving then in the sign for Wakan, medicine. Others, some he did not know, touched his hand briefly and with friendship.

He left then, walking back toward the lodge, blood racing, still with the sense of moving in the circle of a hand. He could not forget the dancing or the drumming. His feet walked lightly the toe-heel step, his hands, of themselves,

147

moved in the air describing the vision—the leaping flames, the dancers, the sinuous shadows, drums, the drummers—the signs a fashioning of form and movement in the air, becoming as he walked the movements of a dance that his whole body joined, creating.

It was a rich new joy the dancing gave him, a strength he had never known—it was a singing past any he remembered from the world of sound, a shaping more beautiful than any of his hand alone. He stopped, feeling that he was watched, and walked on with dignity toward the lodge. But in his vision he danced on, to an unheard drumming.

## 🏮 34 🏮

They traveled north from the agency toward the badlands, avoiding with a common, unspoken consent the houses of the half-breeds and white men along Arrow Creek and the cowboy camp beyond White River, keeping to the hills, even with the Major along questioning every turn in the roundabout trail. But even the Major after the first day had seemed to understand and stopped his questioning, smiling indulgently, almost participating in the child-like joyousness of the people.

Turning Hawk, riding at the head of the column with the counselors, had felt at first a pervasive irritation and a sharp sense of incongruity: the noisy rattle of wagons and buggies; sore-shouldered, collar-marked ponies, ridden now and painted; men with light skins from the wearing of white men's clothes, stripped now to Indian garb; the Major himself and the young white man. But now, nearing the badlands, the feeling had gone and he allowed himself to laugh and talk with the old men, yet with the strange certainty that if he looked back the feeling would return.

It was dry barren country they traveled, grassless, treeless, dusty, but—with no sign of the white man—friendly and pleasant. At the midday pause, some of the women had gone out with digging sticks and from the hard, dry earth returned with a harvest of turnips.

Beside him the old men rode, arguing endlessly but with laughter about the trail, about the best place to camp, about the likeliest places to hunt, all with a boyish enthusiasm that was at once heartening and depressing, resuming their dignity only when the Major or the young white man rode up beside them.

The day was windless, with an unnatural warmth for the time of year, as if the season also had turned backward toward the days of summer. Behind the long stream of people, the dust hung in the air marking far back the curving and jogging of the trail. His eyes followed it backward toward the cowboy camp and the river beyond—till he caught himself and turned again, resolutely, toward the bandlands.

The sun was still high when they reached the edge of the badlands on the third day and pitched camp at White Flat, near a small bitter stream. The grass was poor; there was no fuel but a thin scattering of greasewood. It was the worst kind of camping spot. Yet from the exuberance with which everyone set to work, it might have been the greenest valley, the clearest stream.

Only the old women who looked out for the placing of the lodges complained—as well they might. He saw the young white man following one of them, Mother-of-All, with his ever-present pencil and notebook, trying (as Turning Hawk supposed) to learn the principles that guided her choice of places.

"Ho, Grandson," he heard her say. "Are you becoming a woman that you should worry about such things? Leave them to the women, who understand. It is enough that the men should choose such a place to camp—" she swept her arm indignantly around her—"without worrying about the placing of the lodges. They have gone crazy."

She went on with her work, ignoring him then, muttering angrily to herself. But the young man was not abashed. He continued to observe, writing occasionally in his notebook. And when Mother-of-All finished, she relented and came back smiling to explain her methods.

The young man was a continual puzzle to Turning Hawk —he could not understand in a white man the avid interest in the old ways. Yet he sensed that the interest was genuine, the knowledge valued. Now, listening to them talk—the aged

149

woman and the young white man—he was struck with the thought that these were the only ones in camp who were seeing with clear vision, who were not sunk over their eyes in the unnatural excitement.

Nearby, Blue Fawn had already unpacked her horses and set up the lodge. Before it, Crazy Walking sat on the ground sharpening arrows and, with a grooved stone, straightening the shafts. His old rifle was nowhere to be seen. His hair had lengthened since the mourning; he had extended it with false hair, and the braids, carefully wrapped with fur, hung down his chest, dark beside the whitened, puckered scars of the medicine dance. It was hard for Turning Hawk to remember him as he had been—a white man in all but blood. His ways then had saddened Turning Hawk, foretelling the end of the old life. And even now, through some perversity within himself, they saddened him also.

As Crazy Walking worked, the young white man came and stood beside him, holding a rifle. When Crazy Walking looked up, he extended the gun, speaking in his own tongue. Crazy Walking did not take the rifle or appear to understand the talk. The young white man paused a moment, then slowly, searching carefully for the words, spoke in the Lakota tongue.

"Here is a gun I have no use for. If you need it for the hunt, you are welcome to it."

"The rifle is good for the long shot," Crazy Walking answered, "but hunting on horseback here—" he indicated the badlands—"the shooting will be close and quick. For this the bow is best. An animal gut-shot with a gun can run far; with an arrow, no."

The white man seemed puzzled, but he said no more.

The reasons were sensible, Turning Hawk thought, but they did not really explain the bow and arrows or the refusal of the gun. There was something more, a turning beyond the return to the people, that he did not like or care to examine.

As soon as the lodges were up, the criers went through the camp announcing the sending out of the scouts. All the people moved out onto the flat, assembling in a great crescent with the horned opening toward the west, the badlands. Carrying the sacred bundle, Turning Hawk took his place with the headmen at the tip of the southern horn, while one of the younger men brought wood and made a fire near them on the ground. Waiting for the time to begin, he remembered the hunts he had led for the people before the buffalo had died

—the grassy camps, the clean leather lodges, the power and joy singing in the air. There was joy now, certainly, and a feverish excitement, but not the power of the people. The young men were noisy and full of laughter that was a little derisive, uncertain. It was the old men who were as eager and joyful as boys.

He had led another hunt after the buffalo had died, with only a few of the older men. They had gone into the hills knowing they would find no buffalo, but sending out the scouts, awaiting their reports and, at the last, charging a band of antelope. They had returned without meat but happy and somehow renewed. They laughed at themselves before and after, having no hopes or illusions. But there was a different, disturbing atmosphere now.

When all were seated, he unwrapped a buffalo chip he had found on that last hunt and placed it on the ground before him. After a silent pipe the scouts were chosen, young, reliable men, but not so young as the scouts of those other days; these when they were boys had known the buffalo. Some, like Crazy Walking, who was chosen as head scout, had hunted them.

Not long since, he would have been surprised at the choice of Crazy Walking, but not now. He had been a hunter and warrior of much promise before going east to the white man's school, had counted coups and given the people a day in the medicine dance. But his change to the ways of the whites had been sudden and complete; he had been lost to the people and had returned.

There was complete silence among the people now. Wolf Head, leader of the hunt, talked to the scouts earnestly.

"You belong to the people for today," he told them. "In your eyes, your hands, your hearts you hold their lives. With clear eyes, watch; with open ears, listen; with straight tongues, report. You are brothers to all animals; keep this clear in your hearts and they will help you. It is in your power to make the people glad. Search well."

Turning Hawk unwrapped the sacred pipe and with care filled it. With the ceremonial spoon he took a coal from the fire and placed it in the bowl. He made offering to the four quarters and the earth and to Wakinyan prayed: "Grandfather, Great Mysterious One, you have been always and before you nothing has been. There is nothing to pray to but you. The star nations all over the heavens are yours and yours all the grasses of the earth. You are older than all need, older than all pain and prayer.

"Grandfather, all over the world the faces of living ones are alike. In tenderness they have come up out of the ground. Look upon your children with children in their arms, that they may face the winds and walk the good road to the day of quiet.

"Teach us to walk the soft earth, a relative to all that live. Give us the strength to understand and the eyes to see. Help us, for without you we are nothing."

He smoked the pipe and passed it to Crazy Walking, who placed the hand holding it on the buffalo chip and smoked, with no sign of the old derision but with an earnestness, an openness of feeling that brought to Turning Hawk again, sharply, the fear and unease that had grown in him all day.

Crazy Walking passed the pipe to the next scout, who smoked and passed it on. When the last one had smoked and the pipe returned, all the men were instantly on their feet, laughing and shouting. The scouts were surrounded, congratulated, praised. Even the Major stepped forward and shook hands with Crazy Walking. He spoke at some length in the white tongue, but Crazy Walking made the sign that he did not understand. Turning Hawk was amazed. The Major was clearly impatient. But Eagle Voice, who was standing near, made the translation: "I am glad to see you in the dress of your people for the hunt. They cannot break as suddenly with the old ways as yourself. It is good to stay in touch."

"This is forever," Crazy Walking answered. "I am an Indian. I don't know how I forgot it. But that is done now, finished."

Again Eagle Voice interpreted. But the Major was annoyed.

"This is well and good, to return for a while to boyhood, to play at the hunt. But the future will hold no hunting. The buffalo are gone, they will not return. You were growing. I hope you will not turn back. You can be an Indian without wearing a blanket."

Crazy Walking did not answer. From the look on his face, he might not have heard; the Major might not have existed. He turned toward his horse, which someone had brought up, and mounted lightly and sat among the others, his face shining with a concentrated light.

All the younger men mounted to accompany the scouts as

far as the badlands, even the Major and the young white man. The old men and all the women and children remained in their places to await the return. Turning Hawk stayed where he was, watching the mass of excited horsebacks gallop away past the lodges, raising a dust that spread over the camp as white as smoke. In the distance, through the dust, he saw the scouts separate from the others and disappear in the badlands. The others wheeled and, raising a shout like a charging war party, raced back toward the flat.

"Hoka hey, hoka hey!"

They circled wide and came into the crescent. They knocked over the three bushes that had been set up and, left to right, circled the crescent and emerged again, still running.

It was over then. The people rose and moved off toward the lodges, obscured, ghost-like in the pall of dust raised by the horsebacks. Turning Hawk wrapped up the buffalo chip, but he did not leave. He sat by the fire watching the people move away, coughing and shouting, mere shadows in the white, bitter dust, disappearing finally among the shadowy lodges as Crazy Walking had disappeared in the grey hills. It was a long time before the dust rose, swirling upward slowly, and he could see clearly again.

🦢 35 🦢

In clear moonlight Westland climbed the rise west of camp, the singing and drumming still clear but diminished and soft, part of the night. At the top he turned and sat down facing the camp, grateful for the solitude and comparative quiet.

In the distance the earth was shadowy and dark, but the white flat was brilliant in moonlight, darkened only by the sparse clumps of greasewood and the horse herd beyond, the scattering of wagons around the circle, and the northern shadowed sides of the lodges. Within the circle the fires shone, bright flowers of color in the colorless night. He was tired; his eyes and throat were raw from the alkaline dust of the campground. Above the circle of lodges he could see it now, the dust raised by the dancers, hovering white and misty, tinged faintly below with the red of the fires.

It was the third night now of the dancing, since the sending out of scouts, but the dancers showed no sign of stopping; they were untiring, carried beyond themselves by an excitement he would have called drunken but for the absence of alcohol.

From a distance the music was clearer; he could hear the whole of it above the wild modulation and was caught in its excitement. What had seemed before mere noise and shouting assumed a weird beauty: ecstatic, abandoned, rising in sudden leaps and dropping slowly; straining upward from self and reluctantly falling; individual and varied, yet fusing in a whole harmony.

He felt in the music a statement of his own impressions. Since the announcement of the hunt he had felt a growing strength, a fusion of disparate parts, till the listless, separate families had tightened to a community, an essence of individuals drawn up beyond themselves—the broken cup for a moment restored and from it a people drinking their lives.

He sat remembering the ceremony of the return of the scouts, composing his impressions for the notes he would make in the morning. They had arrived a few hours before, just at sunset, coming not from the gully, as they had gone, but off a high hill, appearing first on its brow, outlined black and sharp against the sky.

A rider detached himself from the group and, dismounting, shook out his blanket on the ground and with his hands raised a dust that bloomed like fire against the sky, the signal for buffalo. Then all charged wildly down, singing. They swung wide around the camp, entering the circle through the opening to the east, riding completely around it from left to right. At the opening again, they turned right to the center, where Turning Hawk and the headmen waited.

When they stood before him, Turning Hawk filled the pipe and made offerings and prayed, then placed it on the buffalo chip, stem toward the scouts.

Wolf Head, leader of the hunt, spoke to the scouts. "You have carried the people in your hands; you have searched the earth; may you have something good to report."

The scouts smoked in turn, and Wolf Head spoke again, "Tell us with a straight tongue what you have seen and where."

Crazy Walking spoke first, holding up the first finger of his right hand. "On the near side of the first big hill, we found buffalo."

Wolf Head stood up, facing the people. "It is good; but perhaps you have more to tell us."

Another scout spoke with the same gestures, "We crossed the big hill right and, in the next drainage, found more buffalo."

"This is good also; but perhaps there is yet more."

A third scout spoke, "We crossed the long hill to the next drainage and saw even more."

Then all the scouts began talking at once and Turning Hawk could not understand. But the Chief cried, "So be it."

And all the Indians around the circle began shouting and cheering.

They would be moving in the morning, Westland knew, breaking up into small parties to hunt the scattered cattle. He intended to ride also and was sorry he could not get some rest. As he sat, someone approached from the direction of the camp, a white man, he could tell from a distance, therefore the Major. He was annoyed at having his privacy invaded, yet glad too that the Major had sought him out.

"I had a hard time finding you," the Major said, breathing hard. "I hope I didn't interrupt a vision."

"You're not so far wrong at that," Westland laughed. "Have you ever noticed that almost any man likes to climb a hill to do his thinking, not only Indians? It's just a thought. But you came too."

"Maybe. But it isn't a vision I came for; it's a touch of reality. Just wanted to talk to a white man to make sure I still could. Sort of gives you the creeps, doesn't it, all that damned drumming and caterwauling?"

"It's strange, all right; but I'm beginning to like it."

"I'm not. I've heard it before, but never at this rate, not even on that last real buffalo hunt. Maybe that preacher was right about reviving old patterns. It's like a dead man coming to life."

"I've felt something like that," Westland admitted, "but this is a godsend for me—though Martin would call it something else. But what I would have learned only at secondhand, they're acting out for me. I'm thankful for that stampede."

"Not I. I'm sorry; and getting sorrier by the minute. I thought I knew these Indians, but I don't think so any more.

155

It's like seeing someone you know from a distance, then coming up close and finding a stranger—or an animal. Did you notice Crazy Walking? He won't speak English any more. And you know I've got a funny feeling he really doesn't understand it. And I thought he was practically a white man." He paused a moment, listening intently to the wild singing, then shook himself perceptibly and went on, "You know, I'm glad now I let you stay, even though I was a little suspicious of you at first. And I still don't see what you hope to gain, digging around in the past of a dying people. What good will it do? Damn it, it seems a little ghoulish, if you don't mind my saying so."

"I don't know," Westland said honestly. "I've changed my mind somewhat since I came. I had hoped to throw light on our own cultural development by studying primitive culture. But the more I study, the less I feel like the final product of a cultural evolution."

As they talked he saw a horse and buggy come out of the shadows beyond camp and move rapidly across the white flat toward the opening in the circle, leaving not a track but a swirling wake of dust that shone like water in the silver light.

The horse slowed and was just entering the circle when a tumult of barking rose above the singing. A blot of dogs moved across the ring, meeting the buggy and spreading darkly around it. The horse turned sharply and broke into a gallop along the outside of the circle, coming toward the hill. In the foaming wake of dust the dogs appeared and disappeared, shadowy as fish. The driver fought the horse to a stop among the darting, yelling dogs, and sat in the buggy striking at them with his whip, reminding Westland of a fisherman on a bright lake. The dust he had raised floated toward him slowly, obscuring him, and for a moment there were only the black shadows of the dogs weaving in and out to show where he was.

Westland stood up and, with the Major, walked down the hill, knowing from the buggy that it was a white man and from the dogs that it was Martin. As they approached, the dogs gave up the attack and straggled back toward the lodges. But Martin did not move. When the dogs were gone, he sat hunched over in the seat, holding the whip. Westland had the impression that he was shaking, though he could not see it. He was surprised that Martin had come, recognizing it as an act of courage.

They walked up close to the buggy before the man saw them and straightened up with a start.

"I didn't expect to see you here, Reverend," the Major said. "But now that you're here, your work is cut out. The devil is rampant."

"I'm relieved to see you," Martin answered shakily. "I didn't know how to find you. Do I have your permission to stay?"

The Major nodded, smiling. "I was beginning to feel outnumbered myself. Did you bring a tent?"

"No. I thought perhaps one of you—"

"Well, we've thrown in together. But there ought to be room for three."

Sleep was impossible. Westland lay awake listening to the Indians, tired but filled to wakefulness with their excitement. On the canvas of the tent, fire shadows moved and flickered, rising and falling like the music.

Across the tent the Major slept. Near him Martin was breathing heavily but was beginning to jerk and tremble as if he were dreaming. He muttered for a moment in a strained voice and was suddenly rolling and twisting on the ground, clutching the blankets desperately. He seemed to be screaming, but no sound came, only prolonged expulsions of his breath.

Westland watched him curiously, becoming alarmed finally when he showed no sign of calming down. The struggles at first had been like those of a wrestler, becoming tense and jerky till finally, when the soundless screaming stopped, they were spasmodic and uncoordinated as the struggles of a dying animal. It occurred to Westland then that it might be some kind of seizure; and he was out of bed kneeling over the man, shaking him awake.

But Martin did not awaken. Instead he seized Westland by the arms and held on with grim, desperate strength, eyes slightly open, lips moving soundlessly.

"What the devil's going on?" the Major exploded. "Isn't there enough racket without a wrestling match?"

Martin awakened and sat up, face contorted.

"You're in the Indian camp," Westland assured him quietly. "Were you having a nightmare?"

Martin did not answer but stared at him uncomprehendingly in the half-light.

"You must have been dreaming," Westland went on. "Anyway, you wrestled a good bout. Was it Satan or an angel?"

"I doubt that he'd take you for an angel," the Major put in dryly.

"I don't remember." Martin expelled his breath in a long sigh. "Won't they ever stop that infernal howling? It's going to be worse than I imagined. You should have listened to me," he told the Major. "It'll be much worse than the beef issue." He paused; then, as if really seeing Westland for the first time, went on, "At any rate, you ought to be glad—if they don't scalp you."

Westland nodded, laughing. "If they do I'll be careful to take notes on how it's done. But I hope you don't exorcise the devils before I've met them."

Martin was not amused. "This is no laughing matter. It's dead serious. You're taking a chance for nothing, whereas it's my duty."

Westland shrugged. "I don't feel any danger. I'm only here to record; you're here to expunge. But it looks like you've got the short straw for now. This'll take more than a burning pyre and a little gunpowder."

Martin snorted angrily and lay back down in his blankets.

Westland went back to his bed, knowing that he would sleep now and Martin would not.

The singing was dying down; it would soon be morning.

Martin had no more than closed his eyes when he was awakened by the barking of dogs and the shouting of children. The Major and Westland were already up, preparing to take down the tent, so he arose in haste and helped them as much as he could—which was little. They worked quickly, as if each movement had been agreed on in advance, and the tent was soon struck.

He was standing alone watching them when Eagle Voice came by and invited him to breakfast. He accepted gratefully and ate with the Indian family inside their lodge, marveling at their mastery of the two modes of life. He thought of their house on the allotment. But having seen the medicine room also, he was not surprised at this; only saddened.

Eagle Voice seemed aware of no ambiguity; he was all Indian now, speaking freely of the old ways and with the disconcerting air of a teacher. Their positions were suddenly reversed. And Martin, in the role of pupil, was irked.

After eating, he started to hitch up to the buggy but Eagle Voice stopped him.

"We'll break up into small bands to go into the hills," he told Martin. "It's rough country. If you go you'll have to ride. I can lend you a saddle."

Martin thanked him and with trepidation saddled the horse. He had never ridden it before, did not even know if it were broke to ride. In any case, he did not trust the animal. He swung on cautiously, but before he found the other stirrup the horse reared and he swung down again. On the next try the horse went sidewise just as he stepped up, dropping him on his back in the dirt. He lost the rein and the horse trotted away, stopping after a few steps to look back with pointed ears.

He got up and brushed off his clothes, expecting laughter from the watching Indians, but he heard none. Eagle Voice caught the horse. He brought it back to where Martin sat, took off the saddle and, holding its muzzle between his hands, blew into its nostrils. He seized one of its ears and, putting his mouth close, seemed to whisper something. Then he sprang onto its back and rode in a tight circle at a gallop. The horse did not attempt to buck.

Martin watched, chilled and revolted by the man's obvious power over the animal; it seemed occult and evil. But he would not try the horse again himself. He had just decided to go back to the agency when Eagle Voice offered to trade him a mule for the horse for the duration of the trip. He accepted and found the mule tractable and easy to ride. But he wondered uneasily if it were the same one that had followed him braying in the night.

The day was bright. In the cool autumn sky was a brilliance that burnished even the clay-colored hills, lacquered the brown skins of the Indians, and glittered garishly on the colors of their beadwork and paint. There was no sober clothing left among them, Martin reflected. Black, the habitual hue of the reservation, was missing—even the broad-brimmed hats. All was buckskin and beadwork, bright calico and colored blankets.

Behind him as he rode, their talk and laughter echoed brightly in the steep-sided gully they traveled, reminding him of the flight of birds. And yet, for all the brightness, he had a vivid sense of darkness, of descending into gloom. The change in the Indians, the very presence of the colors, was a descent, a turning back toward a dark, untutored past; it was this that affected him, he thought, this and the country, the badlands—*mauvaises terres,* as the French called them, with the distinct meaning of evil. His blood quickened with the insight—it was a journey into darkness, into evil.

The land was marked vividly: scarred with washes and gullies like the marks of claws, supporting scant life, peopled in the flats with fantastic wind-and-water-carven shapes of clay and sand. It was a land of violence, jagged, slashed, raked, broken; the work of a huge, metaphysical savagery. Add fire, he thought, and the mind could fashion from this land a fearful vision of Hell.

He rode near the front of the column, beside him Eagle Voice, stripped to breechclout and leggings, explaining with enthusiasm all the customs and rules of the hunt, seeming to have no sense of the violation of Christian precepts in the pagan rituals. He was beyond fathoming, this dark, powerful man, part Christian, part heathen.

Martin shrank inwardly, remembering the buffalo stone he had broken in the Indian's house, wondering if he suspected yet who had done it. Surely he would miss it in the hunt. As if sensing his thought, Eagle Voice spoke with a sudden lapse of enthusiasm, "My power in the hunt is gone now. I believe the buffalo will not return."

For an instant Martin was on the verge of confessing, but he did not. Some overpowering strangeness about the Indian prevented him. And yet he owed this man much: as interpreter, almost all his spiritual contact with the Indians; even his own presence now on the hunt; the mule he rode. He would try to repay—but not at the Lord's expense. He would not compromise His cause. In the meantime, he endured.

To his right, Westland rode with Turning Hawk, plainly engrossed, even taking notes as he rode. He valued his work, however mistaken; his enthusiasm was enviable. Martin was watching the man curiously when he saw him rein up his horse and stop, pointing to the ground off to the side of the trail. Turning Hawk also stopped and at his signal the rest of the Indians halted and were silent.

There was a long pause; then Turning Hawk spoke to the people, reining his horse around to face them. When he finished, Eagle Voice translated quickly, leaving out much, Martin knew.

"Something mysterious is happening. The unseen powers have looked on the young white man and he has pleased them. Therefore, as a token of their approval, he is about to receive a pipe. I will instruct him how to receive it, he being merely a white man, knowing nothing of such things."

Both men dismounted and stood together facing ahead along the trail. Turning Hawk, with raised hands, began a kind of chant that Martin assumed to be a prayer. But Eagle Voice, completely fascinated now, did not interpret. Edging closer, Martin saw a brightly decorated redstone pipe lying on a rock beside the trail.

When the prayer was finished, both men advanced part way to the pipe and stopped, and again Turning Hawk prayed. Westland stepped forward then and picked up the pipe. Turning Hawk called an old woman, who took the pipe from Westland with trembling hands and wrapped it in a piece of bright red cloth, praying in a low, intense voice as she did so.

Martin had a sudden desire to laugh at this solemn and elaborate display of superstition, but something in the atmosphere restrained him, a quality of silence like a finger held to his lips. He thought he could detect a faintly sardonic look on the Major's face, but Westland was perfectly serious; he did not even seem embarrassed. Martin was suddenly furious, seeing the man's attitude as a kind of betrayal. But he said nothing.

They rode on, but in silence. There was no more laughter and only desultory, subdued conversation, even among the children. It was not fear, he decided, but a sense of awe and reverence. But his own reaction was one of increasing tension and dejection. There was nothing in the incident, he reasoned, that should have affected him. It was only a lost pipe, found by accident. There was nothing mysterious about it. Yet he was affected, as if he were joined with these savages in a communication beyond language; he also felt the awe. But under this was a strong, inexplicable sense of dread.

It was just before the noon pause when he noticed the dog.

It was following Westland, though neither he nor the Indians seemed aware of its presence. It was not an Indian dog, Martin knew at a glance: it was well-fed and of a breed strange to the country, large, short-haired, and with a shining copper color. It walked quietly behind the horse, paying no attention to the Indian dogs that ranged along the trail; and what was even stranger, those dogs paid no attention to it.

Eagle Voice noticed the dog then and clapped his hand to his mouth in surprise. His exclamation called the attention of the other Indians, and for a moment a confused murmur moved along the column. Westland stopped his horse and turned to look, and the dog stopped also, dropping to its haunches and looking up at him with enigmatic dignity.

The dog stayed with Westland exclusively after that. During the noon pause it sat close to him but with obvious aloofness. He tried to feed it bits of meat but the dog would not eat, would not even smell of the food. Once Westland put his hand on its head, but only for a moment. The dog did not snarl or in any way alter its expression, but from deep in its chest a low growl rumbled, like distant thunder. Westland left it alone after that, as did the Indians. In fact, they seemed to forget the animal altogether.

Martin could not. It held a curious fascination for him. He could not take his eyes away. But he was grateful that the dog had not attached itself to him. He mentioned the dog to Eagle Voice, trying to find some explanation of its presence, but either the Indian was not interested or preferred not to speak of it, for he would venture no opinion.

In the evening, after the tent was up, the old woman brought the pipe, complete now with a beaded bag, and hung it on the wall of the tent at the back. When she was gone, the dog entered, sniffed briefly at the bundle, then lay down outside the door where it remained on guard. But its presence was not a comfort to Martin. He left the tent briefly before going to bed and on returning was greeted by a thunderous growl. He dared not try to pass till Westland stepped out and stood by the animal while he entered. Once inside again, he felt imprisoned. He was tired and went to sleep quickly, but the red dog invaded even his dreams.

He seemed to awaken in darkness, aware of a powerful presence; with no surprise he found himself looking through the canvas of the tent as through a mist, seeing the dog, red as sunset against the sky, crouched over the tent, mysterious, enigmatic, evil. And as he watched, the dog became an Indian, smoking the redstone pipe, blowing clouds of flaming smoke across the sky. He awakened in terror. But each time he slept, the dream recurred. He was glad for daylight when it finally came. The dog was still present. It attached itself to Westland again and the march into the badlands went on.

The day was again clear, but in the afternoon as they approached the rugged butte country where they would hunt, thunderclouds formed in the west and came toward them swiftly. Dust rose on the hills and through its yellow cloud flashed rapid blades of lightning.

They were just coming off a ridge into a small valley, and when they reached the level Turning Hawk called a halt and ordered the lodges put up for the coming storm. Martin tied his mule and helped stake the tent against the rising gusts of wind that whipped erratically across the flat. As he worked, he saw a crow descend violently from the ridge and alight with ruffled feathers in a dead cedar near the tent. It did not fly even when Westland came near the tree, seeming loath to commit itself again to the gusty air. It sat cawing raucously, neck feathers expanding emphatically with each sound.

In a moment the lodges were all up. With the Indians, Martin stood watching the approaching storm, shivering a little with each flat crash of thunder. The storm crossed the divide, dropping swiftly down the ridge, and the far end of the valley was enshrouded suddenly with dust. Dark clouds boiled over the hill and down. But on the slope the storm seemed to turn sharply and move northward across the buttes. A few pellets of hail struck the camp, but no more. Dust and a strange electric smell filled the air, and the wind slackened.

The Indians stood in a breathless attitude of waiting, not moving even when the dust cleared. There was no sound but the receding wind and a dying rattle of thunder.

Martin looked for the crow, remembering its hoarse clamor, but it was nowhere in sight. The dog too was gone; he could not believe it. Though the tense atmosphere of waiting held him with an almost tangible constraint, he could not bear the suspense. He turned and rushed into the tent, expecting to find the dog. But it was not there. Outside again he walked frantically among the lodges with the urgent feeling that something of vital importance depended on his finding the dog.

163

But the animal was gone, as completely and mysteriously as the crow.

The far end of the valley was still filled with dust. As he watched, it moved slowly upward against the ridge, revealing like a lifted curtain a shadowy band of animals bunched near the middle of the valley. In a moment he knew they were cattle.

There was a sound from the Indians like the exhalation of a long-held breath, and a low, musical cry of joy. The spell was broken. All the men rushed for their horses; guns and bows and arrows appeared. With unexpected orderliness, every man in camp was riding toward the cattle.

Impulsively Martin mounted his mule and rode after them, compelled by a growing fascination. He did not want to watch the slaughter, but he could not sit and wait. He followed Eagle Voice, feeling lost and helpless when the Indian disappeared in the dust of the charge.

❧ 37 ☙

The dust of the storm still hung over the flat, but it was thinning, rising. Above the high butte, the last clouds moved north, leaving the sky brassy yellow in the lowering sun beyond the dust. The flat and the butte beyond, revealed now, were suddenly familiar to Crazy Walking. He had been here more than once, he knew; and yet there was a mystery in the place, palpable as the dust in the air.

There was grass in the near end of the flat, but the far end sloped upward toward the butte, grey and lifeless, ending in a jumble of boulders and a scattering of eroded shapes of clay and sandstone, as familiar to him as people. To the right a precipitous gully curved upward around the north end of the butte, too steep for passage. The cattle were boxed in; there was no way out except past the camp. He recognized the animals, a small bunch, some of the wildest of the herd —they would be hard to get, harder than buffalo.

He rode in the front rank of hunters, holding his horse in, curiously calm in the excitement around him, hearing a song begin within him, faint and unfamiliar as if from a far time, the music complete but the words a jumble.

The cattle were already moving away, noses up, testing the air. An old yellow steer faced them, front feet spread, tail up, blowing through his nose like a wild horse. He whirled suddenly and crashed into the others, stampeding them. And all the riders were suddenly charging.

Crazy Walking was riding the old Nez Percé war horse with the spotted rump, and he expected to be left behind in the race to the cattle. But in the rush the old horse seemed to drop his years and come alive. He stretched out in a long springy stride, bounding like a deer in the rough places, nose out and pointed at the cattle. He struck the wall of dust they had left, burst through it, catching them ahead of all the others. With no direction he picked a big blue steer and ran close on its flank.

Crazy Walking fitted an arrow to the string and, leaning forward, drove it deep and slanting ahead of the hip. The steer bawled and swung out suddenly against him. The horse struck the animal with his shoulder, knocking him over, and ran on without breaking his stride.

Looking back, Crazy Walking saw the steer struggling but unable to rise, and without thinking shouted, "Owee—yuhoo," with all the power of his lungs. The horse had already picked out another, a big roan cow, and was coming up with her.

He lost his first arrow against the hipbone; the next went true but not deep. The cow stumbled and came up again alongside, swinging her horns against him but missing. He swung to the side and slowed and she went on by, running strongly. He shot again, striking the ribs but with no effect.

She was running beside a big steer now, crowding close, the first arrow dipping with each jump. He kneed his horse over beside her and leaned down and forced the arrow in clear to the feather, bringing his hand away wet with blood. The cow went down suddenly, flinging her head aside, catching the horse's leg with a horn.

The horse fell and Crazy Walking threw himself clear, striking hard and rolling dizzily in a welter of dust. He stood up, staggered a few steps, and fell again, eyes blurred, mind confused and dizzy from the fall. He saw his horse, a distorted shadow in the dust, gallop by, following the herd. Near him the cow was kicking in a circle, dying.

He stood up again and was able to walk unsteadily, but his vision was still blurred and wavering. He found his bow and the arrows scattered from his quiver and started after the horse, unable to see him in the dust, knowing only the direction he had gone.

The main bunch of the cattle had spread out in the rough ground toward the butte, circling back now, dodging and twisting among the boulders, each one with a rider or two in pursuit. He saw one jump a narrow wash and a rider behind it go down on the jump. Rifle fire crashed erratically in the flat, echoing high off the butte with now and then the high piercing cry of a kill. Near him he heard another cry, "Hoka hey, hoka hey," and through the dust and the blur of his vision saw an old man dodge spryly around a tall pillar of sandstone, just avoiding the horns of a big red steer.

The steer swung wide on the turn, stopped, and stood shaking his head. The old man stepped behind the pillar and Crazy Walking could see he was trying to reload a revolver, but he kept dropping the bullets, then searching in the dust to find them, all the while keeping an eye on the steer and yelling in a high squeaking voice, "Hoka hey, hoka hey."

Crazy Walking started toward him to help but the old man waved him away emphatically. The steer charged again and Crazy Walking heard horns rattle against the stone as the old man again skipped aside, still fumbling with the bullets and yelling. But the yelling was like a song with pride in it, and a wild joy.

He went on, seeing his horse in the dust ahead, waiting. A steer ran by and, close on its heels, he saw Eagle Voice, grinning widely, reloading his gun as he passed. Behind him, riding dimly in the wake of dust, was Martin, beating his legs wildly on the mule's ribs, trying to catch up. He had lost his hat, and his black coat was streaming out behind his flapping arms like wings. His face was white and intense and he rode as if his life depended on catching Eagle Voice. The steer jumped a small wash; Eagle Voice cleared it also, but the mule slowed on the approach and made the other bank only with his front feet. He scrabbled briefly at the edge and fell back out of sight.

Crazy Walking ran forward and saw the mule trotting away along the wash. Martin was crawling around in the bottom, face close to the ground. He picked something out of the sand and sat up, putting his glasses on.

Crazy Walking climbed down the bank, but when Martin saw him he jumped to his feet without a sound and ran, looking back over his shoulder, his eyes dark and wild under his glasses. He stumbled over a stone and fell but was up again hardly missing a step.

Crazy Walking climbed back up the bank, found his horse, and mounted, still dizzy and shaken from the fall, vision still blurred. The sun was behind the butte now, the shadows dark on the flat; he could hardly see the cattle and riders that galloped here and there in the early darkness. There were only a few cattle left. At the lower end of the flat, the women and children had spread out to keep them from getting away, and were shouting and trilling in a joyous clamor.

He turned toward the upper end and through the dust and the blur of his vision saw a white animal like a faraway light flicker among the boulders and disappear in a gully, behind it swarming the shadows of several riders.

He kicked his horse to a run and in a moment saw a spot of white emerge from the gully into a little flat, disappearing among figures of clay. It reappeared on the slope of the butte, moving upward. Reaching the gully, he saw the riders, one after another, drive at the steep bank and slide back till the dust of their struggles enveloped them in a yellow cloud.

He turned down the gully, crossed, and rode back along the other side toward the little flat. He passed the place where the animal had left the gully and below him saw the riders swimming shadowy in a pool of dust, still straining upward, trying to climb the bank. One after another he saw them surface and again sink, four old wrinkled faces.

When they saw him above, they shouted hoarsely, clamorously, but he could understand nothing; his hearing was as blurred as his vision. Only a single word stood out, separate and distinct: buffalo.

He crossed the flat and at the foot of the slope saw the shrunken carcass of the yellow horse, remembering with dream-like clarity the Blue Cloud riding this same slope; the song rose again to his lips and he knew it was the Blue Cloud's.

Above him the white animal moved steadily, weaving back and forth against the darkness of the slope as it climbed.

He found a narrow, barely discernible game trail and followed it upward, his vision clearing as if with the height.

East, beyond the shadow of the butte, the land burned in slanting yellow light; in the dark shadow below, the flat was quiet, lying in an even, slowly drifting mist of dust. Nothing moved that he could see; all the cattle were dead or gone, the riders stopped. By intense intuition, he knew that he was watched, that all the eyes below rode with him on the slope. He could not turn back: a power lifted him against the impossible climb.

Again he saw the Blue Cloud, the yellow horse balanced against the slope, rifle raised to the white animal above; saw the rifle fire and the horse and rider slide in dust to the bottom. He passed the place where the horse had fallen and, looking down, saw the carcass directly below, almost straight down, it seemed. He had not imagined the slope so steep.

The spotted horse moved carefully now, nose almost touching the trail, seeming to feel for each spot to place his feet, turning slowly and solidly on each reverse of the trail. He showed no fear, only singleness of purpose.

Above, the white animal moved parallel to Crazy Walking, crossing and recrossing the dark butte. He could not say what it looked like. Below, on the flat, even in the deep shadow, the things he looked at were clear, outlined sharply against the grey earth. But above, against the dark butte, the animal blurred still, a source of light, its lines fluid as the edge of flame.

Within Crazy Walking was a flickering of feeling, an alternation between awareness of himself on the slope and the memory of the Blue Cloud; between clarity and a curious blurring. He was aware clearly of the danger of the trail; he was high now and the slope was sharp. One slip and he would fall steeply among boulders. But he was not afraid, even knowing that he should be. In a sense inaccessible to logic, the pursuit was more important than his life.

His horse paused for breath, and above, at the same time, the animal stopped and looked back. And as Crazy Walking watched, the memory of having seen it before, with more clarity, flashed on him with startling impact. The animal moved; he saw it rear with unhurried grace against the ledge at the rim of the butte. In the same instant a rifle crashed from the slope somewhere above. The animal sprang upward and was gone. A stone, loosened by its feet, bounded over him in a tremendous leap, showering him with dirt and sand. The horse snorted and moved on.

At the next turning of the trail, he saw a man climbing the slope to the south. He was hurrying frantically but progressing slowly, sliding back often, scrabbling recklessly on the slope, seeming to advance only when his hands caught on the boulders, like one climbing in a dream. In the shadows Crazy Walking could not see the man's features, but he knew instantly that it was the Blue Cloud.

Reaching the ledge at the rim, the horse stopped and smelled of the rock. It was an impossible leap; but there was no turning back. The trail was not a foot wide, caving and broken on the edges. But Crazy Walking had no thought of turning or even of leaving his horse. He sat waiting while the horse rested, watching the Blue Cloud, below him now, struggling straight up the slope in a nightmare of effort. He was near a curving of the trail but appeared not to notice. His eyes were fixed upward, showing white, his lips moving soundlessly.

Crazy Walking looked at the ledge again, and the horse, with no urging, gathered himself and reared against it and with a tremendous leap caught with his front feet at the top and scrambled up, falling just over the rim.

Crazy Walking stepped off while the horse got up, searching for the animal while he waited. The top of the butte was wide and flat, and at the far edge, black now against the lowering sun, he saw the animal, saw it drop as if sinking into the earth.

He mounted to follow and caught a glimpse of the Blue Cloud still struggling near the top of the slope; he was stopped by sympathy for the man. For an instant he was himself the strange Indian struggling vainly with the dark hill.

He hesitated, then kneeing his horse over to the edge, threw the end of his rope. It slid almost to the man's feet, but he did not notice it. Instead he stood precariously and made the sign for go and for buffalo. Without answering, Crazy Walking snaked the rope closer. But the Blue Cloud only waved it angrily away.

Crazy Walking turned away, heading at a run for the spot where the animal had disappeared. He found a trail that led down into a ravine and followed it, straining his eyes into

169

the shadows below for a glimpse of white, but finding nothing.

While he rode, the sun dropped, reddening the sky; the shadows deepened. Far ahead and down he saw again a moving spot of light and followed with all the speed he could make on the rough trail. But he could not gain. The light curved and dropped, appearing and disappearing; darkness thickened and finally the light was gone. But he kept following, coming at last to the mouth of the ravine where it joined another; and here the trail stopped in a mass of jumbled rocks he could not cross.

He dismounted and climbed over the rocks in darkness, excitement clutching dryly at his throat, and came suddenly on the animal descending slowly at the edge of a stream. It paused, head toward him for an instant, then sprang down lightly and plunged through the stream in a spray of white, climbing the bank opposite him, not twenty steps away.

He fitted an arrow and shot, certain of hitting. But he heard it strike rock, splintering, and saw a burst of sparks beside the animal. He drew another arrow, still with plenty of time; but his hands were slow and numb. He dropped the arrow and drew another, shooting just as the animal gained a ledge above the stream, and knew without seeing that he had missed again.

The animal disappeared behind a boulder, appearing farther on, still climbing. It faded slowly, changing again from animal shape to a blurring spot of light that moved in shadow, fading still. It was gone then. But still a vaporous light seemed to glow and move just at the edge of his vision. He watched till his eyes blurred and stung, and there was nothing but darkness.

He relaxed then, leaning against a rock in sudden, shaking weakness. He was not disappointed; only relieved. He turned and climbed slowly, and with unwonted care, back to his horse.

## ❧ 38 ❧

It was late; the feasting was done. Around the fire the men smoked and talked of hunting and war, reluctant to leave the circle, awaiting with unspoken anxiety the return of Crazy Walking. Some of the young ones were restless, making movements to leave but still staying, listening with ill-concealed contempt to the brave tales of the old men—but with envy, too, Turning Hawk sensed, and bitterness that they had no tales to tell themselves.

The old men were irrepressible. They had argued long with the young men over the white cow, the four who had seen it contending strongly but with good humor that it was a buffalo. It was their good humor that surprised Turning Hawk. They were happy in their certainty, overlooking with indulgence the derisiveness of the young men.

The ancient High Bear, who as a youth had killed a white buffalo, told the story of White Buffalo Woman, who, in the sacred myth of the people, had brought the pipe and the ceremony for bringing buffalo. The way he told it was overlong and the young men did not listen. Turning Hawk could understand their feeling: the buffalo were gone, the ceremony had lost its meaning. But for himself, the story still had beauty and a power to move the heart.

High Bear stood then to tell his own story, touching Turning Hawk on the shoulder and asking him to take the part of the buffalo. Turning Hawk assented and stood. He had heard the story many times, had been the buffalo more than once. But it was a good story with the flavor and strength of the old days.

High Bear backed far out of the firelight, talking all the while in a high excited voice.

"The snow was deep, in the moon of popping trees. Cold. There had been wind but it was still now, and we saw from the distance the breath-cloud of the buffalo. We found them in the shelter of a bluff, all dusted white with snow. Some were dead, frozen.

"We made our meat and were skinning when we saw the white one, a shadow only on the snow. The nose was white and even the horns and hoofs; we thought it a ghost buffalo. But it ran, wallowing in deep drifts, and stopped.

"I ran on snowshoes, carrying only a spear."

He came forward, swinging his feet out as if with snowshoes, hobbling painfully into the light. Turning Hawk bent over and wallowed in the snow. But before the old man reached the fire, he was out of breath and had to stop. Turning Hawk stepped forward and helped him back to his place by the fire. When High Bear caught his breath he said, "The meat is good but it has no strength."

"It is not buffalo, Grandfather," the young man Yellow Bird remarked.

"I killed it," High Bear went on. "My woman dressed the robe and painted it with sacred designs and left it on a hill for the spirit powers. Buffalo were plenty for many snows. It was Wakan; a long time ago when the hoop of the people was not broken. That is how it was."

The Blue Cloud, who had sat by the fire all evening without a word, came to life after watching the action. He questioned High Bear in signs, his face transformed with interest.

"There is another," he signed, renewing unknowingly the argument that had gone before. "It will be so again."

Yellow Bird laughed, not bothering to speak in signs, "A white man's white cow. We will see when Crazy Walking comes. His eyes are young, not full of buffalo."

The old men, who had seen, said nothing but nodded their heads, waiting.

Turning Hawk remembered the evening in this same place when the Blue Cloud had killed his horse following the white cow. Almost a moon had passed now and he still believed and still hunted, following a light from the past that no other could see—except the old men whose eyes were gone. Turning Hawk himself had almost believed, seeing the white animal on the dark hill—as if the passionate belief of the Blue Cloud had altered his own vision. Even now, looking into the past, the time seemed sacred, mysterious. He remembered with a shiver Crazy Walking's harsh laughter that had undeceived him.

Crazy Walking would bring the truth when he came and perhaps the cow's hide, proving the young men right. In the meantime, Turning Hawk did not enter the argument. He could not side with the young ones against the old.

He watched the Blue Cloud, who had settled back again, waiting also, serene, sure of the outcome, eyes shining in the firelight. He was strange, a man apart; witko, perhaps, insane, but Wakan also. His eyes were the eyes of a child, and yet he seemed ancient also. He had not spoken of the Spirit Dance, was perhaps awaiting the outcome of Crazy Walking's hunt.

In a little while Crazy Walking arrived. He would have gone straight to his lodge if someone had not stopped him and brought him to the fire. He seemed surprised and perplexed that anyone should be waiting for him.

After he had smoked, it was High Bear who asked the question, "Grandson, did you kill the white buffalo?"

"No, I shot and missed."

"You saw it close then?"

"I saw it close, Grandfather, but in the dark. I could not see well."

He answered the questions diffidently, seeming abstracted and withdrawn. Turning Hawk was surprised. He had expected Crazy Walking to laugh harshly in his old way at the fiction of the white buffalo. But he did not.

Yellow Bird could wait no longer. "It was a white cow, not a buffalo. You saw it. Were your eyes also full of buffalo?"

Crazy Walking looked at him, blinking his eyes curiously like one awakening from deep sleep. "I don't know. My eyes were blurred when I started—I had a fall. After that it was dark. But it was white and I could see it in the dark."

"Was it the same one we saw before?" Turning Hawk asked.

Crazy Walking met his eyes and looked at him steadily for a long time. He was puzzled and in some way hurt by the question.

"I don't know. It was white." He was silent for a moment, then told of the ride, accompanying himself with signs for the benefit of the Blue Cloud. He described the climb, the pursuit, and the encounter at the stream with exact objectivity, saying nothing of his own thoughts or feelings; but in his story was a spirit life, the reality of dream. The animal was not flesh and blood but a mysterious light receding in the darkness. When the last arrow missed and the light was

173

gone, there was a long pause; even the young men were silent, their eyes in fascination fixed on Crazy Walking.

High Bear was the first to speak. "Grandson, there is mystery here; the animal is sacred, a symbol. Do you think you could find its trail again if we followed?"

"I can find it."

"Good. We will follow as far as it leads." He glanced at Turning Hawk as if expecting some objection. "We cannot move until the meat is cured. By then, our party will have returned."

"Who will go?"

"Myself and three grandsons." High Bear laughed, indicating the three old men beside him, Lean Man, White Hawk, and Red Moon, "and for scout the only two-legged in the party." He indicated Crazy Walking. "And perhaps the Blue Cloud will also come." He turned and in signs spoke to the Blue Cloud. Instead of answering directly, the man stood, advanced into the firelight, and spoke to all in signs, eloquently picturing his meaning.

"I will go. I have hunted the white one many days. Three times I have shot and missed: my bullets have not touched. I have killed my horse, a fine buffalo runner. I have not eaten in many days. The animal is sacred; because of my suffering it has given me a song, a song for the Spirit Dance."

He sang in a low intense voice, not ceasing his hand talk:

> I return, I return
> I whose hump, a hill from the earth rises,
> I whose hump, a hill from the earth rises,
> I return, I return.

He stopped and stood motionless, his eyes fixed in the darkness; and there was no sound in the camp, not a whisper. His power was strong and visible in the white night.

After a long time he went on, telling of the trip west, of the Spirit Dance, as he had done another time in this same place. And again Turning Hawk was moved deeply, involved in the strange passion, his thought rebelling at the vision of the dead returning and the earth renewed, but heart lifting, winging. He put aside the doubts and listened, wholly absorbed.

Done with speech, the Blue Cloud sang again, songs of the

people of the west, flashing their meaning clearly with hands and body, the songs vivid, speaking to the heart.

Beginning quietly, moving out of the firelight, turning his face upward to the sky, he sang:

> The snow lies on the mountains,
> The snow lies on the mountains,
> The spirit road among the stars,
> The spirit road among the stars.

And turning his face to the earth, sang of an antelope, animal of dream, that, moving, became the buffalo and all others born of earth:

> A slender antelope is circling,
> A slender antelope is circling,
> It is rolling upon the earth,
> It is rolling upon the earth.

Turning to the mountains, with sudden violence:

> The black rock,
> The black rock,
> The rock is broken,
> The rock is broken.

Returning briefly to the earth mother and to peace:

> The wind stirs the willows,
> The wind stirs the willows,
> The wind stirs the grasses,
> The wind stirs the grasses.

And again to violence, to the powers of the sky:

> Fog, fog,
> Lightning, lightning,
> Whirlwind, whirlwind.

And to the great change, the new earth coming:

> The whirlwind,
> The whirlwind,

The snowy earth comes gliding,
The snowy earth comes gliding.

And subsiding:

> There is dust from the whirlwind,
> There is dust from the whirlwind,
> The whirlwind on the mountain,
> The whirlwind on the mountain.

> The rocks are ringing,
> The rocks are ringing,
> They are ringing in the mountains,
> They are ringing in the mountains.

And finally to quiet and peace, to the sacred tree, the immortal one:

> The cottonwoods are growing tall,
> The cottonwoods are growing tall,
> Are growing tall and green,
> Are growing tall and green.

It was finished. The Blue Cloud stood like stone in the moonlight. No one spoke; and after a time all left in silence.

Turning Hawk returned to his lodge, spent by the alternations of emotion in his heart. In memory the songs moved and changed; the vision of the Spirit Dance was a light leading downward in darkness.

## ❧ 39 ❧

The day was sunless, the sky a dirty yellow, as if the clouds were partly dust. Above the hills the sky began quite imperceptibly, a far, fading extension of the lifeless land.

Westland sat with the Indians in a little flat at the upper end of the valley, waiting for Martin to begin his sermon.

Below, camp was pitched on the bank of a gully in the bottom of which a spring ran. Drying racks laden with meat were set up around the lodges. Now and then an old woman on guard shouted at the dogs and pounded on the ground with a stick to keep them away from the meat. He saw a small boy pilfer a piece of meat from the rack above her and get away without being caught.

Around the space where the Indians sat was a curious assembly of eroded shapes of clay and sandstone: columns, ovals, bread loaves, none in any recognizable animal form, but as a group giving the impression of a statuary of grotesque beings—the Silent Ones, Eagle Voice called them—drawn together in brooding worship.

The nearest of these Martin had chosen as a pulpit, an oval the shape of a woman's breast, even to the small rounded nipple at the top, and he stood behind it now, just his head and shoulders visible, trying to balance his Bible on the nipple while he turned the pages in search of a text. After a moment he stopped and tried to level it off with a stone, but it was too hard. He held the Bible in his hand then.

Beside him Eagle Voice, in immaculate Prince Albert and white shirt, waited with regal dignity. The clothing, Westland knew, was part of the Indian's medicine. He carried it in a rawhide medicine case along with other sacred objects, taking great pains in its proper care. Westland wondered idly what Martin would think if he knew. Beside the Indian, the missionary seemed colorless and weak: his clothes were wrinkled and dusty, his face was smudged with dust from the pulpit, and he was nervous and harassed. He glanced continually around, as if the presence of the Silent Ones were in some way a menace.

Waiting, Westland turned toward the lower end of the valley and saw Crazy Walking and his party climbing the hill north in a detour of the butte. They were strung out in single file, Crazy Walking in the lead, behind him the strange Arapaho, then the four old men. They climbed the hill and for a little while on its crest were outlined sharply against the yellow sky. With the exception of Crazy Walking, they were bent, round-shouldered, heads tipped forward as if in prayer or mourning. It was not a hunt, he saw with sudden insight, but a religious quest.

Glancing back at Martin, sensing his agitation, Westland

177

felt a quick alternation of sympathy and amusement. Ironically, it was the very presence of mystery, of a strong religious feeling, that confounded the man. In its presence he was afraid, as if he might become infected. Westland was surprised that Martin had chosen this spot for his service, remembering that other ceremony performed here a few minutes since by High Bear and the old men, that of the white buffalo. It had been a simple, reverent acting out of the myth of the White Buffalo Woman, announced by High Bear after some preliminary singing and drumming, and purification in a sweat lodge.

The white buffalo had appeared at the head of the draw, a woman wrapped in a white robe. Among the Silent Ones she threw off the robe and stepped into a small, dusty opening, holding high a pipe, stem pointed toward the sun. Two of the old men approached her. (In the myth, Westland remembered, the two were young, but High Bear had found no young ones in the camp willing to assist.) One of them spoke in a high ceremonial voice, "Brother, here is a beautiful young woman, alone and helpless. Let us capture and enjoy her."

"No," the other replied. "There is mystery here: this is a sacred person."

They stood waiting and the woman approached, putting her forehead to the ground before them, saying, "I am alone and helpless, as you see."

The first speaker dropped to the ground and seized her; in the same instant the other shook out his blanket and the two were enveloped in a cloud of yellow dust. There was a hissing sound, the source of which Westland could not determine. Slowly the dust cleared, revealing the woman, holding the pipe high, as when she had first appeared. But the man had vanished. There was only a low, dusty mound and a scattering of white bones.

"The young man has suffered for his own wickedness," the woman said. "But I see you are brave and kind. Your people are suffering, and I will take pity on them. You may take them this message."

The man returned. Four old men went out with a blanket and carried the woman back to the little amphitheater where the people waited. They formed around her in concentric circles.

Inside the circles the woman stood and spoke. "In your

trouble, I have taken pity on you. I have brought you these four things which, if you hold them sacred, will give you strength and spiritual power: tobacco, red robe, white shield, and warbonnet of eagle feathers. I give you also this sacred pipe which will give you the power to find buffalo."

To High Bear she presented the pipe and a bundle. She left then, disappearing among the Silent Ones to reappear for a moment beyond, wrapped in the white robe, bent over to represent a buffalo. The ceremony was finished. The man who had vanished reappeared covered with dust. The woman returned.

Martin announced then through Eagle Voice that, since it was Sunday, he too would conduct a service. But Crazy Walking and the old men would not stay. They had mounted and ridden off, even as Martin was selecting his pulpit, the old men chattering eagerly as boys.

Martin found his text at last and with shaking voice read the thirteenth chapter of Isaiah, that fierce yet beautiful prophecy of the doom of Babylon. He read it in all its horror and vividness, without introduction or explanation, speaking with such rush and passion that Eagle Voice had no chance to interpret. Martin seemed to be caught up in the passage, unaware for the moment of his audience, as if the fiery revelation were in some way his own. Finished, he paused, not raising his eyes but continuing to stare at the book.

Eagle Voice studied deliberately for a moment, then throwing his head back spoke in a calm, strong voice. The White Robe's power, the book, he explained, had given him a vision of the future and the punishment of the white man. He had seen the Great Spirit gathering all the nations of the dead, leading them along the spirit road, gathering with a great noise in the mountains: the sound of thunder, of great rocks broken and moving. Like a whirlwind would the spirits come; the sun would be darkened, the star nations would not give their light, the moon would cease to shine.

The evil ones would be stricken: a white man would be rare and hard to find as the yellow metal that makes them crazy. None would be spared, neither man, woman, nor child; even the unborn should feel the knife. Their houses would be deserted forever, inhabited only by the animals.

He was surprised, Eagle Voice said, that such a vision should be given to a white man, especially to this man who seemed to dislike so intensely the ways of the Indian. Nevertheless, he hoped that it might be true. He himself believed that it might: in substance it agreed with what the Indian Messiah of the west had foretold, according to the Blue Cloud, who had brought word of it only the night before. Though of course there was no mention of a dance to assist in the return of the spirit hosts. But it was something to think about, something that should be investigated.

He himself favored the idea of a new earth with the white man returned to the land across the waters from whence he had come. The White Robe's prophecy seemed unnecessarily harsh; but perhaps he knew more of the wickedness of the white man than did he, Eagle Voice.

He had no doubt that the white man's God was powerful and fierce. Had he not taken away the land of the Indian to give to the whites and put the Indian on these little islands to starve and to die? Had he not taken the very life of the Indian, the buffalo, completely from the earth? Had he not suffered the white man to overrun the whole land, swarming like maggots on a dead carcass? But perhaps he now repented, seeing the way the white man had treated the Indian. Perhaps he would make amends.

In that case, he, Eagle Voice, would be glad to follow the precepts of the White Robe, since there was much in his doctrine that agreed with the beliefs of the wise ones among the Indians.

Eagle Voice stopped, indicating that he had finished, and Martin, more calm now, went on to expound on the punishment of evil, of the fate of the transgressor, mentioning in particular those who failed to observe the Sabbath, intending his remark, Westland thought, for Crazy Walking. He spoke in shorter intervals now and the translations were also shorter and more accurate, though Eagle Voice explained that the things Martin advocated were things the Indians must do to help out the power of the vision.

The response to the service was enthusiastic. Watching Martin smiling among the Indians, Westland was both amazed and amused. Whether Eagle Voice's speech had been intended as irony, he could not tell. But he was interested in the Ghost Dance reference and its effect on the Indians. He left without speaking to Martin, not wanting to comment on the accuracy of the translation.

In the afternoon, he was once more in the little flat sketching the Silent Ones for his notes, when Martin came up silently and stood watching as he worked.

"Do these have some place in the superstitions of the Indians, that you value them so much?" he asked.

"I don't know," Westland answered, ignoring the sarcasm, "Eagle Voice calls them the Silent Ones but knows of no legends connected with them. It's just that they give the impression of living presences, I think."

"It's part of the evil that's in the air. I try to fight it. You seem only to revel in it."

"I'm interested. I respect the beliefs of these people even though I don't accept them. I haven't seen any evil."

"How do you explain the strange things that have happened, except as the work of the Devil?"

"What things?"

"The pipe you found—and accepted—the dog, the crow, the storm, all that happened on the trip here?"

Westland laughed. "I hadn't thought much about it. The pipe and the dog were obviously lost by the same party— the dog smelled the pipe on me and followed. At the time of the storm he picked up the trail of his owner and followed it. The crow was simply escaping the rough air."

"What about the storm changing its course and the appearance of the cattle; didn't you feel anything strange about that?"

"Just a coincidence."

Martin shook his head and muttered darkly.

Westland went on sketching. He had found the events somewhat eerie himself, though he was loath to admit as much to Martin. At the same time, he felt that his explanation was correct.

Martin watched awhile in silence, then asked,

"How accurate was Eagle Voice's translation of my sermon? It seemed to have a rather extraordinary effect."

"It was fairly close," Westland answered uneasily. "I guess he expressed it as he understood it. My understanding of the language is still hazy."

"I thought he might have added something. The response somehow didn't seem to fit."

"You should learn the language," Westland said, changing the subject.

"I'd like to but I don't seem to have the knack. It's just noise to me."

Westland said nothing. Glancing back toward the camp, he saw Little Wound coming toward him. Part way across the little flat, the boy stopped. He circled until he was downwind, then retreated to the edge of the flat like a horse shying at a scent, and stood waiting.

Martin left, walking away from camp, and when he was gone, Little Wound came directly in toward Westland, when he was close extending his hands. Westland touched them as a recognition of his presence.

Little Wound signed, "Grandfather would like you to smoke with him in his lodge."

Westland signed, "I am coming." The small hands followed his as surely as if they had sight of their own. When Westland stopped, the boy turned and led the way unerringly toward the lodge, avoiding the poles of the drying racks with startling precision.

Westland entered the lodge and found Turning Hawk and all the older men sitting around a small fire. To his surprise, the place of honor next to Turning Hawk had been saved for him. For a little while, as the pipe passed around, nothing was said. It was Turning Hawk who first spoke.

"We are honored," he said, "to have with us as a friend a white man held in esteem by the same unseen powers that watch over the Indian, one who, in our presence, has been given a pipe."

He paused for a moment, then, addressing the group, went over the events of the previous day: the finding of the pipe, the dog, the crow, and the thunderstorm.

"In the past," he said, "many of our people have been killed by lightning; the power of the thunder is great. And yet, at times we have been given a pipe by these same powers as a sign that our prayers have been heard. The white man has received such a pipe, and it was obviously the power of this pipe that turned aside the storm and at the same time revealed the cattle.

"The strange dog that followed, the crow, were merely the symbols of guardianship for this chosen person who was traveling in a strange country among a strange people.

"He has been silent about these mysterious happenings, which is the way, also, of the Indian, and is a sign that he realizes the importance of what has happened. But, without doubt, the powers that have given him the pipe will appear to him in his dreams to give him even greater spiritual gifts.

"Wherefore I am honored by his presence. Until now I have called him friend, believing his regard for the ways of the Indian to be sincere, but with some doubt, since he is white. However, henceforward, I hope he will remain as one of us as long as he cares to stay."

Westland was taken aback but deeply gratified. He could not doubt the old man's sincerity. And while he did not see the events in the same light, yet he did not feel that his own explanation of them had any overpowering virtue. He —and Martin also—had been affected, had sensed the mystery. Three points of view had given three different explanations. And what logic was there that could choose with certainty among the three?

No more was said. The pipe moved around in silence except for the wheeze of the smokers. In a little while he left with a feeling of having felt a truth that was beyond intellectual perception.

## 🦅 40 🦅

By midday Crazy Walking found the trail, bringing the old men across the divide and down to the stream by an easy, roundabout way. He found the crossing and the broken pieces of one of his arrows. The tracks, round and clean-cut as buffalo prints, led downward west and north.

The old men dismounted and studied the tracks, nodding their heads wisely, grinning toothlessly with anticipation. But the Blue Cloud only sat his horse, looking into the distance, eyes alight as if they already beheld the quarry. The day was dark with dust and cloud. Above the hilltops the earth-colored sky slid westward with ponderous, downward motion; among them the wind flowed with the bulk and sound of swiftly falling water.

The trail led downward, following the stream, then crossed the ridge and dropped again, winding tortuously among gullies and washes. It was slow and difficult and they were not in the open yet when the sun was gone. They camped in a sandy wash with no grass or water for the horses and no wood for burning. The Blue Cloud, impatient of delay, almost went on alone, then changed his mind. But the old men were exhausted. They had clung grimly to their horses, but when Crazy Walking saw old High Bear almost fall, he called a halt.

They ate a dry meal and the old men slept, but the Blue Cloud did not even spread a robe. He retired a little way from camp and, building a tiny incense fire with grass from a pouch, sang in a low, pervasive voice.

Crazy Walking could not sleep. He listened for a long time to the Blue Cloud's hypnotic singing, but with an increasing agitation. He could not understand the words of the songs, and yet they filled him with uneasiness and dread. When the sound stopped, he sprang to his feet and walked quickly away from camp. He climbed a hill, toiling upward till he reached a rocky summit, and sat in the streaming darkness, not resting but involved in the turbulent sound and movement of the air. The light died completely; he could see nothing. But the press of the dusty air against him in downward movement gave him a vivid sense of flying, of soaring upward swiftly among clouds.

After a long time, the darkness thinned. A brightness like yellow mist appeared in the east, and he guessed that the clouds were gone and the moon was up. But the dust in the air obscured the light so thickly he could not tell the position of the moon.

As he sat, the wind increased to a thunderous howling, then slackened gradually. The sense of movement slowed and he dozed lightly as he sat. But he was awakened by his own voice singing; the song strange to him, and his voice, singing it, shaken and tense.

> A whiteness of death moving over me,
> A whiteness like snow, sliding above.

He sang it again in wonder and dread, trying to remember the dream in which it had come, but he could not.

Day came slowly, light rising like smoke in the yellow sky, and he descended again to camp, finding the old men already awake, chewing their dried meat as they waited. They took the trail again, finding the tracks only in sheltered places where the dust had not drifted. But there was nothing to turn an animal aside, no grass or browse, so they had only to follow the trail on down.

The day was old when they found the animal, coming on it suddenly in a flaring of the gully in which they traveled. There was grass in the little park and a few clumps of greasewood; and from among them a white animal arose and ran. The old men surged forward around Crazy Walking and he let them go, held back by a lethargy, a sinking of desire. But he could not keep his horse from running. Ahead of him crossing the flat the old men rode, closely bunched, yelling and shrieking like boys. Surprisingly the Blue Cloud was behind them, riding quietly, making no attempt to pass. The gully narrowed again for a little distance, then spread out once more into a valley in which, far ahead, there were willows and a stream. Beyond these Crazy Walking saw the land dotted with cattle grazing.

The horses were tired and they were far out on the level before they overtook the cow, still in the same order. He saw High Bear lean over and drive an arrow into the fleeting form, and in quick succession the other three shot. They swept on and the Blue Cloud followed, not even shooting as he passed. Crazy Walking reined in and the cow was before him, kicking in a circle on the earth. He sat looking down at the dying animal, seeing it clearly and in detail for the first time: a two-year-old heifer, short-haired and slick, its hide a shining white, marked now by spreading stains of blood. She was slim-bodied, long-limbed, and except for the round black hoofs and short curved horns, impossible to mistake for a buffalo.

The old men circled and came back slowly, bent and silent on their winded horses, and sat looking down at the kill. The Blue Cloud came in last of all and, looking briefly, signed, "This is not the one. We have taken the wrong trail."

Crazy Walking said nothing but dismounted and lifted one of the feet, tracing the round edges with a finger. Then he walked a few steps back and pointed to the tracks. The old men followed with their eyes, nodding in resignation and defeat. But the Blue Cloud kept his face averted.

Crazy Walking forced himself to begin skinning the cow, working against a powerful repulsion. High Bear came to help him, but he was slow and his hand shook so hard that he cut holes in the hide. They had not yet finished when something whined overhead, and glancing toward the willows

Crazy Walking saw riders burst into the open and come toward them. One, armed with a repeating rifle, was shooting as he rode, but all the shots were going high.

Crazy Walking stopped skinning and cut a long strip of meat from the back, deliberately staying while the old men got a start, regretting for a moment the rifle he had given away. He tied the meat on the saddle, keeping an eye on the white men. When he mounted and rode off, the bullets were kicking up dirt all around him.

The Blue Cloud was in the lead, the old men strung out behind, looking back. And he saw that they were riding toward the wrong gully and would miss the trail. He shouted but no one heeded, and in a moment they disappeared. He followed, watching his pursuers over his shoulder: three men, well mounted and all carrying rifles.

But he was not worried; they would probably stop after a little; it was not likely they would follow far in search of trouble. He rounded a bend and ahead saw the old men strung out in single file, threading a narrow, boulder-strewn gully that climbed steeply, narrowing and twisting. By the time he caught up they were at the end of the gully where three small washes joined. Only a narrow game trail led upward along a rocky ridge.

It was slow going. The white men were close enough now to be dangerous, but their shooting was bad. They were still riding, shooting from the saddle, wasting their lead. But when they came to the end of the gully where the trail steepened, they dismounted and led their horses, and their shots came closer. High Bear's horse was hit and fell, rolling and sliding on the steep hillside, but the old man jumped clear and was not hurt. They all dismounted and walked then, keeping their horses between themselves and the riflemen.

The trail crossed the ridge and dropped down into a dry stream bed, winding between steep-cut banks and tumbled boulders, and for a while they lost sight of their pursuers. They were safe now and not exposed to fire; all they had to do was stay ahead. But the old men were tiring. Crazy Walking gave High Bear his horse and followed on foot, knowing that the old man could not keep going much longer. He was pale and out of breath, barely able to stay on the horse. Finally, at a pause to rest, High Bear gasped, "Grandson, I am finished. Leave me here by the trail and I will stop one or two of these long knives. This is a good trap and they are without caution, following as if we were rabbits."

He stopped suddenly, out of breath, and slid from the horse. Crazy Walking caught him and tried to set him on his feet, but he was limp and helpless, his legs buckling and jerking. Crazy Walking laid him down on a strip of sand in the stream bed, and the old man did not move or speak. But in a moment his lips began to move and his voice, hardly more than a whisper, lifted in a death song:

> The black road leads to darkness,
> Only the earth lives on.

Below on the trail, Crazy Walking could hear the careless voices of the white men and the sound of steel-shod hoofs on the rocks. Looking at the old men, he knew he could not keep them from fighting.

"The white men are crazy," he said. "But perhaps we can stop them without killing."

He led the way back to a heap of boulders that overlooked a bend in the trail below where the stream bed widened. He left the old men and the Blue Cloud here, telling them to shoot when the white men appeared in the open, knowing the range was too great for the bows and the old musket. Then he went on down till he was not twenty steps from the bend and climbed up to a large overhanging boulder. It was a good spot. They could not climb the steep sides of the stream bed, and if any tried to come on after the warning fire, they would be exposed in easy range. But he hoped they would stop.

In a moment they came into the open, riding in single file. When they were all exposed, he heard the hiss of the first arrow, saw it stick lightly in the shoulder of the lead horse. The Blue Cloud's rifle cracked and another arrow appeared in the ground in front of them.

The little space was suddenly a tangle of rearing, snorting horses. Another was hit by an arrow before the riders got untangled and out of sight around the bend. In the delay, Crazy Walking thought, he could have killed them all. He could hear them swearing at the horses and arguing.

"I told you," one said, "they're dangerous even without guns. An arrow in your ribs is as good as a bullet."

Another answered, "Hell, look here. The last one didn't

even break the hide. They're still too far away to hurt us. All we got to do is get where we can see 'em and we can pick 'em off like ducks. We got 'em now."

"Naw," a third objected, "Ed's right. This won't be healthy. What makes you so set on hurtin' these Injuns, Wiley? That cow wasn't even out of our bunch. We got no white ones like that. What you so het up about?"

"By God, if it wasn't ours, it was somebody else's. I've lost enough cattle to these damn savages. And who's gonna stop 'em if we don't? Nobody. You two càn go back if you like, but I'm gonna make meat. Hell, this is a brand-new rifle and I haven't killed a thing with it. I've gotta baptize it, haven't I?"

The horses had quieted. In a moment Crazy Walking saw one of the men dart into the open afoot and start up the trail. He saw a flight of arrows and a spurt of dust where a bullet hit, but the man was untouched. He dropped behind a rock at the side of the trail and fired a shot upward. Behind him the other two were firing to cover him, but Crazy Walking knew they could see little from where they were. He stayed out of sight hoping the man would go back, deciding to wait till he was directly below before shooting: maybe he would turn in the meantime.

One of the men beyond the opening called, "Wiley, you damn fool, you better get back here. How do you know there ain't a redskin settin' up there behind a rock waitin' for you? There ain't but four shootin'; we saw six come in here."

The man behind the rock snorted, but he made no move to go back. Crazy Walking could see him studying the rocks ahead, planning his next move.

"You get yourself hung up, I ain't sproutin' feathers to bring you back. By God, you can stay there and rot."

"Hah," the man said, and dived across an opening to another rock. Again arrows struck around him and a bullet whined off a rock. His face, as he peered over the rock, was beaded with sweat but lit by a soft smile, as if he were looking at a friend.

Crazy Walking could not understand, could not guess what would drive the man to risk so much for so little. He found a small stone and carefully threw it across to the other side; it struck the bank and rolled down almost hitting the man where he lay. He twisted the rifle upward and fired at nothing; but the smile did not leave his lips. He did not go back.

In a moment he made another rush that brought him beyond the opening visible to the men above. Crazy Walking put an arrow to the string and waited; and when the man came abreast, drew it to the head and shot.

The man saw the movement and raised the rifle with amazing swiftness. The arrow appeared under his raised left arm, sunk nearly to the feather; the rifle crashed and a bullet spun off the boulder, showering splinters of rock. He looked up at Crazy Walking for just an instant with the soft smile; then his legs buckled and he dropped to a sitting position in the sand, head bowed, his left arm curled around the arrow, right hand clutching it against his chest. He fell backward, hands frozen incongruously in the sign for love, on his face still the traces of the smile.

"By God, they got him," one of the men said. "With a lousy arrow, at that. I told him, but he went looking for it and now he's found it. Look at him. One of them damn savages is behind that rock right by him; and no tellin' where the others are. I'm gettin' out of here."

"Maybe we ought to try gettin' him, Ed. He's dead all right, but I'd hate to see him scalped."

"To hell with him. He said he'd make meat, and by God he is—wolf meat. I told him I wouldn't and I won't. The silly bastard; the sad, sorry sonofabitch. Christ, what did he want to do that for? Come on, Goddamn you, get out of here before they feather you too."

Crazy Walking heard the clatter of horses moving hurriedly back along the trail, and slid down the bank beside the dead man. He picked up the rifle, levered a shell, and fired down the trail, catching a glimpse of the two riders as they rounded a bend. He fired another shot to hurry them along. He threw the gun down in quickly fleeting anger, and stood looking at the dead man in puzzlement and wonder. His hat had fallen off and his head was hairless and slick, but there was something familiar in the thin, bony face, something that spoke to Crazy Walking insistently; there was a tenderness and about the eyes a look of gratified desire. He stood looking with a feeling of profound understanding; but his mind was blank.

Red Moon and Lean Man came down the trail and both struck the body lightly with their bows, counting coup. Red Moon danced a few shuffling steps of a victory dance.

"This long knife wanted it bad, to come so far to get it,"

he said. "He makes love to the arrow. But there will be trouble, Grandson. The white men will want to strangle someone for this. They can have my breath; there is not much left."

"No, Grandfather. I gave him the gift and I can die, if need be. We will wait."

Lean Man touched the bald head with his toe.

"No good," he muttered. "He had nothing to be afraid of."

Crazy Walking turned and went back up the trail, finding the Blue Cloud and White Hawk standing beside High Bear. He was dead.

It was night again. Afoot, he followed the trail back down to the valley. The white hide was gone, but in the distance, beyond the willows, he could see a fire. The two men were sitting by it when he came close, hunched over in silence. Behind them at the edge of the light, he saw the hide, spread out on the ground. Neither wore pistols and their rifles were a few steps away leaning against their bedrolls. He watched them a little while and when they continued motionless, decided.

Walking back to the willows, he stripped to breechclout and moccasins and, leaving his bow and arrows with the clothes, returned. With no attempt at concealment, he walked quietly toward the fire. He reached the hide and, stooping, rolled it up, slowly and silently. He picked it up and, without turning, backed out of the light, keeping his eyes on the men.

In a moment he was again among the willows. Looking back, he saw one of the men rise and turn toward his bedroll. In the same instant he must have missed the hide because he made a dive for his rifle and the other followed as quickly. They lay by their bedrolls, peering out into the darkness, their rifles ready. After a little they started crawling away from the fire. Crazy Walking walked quietly back to his clothes.

It was still dark when he roused the old men. They found a trail that led up out of the stream bed and a little way along it found a single, twisted cedar with branching top. From ropes they made a platform for High Bear and put him on it, wrapped in the white hide.

They went on then. Glancing back from the ridge above, he saw the hide shining, a light falling into darkness. He did not look back again.

## ❧ 41 ❧

The wind had blown all night, curling round the house with straining, moaning sounds, eerie voices of the dark world outside. The house moved and creaked in collision with the long gusts; the lamp flame smoked and fluttered, filling the room with oily, reeking odor, marking the chimney with bowed, curving figures of black.

Leah sat beside her daughter's bed, sleepless, exhausted, the tension of her feelings rising and falling between the spasms of Christine's coughing, as if her very nerves were exposed to the wind's gusts. After each spasm the child would whimper and fall back, terror in her wide, violet eyes. The veins of her forehead, distended by the coughing, would disappear; the blueness of her face would fade to chalky white. The small hand that clutched Leah's with such fearful strength during the spasm would relax slowly and Leah's own fears subside.

Light came imperceptibly, greying in the air like dust, oppressive as darkness. Nothing, she thought, could lighten her loneliness.

Martin was stirring. From the bedroom came the droning sound of his morning prayers, rising and falling in waves on the surface of the wind. He had slept well, she knew. She heard him enter the kitchen and build up the fire, then rattle a pan ineffectually to signal without words his annoyance that breakfast was not begun. She remembered guiltily then that it was Sunday; he would need time to go over his sermon before the service. Still she did not rise, loath to leave the frightened child, knowing that Martin could not comfort her. In a little while he came into the room and stood looking at his daughter with a pained, withdrawn gaze. Leah knew he felt uncomfortable in the presence of sickness as if somehow it were involved with evil. He raised his hand to Christine's forehead, held it for a moment poised and almost touching, then let it fall again. The child flinched, then watched listlessly, showing no recognition.

In the dusty morning light he seemed far away.

"I've prayed," he said at last. "I believe He will help."

With an effort, Leah roused herself. "I'd like to bring the doctor."

Martin shook his head. "I think she's better; she'll get well, God willing, without the help of that white medicine man." His voice was full of scorn. "You might expect him to come equipped with drum and rattles and an Indian assistant or two. God forbid that I should bring such a man into my house."

"The Indians trust him," she said, not wanting to argue.

"Because he caters to their superstition, consulting with witch doctors. A doctor is helpless without God's help. Do you think He would truckle with magic?"

"I don't know. It's too much to bear alone."

"You've forgotten Him again. You'd better pray. The Indians themselves are turning to God for help in their sickness. We can do no less."

She turned her face away, unable to contend further, assailed again by the frenzied, oppressive noises of the wind. Beyond the latticed window, grey, changing figures of dust marched the road. Martin left without touching Christine and went back to the parlor to work on his sermon.

Leah rose and, wrapping Christine tightly in her blankets, carried her to the kitchen and put her in the rocking chair by the fire. With tremendous effort and concentration she began making breakfast.

Christine did not eat but sat watching Leah with wide, uncomprehending eyes. Part way through the meal she was struck again by the cough. Leah left the table to hold her, forgetting everything, almost losing her own consciousness in the child's seizure; her chest and throat ached, her eyes burned with tears, terror constricted her heart. When it was done, Martin had left the table, his meal unfinished. The door to the parlor was closed and she could hear him praying again. She took Christine back to her bed, closing the door to the room, and in a little while she heard him leave for the church.

The cough grew steadily worse. Between spasms Christine lay pale and hardly conscious, her breath quick and shallow, inaudible under the wind's breathing. Leah could stand it no longer. She left the house in panic, afraid to leave but afraid also to wait; she could not wait.

The wind was fierce, not a single force but many, whipping in drifting shapes of dust along the road, pushing at her with paralyzing, invisible force, sucking at her very breath. In front of the church a congregation of horses waited, humped up, rumps to the wind, enduring. A buggy top broke loose and blew, flapping and billowing among them, but they did not move or even notice. She had a desire to stop among them as if she might partake of their strange power.

She had never seen so many at the church before. The epidemic, Martin had said, was turning the Indians' thoughts toward the life after death. In the two months since the cattle hunt, they had changed much.

She made her way past the buggies, noticing in the steeple a faint movement of the bell and hearing above the wind a thin and faraway ringing. And for a moment, close to the church, she thought she could hear Martin's voice, exhorting the Indians.

The wind was broken in the square, but it was full of dust, swirling like water, banging and twisting the windmill. She passed the carpenter shop, keeping her face averted from the row of coffins in front, hurrying directly to the doctor's office. But he was not in. Her heart sank; she had not considered such a possibility. In desperation she inquired at the hotel and even at the carpenter shop but was told only that he had gone, perhaps to the Indian camp. At the road she hesitated; then, in final resolution, turned toward the camp.

A pack of starved-looking dogs came at her, barked briefly, and hurried back to the lodges to find shelter from the wind. From far along the circle came a faint sound of drumming and singing and the windy sound of rattles; nearer the sound of women keening, their voices contending hopelessly with the wind's fury. The flapping of lodge covers was the sound of wings.

She found the doctor's buggy near one of the lodges and entered, not waiting to be asked, stooping through the low entrance into a smoky darkness. Instantly she felt in the air a grief more bitter than her own. The doctor was there, haggard and unshaven, working over a boy who was lying on a robe on the ground. Beyond him a woman held a baby, weeping almost soundlessly, rocking. Leah could not see the woman's face or the baby's, yet instantly she knew that it was dead. The doctor did not notice her, and as she waited the boy was seized by a spasm of coughing. The doctor raised his shoulders up and supported them, holding the boy's chin down.

The spell over, he poured some medicine into a spoon and tried to induce the boy to take it, but he would not. He gritted his teeth and twisted his face away, struggling in terror. Only then, coming out of the haziness of her own misery, did Leah recognize the boy as Little Wound.

She knelt beside him, touching his outstretched hands. In his face the frenzy subsided, replaced by interest, then by recognition. She moved closer to sit beside him, and he leaned against her, tension draining from his body.

The doctor looked at her, relieved. "I'm past being surprised by the strange powers of medicine men; but to find the same magic in a minister's wife is something new. I thought he was afraid of all white people."

"I've met him before," she said simply, extending her hand for the medicine.

She held the spoon to the boy's lips, not touching them yet. He drew back a little and raised his hand to the spoon, following it to her hand, making sure that it was she who held it. Then, without hesitation, he opened his lips.

The doctor turned his attention to the two little girls, who were both coughing now. Leah watched a moment and was caught up again in her own panic. Little Wound stiffened and drew away, sensing her agitation. She touched his face and stood up, waiting for the doctor, awareness dimmed in her memory of Christine.

She rode back in the doctor's buggy; and in spite of her panic he drove slowly. Out of her own weariness, she realized that he must have worked almost beyond endurance.

He shook his head wearily. "I don't understand. They die so easily; there is no resistance. But you needn't worry," he assured her. "It isn't the same with white children. Just with these Indians, as if they wanted to die. But with the little ones, that can't be so. With the old ones maybe, but not the kids. I don't know. Since that crazy cattle hunt in the fall, they've gone downhill—as if they were rejuvenated for a while and had to pay for it with their lives."

Church had let out. Along the road they met the stream of Indian buggies plodding dejectedly into the wind. In front of the church Martin and Eagle Voice were talking, both holding their hats against the wind. When Martin saw Leah with the doctor he forgot the hat and it sailed off down

194

the road. He ran a few steps after it, then turned and came back to meet the buggy, his face clouded and stiff. But the doctor did not stop till he came to the gate in front of the house. He stepped down then and went around to the back for his case of medicines. Leah got down and ran to the house, hearing Martin expostulating with the doctor.

In her absence Christine had climbed out of bed and was on the floor now, shivering. When Leah picked her up and put her back in bed, she turned her face to the wall and cried bitterly, as if she had been betrayed.

The doctor came in, closing the door in front of Martin, his face set grimly, and began to examine Christine. She shrank from him at first but in a little while relaxed.

"You should have called me sooner," he told Leah sharply. But glancing at her, he went on with softened voice, "I guess you tried. You look all in. You ought to get some rest."

When he finished, he gave Leah a bottle of medicine and a little packet of leaves to burn as an inhalant. She followed the doctor and to her surprise found Eagle Voice in the kitchen with Martin. It was the first time the Indian had ever come in.

"It is a sacred song that was given me in a dream," he was saying. "It is good prayer in case of sickness of the young."

"No, no," Martin answered, with strained patience. "You see my position. I am a Christian. I cannot compromise my beliefs. This is a kind of magic and no good can come of it to me or mine."

"I am a Christian too," Eagle Voice argued. "But I see much good also in the beliefs of the old ones. My own children had the coughing sickness, but I made offerings to the spirit powers as I was directed in a dream, the same in which the song was given me. They took pity on me and all my children live."

As he talked he took off his coat, then the stiff white shirt, and stood before them, naked to the waist. Leah caught her breath at what she saw: all his chest and both his arms were decorated with dark figures—crescents, crosses, pipes, bird forms—there was hardly an inch of skin not covered. But the designs were not painted; they were dark red, unhealed scars.

He pointed to the scars. "With each I offered a prayer for

my children. The prayers were heard. And with the sacred song I have helped others also. I would like to help you."

"He has some kind of power," the doctor said, "at least with his own people."

"No," Martin almost shouted. "Get out now. I can't stand any more."

The doctor shrugged and picked up his case. Eagle Voice put his shirt and coat back on and stood again in powerful dignity, his dark face puzzled and hurt.

"I can't do any more now," the doctor told Leah. "She has a chance; it's up to her now—and you."

When Leah tried to pay him, he waved it away.

"I'll be asking you for help soon, I think. Will you do it?"

She looked at Martin, seeing him stiffen; but he did not turn to look at her. On the instant, she was given strength.

"Yes," she promised. "Yes."

Eagle Voice and the doctor left; Leah turned with courage to her daughter's room.

※ 42 ※

Though she could not see the sun, Christine could feel the light growing, increasing like sound heard in distance, approaching; a white fountain rising; a blooming of fire. And the light became distance, far to the world's edge where mountains rose, blue and shining as glass.

She was alone on a wide plain of yellow, moving easily as a bird skimming, the grass feathery at her feet, turning under and back; and in the distance the light on the mountains growing, flaring upward shadowless, till her eyes burned and she turned back in terror.

There was shadow now, a spot of darkness in the distance, blurred as a cloud, moving as slowly. And far off, faint, a sound beginning as the light had done, a sound of singing. She had stopped moving; and she could not turn again toward the light.

The shadow darkened and took shape: a horse and rider

coming toward her, the sound of hoofs a drumming to the far-off singing. There was dust behind them, a feathery billow, swirling smoky, drawn toward her, covering the light. And the sound grew like the dust, not singing now but wailing, a sad, darkening sound rising out of the earth. The cloud enveloped her, darkly enfolding, smothering her with dusty, fiery odor. She was seized by coughing that clutched with terrible hands at her throat . . .

Her eyes opened on the dark yellow light of the room. And on the table, near her, the lamp flame glinted, hard as a rock inside a shining bubble.

Dimly, she saw her mother, insubstantial, clothed in light; and her father, a shadow beyond the lamp, dark, silent, his glasses glimmering. Under his hand a match flared blindingly and with sulphurous odor. A dish appeared on the table, born of light, filled with dry leaves. The light lowered toward the dish, fluttering, burned low and went out. But from the dish a ribbon of smoke curled upward. The ribbon was broken and she saw that he was blowing on the dish. Embers appeared, bright ragged edges of red among the leaves. Then the blowing stopped and smoke and yellow flame grew in the dish.

The room was full of curling smoke, consuming the light, and she could not breathe. She reached out her hands and for an instant touched her mother's face; then that too, like the light, was gone . . .

She was at the window, staring out through bars of darkness; and yet she could see the road, illumined with faint blue light, the white tracks stretching into the night. As she waited the darkness rose, like curtains lifting; the bars dissolved in light, and she was moving weightlessly along the road toward the world's edge, seeing far ahead the shining, glassy mountains of light. She could not turn back.

## 43

Martin focused his eyes toward the front of the church and for an instant was aware with brilliant clarity of the scene around him. It was like awakening to a strange place and finding it revealed in glaring light; yet the church was dark. In the pulpit Eagle Voice was speaking—Martin could not tell how long the Indian had been there; had not even been aware that he was to speak. But he was there, his strange vitality surrounding him like a light. And for a moment Martin had the terrifying impression that the man was performing some heathen ritual in the church: with hypnotic grace and dignity, he moved back and forth behind the pulpit, pausing each time to speak, and again moving. And suddenly Martin realized that he was carrying two roles: speaker and interpreter. It was like him, Martin thought; heathen-like, he considered the ceremony more important than the thought.

He watched the Indian in fascination, not listening to the words—it was one of his own sermons—but carried along by the performance, seeing himself reflected in the man's mimicry. Inside the pulpit, the Indian's demeanor assumed a subtle haughtiness, almost a fierceness, and he spoke in clipped, austere English; but moving out to the place of interpreter, a warmth came over his face and his tones softened; his words became musical, almost a singing. The contrast was clear and disconcerting.

Martin tried in confusion to compose the scene around him. He had a feeling of helplessness, as if he had been dropped abruptly and unprepared into the midst of an ordeal. He had not made arrangements for Eagle Voice to speak; remembering hazily what he had done in the past few days, he realized that he had made no arrangements at all. Leah must have done everything alone. He would not have thought it possible. With detachment, he wondered if he had been ill. In any case, he would not have chosen an Indian to speak at his daughter's funeral; yet he knew of no one else. There were almost no white people in the church—since the epidemic they stayed close to their homes—only Westland and the doctor, neither of whom had been inside the church before. He glanced at them and saw them watching Eagle Voice's unusual performance with intense interest. He resented their presence, yet at the same time was glad of their company.

With renewed shock, he saw the small coffin below the pulpit, resting on two chairs, and in vision saw the white, waxen face of his daughter. The coffin was open; and he was possessed by an urgent desire to close it, to shield her from the staring of the Indians. Yet instantly he felt the darkness and oppression of the box and was seized by terror. He could not accept her death.

The services were finished. He saw Leah standing over him, her hand under his arm to help him rise. Her face looked down at him as from a distance, white, drawn, her skin of waxen transparency. In her eyes he saw concern for himself which was yet cool and impersonal. He stood and she was suddenly gone; seeing her in the aisle, he followed in panic, clutching at her arm. And as he touched her he remembered the blind Indian boy running away and was himself for an instant lost in darkness.

The day was cloudy and windless; as he stood beside Leah outside the church, a silent, heavy snow began, curtaining the distance, flakes disappearing instantly as they struck. He saw Eagle Voice drive up in a spring wagon and stop before the gate, and in a moment two men—the doctor and Westland —carried the coffin out and placed it in the back. The lid was on now and the new wood darkened and shone with beads of melted snow.

The Indian drove slowly away, sitting straight and rigid in the seat, conscious of his power and leadership, Martin thought resentfully. With Leah he walked behind, aware of the Indians following, yet with a sense of loneliness, of lostness, as if the enclosing fall of snow shut him off from them, and from his wife as well. He could hear her beside him, could even touch her; yet with white, altered face, she seemed distant and untouchable as a stranger.

The air was heavy with the smell of wet earth and, oddly, dust, uncovered and raised by the wagon wheels. There was no sound save the muffled rattle of the wagon and a soft whispering of moccasined feet behind him.

Following the wagon, aware of Eagle Voice ahead, riding

in dignity and poise, he felt submerged in breathless depths, as if the snow had become suddenly liquid, impeding his movements. He felt like falling down in the road and weeping.

Hearing hoofbeats on the road ahead, he glanced up and through the snow saw a rider approaching. Instantly he recognized the man as Crazy Walking, who had not been seen since the cattle hunt, when he had killed the white man. He was riding a spotted horse that looked as if it were covered with a blanket of snow through which little round patches had melted. He was wrapped to his ears in a red blanket; his face was marked with designs of red and in his hair were two eagle feathers, symbols of coups. (Martin wondered uneasily if one stood for the white man.) He who had been as near as any Indian to becoming civilized was suddenly the very embodiment of savagery. The man greeted Eagle Voice, but seeing the coffin his eyes dropped and his face became serious.

Martin avoided his glance, but he was shocked to see the Indian look at Leah with direct, open gaze. He made a hand sign Martin could not understand and rode on by, not looking back. Martin glanced apprehensively back along the line at the Indian policeman, Four Guns, wondering if he would make the arrest now, but found him assiduously looking the other way. Martin was grateful for an instant, not wanting an interruption. But as Crazy Walking rode on toward the agency, he was seized by anger; he hated the Indian in the red blanket more than he had ever hated anyone before.

"He'll get away from them again, you'll see," he said to Leah, aware as he saw the startled look in her eyes that he had almost shouted.

"What are you talking about?" she asked.

"Crazy Walking. They'll look the other way, these Indian police, and they know he killed a white man."

"His children are dying," Leah said. "That's why they look the other way."

He said nothing more. His surprising anger was gone now, leaving him shaken and slightly nauseated.

Eagle Voice turned off the road into the cemetery and drew up beside a newly made grave. He got down from the wagon and stood beside the grave facing east, his dark face and glossy black suit glistening with fast melting snow flakes. He did not look at anyone or speak, but when the two men had lifted the coffin from the wagon and placed it by the grave, he raised his hands to the sky. He threw his head back, exposing his face to the direct fall of snow and, in his own tongue, prayed.

Martin was shocked. In the church he knew the man would not have committed such a breach of form; he would have prayed with lowered head, submissively, as a Christian. But never having experienced a white funeral, he had reverted, Indian-like, to the ways of the pagan. Martin listened in indignation, but there was nothing he could do.

Then, without changing his attitude, Eagle Voice gave the translation of his prayer: "God, mysterious one, look down in pity on this small white child; with tenderness show her the far spirit path among the stars to that last home of her people; she who knew the loneliness of the small island in a sea of alien people; who knew no other young ones like herself, being different from the children of the Indian. Spread for her small feet the wide, easy path. And the long journey finished, among friends let her rest in joy."

Finished, he remained with hands outstretched for a long time, face still exposed to the fall of snow, bright with its beaded moisture. And his eyes were filled with tears.

Again the weakness and nausea seized Martin. He could not believe the man's tears were genuine; yet they affected him deeply. He was at once resentful and possessed by a necessity to weep. But he could not open his heart to grief. He stood numbly, in tension, hardly aware of the lowering coffin, starting in agony when he heard the first sound of dirt raining on the wood.

Beside him Leah was crying, her head uncovered to the thickening snow. In her white face, revealed by grief, he saw an unlooked-for beauty that struck him as deeply as the death of the child. He looked away, shutting his eyes to the fall of snow, his ears to the final relentless sound of the raining dirt. A dark weight descended on him, buckling his knees, crushing out his breath . . .

He felt himself being led toward the wagon, and with tremendous effort climbed into the seat.

## 44

Little Wound awakened slowly to the still, odorless lodge, with consciousness returning a sense of emptiness, aloneness —not loneliness, but of himself as the only presence in all the world. There were odors in the lodge, he knew, but he could not perceive them—the sickness had taken away his sense of smell. He could feel the air in movement, but it was flat and meaningless in his nose, telling him nothing of its origin or the ways it had gone. There was a fire, burned down to coals—he could feel the slight and steady heat on his face —and not enough to warm the air that was cold with the dampness of snow. He stretched his hand toward the wall of the lodge, intending to feel the snow, but he could not reach it and suddenly it seemed far away. He sat up to move but was seized by dizziness and a fit of coughing that dropped him back breathless on his pallet.

For a long time he lay in suspension; he wanted to sleep, to release all holds, to sink splashless in quiet waters. Yet he held to the edge of consciousness, trying to probe the blankness and silence around him with only touch and the tenuous vision of his skin. He knew his mother was there, motionless, asleep or awake he could not tell, but he could feel her presence. This and the fire, like faint sunlight on his face, he was sure of, but there was a blankness, an emptiness beyond the failure of his perception. The conviction brought him fully awake, and he lay gathering the strength to move, not the weakness of his body alone holding him back but a pervasive dread. He tried to imagine what seemed a journey across the lodge but each time was seized by coughing and had to begin anew, lying back in exhaustion. And each time, floating in weakness, a vision recurred of a bright yellow field with brown animals fleeing; and each time he was drawn backward as into a tunnel, the light in distance shrinking and himself struggling upward in darkness.

The violent alternation continued and he did not move from his bed. But after a time he recalled the night of the drumming, finding strength in the strong tactile memory of the drums, of himself lifted by the beat and rhythm, possessed of a power beyond his own. He found himself sitting, the robe thrown off, and for the moment there was no cough to throw him back without breath. He moved slowly, holding the vision of the drumming, the dancing. He could not stand; his legs would not lift him, so he crawled, not anticipating what his search would bring. And as he crawled, his hands explored with hunger the dusty floor of the lodge, drawing from it comfort and strength.

He found the pallets of the two small sisters, expecting them to be empty, but they were not: cold doll-forms wrapped in blankets were there; the girls were gone. He did not examine the dolls further, but lay on his face in a fit of coughing, and when he was able, went on to find his mother and the baby. He could not find the baby at all; but he found his mother sitting by the fire, not asleep but distant and quiet. He touched her face lightly and moved back in wonder when she did not respond, not hurt but more intensely alone. In her aloofness, with no familiar person odor, she seemed a stranger. It was a sickness, he decided.

He started back to his pallet, the short distance stretching out interminably to his tired body. He had to pass the pallets of his sisters and, passing, was seized again by coughing. When it was finished he tried to go on but could not—he was compelled to stay. In dread he touched one of the still forms, letting his hand this time explore the face, holding his breath against the cough.

His fingers recoiled at the coldness—a coldness of stone —but he could not take his hand away. It followed the small features, fingers not touching but skimming the surface, knowing of themselves the contours, building in his heart the touch-image of the known face, Her Eagle Robe.

Again the coughing racked him—he could not control it— and he lay face down, fingers gripping the cool, foot-packed earth, grains of sand and the powdery, smooth dust familiar and comforting. He was shivering when the spasm was done, muscles trembling and jerking as he raised himself to hands and knees, breath chittering in his throat. But he could not leave till he had touched the other—not touched (he could not bear the coldness) but perceived the face with his hands, as Pretty Shield, and he could leave.

He found his robe and burrowed under it, coughing, chilled, desiring sleep with all his heart; but it would not come. He saw himself wrapped unmoving in a cold blanket, and he knew that they had lost more than light and sound and smell. They were dolls only now, unfeeling, unperceiving.

His hand reached out to touch the cool, solid earth while the cough shook him in crushing unending spasm, dropping him finally into numbness and a kind of sleep. But his hand moved on the earth, separating, examining sand and dust and grass, following with fascination the bending, curving surface around his pallet . . .

He awakened again, perceiving a faint odor, unrecognized, yet familiar, realizing only after a time that his sense of smell was returning. Fire fluttered warmly at the center of the lodge—his fingers on the earth caught faintly its little explosions; smoke was sharp in the air.

His hand walked around his pallet exploring and was caught in a warm, firm grasp. The faint odor returned and he knew the hand as that of the white woman who had given him relief from the cough, who before that had brought him back when he was lost.

He sat up weakly and touched her face and found her lips smiling. He made the question sign, asking about the empty lodge, but she did not answer; her hands were dumb. And yet he found in them comfort and reassurance.

She washed his face with a warm cloth and gave him food that for the first time in many days he could taste. And when he had finished, she propped him up with robes and placed in his hands a lump of pliable, odorous clay. He tried to taste it but she put her hand over his lips preventing him.

He made the question sign again, and she took the clay from him and, holding it close so his hands could follow, began working it with her hands. He was puzzled at first, but his hands followed the deft movements, perceiving with joy a form growing out of the clay, an animal with blunt, flat nose and curving horns, humped shoulders and sloping back, curiously like the stone his grandfather had shown him. She stopped and gave him the figure to hold; and when he had examined it, took it again and rolled it into a ball.

He was surprised when she gave him back the shapeless lump; but in a moment his hands were busy, shaping it to his own vision; and he was smiling, dreaming with delight of all the forms of earth his fingers could fashion.

Beside him, the woman sat quietly, and he could feel her presence warm as an emanation of the fire.

## 45

"I realize," the Major told Westland, "that you're here to study these Indians, not get involved with them, and I wouldn't ask you if there were anyone else who could do it. But my police can't find him—and I can't say that I blame them."

"It's all right," Westland answered reluctantly, "I guess I owe it to you. But I really don't see that I can help much. I don't think Crazy Walking will come in; he knows as well as you or I that he'll never get a fair trial in a white court."

"Maybe. If it were any other Indian I'd say you were right. But this man is different. All he has to do is put on civilized clothing and talk English and you can't tell him from a white man. He's got a good case; it was in defense of the old men. Any court will acquit him if he'll just do as I say."

"That's just it—he won't. I don't think you'll ever see him in white man's clothes again. I can't really say why. I just know it."

"Well, you may be right, but I've got to try. Here it is, the middle of December—two months it's been now. If I don't bring him in soon, the army will send troops; if they do, some innocent people will get killed. He ought to see that. It's only reasonable for him to come in."

"I don't know. I don't think reason has anything to do with it. The whole thing is unreasonable, not only the Indians chasing the cow but those cowboys chasing the Indians. And what's reasonable about this eye for an eye kind of justice? The Indian way of making reparation to the family of the injured is more reasonable. Look at it from their point of view: what good will it do to kill Crazy Walking? No one can eat him or use his hide. It wasn't an act of war, that calls for revenge. On the other hand, they've offered almost the entire wealth of the band as reparation—ten times what would be paid in the death of another Indian. And I think they would even offer him as a substitute if they didn't realize the extent of the white man's prejudice."

"Well, maybe it isn't reasonable, but justice is justice, that's all there is to it."

"No, you've already admitted, justice is only justice for someone in civilized clothing. But there's no point in trying to reason it out, no more for us than for him. If I find him I'll explain as well as I can; but there's really no explanation. It's not a pleasant task—especially since he's in mourning."

"No. But anyway, tell him what I said. I can promise to get him off with no more than a light sentence if he'll do as I say. And, by the way, stop in and see his boy at the minister's house before you go so you can take word about him. I think he's about well, though. You know, I wouldn't have thought Martin would take in an Indian like that—it's big of him."

"He didn't do it," Westland said sharply. "His wife did. And I'd have stopped anyway."

"What the devil," the Major laughed. "What did I say to pique you like that?"

"Nothing," Westland said, leaving. "Nothing at all."

It was Martin who met him at the door, looking peaked and woebegone, but he seemed pleased at having company.

"It's like living alone, having the boy here," he said, gesturing toward the bedroom. "She spends all her time with him—when she's not helping the doctor."

"How is he?"

"Better, I think. How can I tell? I can't communicate with him any more than with an animal."

"There's sign talk, you know."

"I know—Leah is learning it, but it's impossible for me. I think the boy should learn the finger alphabet, but she has no enthusiasm for it, and I certainly can't teach him. It's a pity, but what can the world mean to him without light or sound?"

"Everything in the world except light and sound. Is he asleep?"

"How do I know? He never makes a sound anyhow. It gives you the creeps; he's as likely to be up exploring the house in the night as in the day, moving around in perfect blackness like a ghost; he won't sleep in a bed. I'm ashamed to feel so—after all he's only a child—but I don't see how she can stand it."

Leah came out of the bedroom and beyond her Westland caught a glimpse of Little Wound sitting on the floor. She was looking better than he had expected, pale and tired, but in her face he sensed a new strength and warmth. She smiled and, without a word, led him to Little Wound.

The boy recognized him and was on his feet instantly, hands fluttering with questions. But there was nothing Westland could tell him of his family, only that he was going to them now and would bring word.

There were a number of clay figures on the floor where Little Wound had sat, crude animal forms with simple, massive lines that made him think of monuments. Some were damp and unfinished, some baked and rubbed smooth. Little Wound picked up one of them, a simple humped figure—not a buffalo, Westland knew, but a buffalo stone—and making the question sign to Leah, pointed to the figure, then to Westland, finally making the sign for father.

She nodded, at a loss for the sign for yes. Westland showed her; Little Wound, standing near, followed the movement and, sensing the shift of attention, touched Leah's hand in mid-air, catching the sign with delight—not at the answer, but at Leah's having made it.

He handed the figure to Westland then, catching Leah's hand, moved it through the sign again, shaping the fingers, guiding them through the graceful bowing movement. He patted her hand with approval and made the sign for good —level with the heart. Catching his meaning, she flushed with pleasure, as Westland did also; and for a moment the three of them, hands touching, were joined in understanding.

When Westland was ready to leave, Leah accompanied him to the kitchen; but Little Wound did not follow. Westland talked with Martin and Leah for a while; and only after he was on the road did he realize that he had spoken in words to Martin only; to Leah he had spoken in sign. He found himself remembering not what she said but the movements of her hands and body, seeing her more intimately than ever before, revealed as in a dance.

An Indian policeman came along as guide, taking him to the edge of the badlands beyond White River, where he supposed Crazy Walking would be camped. They found an old campsite and, by some logic mysterious to Westland, the Indian said that the latest camp would be at the next stream. Then he went back, leaving Westland to proceed alone.

He found the camp as the guide had predicted and Crazy Walking rode out to meet him, greeting him with a cordiality that made him self-conscious about his mission. He was unwilling to enunciate the Major's message. A few weeks since he would have done it without hesitation; but something had changed. He sensed a new integrity in Crazy Walking that would admit of no compromise.

He was surprised at the man; he had expected to find him broken and hopeless, having lost his family and come face to face with death because of the killing. Instead he seemed like one just come to manhood; his presence was vital, galvanic. He led the way to the camp, helped unpack and take care of the horses, observing with enthusiasm the immense pack of meat Westland had brought. He was both pleased and startled by the clay figure; he turned it over and over in his hand with a kind of reverence, giving it at last to Blue Fawn, who wrapped it in a piece of cloth and put it in a medicine bundle.

"It has some kind of power," was all he said.

It was Blue Fawn who showed most the effects of grief. She was numbed and distracted, hardly aware of her surroundings. Her eyes moved incessantly with an expression of fear, as if with each glance she expected to encounter some new horror. After greeting him briefly, she went about her work, moving always, but mechanically and without vigor.

Turning Hawk seemed unchanged, his dignity and reserve unbroken; there was only a tightening around the eyes, almost a crossing, a subtle expression of pain and sadness. It was he who questioned Westland at greatest length about Little Wound and how he was faring under Leah's care. He was comforted by what Westland had to tell him, expressing such a deep and earnest gratitude—as if Westland had come only for that purpose—that he was again discomfited and prevented from mentioning his mission. He felt awkward and callow in the old man's presence.

It was evening. Westland had brought his tent but, invited into the lodge, he did not set it up. Instead, he turned all his supplies over to Blue Fawn, and in a little while a pot of meat was boiling over the fire. And by the expectant, eager attitude of the two men, he knew they had been hungry. They had made no complaints, but now, with food in prospect their spirits rose.

Still Westland did not say why he had come but brought out his notebook and began again his questioning about the old ways. Always before the two men had been able, though slightly reluctant, informants. But they were changed now, become eager for him to get it all down with no error. They moved from one custom to another, each supplementing the other and with such logical organization that Westland suspected they had been planning his lessons. It was late in the night when they finally stopped; but he could not sleep, lying engrossed in what he had learned, bothered by an uneasiness, a deep reluctance to face up to his task.

The next day he hunted with Crazy Walking, and in the evening they did not come back but made camp in the badlands. They sat around an open fire in the twilight, and Crazy Walking went on with his lessons, explaining the hand game, singing an intricate, meaningless song as he swung his hands and arms, changing the two small sticks from one hand to the other. The rhythm of the song started and stopped, moved slow or sprinted in surprising ways, but always in perfect accord with the movement of hands and arms. It was more than a game, Westland perceived; it was an art with a rich emotional content and beauty of expression.

After he had learned some of the movements and a few of the songs, Crazy Walking suggested that they play for small stakes, and made some peeled willow counters to keep the score. It was then that he anticipated Westland and spoke about the Major, changing unaccountably from his own tongue to English.

"I suppose there's nothing except stretching my neck that will satisfy him?"

"It isn't him. He knows as well as I that you did only what you had to do. It's the government that wants you—to stand trial. That doesn't necessarily mean that you'll hang."

Crazy Walking was amused. "You don't really believe that, do you? An Indian get a fair trial in a white man's court? No, you don't believe it and neither do I. I'd play the hand game with the judge—even though I did no wrong. That would at least be interesting, and I'd have a chance."

"No, he couldn't do it. What the Major had to say was this: If you dress up like a white man and speak English as you are now, he's sure you'll be acquitted or at worst get only a light sentence." He paused, then added quickly, seeing a clouding of the Indian's expression, "It wasn't my idea—I didn't think you would. It's just a suggestion. What the Major is really worried about is the army; if you don't come in, they'll send troops and someone is likely to get killed."

"He means if I don't come in, someone will die in my place?"

"Something like that. It's hard to explain."

"If I were white, I'd come in. But I'm not. And I'm not afraid to die; but to strangle like a dog at the end of a rope is a hard thing for an Indian. With his last breath the Indian's soul leaves his body; to choke him imprisons his soul. This is something I have heard from the old ones. I don't know."

"Then you won't come in?"

"I don't know. Maybe, if others must die in my place."

He paused; then, laughing, suggested, "We can decide it with the hand game. If you win all the counters I come in; if I win, I don't." He hesitated, and shook his head. "No, that's no gamble. You risk nothing; I risk my life. If I win you have to do something for me. There is Little Wound— when I die he will have no protector. You will do what you can for him. That will be your gamble: to be an uncle to a blind deaf Indian boy."

"That's no gamble either," Westland told him, "I'd do that anyway."

"No matter. You can't really expect to win. This is an Indian game—as your court game is white."

He counted out a dozen each of the peeled sticks for himself and Westland; then, taking the two small ones—one colored, the other plain—began shifting them back and forth, swinging his hands and arms, singing in a strong, nasal baritone. He was smiling, enjoying the performance. Yet Westland felt an artistic intent that was purposeful and moving. He was himself interested in the game, its cultural uses and significance, but he could not concentrate on that. There was an involvement greater than scientific interest and beyond a participation in a mock-serious gambling game. In some way he was joined with this Indian who was at once a friend and a fantastic stranger, almost another species. He had never felt so strongly the closeness or the distance.

Across the fire from him Crazy Walking stopped singing, hands extended, waiting for him to guess which held the unmarked stick. Bemused, he had not tried to follow the movements, so he only guesssed now and guessed wrong. He surrendered a counter and Crazy Walking began again. He was not smiling now but was intent and serious. He had thrown off his robe and was naked to the waist, the skin over his

supple, smoothly sliding muscles glinting coppery in the firelight, his eyes feverish, face expressionless as stone. His hands
and arms moved in graceful bird flights, the incantatory syl-
lables following in perfect accord. Again Westland did not
try to follow the unmarked stick but sat entranced, yet with
a feeling of apprehension.

To the west the sun had dropped; and though all the sky
was solid with heavy clouds, the tops of the hills were struck
with a brilliant brassy light slanting upward from an unseen
rift beyond. Mist coming up over the sharp, bright edges
flared up like flames, dispersing upward white as smoke, the
color lost. The mountain itself—the very rock—seemed to
burn. But on the near side was only cold and darkness, the
horizon a sharp fiery edge of division.

Again he guessed and lost, but with an ambiguity of feeling he did not understand. He did not especially care to see
Crazy Walking come in—he would feel a certain responsibility, though he had no power to help. As for himself, losing
would mean little; he was committed to nothing he had not
intended before. Yet with each new movement of the game,
he became more tense and apprehensive. And suddenly he
was paying strict attention, trying to follow the fleeting sticks
as if his very life depended on it.

At last he made a lucky guess and took the pieces in his
own hands. But he was awkward and self-conscious, the be-
ginner, the novitiate, forgetting the words, dropping the sticks.
He was given several chances, sensing that Crazy Walking
was guessing wrong only to encourage him. Then he lost the
sticks and sat again as the loser, his care deepening. At the
same time he sensed a rising of the Indian's spirits, as if
somehow in the game he were losing his troubles as he gained
the counters.

At length, Westland lost all his counters, surrendering the
last one with despair. And yet he was glad that Crazy Walking had not agreed to come in.

Crazy Walking laughed, reading his feeling at the loss:
"It's only a game; you have lost nothing; I have gained nothing. I could not come in and give myself up to be strangled
like a dog. And yet I think it has helped me decide what I
will do." He stood up, a radiance in his face, almost a happi-
ness; yet Westland was struck with dread.

"The Major is right—I can't let others die in my place,
so I will come in; but not to surrender. Tell the Major to

211

have a troop of cavalry in the little valley at the mouth of Yellow Creek—that's near Fort Summers. I'll fight them there, and they can kill me. If they think this is a joke and don't show up, I'll attack the fort and kill anyone I see."

Westland nodded, heart sinking. "When?"

"Right away." Crazy Walking paused, counting on his fingers. "Say four days from now—the first day of winter. A good day to die."

The next day Westland packed up to leave. Sensing his despair, Turning Hawk told him, "You do not understand: it is what he has to do. It is one of the changes within the cup. In the past he would have gone against the enemy until he died, would have gained honor and strengthened the people. Now—he cannot hurt the enemy; but for a little while he can lift up the hearts of the people."

Westland left then, riding toward the agency in sorrow, and yet with a new serenity of feeling.

## 🌿 46 🌿

It was still dark, but in the southeast a bright star shimmered in a pale blue pool among dark hills of cloud. Crazy Walking stood outside the circle of the camp, watching the star in its brief shining, heart open and alive to wonder and mystery.

There was still drumming and singing in the camp; he could hear without attention the strains of an honoring song, for himself, he knew. He had been honored much by the people; his heart was full. Yet he could not stay in camp. It was not a restlessness in him but a need—a necessity to travel a road he did not yet know—that drew him away.

He caught his horses, the old one with the spotted rump and a young bay to ride on the trail, leaving them at the edge of camp while he returned to the lodge for his medicine bundle, bow and arrows, and a little meat. It was all he would need. He left quietly as if going on a raid, though he knew no one would stop him. The road he would travel now was his own; he could only follow it alone.

He struck directly south, though there was no trail; and on his left the star shone fitfully as the clouds broke and closed and again broke. They showed red as the sun rose, then closed solid, and the star was gone. But he knew now where he was going; it was a long way and there was only a day and a night to go and return.

The weather was cloudy and cold, the roads deserted. He saw no one till in the afternoon when he left the reservation and turned west along the railroad. He began to pass white men's houses then, far spaced along the road, and traveled uneasily long stretches that were fenced on both sides. Children playing outside the houses ran at sight of him, and from the windows he saw white frightened faces peering out. At one a man, holding a rifle nervously, stepped out to watch him pass. He half expected the man to shoot, yet he did not hurry or look back.

He watched all with avid interest and was yet detached; he seemed to move in two lands, the one of memory and the one he traveled, this one clear to his eyes, his nose and ears, yet fading intermittently to that other, different land that it had been. Only the hills, the streams, the contours, and in the distance the red, blue edge of the world, like a divide between the two, were the same. All else was different, even the seasons. The land of his memory was one he had known at all seasons of the year, yet now he saw it only in the green of spring. The grey, bleak land he traveled was one of winter; it could never green again.

He crossed a valley and rode into the hills, the colored distance receding before him, and in the evening came to the butte where he had made his vision quest. But it was south of the tracks and his horses would not cross. He left them tied in some brush and on foot followed the gash the road cut in the side of the hill till he found a place he could climb out. In the dusk he made his way upward, reaching a flat, out-jutting point of rock above the railroad. He stepped to the edge of the rock to rest, seeing his horses below and hearing the first faint rumble of the train.

It came slowly, laboring on the grade, its thunderous puffing interspersed with short, sharp reports, like random gun-fire. After a long time it came into view, snaking slowly around a curve. Smoke billowed out of the stack into the quiet air and hung spreading, a widening dark road above the line of cars below.

The engine passed and the smoke drifted slowly toward him, boiling and swirling, opaque as mud. A gravel car came abreast, carrying a crowd of men. Seeing the horses below, some of them began yelling and throwing rocks. One with a gun looked up and, in just an instant before the smoke boiled between, saw Crazy Walking and raised his gun and fired. The bullet spun harmlessly off the rock; Crazy Walking did not move. The car was out of sight now under the smoke but the firing continued. He could hear the bullets whine high overhead, glancing off the rocks, and the men shouting below, lost under the smoke. The engine curved around the hill, dragging a black wake, and the whole train was lost as in a tunnel. He could see nothing but the smoke, so dense it seemed he could walk on it. It rose slowly, spreading till it blotted out the whole land, enveloping him, searing his lungs flame-like, sulphurous, bringing tears to his eyes. He held his breath and moved down the hill and the smoke thinned, dissipating upward. The noise of the train faded, but before it was gone the whistle floated back to him, drawn out, descending, a strange, mechanical cry, dying in distance. He started upward again, but stopped, no longer drawn; something had changed.

Night had come suddenly as if the smoke had turned to darkness, blanketing the whole earth. Above, the hill faded into the black sky, invisible now. Below he heard the horses struggling and snorting, and turned and went down the hill.

He found the spotted one down and tangled in rope and brush, no longer struggling but snorting with distended nostrils, rolling white, terror-stricken eyes. The bay was hanging back on the rope with braced feet, infected by the fear of the other, breath coming in snoring gasps. He sat by the spotted one, talking and stroking the trembling neck till his breathing quieted, then untangled the rope and let him up.

He started back then, released from the need that had brought him; yet he took another trail, not realizing till later that it would take him past the place where he had danced the medicine dance and had given a day to the people.

Darkness was complete now; he could see nothing of the trail, but the horses moved with confidence, so he let them go. The country was familiar; he could tell where he was even in darkness by what he perceived through the horse, his mind

214

fitting in the shapes he could not see. But when he tried to remember it in the green of spring, he could not. He knew how it looked now: burned and dust-drifted after the year of drought, gashed by the plow in the little valleys and in the hills by the sharp hoofs of crowding cattle. But in his mind the past would not return, as if the smoke, the darkness had spread within him.

Before he reached the place he saw a fire, taking it at first to be a campfire. But it was too large; and in its light he saw a building that might have been a house. He had not expected a house; he thought perhaps he was lost, yet knew he was not. The fire was fitful, dying down, then flaring up brightly, but growing. White smoke poured out of it, hanging low to the ground and moving off slowly like river mist. Closer, he saw figures moving in and out of the light, and now and then showers of sparks rising and sudden puffs of white.

It was a house burning, he saw now; the puffs of white, steam from buckets of water thrown on the blaze by the running figures. The building he had seen was a barn by a corral, where the dance circle had been. There was a stream near the house with a smooth slope up the far side on which the figures ran, carrying water. On the near side the bank was high and steep with clumps of willows and bushes rising along its edge.

He rode in among them to the bank overlooking the fire and stopped to watch, fascinated by the frantic labor of the shadows that rushed back and forth in the light, throwing futile showers of water. The whole creek would not put out the fire, he thought.

As he watched, the roof caved in, a whirlwind of sparks towered in the air, and the whole house was aflame, lighting a wide circle in the night. He saw the corral clearly, a circle like the circle of the medicine dance, at the center a large post —the sacred tree—chopped off short and used as a snubbing post. He tried to recall the dance, himself swinging on the bloody thongs, but he could not. His vision was dark.

The two still ran with their buckets, the woman throwing the water from far back now, scarcely touching the flame. But the man ran in close, and puffs of steam, like signals, rose with each bucket he threw. Only over the fire the smoke rose; around the edges it drifted, clinging to the ground. It followed the creek bed, flowing whitely over the water, dimming the reflection of the flames. It crept in wisps over the bank where he sat, rising around him and moving off among the bushes, tenuous, changing wraiths.

The woman ran down the bank through the smoke and collapsed at the water's edge. But when the man kept working doggedly, she rose to her knees, sobbing, and tried to fill the bucket. She gave it up and sank back, as she did so raising her eyes toward the high bank where Crazy Walking sat. For an instant the smoke cleared and he sat quietly watching her, knowing she had seen him also.

She looked at him for a long time frozen in a half-reclining position. Then suddenly she was on her feet running up the bank to meet the man. She grabbed his arm and tried to stop him, but he thrust her aside and went on. She trotted after him trying to speak but it seemed a long time before she found her voice. She seized the man's arm as he dipped water and pointed across the stream.

"Over there—there's an Indian over there."

The man glanced up, but the smoke was thick between. Again he pushed the woman aside and trotted back up the bank with the sloshing bucket. The woman followed, clutching at his arm. When he tried to throw the water, she caught the edge of the bucket. The water flew upward in the firelight, drenching them both.

"Damn it woman, stay out of the way. Have you gone crazy?"

"It's no use," the woman said in a broken, chattering voice. "The house is gone. Stop it now; you've got to look. There's an Indian over there. I saw him plain, and I'm scared."

She was pointing again. The man looked but shook his head, walking back toward the creek. "Hell, there hasn't been an Indian here in ten years. You're seein' things. Set down and rest."

"But I saw him. The smoke cleared and I saw him plain, sitting there on a horse in blanket and feathers."

The man strained his eyes through the smoke for a long time and Crazy Walking was sure he could see. But he turned toward the fire again.

"It's your imagination, woman. Hell, the Indians are gone from here. They're rare as buffalo. In a few years there won't be one anywhere; they'll be extinct. But this is one hell of a time to be worryin' about Indians—no roof over our heads and a snowstorm settin' in. That's something to worry about."

The smoke was clearing now but the snow was beginning.

Once more the woman looked at him, through an avenue clear of smoke, laced only with lightly falling snow. She seized the man's arm once more and turned him from the fire. He looked directly at Crazy Walking, then laughed and turned away. The woman turned also and did not look back. He left, riding down the creek to find a crossing, emerging finally from the drifting smoke with a haunting sense of having been invisible.

It was snowing steadily now, yet there was light, an emanation from the snow itself. He could see nothing by it, not even his horse's head, only the white, gently swirling dome of snow that enclosed him, moving with him as he rode.

After the train and the fire, he was glad of the quiet and darkness, finding in it a peace, an answering to the quiescence within himself. The snow touched his face coolly, whispering around him like gentle rain. He could feel it building on the ground, muffling the sound of the hoofs. Closing his eyes, he could still see the swirling, falling white and feel a building within his heart.

It was daylight when he reached the little valley of Yellow Creek. He rode to the upper end, finding a grove of small cottonwoods for the horses to browse on, and climbed the hill to sit in the quiet snowfall, waiting. He was still at peace: his body was relaxed and quiet as after a long sleep; but within him was a stirring, a beginning movement like water flowing, swirling gently, imperceptibly increasing.

The sky was clearing. The clouds moved off, leaving a gentle afterfall of snow lacing the sky in thin streaks as the sun came out. The land was revealed in blinding white, the blanketed hills moving off to the world's edge, to blue and purple distance. He stood, awareness increasing to a painful vividness he had never known, like blood returning to frozen limbs, within him the strange movement increasing, expanding like a sound, gathering to a powerful, irresistible force. He stood, raising arms and eyes to the blinding sun, staying so till he found the strength to control the torrent, the wild blind rushing in his heart.

Across the valley, beyond the first low hills, white smoke ascended. In a little while people appeared on the hill, spreading out along its crest, forming a dark crescent against the snow. Below and to the right the cavalry came into sight around a hill, riding two abreast in a long line. The line curved to cross the creek, riders and horses disappearing momentarily against the black water, their passing marked only by the white splashing of their feet. The leaders appeared against the snow and curved out onto the flat, the mist of their breathing like scarves blown. Behind the troopers in the broad black trail they dragged came an ambulance, drawn by mules, its wheels leaving sharp, precise tracks in the muddy earth. The horsemen halted below the hill and with stiff, mechanical movements arranged themselves in a pattern on the snow—a straight line behind which the horses clustered in little round groups, heads to the center, like large black flowers.

Crazy Walking went back to his horse then. He built a small fire; bringing his medicine, he hung it on a limb. He took out the pipe and, lighting it with a coal from the fire, made offering to the four directions, to the earth and sky, and smoked slowly and deeply. He stripped to breechclout and moccasins, combed out his hair and rebraided it, replacing the coup feathers and wrapping the braids in red cloth. He painted his face and body finally, letting his hands remember the designs they had not made since the fight on the Greasy Grass, a long time ago. Finished with himself, he brought the spotted horse and painted a thin, single crescent in blue on the white forehead. He hung the quiver to his shoulder, strung the bow, mounted, and rode back up the hill.

He rode slowly, saving the horse, out onto the open, treeless hill and below him saw the troopers dismounted and spread out, behind them the horses drawn together in little knots around the horseholders. His horse looked down and, seeing those below, whinnied loud and long.

He began the death song then, his voice coming free and loud from the new power in his body:

> A whiteness of death moving over me,
> A whiteness like snow, sliding above.

The singing held him steady, gathered and pointed him arrow-like.

Across on the other hill, the people picked up the song, low at first but building in strength as he rode toward the hilltop until, as he stopped his horse and faced down, the valley seemed to fill with sound as with water. Below, a bugle picked up the first notes of the song, rising clear as a bird flight and suddenly stopping.

218

He reached forward and pulled the bridle off the horse and tossed it aside and with his knees sent the animal plunging downward into the shadow of the hill. He let go then, releasing the power he had held so long, dropping downward through the singing, his own voice sharp and clear as a thrown spear preceding him, "Hoka hey, hoka hey!"

## 47

Leah had stood on the bright hill beside Blue Fawn waiting for Crazy Walking to reappear, eyes almost closed against the painful brilliance of the light, her anxiety intensified by the white, unmarked snow, the cloudless sky. For a moment all was still, and she had the feeling that what she saw was not real: it was a stylized charcoal drawing on an immense field of white. It was too formal, too vivid in black and white: the crescent of Indians on the hill where she stood, the precise figures of the men and horses below, their sharply drawn black road in the snow; the creek itself, black and curving, and, where it emerged from the hills, the grove of trees, the bulk of their limbs concealed by snow, a delicate tracery against the white. It was a setting, a backdrop. But with the thought of the scene to be played, the anxiety returned. She was alone and a stranger, standing at the back of the crescent among the Indian women, herself wrapped in a blanket with only her face exposed, yet with the frantic feeling of an actress who has forgotten her lines.

She had been certain, offering to come. She remembered Blue Fawn as she had been the day before, appearing at the door like one in a dream, saying in signs that she would take Little Wound on the trip. Leah tried to dissuade her, knowing he was too weak yet for the exposure. But Blue Fawn was adamant; and Leah had decided, though she regretted it now.

Below, near a tip of the crescent, she saw Little Wound beside his grandfather, absorbed, never turning; and her loneliness sharpened. She wanted to touch him, to see that he was warm; and realized, with chagrin, that it was reassurance she wanted.

The Indians all had their eyes fixed on the little grove of trees. Through their silvered screening she saw slight movement and little flashes of orange from a fire. Above the trees a thin white smoke grew straight and high.

Crazy Walking appeared then, emerging from the trees transformed, another person, heightened, enlarged, though small in distance. He rode diagonally up the hill, a living fire of color against the white: skin shining copper, showing small gleams of yellow and blue; horse sorrel, almost the color of the rider's skin, rump covered by a sheet of white, through which round holes of color shone. He rode slowly, head thrown back, with controlled, stylized grace; even the horse moved with slow dignity, as if with conscious part in the strange ritual.

She found herself breathless—trying not to breathe—straining to catch some sound from the figure across the hill. But there was no sound, even from the troopers below, only a faint whispering of the Indians' breathing.

The rider paused briefly on the hill; the horse's head turned, ears forward. A faint puff of white appeared over its head and the head of the rider, and in a moment she heard the sound of its whinny, unexpectedly loud and clear.

Crazy Walking went on and she heard his singing, far off, bell-like, of a sharp, painful beauty. Her eyes blurred; for an instant she was chilled, seized by the wild sadness of the song. All the Indians took up the song, lifting it over the hills, repeating, building it irresistibly. Beside her Blue Fawn sang, robe thrown back, eyes and face shining and open.

The rider emerged from the hill shadow into the brilliant sunlight at the top and paused there, dark and sharp against the morning sky. From below a bugle rose sharply in the first notes of the song, piercing the singing, like a hand raised in salute, and stopped abruptly.

Crazy Walking leaned forward, touched the horse's head, and threw something aside. The horse sprang downward out of the light into the hill shadow, moving in long leaps, feet sliding as they struck, throwing up white fountains of snow. The singing seemed to increase in volume, though some of the men were shouting now instead of singing, "Hoka hey, hoka hey," blankets thrown off, bare backs and shoulders knotting and straining as if they too rode and fought. Where the hill sloped out at the bottom, the rider emerged into sunlight, turned parallel to the line of troops, and Leah could see him shooting, the curve and snap of the bow, the thin glint of the arrows.

The troops were standing, rifles aimed. The sharp lines of the gun barrels converged, moved sidewise slowly, finding the fleeting figure. Flame spurted from the tips almost in unison; but the rider did not go down. In a moment the sound of the gunfire crashed deafeningly around her. The rider turned in a graceful circle, miraculously alive, away for a moment, then back again toward the line, the tracks a delicate pattern in black against the snow.

A cry went up from the Indians around her, the men shouting, the women calling high and clear, tapping their lips with their hands to make a wild tremolo. The singing began again; the air was fleshed with sound. She felt herself enclosed in it, joined with this strange people, her whole self drawn together and focused on the bright moving figure below. In some mysterious way she had faced death in the man's brief ride, had escaped, turned in the figured circle and again faced it, without fear.

Below, the rider again charged straight in toward the troops. The dark figure of a man in a black coat left the line, moving directly to meet the rider. Again the guns flared. And even as the sound reached her, Crazy Walking dropped from the horse, appearing spread-eagled under a mist of snow, and the horse ran on unwavering toward the line, met the man running, passed over, leaving him writhing on the snow, and in a rattle of rifle fire struck the line and went through. The line closed and the horse fell on its side, continuing to gallop, leaving dark half circles where the hoofs plowed the earth.

The firing stopped. For a moment there was silence and no movement at all except for the black figure in front of the troops, crawling worm-like back through the snow. Leah thought she knew him, but she could not call his face to mind; he was lost in the cry of grief that rose among the Indians like a wind rising.

For an instant the troops seemed to shrink together, clotted by the sound. Then they were scattering, finding their horses, swarming darkly over the snow, all the stiffness and precision gone from their movements. A few had gone forward to the fallen Crazy Walking to stand in a circle around the bright colored figure, though none came close. The circle dissolved and these too returned to their horses. Two men, not troopers, were helping the black-coated man toward the ambulance—she recognized one of them as Westland.

The troops were standing by their horses, again in a line, and at some signal mounted, formed into a column, and moved off the way they had come. The ambulance remained.

The Indians moved down the hill. They had taken up the song again, singing with a low moaning sound like wind in the trees. Blue Fawn was crying now, shedding tears for the first time Leah knew of in all her recent grief. She held blindly to Leah's arm, walking with difficulty on the steep slope. Below, the Indians reaching the dead man formed a widening circle, hiding him from sight as she came down. She crossed the creek on a fallen tree, surprised to see that the water was not black as it had seemed from above, but clear, sparkling over colored pebbles.

With Blue Fawn she entered the circle and saw Crazy Walking, face up in the snow, body torn and shining darkly red. On the white snow blood had spattered in little sunbursts, the drops staining the snow in bright red rays. His face and chest (where blood had not concealed it) were covered with symmetrical marks in blue and yellow and red. By his head a quiver lay, a few arrows fanned out from it like rays, and near his outstretched hand, the bow curved gleaming in the snow.

She looked at the quiet face for a long time, trying to discover any bitterness or pain. But there was none—only peace and, faintly shining from the weirdly painted features, an exaltation.

Some of the men stepped forward then and placed a red blanket on the ground and lifted the body onto it. But as they stooped to lift it, a black-coated figure hobbled into the circle and she saw with shock that it was Martin. As he approached, the men stepped back quietly and he said a short incoherent prayer over the dead Crazy Walking. Finished, he came toward her and she thought he had recognized her under the blanket. But he passed without speaking, looking bewildered and lost. Outside the circle Westland met him and helped him back toward the ambulance. She realized then with revulsion that the figure knocked in the snow by the riderless horse had been her husband. Watching him now, an unexpected pity welled in her heart; yet she did not go to him. She could not.

Blue Fawn had abandoned herself completely to grief, released from her former numbness; she left Leah and followed close to the body wailing loudly. Turning Hawk was exhausted; when Little Wound left him and came to stand beside Leah, the old man looked at her in gratitude, his face grey and drawn. She thought he might collapse in the snow, but he turned and followed the body, wading the creek as if unaware of the water.

Leah followed with Little Wound, thinking to cross on the log, but deciding suddenly against it. Instead she picked up the tired child and carried him, feeling the shock of the icy water on her legs with a perverse kind of joy, a consciousness of new strength.

Across the creek, the boy struggled out of her arms and walked beside her with dignity and independence—yet holding her hand. He was still weak from sickness, exhausted by what he had gone through. With sudden perception she felt the growing strength within him and with the insight felt a twinge of pain. But it was fleeting; and she was no longer a stranger or alone, even in the midst of grief.

The sun was high and warm now, melting the snow miraculously from the slope they climbed. At the top she looked back and found the little valley completely changed. Except for the slope across, the snow was gone. Of the wide black trail left by the cavalry and the flowered circular path of the running horse, nothing remained. Only the far-spaced prints on the snowy slope across and, in the flat, the body of the spotted horse gave evidence of what had been.

### 48

Stepping down from the ambulance, the first thing Westland had seen was the dark crescent of Indians on the slope and on the hilltop across, touched with fire from the rising sun, the strangely magnified figure of a lone rider motionless against the sky like one in prayer; the singing of the Indians was a strange wild sacrament. He knew the rider was Crazy Walking; yet for a moment he found it hard to believe—this was a figure of dream, of meaning, but no proper reality; it would dissolve.

Behind him the derisive cavalry officer stepped down from the ambulance and Westland heard his indrawn breath as the sight and sound struck him.

"By God," he said, "I didn't think he'd come. He's alone too. He better make strong medicine with a hundred men to fight."

"It's strong," Westland said. "Can't you hear it?"

As he spoke, a bugler in the line picked up the first notes of the death song and lifted them clear and strong above the voices. The officer rushed forward angrily and the bugler stopped.

The rider leaned forward, took off the bridle, and tossed it aside, and in that instant became for Westland the man he knew as friend.

Crazy Walking sent his horse plunging down the slope, and Westland found his own hand raised palm outward in salute —or as if, he thought, he could hold back death.

Crazy Walking reached the bottom of the hill and turned broadside to the line, and in an instant Westland heard the whispered flight of an arrow and thought he saw the shine of its passage like a cobweb in the sun. He saw the Major and the officer move behind the ambulance, but he himself had no desire for shelter; he did not move. Nor, strangely, did Martin. He stood in the open, white-faced and breathing hard as if from exertion.

"It's barbarous," he said shakily, "worse than the Indians. It ought to be stopped."

From behind the soldiers Westland saw their guns align magnetically with the running horse and, in the staccato of gunfire, saw the buck of the muzzles, the jar of shoulders, and the smoke rising. He was himself jarred, almost thrown to the ground. But Crazy Walking rode on untouched, circling. The cry of the Indians, the weird tremolo, descended like water falling, and he found himself cheering wildly, trembling and sweating.

Martin was moving forward to the line, slowly and carefully, as if afraid of falling. As Crazy Walking charged again, this time straight in, Martin broke into a run and passed through the line, going directly to meet the rider, arms up-raised, shouting. But Westland could not hear his words.

A shout of anger rose from the soldiers, drowned by the guns crashing. Crazy Walking was lifted suddenly from the horse, hurled downward into snow, but the horse came on toward Martin, ears fiercely back, a wild glaze on his eyes. Martin halted, paralyzed, and the horse shouldered him down, passing over and charging straight into the line. Westland could hear someone shouting, "Let him go, let him go," but the troopers were already shooting.

He saw round spots of darker color on the horse's hide where the bullets struck but the animal kept coming, striking the line, scattering soldiers. It fell near Westland, striking the earth violently, blowing bloody froth on the snow at his feet. Hoofs, still galloping, cut black arcs of mud in the snow.

The line dissolved and the soldiers ran forward to surround the fallen Crazy Walking. Westland tried to follow but he was paralyzed, breathless. For a little while he could not move. From above, the Indians' cry of despair fell, darkening the day.

He saw Martin crawling toward him through the snow, unhurt but wild with terror; and for an instant he was himself sickened with fear. But the fear became unreasoning anger at the man, releasing him. Yet he could not leave Martin fallen in the snow. He was ashamed, as if he had had some part in the man's action. He helped Martin to his feet, finding him incoherent and scarcely coordinated. The Major helped guide him back to the ambulance, scolding, "You might have been killed. What the devil were you thinking about?"

But Martin did not answer. His face was contorted as if he might cry, but he did not.

The troopers who had gone forward to look at Crazy Walking came back now, running toward their horses, glancing nervously at the Indians descending the bright slope. In a moment a young lieutenant shouted the order to mount and the troop moved off, making a little bow bend around the dead horse.

Behind them the dead Indian lay, a blinding spot of color on the white earth. Westland looked at him, not going nearer, trying to remember the man alive, to think of him in

225

any other role, but could not. Yet somehow he had triumphed over death.

With brief insight, he thought he understood the wild joy of the Indians at Crazy Walking's first charge and escape from the bullets: they had for the moment been invincible, unkillable, seeing in that brief moment an immortality. But with his death the illusion had shattered. It was death they knew. And their cry of grief and despair was for more than a man alone.

The first Indians crossed the creek and surrounded Crazy Walking, hiding him from view. The women came last, and he saw the circle of men open for Blue Fawn and Little Wound and one he recognized (after she disappeared) as Leah, wrapped in a blanket, wearing moccasins and leggings. He was startled but not surprised, as if he had expected her there, negating her husband's fierceness, making Westland's part in the death of Crazy Walking less bitter.

Martin moved toward the Indians as if he had seen Leah, and Westland let him go, yet feeling that the man was again in danger. There was an air of darkness about him, an indefinable aura of death. Westland followed to the edge of the circle, but when it opened to admit Martin and closed again he did not go farther. He watched Martin pray over the dead Crazy Walking with a shrinking in his heart, a shame, as if the prayer were a sacrilege, a subtle injury to the dead.

The prayer finished, Martin stumbled out of the circle, passing within arm's length of Leah without recognition. Westland went forward to guide him to the ambulance, catching Leah's eyes and finding in them relief and visible gratitude.

It was not a long ride back to the fort, but, riding, Westland was sorry he had not come alone. He was acutely uncomfortable now in the presence of these men and knew that they too were uncomfortable. A strong repulsion had grown between them. Even the cavalry officer had lost his aplomb and smoked with jerking hands.

"By God," he said, "I've never seen anything like it. I've seen men executed and felt sorry for some of them, but not this one. I think I feel sorry for the men who shot him."

"It wasn't an execution," Martin said. "It was a pagan rite. You were the sacrificial priest, not an executioner. I was a heathenish, evil thing."

"It was a battle," the Major said irritably. "He died like

a man, as he chose. He hurt no one, as he might have done. He shouldn't have died at all."

"There was nothing else for him," Westland said. "He was an Indian. What is left for them? Martin is right. His death had a religious context, though I don't think it was evil. It was a rite for a doomed people."

"Not doomed," Martin objected, "but ripe for salvation."

"It's the same to them."

"Well, by God, I don't mind a good fight," the officer said, "but this thing gave me the creeps—I felt like an actor in a play gone suddenly real: finding he had bullets in his gun in the place of blanks. It's the way I felt, damned strange."

"I failed," Martin said. "I might have stopped it. He should have been arrested and tried."

"And hanged," Westland supplied. "He's dead. What more can you ask?"

"I didn't want him killed; I only wanted him civilized, saved."

"Do you think there's any difference? In his own way he was a true believer, not in need of salvation. He signed his belief with his life. Can a Christian do more?"

"You are as mistaken as the Indians," Martin said severely.

But Westland declined to argue further. He had been shaken by the Indian's death, and with these men he shared a disquieting sense of guilt that caused him for the moment to detest them. He needed desperately to stop the ambulance and get out, to walk by himself. But he did not; he only sank deeper into his seat, refusing to talk.

The next day the Indians came back, camping near the agency, waiting for rations though ration day was still a week off. The weather was cold, the sky as grey as the bare hills when Westland entered the camp again, searching for Turning Hawk and Blue Fawn. They had given away the leather lodge, and it was only by the sound of the woman's grief that he found them in a ragged grey canvas tent, patched with red Indian cloth like spots of new blood. They had no food or even robes, nothing but the medicine bundle with its tripod and the body of Crazy Walking wrapped in a red blanket.

"It is like ourselves," Turning Hawk told him. "Empty. There is nothing left."

Westland sat with them in silence, finding no way to express his feelings but knowing he was understood.

Martin brought a coffin, leaving it outside the lodge and going away with no word. And after a while the people gathered and, placing the body on a drag, moved off toward the hills—not just a few friends and relatives but the whole band, bringing lodges for camping, as if all possessed a blood relationship to the dead man.

Westland walked in the procession, feeling in the air, beyond the personal grief, a people's sadness, a greyness of mood as of earth and sky. They turned off the trail far from camp and climbed a hill to a platform of white poles, covered with colored pictographs of the dead man's deeds. And, when the body was lashed to its top, made a cold camp in the hills beyond.

In the evening Westland sat in a circle of men in Eagle Voice's lodge, knowing their depression by the silent passing of the pipe. Only one spoke, Walking Bear, an old man grey-headed and blind. "My day is past, my sun is set. I have walked the black road from the place of the rising sun to the dark edge where it sinks. Now in my heart the darkness springs. But before it covers me, I would speak to my people. Hear me, for this is a time of truth.

"Wakan Tanka made us. He gave us this wide land and placed us in it to be brother to all, all animals that walk or swim or fly. He gave us the buffalo for our food and clothing. He gave us our lives and the power to live in a sacred manner. He gave us wisdom through dreams.

"We fought our enemies and feasted our friends. Our children were many, our herds large. Our old men talked with spirits and made good medicine. Our young men dreamed and hunted and made love to the girls. Where our tepee was there we stayed and no house imprisoned us. No one said, 'To this line is my land, to that is yours.' In this way our fathers lived, and were happy. Then the white man came to our hunting grounds, a stranger. We gave him meat and presents, and told him go in peace. He looked on our women and stayed to live in our tepees. His fellows came to build their roads across our hunting grounds. He brought among us the mysterious iron that shoots. He brought with him the magic water that makes men foolish. With his trinkets and beads he even bought the girl I loved. I said, 'The white man is not a friend, let us kill him.' But their numbers were greater than blades of grass. They took away the buffalo and shot down our best warriors. They took away our lands and surrounded us by fences. Their soldiers camped outside with cannon to shoot us down. They wiped the trails of our people from the face of the prairies. They forced our children to forsake the ways of their fathers. When I turn to the east I see no dawn. When I turn to the west the approaching night hides all."

The old man sat down, his face grey with the earnestness of his vision. There was silence for a long time, only the breathy, whistling sound of the pipe.

Westland wanted to leave, but he could not. He was immobilized by a vertigo, a sense of height above a dark, night-shadowed chasm. He could not move for fear of falling. ·

Finally a young man spoke. "We have heard wisdom from one old and full of honors, one who has feared nothing and having lived long, can even welcome death. The past is before him; the future in the darkness behind.

"What he has said is true, the world is dark. Our children are dying; if all are to die, it will be better for us to die also. But there are many who live, who have need of the future, who can seize it only with hope.

"Wakan Tanka made us; he will perhaps save us. We have heard of a Wicasa Wakan, far to the west, an Indian of great power who has died and gone to the spirit land and returned, bringing a sacred dance to renew the earth and all the ways of the past, to bring back the buffalo.

"We do not know that this is true. We should send someone to verify or destroy the hope. Someone must make this journey; it is all the hope that is left."

There was approval from all the young men, even from a few of the old. One of them spoke dreamily, "To bring back the buffalo, that would be good. But the white man in all his numbers, what of him? It is well known he cannot live with the animals; he must kill all. While there are white men, the buffalo will not return."

Another answered, "The new earth will come; the white man will be no more, or only in his own land across the water. It is what I have heard."

Enthusiasm grew and, in its growth, Westland was released. He left the lodge. There was moonlight, marking the earth with strong patterns of light and shade. He walked with his own solid shadow, feeling it as an eerie presence, a being of fierceness and evil. He was anxious and afraid.

He climbed a shadowed hill, emerging at the top near the

scaffold. The poles were stark against the sky, shining coldly on the moon side, yet showing the painted symbols clearly, black against white. He stood silently for a long time, roused at last by sounds from the trail below. In the hollow, he saw a knot of riders moving at a trot toward the agency; soldiers, he knew. He almost hailed them, feeling an intense need for company, but he could not bring himself to break the silence. As they passed below, close now, one looked up and shouted, pointing at the scaffold. In a moment a gun burned in the darkness; a bullet struck the pole beside him, splintering wood.

He shouted and ran along the hill away from the platform, hearing a quick succession of shots, knowing they were aimed at the platform and striking it, but feeling a violent jerking in his body as if it were himself the bullets struck. He ran slanting down the face of the hill, his eyes on the riders. And in a moment he knew they had seen him. The firing stopped and they spurred down the trail, their faces turned toward him in the moonlight, white and intense as if he were an enemy pursuing. They rounded a bend; the sound of hoofs died slowly in the distance.

He turned east alone, beginning the long walk to the agency.

## Book III

# JANUARY-DECEMBER
# 1890

### ⧓ 49 ⧓

MANY DAYS Turning Hawk had traveled in winter wind, seeing each evening the sun set far to the south beyond the white, empty land, and ahead, the evening star shining clear and icy over the dark hills. And always in his heart, like a weight of stone, the thought that it was folly and the vivid memory of Crazy Walking and the white cow.

They were hungry often; game was scarce and there was little grass for the horses, and that thin and bodiless from the dry year and buried in snow. And always the bitter cold.

They made short camps, traveling night and day till one of the horses died and the others were footsore and gaunt. Turning Hawk would have stopped then to rest and hunt, but Eagle Voice would not pause. He was a man burning with thirst, seeing in the distance the tremulous, blue lakes of the air. He was tireless and undiscouraged.

At Wind River they rested among the Blue Clouds and the Snakes, hearing much talk of the Messiah in the west and the Spirit Dance. Among the Snakes, Turning Hawk recognized old enemies, men he had fought in the past, but they were friendly now, full of the wonder of the new dance, seeing in any Indian a brother. The peace was good, Turning Hawk knew; yet he looked back on the days of the fighting with downcast shrinking heart.

He would have lingered long at Wind River, but Eagle Voice, filled now to bursting with the new vision, would not stay. They pushed on, south now, after several days reaching a small camp of white men's houses that Eagle Voice called Rawlins, beside an iron road, waiting in uncertainty, till in the evening a train came and halted with hissing and thunder at the edge of the camp by a shining, ice-encrusted water tank.

Some cowboys emerged from the small house car at the back and, after talking with Eagle Voice, helped load the ponies into one of the cars. It was a wild struggle, the ponies plunging and bawling in terror, the cowboys laughing and shouting, some of them foolish with whiskey, falling from the car or getting tangled with the horses. Turning Hawk did not help but watched bemused, feeling a curious sympathy for the frightened animals, himself reluctant to enter the train. He wanted to turn back, setting his face again toward home, but he could not. And again they moved west, carried headlong now by the tireless, fleshless power of the whites into a country he had never seen before, toward the dark, nightward edges of the world.

It was a strange journey, Turning Hawk knew, a search for light in the darkening west, a hope of life at the end of the black road. He remembered that other journey with Little Wound on the iron road when he had hoped to bring light to the boy's darkness, finding in it a disturbing parallel to this journey now.

They traveled sleeplessly in the rocking, rattling car with dim lanterns swinging and smoking, filling the air with oily stench. Some of the white men shouted and sang with the depressing joy of drunkenness, heedless of the power of the train burrowing the darkness or of the land they traveled. One tried to cook meat on the bare iron of the stove and filled the car with smoke. One of the others opened the door at the back and threw the flaming meat out.

Turning Hawk stepped out onto the little platform at the back, closing the door after him, and watched the burning meat recede like a hole drilled in the darkness till it was gone and there was nothing but a cold glint on the steel tracks and the feel rather than the sight of the land rushing by. And for a moment he was stricken with panic, feeling the train no as a physical but a spiritual power drawing him relentlessly into an unknown country and into darkness. Before dawn the train stopped in another white man's town and the cowboys helped load the ponies into another car, and as the light came they were moving beside a wide, treeless lake bordered with white like snow, smelling of salt.

And beyond the lake was a dry, grey land of sage and black rock, broken by low treeless mountains, showing little life save coyote and jack rabbit and wheeling hawk. Through the day and the night and the next day they traveled, stopping only once among strange Indians who lived in round grass lodges and painted their faces white with black spots. They were welcomed and fed, and overwhelmed with news of the Spirit Dance and the Messiah, and learned that even the whites were dancing here.

Again they took the train, coming at last to the agency of the Fisheaters, the Paiutes, on a river and a lake. Yet it was not the end of the journey; the Messiah was at another camp. They unloaded their ponies and rested and again set out with an old man as guide and interpreter. They traveled all day through snowy sagebrush plain and at night still had not found the camp. And after wandering for a long time in the dark over a maze of cattle trails, the old man confessed that he was lost. He had not been here in many years; his eyes were bad; in the night he was blind.

In the end it was Turning Hawk himself who found the camp, remembering vaguely the Chief's directions, coming on it in darkness, having seen from a distance the sparks rising from the open-topped grass lodge when the fire inside was replenished.

Eagle Voice and the old man went immediately into the wickiup, but Turning Hawk found himself lingering. He was lame and weary from the long ride and, now that it was finished, in a ragged grass lodge in a desert of snow and sage, it seemed he could not move the last few steps. He leaned against the wagon where the horses were tied, with the smell of burning sage in the frosty air, till the weakness passed; and followed, stooping stiffly through the low doorway.

The wickiup was full of people. Near the entrance a large, solid man of heavy features sat; the Messiah, he knew; and beside him a young woman with a child asleep in her arms. On his other side were the old man and Eagle Voice. They were smoking a pipe and Eagle Voice was gazing intently at

233

the man, his face alight with awe. Across the fire a woman sa
beside a sick child that lay in a bed of rabbit skins, and ove
it a medicine man chanted and prayed.

Turning Hawk sat between Eagle Voice and the old mar
grateful for the warmth and light, the smell of sage comfort
ing and familiar in the strange lodge. It was not grass, he sav
now, but tule rushes tied in bundles and laid over a frame
work of poles. From the outside it had looked like a larg
snow-covered sagebrush or merely a heap of grass blendin
into the landscape. The top was open but there were n
flaps to control the smoke; changes of the wind filled the ai
with smoke; the rushes inside were black with soot. Ther
were scant furnishings in the lodge—a few baskets and bow'
of woven grass but no pots and pans, nothing of the whit
man's things save a small rifle leaned against the wall and th
clothing they wore under the rabbitskin blankets.

The pipe finished, Eagle Voice spoke to the Messiah i
the white man's tongue, the old man translating into th
Paiute, explaining, Turning Hawk supposed, their missio
and whence they had come. It seemed at first that the tw
men were chanting or changing the words of Eagle Voice to
song. Then he realized that the Messiah was repeating eac
statement after the translator, waiting each time for th
latter's approval. Yet the effect was of a ceremonial chant.

Across the fire the man still sang to the child. It stirre
faintly and he increased the volume and intensity of h
singing. And for a moment all eyes were on the child, but
made no further movement, seeming to sleep.

The Messiah began to speak then, the old man repeatir
then translating to Eagle Voice, who in turn spoke to Turi
ing Hawk. And again the effect was of ritual, of singing.

"I was in the mountains on a day the sun died and hear
a noise like thunder or of rocks breaking and a roaring c
wind among trees. I turned toward the sound fearfully, an
as the sun darkened I also fell down dead and was taken uj
ward to the land of spirit. I saw my mother and father ar
friends, living as they had lived before in a green worl
hunting and working and playing the old games, happy ar
forever young.

"I saw the great Father, who showed me all and told n
to return and make a road for my people, a road of love ar
peace. He said that if they walked this road in faith th
would arrive at such a land as he had shown me.

"He gave me a dance then to bring back to them, a dance to renew the worn-out earth, to bring back the animals and green the land again as it had been before the coming of the whites.

"Friends, we are dancing this dance. If we do it faithfully, the new world will come. It will come in a dust, in a whirlwind; the white man will be no more, the dead Indians will live again and be happy and young forever.

"Friends, you will see this dance and be part of it and take it with you when you return to your own country."

He stopped speaking and for a while there was silence except for the continued chanting of the medicine man. Then the Messiah placed a large hat on the ground before him and, with an eagle feather, made a few slow passes over it. With a quick movement of his hand he drew something dark from the hat. For a moment the object seemed to live, a furry, moving animal, and he dropped it again into the hat and it was gone.

Turning Hawk was impressed; the man's powers were good, yet no better than others he had known. But Eagle Voice continued to stare at the hat without speaking, his expression intense but changing and mobile like that of one watching some vivid action.

For a long time there was silence; and suddenly the sick child sat up in his bed of skins, shrinking against his mother, pointing to a spot in the air above him on which his eyes were fixed in terror. He jerked his head from side to side, blinking his eyes as if dodging blows from some unseen assailant. The mother held him, herself terror-stricken but murmuring softly, and in a little while the jerking stopped and the child slept again. The medicine man left and gradually all the others slept, lying back in their robes. Even Eagle Voice at length lay down.

But Turning Hawk could not sleep; doubt like a stone still lay in his heart.

"Numa Naha, he's called now, Our Father," the Paiute agent told Westland. "But he's just an ignorant Indian—though better than most. Works for a white rancher over in the Mason Valley, and strangely enough is a good worker. Doesn't steal or drink whiskey, and insofar as the others follow his example, his influence is good. But this Messiah thing is a hoax and ought to be stopped. An Indian Christ! It's a joke."

"Nevertheless, I'd like to meet him, if you've no objection."

"Not at all. I pay him no attention, myself. Don't want to give him any notoriety. This nonsense ought to be discouraged."

The next day, with the help of an Indian guide, Westland found the dance ground, a large circle cleared of sage and snow, ringed by small, oval shelters of willows that from a distance looked like clumps of sagebrush on the snowy plain. To the side was a larger one, for Our Father, the guide said. Indians were already gathering, putting up small half shelters of white cloth—not canvas—around the circle, clustering in small, dark groups on the snow.

Westland waited most of the afternoon, sitting in the buggy with the guide, watching, absorbing the excitement and anticipation of the Indians. The guide was not communicative; he was inclined to ridicule the dance, affecting a kind of white man's derision. But when the Father finally came, riding alone on the seat of a high spring wagon, he averted his eyes and became silent, losing his affectation.

It was a red evening of sun and cloud. In the gathering dark, small fires of sage appeared around the circle. The shelters, the white sheets, the bodies of the Indians in grey rabbitskin blankets seemed to fade, to merge with the snowy sagebrush land, till only the fires and the shining brown faces were left.

The guide would not approach Our Father as messenger. He was reticent; and about him Westland sensed an air of guilt—as if he expected, in the face of righteousness, to be struck down. So Westland walked alone to the large oval shelter where the Indian had gone, feeling conspicuous and somewhat guilty himself, as if his very presence were a profanation.

The Indian was seated by a small fire, eyes closed, but hearing Westland he rose quickly, shook hands with unexpected warmth, and with dark, child-like eyes fixed on Westland, asked what he wanted. Westland was disconcerted; he did not at first recognize the man's speech as English. The pronunciation was guttural and broken with each syllable, giving the effect of a separate word. Then the meaning came to him, its import without words, and he was relieved out of all proportion and taken by a desire to laugh. He felt released, as if the awkward pronunciation had broken an invisible fetter.

The man seemed to grow smaller, to shrink perceptibly, to the average, indeterminate figure of an Indian in white clothing. Yet Westland knew the change was within himself; about the man a gentle power remained. He stood smiling while Westland explained his interest in the ways of the Indian and the new dance, inviting him at last to sit by the fire and talk.

"I do not see how you can use what I will tell you. A broken cup holds no water; our cup is broken. All the white men I have known have been interested only in the breaking. It is done now."

"I only want to write down what you say so that men may read and understand."

The Indian shook his head slowly. "I do not understand. But because my brothers from across the mountains have spoken of you with trust, I will tell you what I can."

He looked at Westland with unwavering eyes till Westland looked away, at the fire, at the red willows of the shelter, and finally at his own hands, which were plucking nervously at his coat.

"I know," the Indian went on, "that the only road is the road of the white man. His God is strong and without pity. My people must send their children to school to learn that road or they will be lost in a white man's world. I teach my people this. Perhaps someday they will be white—there are even white men who say this. I do not know. But it is plainly the only road for the young."

He paused again, having spoken in a dry, toneless manner. But as he went on his face brightened and his voice quickened with feeling. "But I am not young. I cannot forget the road of my people; it runs unbroken in the heart.

"The road began far back in time when the earth was young, not old and burnt and wrinkled as it is today. This land between the mountains was green and pleasant, a land of rivers and blue lakes. The people were a race of giants, light of skin and peaceful in their ways, fighting only to protect their land from the lean ones beyond the mountains. But when these attacked, battles were fought and won. And when they were finished, the dead and wounded were carried to the sacred mountain of fire at the center of the land, where the wounded were healed by its vapors and the dead reclothed in flesh and set on the star path to the land of spirit. Thus they lived and were happy and died.

"Then among this handsome race of giants, a cripple was born, a boy deformed and ugly, who could not be healed or straightened even by the vapors of the mountain of fire.

"He was laughed at and tortured by those whole and beautiful till his life was an agony. Alone he climbed the fire mountain to throw himself into its flames. But as he stood on the precipice, the earth trembled, lightning and thunder shattered the darkening sky, and from a cloud the Great Father stepped, clothed in brilliance, and from the mountain cursed the people for their cruelty.

"Then with hand of light, he dipped the boy three times in the fire, bringing him forth transfigured, a child of beauty; and both vanished in thunder and blinding light.

"The earth heaved and shuddered, the mountain split, and molten rock in fiery rivers flowed over the land, burning it brown, drying the lakes and streams.

"The race of giants fled before it, burned brown, shriveled in the heat till they were small and pitiful as men.

"Then came the lean ones from beyond the mountains to attack and destroy till at last only a man and woman remained. The man's name was Paiute and he was the father of our people.

"His children learned to live in the dry land, to hunt small game, to harvest the seeds of the grasses and the pines.

Thus they lived and grew strong. And always they were kind to the crippled and unfortunate ones among them.

"They were kind even to the white man, though like the lean ones before him he came only to destroy. He has taken our land. His animals feed on our harvest of seeds. We work for him for little wages; he feeds us in troughs as he does his animals, outside his houses. The cup of the people is broken.

"But it will not always be so. I have died and talked with the Great Father. He says the earth has grown old and worn; it will die, but it will live again. Thunders will come and smoke and lightning, and in a whirling dust the new earth will slide over the old. The dead will return and all be young again, and this land belong to the Indian as before.

"The Great Father gave me a dance through which we can bring the new earth into being. I have brought this dance to my people and even now they are preparing to dance. You are a white man, but if you wish, you may stay."

He turned back to the fire, dismissing Westland. His shadow cast by the fire on the curved wall of the shelter was immense and dark.

Westland turned quietly to leave, accepting his dismissal. But at the doorway he turned and saw again the indeterminate figure of an Indian in ill-fitting clothes and spoke in quick resentment, "You have not spoken honestly but with two minds; with one of the white man's road, with the other of the Indian. You cannot believe in both."

The Indian answered without looking up from the fire, "I have spoken not with two minds but with heart and mind. What I believe is from the heart; it is the wisdom of the Indian. The white man's wisdom is from the mind; I believe he has no heart."

Westland did not answer. He was embarrassed somehow by the man's duality, yet he felt that he was wasting the time of someone more important than himself. The people were waiting. He turned away again and was startled by someone speaking just outside the lodge.

"Oh, Jack, come here a minute, will you?" There was a familiarity, a tone of command in the voice that was incongruous and shocking.

The Indian stood quickly, face and eyes losing their intensity, and stooped out through the low doorway. As he passed, Westland saw the strong features compose themselves into a bland, smiling expression. He followed, resenting the unseen speaker's presence and arrogance, expecting to see some large, commanding figure. Instead he found a small bearded white man on horseback, looking down with familiarity on the Indian.

"We're out of wood, Jack," he was saying. "Will you bring an Indian or two and cut us some more?"

The Indian nodded.

"Right away?"

"After the dance," the Indian said apologetically.

"Well, all right, but hurry it up."

The Indian went back inside.

"Ordinarily, he does what he's told," the man apologized. "Have to overlook a few things; after all, he's just an Injun. Anyway," he laughed, riding off, "if he rearranges things the way he intends, I won't be needing any wood."

Westland turned away without answering, hating the man, barely controlling his anger. Yet he knew he was wrong: in the stranger he perceived a gentleness and kindness beyond the ordinary.

He walked back to the buggy in confusion, doubting his right to be here, doubting even the value of what he was trying to do. He wanted to retreat to the agency. But he would not. He forced himself to sit quietly in the buggy, and in a moment saw the Father emerge from the shelter, dressed now in an odd white and black striped coat that seemed for a moment in the firelight like a source of rayed light. The Indian made his way slowly to the edge of the circle and sat before a small fire, disappearing as the Indians gathered around him.

The fire brightened within the enclosing circle of Indians, sending up showers of yellow sparks as armfuls of sage were thrown on it. Burnt leaves and bits of white ash floated above, catching the light in a wide ring. The circle expanded away from the heat and the Father appeared again, standing now, and spoke briefly in Paiute, which Westland could not understand and the guide would not translate, being as absorbed as the others, listening with a kind of glaze over his eyes.

When the Father finished speaking, he moved around the circle, painting the faces of those who stepped forward with simple designs in red. Waiting, Westland moved around the circle, searching for Turning Hawk and Eagle Voice knowing they had not yet returned to Arrow Creek though it was two months now since their departure. He found them and was greeted warmly. But both were too abstracted to talk. Eagle Voice was like one in a trance, following every movement of the Father. Turning Hawk was morose and withdrawn; after the greeting he would say no more, and Westland went back to the buggy. It seemed hours before all the dancers were painted and arranged in a ring on the cleared circle of ground. The small fires were gone, but a large one still burned at the edge of the circle.

They began dancing then, alternate men and women, holding hands, moving clockwise slowly while the Father sang from his place in the firelight. As he finished each song, the dancers took it up fervently, repeating with wailing, wind-like tones, the wheel their bodies made revolving through the edge of the firelight.

The songs were familiar; Westland remembered them from the singing of the Arapaho during the cattle hunt. He had taken the words down in phonetic script; the melodies he remembered clearly. But the meaning came to him in imagery rather than words—the vivid sign talk of the possessed Indian—woven inextricably with the memory of Crazy Walking and the white cow. The songs and a sense of parallel meaning made the scene for a moment familiar, as if he had experienced it before.

He was moved by the songs, surprised by their unexpected power: on the first hearing they had seemed meaningless and simple, mere statements of fact; he had looked for simile or metaphor and had not found it. But the meaning emerged now, organic, alive.

The moon had risen, whitening the night, plating the snow with metallic sheen. In the distance, west, the high Sierras, the Snowy Mountains, shone, and above them, an ethereal extension in the cold clear sky, the misty reaches of the Milky Way. It was this he found now in the first song:

> The snow lies on the mountains . . .
> The spirit path among the stars.

A statement in the language of the heart, a singing of the continuity of earth and sky, of flesh and spirit. And in the second, a continuing unification:

A slender antelope is circling . . .
It is rolling upon the earth.

The antelope in its actions (rolling in the manner of the buffalo, circling), a symbol of all things living. Turning Hawk had told him, "For the Indian the circle is sacred. All that lives is round: the body of a man, the stem of a plant. The sun and the sky, the earth and the moon are round like a shield. A circle bounds the edge of the world where the four winds travel and is the shape of the whirlwind. The day and the night and the moon circle in the sky; the seasons of life and death follow. It is a symbol of life and the world and time. Only the rock is not round; it is destruction, the opposite of life."

The black rock, the black rock . . .
The black rock is broken.

The sacred mountain, the mountain of myth, broken, split; the spirit powers invoked; the resurrection foreshadowed.

The wind stirs the willows . . .
The wind stirs the grasses.

And all the powers of the air unite in the transformation:

Fog, fog,
Lightning, lightning
Whirlwind, whirlwind.

Then the change, the new earth of the Indian:

The whirlwind, the whirlwind . . .
The snowy earth comes gliding.

Dust in the whirlwind, dust in the whirlwind,
The whirlwind on the mountain . . .

The rocks are ringing . . .
Ringing in the mountains.

The cottonwoods are growing tall . . .
Growing tall and green.

The earth renewed and death defeated.

He knew there was much that escaped him, that beauty of language could not survive translation. But through the imagery he perceived a poetry that was different in kind from what he knew, spoken from a different world, a poetry of complete identification with nature, a looking from within that obviated all simile; it was emotion objectified.

And understanding this, he thought he could better understand the dance: a people facing death but unable to accept, seeing in nature no counterpart. Earth renews herself; being part of the earth they could not die. Death as a people was a reality they could not comprehend. The dance was a turning away, a facing toward the past and, ironically, toward death. It was a painful and troubling thought and he brushed it away with distaste, but it recurred, giving to his perceptions a darkened, somber cast.

He got down from the buggy and built a fire, using sagebrush from the clearing of the dance ground, finding in the exertion, the feel of the wood, the warmth of the fire a physical reassurance.

The dancers kept on far into the night, turning and turning from the darkness through the light. He watched the Big Dipper turn in the sky, saw the shift of the stars toward morning. The singing continued, as repetitive and monotonous as the single drag step of the dance. Westland sat wrapped in a blanket by the fire, trying to stay awake, to miss nothing of the dance. Yet he dozed and dreamed.

He was looking down from high up onto a wide white plain sprinkled with tiny spots that might have been bushes or animals or men. The light was strange and frightening: he could not find its source; there was neither sun nor moon.

As he watched, the earth moved and he found that he was mounted on a great white horse that ran with ponderous, irresistible motion. He tried to check the animal but found he had no bridle. He remembered then with terrible regret that he had thrown it away. The horse plunged downward toward the plain and a sound rose around him in wailing, wind-like tones, a wild sad singing.

The spots on the plain below became Indians, looking toward him, their faces vivid with grief in the strange light. And he knew with shock that the source of the light was the animal he rode, that carried him headlong and in terror toward the plain below.

The faces came toward him with fearful speed, brighter and clearer, rising toward him in the increasing light, dropping suddenly under the battering hoofs and with long receding wails of pain, falling away in darkness.

He cried out in sorrow, and the light and the horse were suddenly gone and he was alone in darkness and silence, looking far down on a small fire. But on his face he could feel its heat and the movement of flames. It grew, becoming a conflagration, but he could not move and the flames blew above him in the wind till he was small and shrunken in the heat.

He awakened, slumped over the fire that was burning brightly with fresh wood. The dancing had stopped and all the Indians were shaking their blankets with windy, popping sounds—to drive away evil, the driver said. They dispersed slowly, the Father leaving first, driving in lonely dignity on the high seat of his rickety wagon.

Westland went back to the railway station then, taking no notes, unable to sustain his curiosity. He did not try to talk to the driver.

## 🦌 51 🦌

Martin stood beside the pulpit, in agitation that was like stage fright, though it was long since he had been afraid of crowds. For the moment he could not remember what he intended to say, could not anticipate what would be expected of him. He was immobilized, as in the face of danger, wanting to call out for help; but there was no one to help him.

He glanced toward the organ, seeing that Leah had not arrived, knowing now that she would not; she would be helping the doctor. The interpreter, Sun Ray, stood beside him fidgeting, reflecting his unease. He was filled with sudden dislike for the man, an aversion so violent that he dropped his eyes and passed his hand before his face in an involuntary gesture of hiding, and from the corner of his eye saw Sun Ray also raise his hand.

Martin kept his eyes averted, trying to analyze the feeling; but he could not. There was nothing about the man he could object to: he was well dressed—he could pass for white, Martin thought, though he was a half-breed. He was a dedicated Christian—too dedicated, if such were possible, too quick in denouncing all that was Indian. There was something hollow in his conviction. He spoke good English and his interpretations were accurate and literal. Yet Martin could not help comparing him, unfavorably, with Eagle Voice; he did not have that Indian's power, his vivid, moving effect.

In the terrible winter of sickness and starvation, the congregation had doubled. And yet, he reflected, with the loss of Eagle Voice he had lost touch. It was perhaps his own failure, he thought, that made him resent Sun Ray. But he was not convinced. He resolved to think more highly of the man in the future.

The services were late; it was time to begin. And with surprise (how, he wondered, could he have ignored it so long?) he realized that, with the exception of the police, there was not a single Indian in the church. There were more white people than usual—perhaps, he thought, at the insistence of the new agent, who was a man of strong religious convictions. But there was not an Indian.

He walked hurriedly down the aisle and onto the porch, sure that they would be waiting outside. But they were not. The morning was grey, with a misty April rain obscuring the distance. He felt imprisoned, as if the white mist were a wall, impenetrable to himself, beyond which the Indians waited.

He was shaking with fatigue, as if released from some heavy burden. And he realized that he had expected this and feared it. Eagle Voice and Turning Hawk were back from their three-month journey west; he had felt the excitement their homecoming created. But he had not believed they would hold a meeting on the Sabbath. Indeed, they had been meeting now for three days, crowded together in smoky lodges, alternately talking and singing, the weird music of the Ghost Dance sounding far into the night. They should have finished by now.

He returned to the pulpit, almost running, furious with Eagle Voice; it was his power, Martin knew, that was holding the Indians away—a vicious kind of spiritual blackmail. He remembered the Indian's absurd suggestion that he report in church on the new Christ in the west. He had been serious and seemed genuinely hurt when Martin pointed out the absurdity, the wickedness of the thought. Now he was retaliating, Martin was sure.

He entered the pulpit, still in fury, calming quickly, with painful guilt, when he realized where he was. He opened the Bible with fumbling fingers to his text, remaining silent for a moment, head bowed, praying for the strength to continue, to collect his thoughts and feelings to a semblance of piety. He gave the text without raising his eyes, and was startled to hear Sun Ray interpret his words—as if the church were full of Indians. It was something Eagle Voice might have done.

Martin looked sharply at the Indian, hardly believing his ears, filled again with anger. Controlling himself, he realized that, had he not been confined by the pulpit, he would have kicked the man off the platform. Laughter burst in his ears, checking his anger, bringing him forcibly back to a sense of the occasion. He looked sternly at the laughing faces, seeing with a certain satisfaction the guilty lowering of their eyes as his gaze moved across them.

Sun Ray looked at him in puzzlement, moving reluctantly when Martin waved him toward a seat on the empty side of the church. He sat there flushed, glancing often at the empty seats around him or across at the gathering of white people. Martin, as he spoke, could see the man moving slowly and surreptitiously along the bench toward the white side.

He gave his sermon mechanically and in distraction; he could not keep his mind from the perfidy of Eagle Voice. He glanced continually at the entrance, hoping some Indians would arrive, but knowing they would not. Without the usual pauses for interpretation, the sermon was extremely short. Finished and looking at his watch, he realized that he must have spoken rapidly and wondered uneasily if he had even been understood. He led them in song, but without Leah at the organ it was tuneless and without feeling. He had not realized before how much the effect of the services depended on her. Everything had failed him, he thought bitterly, even his wife.

He finished the services in a rush, remaining at his place in the pulpit, hoping that all would leave and he could be alone. But the church emptied slowly, as if all were as loath as himself to face the bleakness of the world outside. The image of Indians waiting beyond the ring of mist recurred. He read a passage from the Bible with determination, not looking up till he was done and finding, when he did so, that nearly all were gone. But some were waiting; he would have to face them.

He stepped down and at the back of the church joined the three men who were waiting: the agent, Sun Ray, and a well-dressed stranger he did not know. But he knew immediately that he did not like the man. He was smoking a pipe, even in the church. Sun Ray, standing beside the stranger, imitating precisely his manner of standing, had begun filling his pipe also. But seeing Martin, he put it away, still affecting however, like a distorting mirror, the worldly air of the stranger.

The agent introduced the man as a reporter from one of the eastern newspapers.

"Just traveling through—looking for news or a way to make it." He laughed. "It seems your heathens have fled the fold."

Martin did not answer him but turned instead to the agent. "It's Eagle Voice—he has them spellbound with this crazy Ghost Dance. He ought to be stopped."

The reporter nodded. "I've seen it everywhere in the west. These savages simply go crazy. You can't imagine it unless you've seen it. Reel around and fall down in a faint. They think by dancing they can destroy all the whites. Who knows when they'll try a more conventional way and start harvesting hair? The thing is dangerous."

He spoke seriously, but in his tone Martin sensed a falseness that made him uneasy.

"Do you think so?" the agent asked. "Don't you think it'll just blow over?"

"Not from what I've seen. It's a disease that'll spread if it isn't stopped. It's up to you." He paused and from the pocket of his coat extracted a folded newspaper which he handed to the agent. "One of my own poor paragraphs," he said. "It's what I saw at Wind River. Dressed up a little, you understand—have to cater to the customer."

Martin saw the headline, "Six Thousand Savages Dance Destroy Us," and read the story over the agent's shoulder envisioning a mass of Indians gone mad. But he could no really believe it.

"You saw this at Wind River?" he asked.

The reporter nodded.

"There are only about two thousand Indians there."

The man shrugged. "They're dancing in other place enough to make up the difference. It's the poetry of th thing. Reverend; six alliterates with savage. It doesn't disto. the facts as much as two distorts the line. Have to please th people, see?"

It was not logical to oppose the man, Martin thought; h himself did not want to see this new madness flourish. Th agent was listening, being convinced; and Martin knew h should not oppose the man; but he could not help it.

"No, I don't see. The truth is the truth; two is not si And I've heard they dance not so much to destroy us as bring back the old life."

"My God, Reverend, are you defending this dance, th counterfeit Christendom?"

"No, didn't I say I wanted it stopped?"

"Then your tactics are weak. If a thing is bad, sho up its vices, not its virtues. I'm only trying to help. And I get a story, well so much the better."

The agent was clearly bewildered, looking to Martin f advice.

Martin nodded reluctantly. "It ought to be stopped."

"What can I do? I can't arrest the whole tribe."

"Arrest the agitators," the reporter said. "Stop it fro spreading. Show them you're serious." He paused, and Mart could see that he was laughing to himself. "Say, there's start for a story; a heap of headlines."

Martin turned away from the man in disgust, forcing hir self to say, "It's Eagle Voice and Turning Hawk; maybe you arrested them as a warning . . ." He did not go on.

"Well, I could do that. But it's probably too late."

"Have they started dancing yet?" the reporter asked.

"Not that I know of."

"Then it's not too late. That's when they go crazy—whe they dance. You can't tell what they'll do then."

"Well, maybe I ought. But I don't like it. I'm new her

and I hate to start off wrong. But they ought to be in church, not dancing and caterwauling."

They drove to the camp, the agent in the lead with his police, all riding in a spring wagon, Martin following in his buggy with the reporter and Sun Ray.

There was no rain, but a patch of mist still clung to the earth, moving slowly toward them over the camp in an increasing light. They entered it just at the edge of camp, moving into the circle as into another country.

The Indians were assembled in the open, the whole band seated in a crescent, their blankets pearled with beaded moisture, as if they had sat unmoving for a long time. At the opening in the crescent, Eagle Voice was speaking, his strong baritone rising even above the noise of the dogs that barked around the vehicles. Martin was startled somehow by the clarity of the voice, as if he expected it to be muffled by the mist.

The agent stopped at the edge of the gathering and, after some hesitation, got down from the wagon with his two policemen. He turned toward Martin immediately, beckoning, and for the first time Martin realized that he was afraid. He tied the lines to the dash, trying to conceal the shaking of his hands, and got down. Walking toward the Indians, forcing each step, he realized he was carrying the buggy whip, though the dogs had already departed. Beside him Sun Ray walked, his face grey in the misty light.

The agent was nervous. "I thought in case of trouble, you might be able to talk to them," he told Martin. He stood wringing his hands while the two policemen moved through the crowd toward the opening where Eagle Voice stood. But there was no trouble. The two Indians came quietly, climbing into the wagon where they sat in dignified silence, their blankets drawn up around their faces. The crowd did not move, remaining in ominous, oppressive silence. Martin could hear nothing but the straining, windy sound of his own breathing.

The agent climbed into the wagon then and the driver pulled the team around and drove away at a trot, leaving Martin alone—he had not seen Sun Ray leave. He turned toward his buggy in time to see it disappear in the mist, ahead of the wagon. He started to run, assailed by blinding fear, but he could not move; there was nowhere to go. He stood unseeing, drawn up, expecting to be attacked, struck down.

But there was nothing. And in a little while he was aware of the Indians moving by him quietly, some watching him with covert, curious eyes. He was able to move then, but he did not breathe freely till he emerged from the mist into sunlight beyond the circle of the camp.

## ⚛ 52 ⚛

"He'll die sure if they leave him in that damned cell," the doctor told Leah as they entered his office.

"He doesn't seem so ill. What does he have?"

"Nothing. That's just it: nothing, not even hope."

"Don't you think the agent would let him go if you told him?"

"Why should he? I just told you, that Indian isn't sick. He's just got nothing to live for. How can I tell a politician that? Oh, no, I stay out of politics. You tell him . . . or tell your husband—he's the one."

"I'm sorry he's that way, doctor. It's just that he's so—religious."

"Sure. And the agent too. From a savage you could expect a little tolerance—but these religious caterpillars? Oh, hell no."

He paused and looked at Leah, face softening, and for a moment he seemed very old. "Hell," he said, "it's no fault of yours. Don't look so hurt. You know by now, I'm not as mean as I sound. I'm tired, that's all."

He slumped down in his chair closing his eyes, all the humor gone out of his face, leaving only exhaustion and a blurring of features from too much whiskey.

She caught his shoulders and pulled him forward in the chair, shaking him till his eyes opened and he stood up. Supporting him, she led him to the couch at the back of the office, feeling sharply the weight of his dependence. She took off his coat and, making him sit, unlaced his shoes. He fell back with a deep sigh, and she knew he would sleep for a long while. She covered him with a robe and, without hesitation, picked up the bag of medicines and went out, blowing out the lamp as she left. She moved quickly, feeling that if she paused she would not be able to go on, would collapse under the sudden responsibility.

It was almost dark. The wind had died and there was a softness, a silence in the air, a sense of transition. For a moment the grey-black land was less harsh and forbidding. Yet nothing she could see had changed. The hills were pied with late-melting snow and dark rocks; the green of the new grass was not yet showing, or even the yellow of the old. The pines and cedars on the low hills were black in the early dark, all the colors of the earth cold. But high overhead a mackerel sky caught fire; color in waves, curving high, with interfering patterns as on a pool's surface, caps of fire and in the hollows smoky red and purple.

She stood by the buggy looking upward at the changing sky, herself warmed, in flux. The sky darkened; she climbed into the buggy, placing the bag beside her on the seat, took the lines and, for the first time, drove alone to the Indian camp.

She made the doctor's rounds, finding within herself unexpected courage and strength; she would not have thought she could face the suffering of the children without the bulwark of the doctor's presence. She had thought of herself only as a helper. But alone now, giving the simple medicines she had learned to use, she knew she was more. In the faces of the children and their mothers she saw, as in a mirror, a self unrecognized before; a giver, not of medicine, but of love. And seeing this, she knew she could endure.

She made the last stop at the lodge of Eagle Voice, finding all four of his children down with the whooping cough— they had stayed miraculously well till now, the only family in the whole camp. As she worked with them a memory of Eagle Voice came to her, a vision of him, stripped to the waist in the yellow lamplight, clothed in the red and unhealed scars of his sacrifices for these children, offering his song to help Christine. She realized now that she had believed them immune.

There was little enough she could do. But under her hands she saw a change in the small faces, saw the terror die and peace return. And the power she felt was like a singing. Finished, she left the camp and drove back to the office. She lit the lamp and renewed the fire, deciding to stay till the doctor awakened. She had done all she could, but her mind returned continually to Eagle Voice and Turning Hawk, seeing their faces beyond the dark bars of the jail. They were not sick; there was no medicine she could give; and yet she felt that there was something she should do. She sat for a long time considering, finding no logic or knowledge to guide her, but driven finally to act.

She found tobacco in the doctor's desk and, taking it as a present, left the office and walked across the square to the jail; as a kind of official passport she carried the doctor's medicines. The jail was locked, but a policeman came from the hotel and, after some hesitation, let her in. He lighted a lamp and, setting it on the desk, stepped back to wait, keeping a nervous eye in the direction of the agent's house.

Eagle Voice came from the back of the cell, watching her with unsmiling face, and she knew he had heard of the sickness of his children. For a moment in the poor light she could not see Turning Hawk. She searched the barred darkness of the cell, finding him in a far corner, sitting cross-legged on the floor staring at nothing. On a small table across from him she saw a tray of food untouched. He did not move or raise his eyes to the light.

"Is he any better?" she asked Eagle Voice.

"He is not sick, only suffocating. The whole reservation is not breathing space for a man like that."

"Is there anything I can do for him?"

Eagle Voice nodded. "Get him out. He's done no wrong."

"I can't. Being a woman I have no voice in these things. But I can try."

She divided the tobacco and gave it to Eagle Voice, who received it with gratitude. He put half on the floor in front of Turning Hawk and the old man looked up at her and smiled distantly, but he did not take the tobacco.

"Even if I fail," she said to Eagle Voice, "I hope there will still be friendship between us."

He did not answer but made the sign for good—level with the heart. She turned away and the policeman moved toward the door to open it. He seemed anxious for her to leave and she suspected he had broken a rule in admitting her. She did not like to cause him trouble, but there was no other way.

She took her coat off and, not looking at the policeman, turned her attention to the fire. It was almost out, but there was wood. She built it up methodically and, when it was burning, sat in the chair before it to warm her feet. The policeman could speak no English, but he spoke volubly in Sioux to Eagle Voice, watching her nervously the while.

Eagle Voice translated, "You have to leave. The little father—the agent—will come and make trouble. You have to go quick."

For answer she settled deeper in the chair, propping her feet against the front of the stove. But she did not feel so secure. She could see that the policeman was really perturbed and, being an Indian, might throw her out.

The bag of medicines was on the floor beside her. She opened it and, finding a vaccinating needle, held it up to the light, glancing significantly at the policeman. He understood and withdrew, chattering excitedly as he closed the door.

She did not have long to wait. The agent burst angrily into the room, just as she expected. But she was surprised to see Martin with him. He did not speak but stood looking at her indignantly, awaiting an explanation.

"The doctor's not well tonight," she explained. "I'm taking his place the best I can. There's a patient here I have to watch, even if I have to stay in jail."

"That old Indian? There's nothing wrong with him. He's just making trouble."

"He hasn't eaten since he's been here—more than a week, isn't it? The doctor says he'll die if he stays. So even though there's nothing I can do, you can see I have to stay."

"No, you can't stay. A woman in the jail—it's impossible."

He turned accusingly to Martin, who was also looking at her in anger; but there was a pathetic appeal in his face. A long time ago he would have taken her out by force. Now he would not, she was sure; she was no longer afraid of him.

"You ought to be reasonable," he said. "You're interfering in something that's none of your concern. An agent's job is hard enough; don't make it harder."

She did not answer but pushed her chair back against the bars of the cell, shaking her head. "I don't mean to be difficult. But what he's done is not a killing matter, is it? Just to hope for an Indian millennium? And not even expect to fight for it?"

"That isn't for you to judge," the agent told her. "In any case it can't be settled by a woman's whim."

"I'm sorry it seems a whim, but I'm really serious. I think he needs my help, so I have to stay."

"But he doesn't need any help—not medical help."

"You may be right. But you can see I have to follow my own conscience. If he were home in his own lodge it would be easier for everyone."

"You mean you want me to let him out to make more trouble?"

"No. But you should think what your trouble would be if he died here. He's an important and respected man among his people. They would resent his loss; this would be a place of death where no Indian would come without a fight. That would be trouble worth mentioning."

The agent was looking doubtfully at Martin, as if waiting for advice. But she could see that, because of her own actions, Martin had fallen in his respect.

"Well," Martin told him, "he isn't really the leader of this Ghost Dance. Eagle Voice is. And in his present condition he isn't likely to do much harm."

"You can't stay here," the agent told Leah. "That's final. If I turn him loose will you try to persuade him to forget this Ghost Dance foolishness?"

"No. I'm only concerned with his health. In any case, I would have no influence."

"You're hard to deal with. But I'll let him go anyway."

He opened the cell and Eagle Voice said something to Turning Hawk in Sioux. The old man stood with difficulty and walked out. He did not look at anyone and, though he seemed weak, he walked with a regal dignity.

Leah rose and put on her coat; but before leaving she turned to Eagle Voice. "Your children are not in danger now. I'll do what I can for them, and promise to let you know if they get worse."

He thanked her, but in sign, knowing she would understand. He went on moving his hands so rapidly that she could not follow, but when he began singing she knew what it was he wanted.

She listened intently to the short repetitive phrases of the song till she knew she could repeat them even though she did not know their meaning. When he stopped she sang, forgetting neither the words nor the music, but repeating only once, aware with repressed glee of the shock in the faces of her husband and the agent.

Eagle Voice smiled at her in approval, holding up four fingers to indicate the number of times the song was to be sung. He made the sign for good and moved back into the cell.

"What was all that about?" Martin asked.

"A song he gave me. He thinks it will help his children."

"You're not serious; you were just humoring him. You don't intend to use it, do you?"

She picked up the medicine without answering and stepped out the door. She did not want to hurt him any further in the agent's eyes. But in her heart she could hear the song; she would sing it for the children of Eagle Voice, she knew.

## 🎋 53 🎋

The square was full of Indians when Westland got off the stage at Arrow Creek. It was afternoon but dark, the air heavy with misty spring rain that moved like dust on the wind.

He left his bags at the hotel and walked along the square toward the Major's office, wondering what had brought the Indians together. After the long trip, Westland was glad to be back but, for no reason, anxious too. His throat was dry and he found he was hurrying, not to arrive anywhere but as if to face something while he still had the courage.

He passed the doctor's office and in a moment heard a door slam and footsteps hurrying after him. Glancing back he saw a woman running toward him, and in just the instant before recognition, he had a sharp impulse to run. He could not see her face—she was shielding it from the wind and rain with her hand. But even before she uncovered it, he knew it was Leah.

He saw a shadow cross her face, an evanescent change of feeling in response to his own, and yet she hurried on, driven by what it was she had to say.

"You came just in time; if you hurry you can still help."

He said nothing and she stopped suddenly. "I'm sorry,

255

you don't know what I'm talking about. It's the trial of Eagle Voice—a kind of trial—about the Ghost Dance. You've been there—you ought to be able to say what it's all about and maybe it will help get him free."

"Free?"

"Yes. He's been in jail ever since he got back, two weeks ago. They let Turning Hawk go a few days ago, but they're still holding Eagle Voice. His family's sick and they won't let him out to doctor them. Now they're having a trial."

She began walking on along the square, and he fell in beside her—but with a strong reluctance.

"You still haven't told me why they're in jail."

"Yes. The Ghost Dance—they're afraid it will cause trouble."

"Why?"

"Have you read any reports in the newspapers?"

"Yes, but just wild-west stories no one could believe. Surely the Major wouldn't."

"Oh, that's something else you don't know—there's a new agent. I guess the Major was a Democrat."

Westland stopped reluctantly. "Wait now. I don't even have a permit to stay here yet—I'm a stranger to the agent—and you want me to burst in there and testify. What does the new agent think about it, anyway?"

"I honestly don't think he knows anything about it. He seems kind of timid, though. I hate to say it, but I think Martin has too much influence with him—and you can guess how he'd feel about it. Besides that, a reporter was here doing his best to stir up a story. So there's no one really with an honest point of view—except yourself."

The directness of her gaze embarrassed him. "I don't think I'm very honest either. I try to be, but how can you be honest and an advocate too? Or testify and still be an observer?"

"I guess you can't. But do you think they ought to be in jail? Is this Ghost Dance really a rebellion?"

He did not answer but stood looking at her in confusion. She had changed; she was thinner, her face was less round. And yet there was a fullness in it and a power he had not felt in her before. It made her very beautiful to him; yet for the moment he felt only resentment, almost dislike.

She reacted instantly, turning away, her eyes lowered "I'm sorry. I wasn't thinking about you or your work. It's

256

important too, I know. I guess I'm caught too deeply in their troubles to be fair. Maybe you'd better not do it."

Without looking at him again, she walked quickly back toward the office. He wanted to follow her but knew he would have to run to catch up. He checked himself and went on along the square. He found the place of the trial, the same large room in which the Major had held meetings; but it was full of chairs and benches now on which the Indians sat, uncomfortable and self-conscious. There were no seats left, so he stood alone at the back of the room.

At the front of the room Eagle Voice sat stiffly on a backless chair. His robe was wrapped tightly around him, his face expressionless. Yet, in spite of his defensiveness, there was about him an air of dignity and power. To his left a small, bald-headed man—the agent, Westland guessed—sat before a table; to his right Martin stood. Martin was questioning the Indian, filling perfectly the role of prosecutor.

"The real purpose of this dance then, is to destroy the white race?"

"No. It is to bring back the buffalo and all the dead Indians, to restore the earth as it was before. The Indian is part of this land; he is born of the earth. The white man is not. How he will be destroyed, I do not know. But in this place it will be as if he had never been."

"How will all this come about?"

"Our Father will cause a great whirlwind to come; a new earth will slide over the old." Eagle Voice moved one hand above the other in a sign very similar to the one for death.

"Suppose some white men survive this catastrophe; will the Indians then assist providence and finish them off?"

"No. Our Father says, do not fight. Do no harm to anyone. There will be no white men left; Our Father will do just as he says."

"When will he do this?"

"In the fall or perhaps in the next spring. I do not know."

"It's impossible, of course; how anyone can believe such nonsense is beyond me."

"If you believe it impossible, why do you worry? If it is good it will prevail; if it is bad it will fall to the ground."

"It's no good to argue. If you're released, will you promise not to cause trouble teaching this fantastic nonsense?"

Eagle Voice shook his head, looking directly at Westland.

"Here is one of your own people," he said, "who has seen Our Father and talked with him. If he says it is bad, I will lead no more dances."

Westland was shocked; he had not intended to say anything. He was seized again by the desire to escape. But he was trapped now. Martin did not so much as look at him; but the agent smiled as if greeting a friend.

"Would you give us your opinion?" he asked Westland.

"This is none of my affair. I try not to interfere with the religion of others."

"This is not religion," Martin snapped. "It's utter nonsense."

"Nevertheless," the agent persisted, "will you give your opinion of this as a cause of trouble?"

"It's not a cause but an effect; it's a religion of despair. I see nothing bad in it."

The agent scowled downward at the table.

"I could have told you beforehand what he would think," Martin said. "He's in love with savagery."

Westland said nothing. There was a ripple of whispering among the Indians; and as the word passed, he saw them turning toward him, one after another, in gratitude. He felt a deep sense of relief, now that he had spoken, though watching the agent and Martin, he knew he would not be able to finish his work.

Martin went on questioning Eagle Voice; but the agent was impatient. "I don't want to hold you any longer," he said to Eagle Voice. "You can go free. But I will break up any dances with my police. This will not be allowed."

He went out then, not waiting to adjourn the trial.

Westland followed him into the office, and made his request to stay, putting the letters of introduction on the table. But the agent would not look at them.

"You can stay the night, of course," he said. "But no longer. You can see these are troubled times. I have enough to worry about."

Westland left, disappointed but with a strong sense of release. He went back to the hotel and after supper stepped out into the darkness, intending to go to the Indian camp; instead he crossed the square to the doctor's office, hoping to find Leah. But she was gone.

"Probably Eagle Voice's lodge," the doctor told him.

In the darkness it took him a long time to find the right

lodge. And when he did, it seemed to be dark. But stooping through the entrance, he saw a small fire glowing redly on a stone altar. The air was heavy with a bittersweet smell of burning grass.

Just as he entered, a child began coughing, a breathless, whooping spasm so racked and tortured that he felt a contraction of his own chest. He found the child in the dim light; and not till the spasm was finished did he realize that the woman holding him was Leah. She did not look at Westland, whether from intent or because she was engrossed with the child, he could not tell.

At the back of the lodge Eagle Voice sat, praying quietly, pipe in hand, eyes intent on the altar before him. His face was painted and from his hair an eagle head stared with eyeless sockets. He was wearing the black suit and in the darkness it shone with blue and purple lights. Beside him an assistant sat, drum on his knees, waiting.

No one noticed Westland as he stood at the entrance; and he was on the point of leaving when he saw that Leah needed help to hold the child—he was jerking and struggling in terrible choking efforts to breathe.

Westland sat beside her, putting his arm behind the child; and though the fire was small, the lodge cold, he began to sweat immediately. Something of the boy's fear and suffering seemed to flow into him through touch. His own muscles became tense; he was breathing hard and deep. He glanced at Leah and found her looking at him now in surprise. She let the child down between them, her arm also behind his back.

Immediately the small body straightened in a spasm, thrusting backward against the lodge cover, almost falling, though both their arms held him. Westland caught Leah's hand, interlacing his fingers with hers behind the boy's shoulders to make a back rest.

Eagle Voice stood up in the smoky firelight. In one hand he held a rawhide rattle, in the other a polished buffalo horn from which furled a white ribbon of smoke. As he stood, the assistant began a quiet rhythm on the drum, scarcely touching its surface at first, building slowly as Eagle Voice moved toward the sick child, not dancing yet but, as he walked, keeping time.

Stooping, he passed the horn back and forth in front of the child's face. Then, putting his mouth to the tip of the horn, blew gently, and a heavy cloud issued from it, enveloping the child's head, sending him into a new spasm, spreading till Westland was also coughing, eyes dimmed and burning till he could hardly see the child. He could not see Leah through the smoke, but he could feel through her fingers that she too was coughing.

Four times Eagle Voice blew the cloud of smoke, keeping the time of the drum, retreating finally to leave the smoking horn beside the altar. He began singing then, shaking the rattle, movements becoming quicker, though still as quiet as the flickering of the small fire.

Westland could hardly see him through the thick air and the tear-blurring of his eyes; he was a phantom only, silent and sinuous as the shadows on the walls. He approached through the smoke, turning, twisting, bending, drum and rattle growing louder, till he was solid and startling, more than himself.

His face shone in the firelight; sweat in clear beads glassed his forehead over the red paint; and even through the heavy smoke smell in the lodge, Westland caught the odor of his exertions. His singing rose clear, hypnotic, seeming apart, unaffected by movement, a presence in itself outside the sweating, straining figure of the dancer.

The child had stopped coughing; the jerking muscle tension in his back subsided, becoming a steady trembling. The small body seemed to shrink, emptied of terror. Breath became quick and shallow—Westland could not see or hear it, could only feel it through his hand. The eyes, closed till now, opened, shining dryly in the firelight, growing brighter as they followed the shadowy dancer.

Eagle Voice, as if sensing the change, became quicker, more vigorous in his movements. The song became a chant that Westland could not understand, rising in pitch to the limit of his voice, then dropping back. Something in the chant, in the turning, rising movements of his body, suggested wings, a high spiraling of flight. And through the trembling of the boy's body Westland felt tiny, incipient motions as if the very muscles perceived and followed the movements of the dance. The motions increased till the child was again jerking and struggling. He was seized by another fit of coughing; but it was different, not the dry choking sound but free, as if the lungs had expanded. He stopped coughing and lay back limp and motionless. Looking closely at the relaxing face, Westland knew that the child was asleep.

Eagle Voice did not pause but his movements became quieter; the drumming died slowly till it pulsed no louder than a heartbeat, the rattle to a whisper of rain. Westland's hand was numb from the boy's weight; he could not feel but only remember that Leah's hand was in his.

Then it was over. Eagle Voice sank to the ground; the rattle rolled from his grasp; the drumming stopped. Leah and Westland laid the sleeping child back on the pallet, both leaning over to bring their still joined hands from under his head. Westland tried to release Leah's hand, but he could not move his fingers. He glanced at her and found her looking not at her hand but at him. Her eyes were luminous in the smoky darkness, her face very white and rapt.

He stopped trying to move his fingers and sat looking at her, the feeling returning to his fingers, sharp needle points shooting through the nerves, a stinging like nettle. She looked down then and, with a softness in her face, undid his fingers as if they were jointed sticks. Again they sat looking at each other, rubbing their numbed hands to bring back feeling. And strangely, when he could move his fingers and the tingling stopped, he felt again—so clearly that he looked to see —her fingers laced with his. Glancing up, he found she too was looking at her hand in wonder. She did not look at him again but turned her attention to the child, covering him with a robe.

The drummer was gone, though Westland had not seen him leave. Eagle Voice still lay on the ground as if asleep. His face was still exuding sweat that ran slowly down the sides of his face. The painted designs were smeared, giving his face a wild, formless expression. The black suit was dusty and limp with sweat. His wife came into the lodge and covered him with a robe, then sat on the ground beside the sleeping child.

Westland and Leah left then together. Beyond the camp darkness was complete. The sky was clouded and the wind flowed around them black and palpable as water. They moved slowly, just their arms touching, and he knew she was trusting him to find the way. He found the path with his feet, following it by touch till they were almost to the square. But before he found the entrance, he lost her; and for a moment was filled with panic, as if the darkness between them were suddenly impenetrable.

He called to her loudly, and hearing her voice clear and unexpectedly close, felt foolish and yet immensely relieved. She gave him her hand then, and they found the way.

## 🕊 54 🕊

Turning Hawk sat on the hill, the sun behind him nightward, but hot, burning his shoulders. Below, beyond the camp circle, the flat lay dry and hot, little wisps of dust riding the breeze like smoke. Against the grey hills, far out, a whirlwind crossed a drought-stricken field of grain, bending and turning, lifting its stem of smoky dust, blooming, a yellow flower against the sky. In the heat the land shimmered, fading and clearing, the alternations extreme, not different from the fading and reviving of his own vision, waves of weakness that moved continually through him, changing his perceptions.

A long time he had fasted, praying for guidance in his perplexity; but none had come. Now he would finish and go down again. Below, within the camp circle, the dancing for the fourth day was about to begin; and he found himself looking forward expectantly. For Eagle Voice had promised a wonder in the sight of the people at this dancing, a thing he had learned at Wind River on his trip during the summer. Turning Hawk could see him there below, speaking to the people, arranging the ceremony. Beside him the tree spread, leaves dusty and prematurely yellow from the drought. Bright bits of cloth fluttered among the leaves, prayer offerings to the sun.

Around the dance ring the people were gathering with a quiet murmuring, stirring small puffs of dust with their feet. A young woman stepped from among them and crossed the circle to stand beside the tree, in her hands, barely visible from the height, a bow and arrows. Facing the west, she shot an arrow; he did not see its flight, but a group of young men followed it, running. To all the quarters she shot; the arrows

262

were returned and hung on the tree beside the pipe and the hoop given Eagle Voice in his vision.

At the edge of the crowd, a small group formed and began a march around the circle of lodges, singing, moving left to right, sunwise, growing as others fell in behind. The circuit complete, they returned to the center, forming in a single line that moved around the tree in the beaten path of the dance circle to make a complete ring. They stopped and stood motionless while Eagle Voice prayed, facing the west toward the land of the Messiah, from whence, as they believed, the buffalo and all the dead Indians would return; the direction also of the black road that, at the last, all men must travel.

The prayer finished, they moved slowly around the circle, the hands of each touching the shoulders of the person ahead, all singing, and he could hear the words now, "Father I come, Father I come." Four times the ring turned, then stopped.

For a moment there was silence. Dust from the movement cleared and trailed off, spreading to thin white streamers across the flat. Then from the depth of silence, the crying began, the people wailing and moaning as at a new death, crying to those who had died, the sound one single cry of pain and sorrow, rising and falling like wind in the trees. His vision blurred; and over the ring, dust bloomed and drifted as he dancers took up dirt and tossed it skyward.

The crying stopped. In silence, all raised their arms and faces to the western sky, standing thus for a long time, praying, as he knew, that they might see again their kindred.

They sat down then in the ring and Eagle Voice spoke. Turning Hawk could see him moving slowly around the tree addressing all, though he could not hear the words. As they sat, the sun went under, the sky reddened slowly. The dancers rose and, in the dimming light, widened the circle.

They joined hands again and sang, softly the first time so that he could not hear the words but only an intense humming, then repeating loud and clear as they moved, turning slowly.

> The Father says it,
> The Father says it,
> You shall see the Grandfather,
> The Father says it,
> The Father says it,

You shall see your kindred,
The Father says it,
The Father says it.

Dust rose up, slanting on the steady breeze, engulfing the base of the tree and one side of the ring of dancers, moving off in the dim light, tinged with red.

Turning Hawk stood shakily, weak from the long fasting, and turning found the western sky a haze of red. High overhead thin clouds lay in a wide red sheet, rippled evenly like sand on a flat, and below, from a source beyond the black mountains, the red dust rose, bright at the hilltops, fading high to the rippling clouds: dust of the spirit nations, the dancers beyond death.

He stood at the edge of the bluff, wanting to join the dancers, but something held him back, a reluctance, a powerful weariness. Only with intense effort was he able to move his legs and begin the descent. He moved slowly into the dark shadows of the hill, watching the dancers, with difficulty perceiving them as real and not figures of dream. Only one edge of the ring was visible, whirling wildly into a steady burning of dust, voices high and straining with the straining bodies and tensely swinging arms. The sound came to him in gusts, drifting away and renewing.

Closer, the singing was loud and strong, drawing him powerfully; he had a fleeting image of a small figure drawn like a mote of dust to the heart of a whirling wind. He stood at the edge of the circle, waiting for an opening, and as he waited a woman burst through the ring, rotating her arms wildly, lifting her knees high as if wading in water. Her hair, grey with dust, was blown over her face, and through it her eyes shone, bulging and sightless. Beside him she stopped, arms still spinning; but her feet seemed to freeze to the earth. She tilted backward, falling as stiffly and slowly as a tree. The flailing of her arms stopped and she struck the ground with an audible expulsion of breath and lay still. He stooped to touch her but caught himself and drew back, remembering the promised miracle: perhaps it was this.

He found an opening then between two women and, fitting his fingers to theirs, joined the dance. The women were strong, their movements jerky and violent but in perfect accord with the singing. He could hear their voices, strained and hoarse, singing the intense involvement of their bodies

He was drawn into a darkness of dust, emerging after a time, choking and out of breath, on the windward side, caught up now in the intensity of the action, though he had not yet joined the singing.

Before him the tree was a peak of light floating above the dust. Among the fluttering leaves the bright offerings of cloth shone, the last color of day. Around it in the circle, fallen dancers were scattered as randomly as rocks, hardly visible in the dust that flowed above them. Moving on the windward curve he was in clear air; dust rose at his feet, slanting upward, a strange river of the air.

In front of him, beneath the dust, he saw the figure of a man approach, recognizing Eagle Voice as his head and shoulders emerged into light. He walked to the woman on Turning Hawk's right, his step light and graceful, adapting as he came close to the sidewise movement of the dance. In his hand a blue cloth fluttered and shone. He looked intently into the woman's face, matching his step to hers, moving the cloth with circular motion, increasing the speed till it became a perfect hoop of blue. He was chanting now, expelling his breath in short breaths like a winded runner, "Hu, hu, hu."

In the woman's fingers Turning Hawk felt a tremor, slight at first but increasing to a violent trembling. She still sang, but he could hear a slurring of the words.

They moved into the dust again. Eagle Voice seemed to sink, as if wading into roily water; the colored circle of cloth faded to grey. Turning Hawk himself sank into the dust, vision blurred, but he could still see the circle of cloth and the face of Eagle Voice, seeming to shine in the darkness, to cast a light on the face of the woman. She watched him in complete fascination, eyes unblinking even in the dust. He moved backward slowly toward the tree, changing the circular movement of the cloth to short vertical strokes.

The woman's hand left Turning Hawk's and she followed Eagle Voice toward the center, though still moving sidewise with the circle. She had lost the words of the song and was moaning, still with the melody, an intense projection of its meaning. She was staggering; and suddenly she stopped and stood rigid, leaning slowly to the side.

Turning Hawk moved on in the circle; dust flowed between till Eagle Voice and the woman disappeared. He did not see her fall. He moved on and on in the dance, drawn beyond his own strength, in and out of the dust, from darkness to light

265

and again to darkness, his vision clearing and dimming alternately as if the dust moved within him as it did without.

Under the rising hill of dust, the fallen dancers grew many till Eagle Voice was moving with difficulty to avoid touching them. He stopped the dance then.

The dancers sat where they were in the circle. Turning Hawk sank into the dust, grateful for the pause, clutching the ground with his hands to fight off a darkness that seemed about to engulf him. The dust cleared, rising and drifting off. The last daylight was gone, but the moon was up, revealing the fallen dancers in a blue light. Some were sitting, moaning softly, staring around them at the shadowy ring of people. Others still lay as they had fallen, yet subtly changed in the new illumination.

Eagle Voice stood by the tree, facing the west, and with arms outstretched prayed, "Grandfather, have pity on us. Give us to see our kindred who have walked the black road west before us: all those young ones dead of the white man's sickness; all those starved on his bitter food who might have lived had the buffalo lived.

"Give us to see again the buffalo and all the animal nations fallen to the hunger of his rifle. Give us to see the new earth as Our Father has promised.

"Those who have died in the dance, let them return with visions to lift up the hearts of those who remain; let the new moon guide them on that far spirit path across the sky, the morning star shine unclouded to light their way.

"Grandfather, look down in pity on these who cry to you from darkness and dust."

Several of the fallen ones were sitting, looking around in bewilderment. One by one they stood and staggered out of the circle. Near Turning Hawk a woman was stretched rigid on the ground; but as he watched, she was shaken by a violent tremor. She opened her eyes and sat up trembling, gazing wildly about, moaning softly and continuously. Her face slowly lost its tenseness; tears dimmed the feverishness of her eyes. She stood and moved unsteadily toward him; and only then he recognized her as Blue Fawn. She did not look at him but moved through the circle, weeping with complete abandon.

Only a few of the fallen ones remained in the circle. These Eagle Voice approached, one by one, drawing from them distracted, incoherent accounts of visions. A woman who had seen her dead children smiled and wept and with broken voice tried to sing.

An old man spoke in a whisper to Eagle Voice, and Turning Hawk could not understand him. The two men conversed for a while; then after a long silence the old man stood and sang:

> The whole world is coming,
> A nation is coming, a nation is coming,
> The eagle has brought the message to the people,
> The Father says it, the Father says it.
> Over the whole earth they are coming,
> The buffalo are coming, the buffalo are coming.
> The Crow has brought the message to the people,
> The Father says it, the Father says it.

The dancers stood and took up the song, softly the first time, then—moving again in the dance—loudly.

Turning Hawk could hardly stand; his body was alien to him, weak, worn-out. And yet he moved in a clarity of perception such as he had never known. He seemed to float easily in the circle, yet to know at the same moment that he was stumbling. They went on singing the new song, turning again in the dust and moonlight, and it was oddly familiar, coming to him with no effort of memory as though he himself had dreamed it. The images it brought merged dimly with the memory of his first vision: the buffalo moving under him solid as earth, himself borne lightly as a breath. Beyond them in distance, a mass of figures advanced: people, he knew, yet strange and terrible.

He came to the present suddenly, having fallen to his knees, feeling himself pulled violently along by the dancers. He emerged from dust into clear air and found Eagle Voice in front of him, turning the strip of cloth in a hoop of blue. He watched the man's eyes, shining in moonlight, heard his rhythmically expelled breath, "Hu, hu, hu," but as if from a distance. He had a sense of someone—a friend—calling from far away and himself trying but unable to answer. The circle turned, curving past the ascending white hill, drawing him relentlessly into the darkness again. And he was suddenly blind, choked with fear.

He seemed to rise then, borne up by the dust; to look back from a great height at the revolving hoop of dancers: figures of light emerging from earth, turning and returning again to earth. He floated in loneliness, drawn downward by all desire but unable to descend.

Beneath him the circle turned, in and out of the light, a hoop half buried in the earth, dimming, turning faster and faster, becoming a round blur of light, a whirling wind. It burst at the center: small figures flung outward, and he was falling toward his desire, spinning dizzily downward into the whirling vortex of the dark.

## 🐚 55 🐚

Little Wound sat beside his grandfather in the sweat lodge, following the movements of the ceremony, aware clearly in the small enclosure of all that went on. In the quiet air he could identify the person odors of all those present—six besides himself—knowing clearly their order in the circle. The close dome of the lodge seemed to touch him from all sides and above so that his perception of it was direct and with his whole body. It was the shape of the world, his grandfather had said, the sky arching over and the earth flat beneath; he perceived it now with secure, solid knowing.

The pipe had been offered; smoke circled in quiet currents about his head; the taste was a sharp tingling on his tongue. The pipe was passed out now to the women, and the blankets were lowered around the sides of the lodge, cutting off the flow of air and the sense of the world outside.

He touched his grandfather's arm, finding him relaxed and tranquil, as he had not been in a long time. Little Wound was himself strengthened, drawn close, and quieted. A hard, wrinkled hand closed over his; his whole body seemed for an instant enclosed in it as palpably as in the sweat lodge.

A hot stone was passed in; he followed its passage by the movement of heat on his face, felt the impact as it dropped into the hole, smelled the scorched wood of the sticks that had carried it. From the hole the sweet smell of vernal grass mixed with tobacco rose. The pile of stones grew to a hot, expanding presence in the small space, brought quickly the smell of sweat and the savor of heated earth. The last opening was closed and the bowl of water was passed, revealing its presence and circular path by a sweet, wet-wood odor and a breath of coolness on his face. The smell of wet hair filled the lodge.

He took a mouthful of cool water from the bowl, passed the bowl on to his grandfather and, spouting the water into his hands, rubbed it in his hair. He leaned forward then, face close to the earth to escape the fiery heat at the top of the lodge.

Water exploded on the stones, a slap of air against his face and a tongue of steam flashing over him. He was sweating, large drops falling from his face onto the ground, releasing a rich and faintly female smell. And for a while he was squeezed, pressed tightly by the steamy heat and the small space. The blankets were raised and cool air flowed over him, releasing for a moment the pressure; then they were closed and again the heat grew.

Four alternations there were of heat and cold, of pressure and release, before the blankets were thrown off and he emerged into cool air and open space. He swam in a pool at the creek, coming out with a vivid sense of morning or of spring.

This was his first preparation for the dance, and he sat reluctantly before his grandfather, enduring the painting. Always before he had liked this ceremony: having his hair brushed and braided, his face touched with the smooth, pleasant-smelling paint. But that had been before the dancing. He did not like it now and had stayed away from the dancing as long as he could. Something had changed in his grandfather; he was drawn up and distant, touching him with hands only, softly but without gentleness, involved completely in the designs he painted. He finished and Little Wound stood up and was brushed aside firmly by the next person in line. He moved away to search for his mother. But when he found her she was sitting before Eagle Voice being painted also. When he touched her she drew away with a quick impatience, giving him the pushing-down sign for wait.

He turned away, hurt by her impatience, yet, in the unusual excitement of the people, finding a reason for it: they were all caught up in the dance. He remembered the cattle hunt of a year ago, the drumming and singing that had lifted him up and held him strongly. There was the same sense of excitement now—an intense anticipation that submerged all else. But he missed the joy, the beat of the drums.

A dog nosed his hand and stood beside him, but it turned and fled suddenly; and feeling the beating of sticks on the earth, he knew that all dogs were being driven away lest they disturb those who would die in the dance.

His mother found him and led him to the dance ground, giving him no words or attention. He walked beside her reluctantly and with a sense of traveling in unknown country. And though he walked so close that he could feel her presence on his face, she seemed to move on ahead of him into impassable distances. But he did not feel like hurrying after her; he wanted to stop, to stay quiet awaiting her return.

She stopped and he recognized the dance circle by the dust that puffed under his feet, the depression in the earth that reminded him of buffalo rings his father had shown him on the prairie. Others joined them; and after a wait there was prayer and the line began to move. Walking beside his mother in the dusty circle he could feel the singing against his face.

The ring stopped; he touched his mother and found her standing with arms upraised. And suddenly she was crying, sobs racking her body, bursting like living beings from her lips. He had not known her to weep so violently since the death of his father. He drew his hand away trembling, himself weeping at the vividness of her grief. He touched the person next to him and knew that all the people were crying Only death, he knew, brought such grief; yet no one had died. He wanted to run, but he could not move. It seemed an endless time before the crying stopped and the singing began again.

His mother took his left hand, his right was seized by someone he did not know, and he was drawn to the left in the circular path. Dust rose around him, spoiling the delicate skin sense, obliterating all odors but those of the earth, reducing his awareness. He walked with difficulty, jerked violently from side to side by the swinging hands that held him Through his hands he was aware clearly of the feelings of the persons he touched. His mother held his hand; he knew that his grandfather was within the circle with Eagle Voice leading the dance. Yet the feeling grew that they had gone where he would not follow. In fear he tried to escape, but the two hands held him, drew him onward unceasingly into the dust.

The fear became terror with the violent trembling that came to him through his mother's hand. Her body grew stiff and awkward, unresponsive to his touch. And suddenly she dropped his hand and staggered forward into the circle. He jerked his other hand free and followed her, not touching her but staying close. Someone tried to catch him but he broke away and retreated to the other side of his mother.

He brushed against someone and recognized his grandfather instantly; but he was given no recognition. He stood for a moment touching both—his mother and grandfather—perceiving a tense communication between them that excluded him coldly. He stepped back repelled, not understanding.

He could feel faintly the movement of the cloth his grandfather fluttered in the air; its rhythm increased, and after a time his mother fell heavily beside him. When he stooped to touch her, he was lifted back and released to stand before his grandfather.

"She is dead and talking now with those who have died before. She will return. Wait."

Turning Hawk moved away, and Little Wound was frozen with shock. And yet his senses told him there was no death. Dust was thick in the air, but within the circle, over its clogging smell, he could still detect the person odor of his mother, untainted by death. He bent down close above her and was reassured. But there was a sharp, increasing odor of fear about her that frightened him almost as much as the prospect of death; he could not refrain from touching her.

Her face was stiff, as still as death, but her skin was warm, damp with sweat and smooth with paint. He moved his hand lightly over it, finding her eyes closed. But with half-terrified relief, he felt movement under the lids: the eyes were moving as if following some action, though he knew that, closed, they were sightless as his own.

He was puzzled and touched them again, this time too firmly: she shuddered violently and sat up, flinging her arms wide and almost knocking him down. She struggled to her feet and, when he touched her tentatively, she pushed his hand away and, turning, moved off, almost running. He followed her and felt the ring of dancers opening to let them through.

Outside the ring she stopped and stood weeping; and he waited, himself on the verge of tears, till she was again quiet.

But when she took his hand and led him back toward the dance circle, he was filled with dread. Waiting till her hand relaxed, he pulled free and ran, not stopping till he tripped and fell headlong on the ground. He paused, his hands and body pressed intently against the earth to catch the feel of her footsteps. But she was not coming. He remembered then that it was night; in the darkness she had lost him. He had not run far; he could still feel faintly the rhythmic stamping of the dancers. But he would not go back.

He sat up and a dog nosed his face; he recognized it as the one that had touched him before the dance. He stroked its head and it lay beside him on the ground, nose pointing intently toward the dancers. Now and then the hackles on its neck would rise and a growl vibrate in its throat. Something in the air frightened and repelled the animal also.

Little Wound moved closer, giving comfort to the animal; and in the giving was himself comforted. The dog stopped growling and, in a little while, slept.

## 🐉 56 🐉

Martin was standing at the window of the agent's office when the six policemen rode across the square and tied their sweating horses to the rack. They had not brought Eagle Voice or Turning Hawk; and yet in their faces he could see no consciousness of failure. But there was something unusual about them, an air of somnolence, an indecisiveness of movement, as if they were tired or ill. They came toward the building slowly and in silence, following the lieutenant and Sun Ray, the interpreter.

The agent, at his desk writing, had not seen them through the window. But when the lieutenant and Sun Ray entered and stood before him he merely nodded and, without ceasing to write, asked, "Where are the prisoners? Did you leave them at the jail?"

"No. No prisoners. We could not touch them; they are

sacred." Sun Ray interpreted directly, with no disdain nor derision.

The agent looked up, startled. "What do you mean, sacred? They're only men—like you or me."

"No. They have done what you and I cannot do: they have caused many to die in the dance and have brought them back after they have seen and talked with their relatives in the world of spirit. We have seen them do these things and are afraid to interfere."

"That's humbug," the agent said angrily. "I thought you were civilized enough to know that. The dancers have merely fainted and dreamed. Spirit world? How can you believe such nonsense?"

"Some of the dancers, young people, have seen men who died long ago—Old Lone Horn, Bone Man, Long-haired Wolf, Black Sun, Buffalo Road—all these and many others, all brave men when these who dreamed were small four-legged ones crawling among the lodges. Yet these have described them as I myself knew them and remember—the clothes they wore, their medicine, the coups they counted. These young ones have seen them in that other world and bring back word of them and how they live. There is mystery here and power. I am afraid to oppose it."

"Do you believe this nonsense also?" the agent asked Sun Ray.

The man colored and squirmed uncomfortably under the agent's gaze. And yet he said, "I think they have some kind of power, I don't know what."

The agent called the others in and questioned them, but they were dumb—half dazed, Martin thought, and half afraid.

"Now what can I do?" the agent asked in desperation. "I have an order from Washington to stop this foolishness, but now these vaunted police have failed me. And I can't ask for troops." He looked accusingly at Martin, waiting for an answer.

"I don't know," Martin said slowly. "It ought to be stopped; but if it comes to fighting, I don't know." He had wanted the dancing stopped. It had robbed him of his congregation; not since April—six months now—had any except half-breeds and squaw men been in the church. But now, faced with the actual suppression, Martin was not sure. He felt exhausted; he wanted desperately to leave the reservation, to

273

turn his back on it forever. Yet he knew he would not. There was nothing to hold him, only a sense of incompleteness that would never let him go.

"Well, I'll have to go myself; at least I still have a few men who haven't been hypnotized. Will you and your men stick by me?" he asked the lieutenant.

The Indian nodded.

"Will you go along, Reverend?"

"No, I'll go by myself."

It was afternoon by the time he was ready to leave. But the weather was warm, the sky clear; he could camp on the way.

There were no small camps of Indians along the trail as in the past. All the allotments except those of a few squaw men and half-breeds were deserted, the houses already falling to ruin. They stood with doors open, the windows gone. From the darkness of the interiors he could tell that the white tepee canvas had been stripped from the walls and ceilings—to make ghost shirts, he knew. Stunted, dry weeds grew in the yards and on the sunken dirt-covered roofs.

But it was the house of Eagle Voice that had changed the most. He came to it about sundown, realizing as he approached that he was looking forward to the sight of it; in the past it had lifted his spirits with its neatness and quiet air of civilization. But he was shocked by what he saw now. It loomed darkly on the evening sky, sagging, twisted, its roof touched with red western light. The single cottonwood in the yard had blown over against it and leaned heavily above the broken roof, shedding yellow leaves. It swayed back and forth in the wind, rubbing against the house with a weird bellowing sound that filled him with loneliness and dread.

The windows were broken, the white paint blistered and peeling. As he passed, the door blew open, and the movement struck him with terror. Yet he stopped the horse and with a shortness of breath—as if fighting a high wind— walked across the weedy yard. He touched the rusted knob, and for a moment some fierce compulsion drew him inward. But he could not move. He stood in balance on the doorstep, touched lightly by falling leaves, intensely aware of the tree slanting above him, the sound it made against the roof, a voice of terror beckoning. The horse whinnied from the road, releasing him; he closed the door and walked back to the buggy.

He drove on then, shaken, remembering vividly the house

as it had been, the medicine room, the bundle he had violated, the terrible braying of the mule as it followed him along the dark road. All of it, the memory, the image of the broken house, filled him with anxiety. Though it was past, there was a quality in it of revelation: if he could understand it, he could see the future. He put a long way between himself and the house before he camped.

Knowing the police would be back, the Indians had moved into the badlands. So it was evening of the next day when Martin found the camp. And having found it, he could not tell why he had come. He had small welcome from the Indians, and for the first time waited by himself outside the camp circle. They were not hostile, only preoccupied, involved in the wild ritual of the Ghost Dance.

The circle had already formed, so he had no chance to speak with Eagle Voice. He left his horse tied to the buggy and, surrounded by barking, circling dogs, walked toward the dance ground, feeling a sharp premonition of danger. But no one paid him any attention. As he neared the dancers, the dogs halted and he was again alone. He recognized the place; he had camped here with the Indians before the cattle hunt, a year ago.

The dancers were marching in a circle, singing, raising a white dust that blew over him chokingly. He moved with them till he reached the west side, where the dust cleared, and stopped. He saw Eagle Voice then, under the yellow cottonwood at the center of the circle, partly buried in the rising dust, only his head and shoulders visible, still and immovable as stone. Above him the tree seemed to tilt; suddenly, in vision, Martin saw the house crushed under that other tree. And the vision and what he saw now were composite, a single image of terror and portent that mysteriously involved himself.

The dancers stopped and turned toward him, facing the lowering sun. For a moment there was unbroken silence, only a windy, hissing sound that might have been wind in the tree or the sound of their breathing. Though Martin knew their gaze was above him on the sky, he was impaled, transfixed. He could not move or turn away.

Then the air was rent with crying, a single wail of grief rising wave-like above him, breaking to myriad voices of sorrow. The sound struck him with awe: it was more than weeping from the lips of men—it was a wordless cry of all the pain

275

and woe of the world. Something within him stirred in answer.

The sound died and again there was silence, only the quiet hissing and the violent beating of his own heart. He was breathless in a suffocation that was like grief. He saw the Indians raise their arms to the sky and stand in silence, faces shining in the brilliant slanting rays of the sun. They were painted garishly in red, blue, yellow, and white. Blue-black, sheeny feathers stood in their hair or fluttered at their elbows. Most wore ghost shirts of white cloth, blue at the neck, covered with curious symbols, also in blue: sun, moon, stars, animals, birds, pipes. Against the grey, dusty flat, the ragged tepees, they shone, a living wheel of color, at once beautiful and alien. They joined hands and sang, softly at first, the music simple, repetitious, but growing in power as the circle turned; he had never heard their singing as music before.

He was drawn toward them with strange yearning, though he did not move. And in his vision rose incongruously the image of a painted serpent coiled around jeweled eyes. He shook his head and turned away, closing his ears to the singing. He went back to his buggy outside the camp circle, accompanied again beyond the tepees by the dogs. They followed at a distance, barking but not trying to bite. He sat in the buggy and they encircled him, sitting in the dust. And he was grateful for their presence. He thought they had changed, were less fierce and savage; and he did not hate them now.

It was nearly dark when he saw the dust of the police approaching from the east beyond the creek bed. But before they were near enough for him to see individual riders, the singing and dancing stopped, and suddenly all the space around him was filled with running, crouching Indians all carrying guns or bows. They scattered out along the creek bed between the camp and the approaching riders, hiding behind boulders or the steep-cut bank of the creek. In a moment all was quiet; and he knew that not an Indian save the women and children in the camp could be seen from beyond the creek.

The police came in a compact group across the open flat. He could see the agent now, riding in the lead with the lieutenant, showing no caution or awareness of the Indians in the creek. But at perhaps two hundred yards they stopped.

Martin got down and, hearing one of the policemen shouting, knew they were aware of the danger. He descended to the creek bed and walked along it, followed by the dogs, splashing through puddles of yellow water till he found both Eagle Voice and Turning Hawk crouched behind two boulders on the far bank. He stopped and Eagle Voice came down to where he stood.

"I know they have come to arrest us," he told Martin. "But we can't go. The people depend on us now. So there may be a fight. You can stay here in the creek and you will not be hurt."

Martin shook his head but said nothing.

Eagle Voice went back up the bank and looked carefully over between the two rocks. What he saw made him stand, climb out of the creek, and walk away toward the police.

Martin climbed up beside Turning Hawk and, peeking carefully over the bank, saw the agent and two policemen walking out to meet Eagle Voice. When they met they were too far away for Martin to hear words, but he could tell by their actions and the tone of voices that an argument had started.

The lieutenant would step in front and speak to Eagle Voice, who would listen, gradually assuming a position of ease; then the agent would step out, gesticulating sharply. Eagle Voice would stiffen and bring his rifle into firing position, forcing the agent back. Then it would start all over again.

There was a dream-like quality about the situation, a ludicrousness that Martin knew could change suddenly to horror. He climbed out on the bank, walked a few steps out toward the little group, and stopped. He had not thought what he would do; he only stood there, numb. But he knew they would not try to take Eagle Voice while he, Martin, stood exposed.

He saw the lieutenant and the agent look toward him in surprise; even Eagle Voice glanced back, though still keeping his gun at ready. The talk went on then but Martin could see that the gestures of the agent had lost their sharpness. He kept motioning for Martin to come on. And afterwhile the three men turned and went back toward the waiting police.

The tension went out of the air and Martin felt suddenly weak and empty. He turned, without waiting for Eagle Voice, and walked back toward the buggy.

## 57

Leah had just got into the buggy beside the doctor when she saw the agent hurrying toward them across the square. She knew the doctor had seen him also but he swung the horse away from the rack, keeping his eyes ahead, and the agent had to run to intercept him.

"Are you going to the Indian camp?" he asked the doctor.

The doctor nodded without looking at him.

"You can tell Eagle Voice and Turning Hawk that any time they'll submit to arrest, I'll issue rations to the band—not before."

"You tell them."

"I can't. They won't even let a messenger in. You're the only one who can come and go."

"I'm a doctor, not a politician. That's why they trust me. I'll tell them nothing."

"All right. You can be replaced, you know."

"Replace me, then." He drove away without looking back, not speaking till they were almost to the camp.

It was mid-November, the weather cold. Wind from the north moved with a constant current of dust over the ragged lodges, whining bleakly through the tops of the poles. Inside the thin canvas shelters, children cried and coughed with a sound not different from the wind.

"It's not the germs," the doctor told her angrily. "It's starvation. They're too weak to withstand the diseases. It's not right. They paid for the rations with their country. We've no right to withhold them because we don't like what they believe. It's these preachers, they're fiercer than the army; and this new agent is one of 'em."

He had pulled into the camp circle and turned toward the lodge of Yellow Bird when two Indians galloped in shouting, "Wasichus, Wasichus!" They made the circuit of the camp and without stopping galloped off toward the horse herd.

Immediately the camp was in uproar. Armed Indians swarmed out of the lodges, running out of the circle and hurrying off to meet the horses that were already moving in toward camp.

"Troops," the doctor said bitterly. "I had a hunch he'd sent for them. There'll be hell to pay now."

"You think there'll be fighting?"

"No, a stampede. How can these Indians fight? They'll head for the hills and go on dancing—and starving. They've got no chance in a fight and they know it."

Already lodges were being struck. Women, followed by crying children, were running back and forth piling their belongings onto rickety wagons and buggies or struggling with lodge covers in the wind.

Yellow Bird's wife ran out with a sick child wrapped in a blanket and laid it on the seat of a high-wheeled wagon. Immediately she ran back and began pulling the pins around the lodge. When she undid the fastenings up the side, the canvas flapped free, almost pulling her off the ground.

By the time she had it folded, Yellow Bird was back with two bony horses. With unbelievable quickness he had the team harnessed and hitched to the wagon and was loading the lodge poles. In a few moments the lodge and all it had held was loaded, and with one accord the two of them ran toward the ragged leather tepee of old Walking Bear, the woman's father. They disappeared inside and a moment later hustled the old man through the entrance. But he was protesting. Outside the lodge he sat down suddenly, jerking away from them both, pulling his arms and head into his blanket like a turtle. The two stood over him, Yellow Bird talking in imploring tones. But the old man would not move.

They spoke together a moment, then left him with reluctance. As they walked toward the loaded wagon, Yellow Bird saw Leah and the doctor for the first time, and came over to them.

"He says his time has come to die; he will run away no more. Will you watch over him till he is dead? And perhaps wrap him in a blanket and leave him on a hill in the sun? We cannot wait; soldiers are coming."

Leah nodded. The doctor had been digging in his bag. He handed some bottles of medicine to Yellow Bird.

"It's for all the young ones who cough. You know how it should be given. It would be better, I think, if you stayed. But I can promise nothing, having no power with the soldiers or the agent either."

"Thanks, friend. But whenever soldiers come, there are soon dead Indians. We cannot stay."

He ran to the wagon where his wife was waiting, the sick child in her arms. They pulled away at a trot, joining the long line of wagons and horses already hurrying away toward the hills.

It was incredible how quickly the camp had got in motion; the few minutes since the riders had come seemed in retrospect all confusion: dogs barking, horses whinnying, children crying and shouting, women shrieking and hurrying about their work. Yet already the last wagons and pack horses were moving away. A few tripods of poles, the oval willow frames of sweat lodges with their white buffalo skulls, and nearby a weathered buggy with no seat; these and the ragged lodge of old Walking Bear were all that remained. In front of the lodge the old man still sat unmoving, completely covered in his blanket. Near him, on its tripod, his medicine bundle swung in the wind.

The doctor turned the horse roughly toward the agency. "There's no way we can help them now. We might as well go back."

"You can take me home," Leah said. "I'll bring some food to the old man."

"He won't need food. When they decide to die, it's what they do. You can do what you like, though."

She made soup for the old Indian; waiting, she remembered the medicine whistle he had given Martin and searched for it, but it was not in the house. She went to the barn knowing that somewhere Martin had hidden it with the bundles he had collected; he had destroyed no more, she was sure, after the one with the lice and gunpowder.

She found them in a feedbox; when she opened the lid a musty odor of mice and moths, fur and tobacco and sage rose in her face. The box was full of bundles; she had not imagined he had got so many. With some misgiving, she searched among them till she found the whistle.

The soldiers had already arrived when she reached the campground; cavalry, she guessed, seeing the many horses picketed. Tents were going up, men were hurrying about bringing food and water, working with horses, building fires. They had pitched their camp between the agency and Walking Bear's lone tepee; a group of them had crossed over from their camp and gathered around the old Indian. She could hear them laughing and talking as she approached. Seeing her, they moved back toward their camp, watching her with astonishment.

Walking Bear had not moved since she saw him last; he sat beside the tripod wrapped in his blanket, alone but not withdrawn. In the way he sat, she sensed dignity and defiance, a strong personal power. She gave him the canteen of soup and he drank it hungrily, touching her face and hair when he finished.

"Granddaughter," he signed, "you have taken pity on me, white woman though you are. It will give me strength."

She gave him the whistle then. When he recognized it, he sat turning it over in his hand with an intense joy in his face. Again he thanked her but immediately dismissed her from attention.

He threw off his blanket and looped the whistle over his neck, then took the bundle from the tripod, addressing it in low, reverent tones before opening it. Holding it on his knees, he unbraided his stringy hair, brushed it with a porcupine tail, and rebraided it, wrapping it with fur and fastening several eagle feathers at the back. He mixed red pigment from a small, stoppered horn with tallow from another, rubbing them together in the palm of his hand. He painted his wrinkled cheeks, smearing them evenly, then making curious swirling designs with his fingernails. He rubbed it around the puckered sun-dance scars and a long jagged one along his side, producing a startling impression of fresh, bleeding wounds. The paint that remained he rubbed carefully on hands and wrists. He mixed yellow then, with which he painted zigzag stripes on his arms and shoulders, and finally blue for a crescent on his forehead. He fastened a small, bedraggled bird skin in his hair so that it swung just over his ear.

Finished, he stood, leaving his blanket on the ground, transformed from a wrinkled shapeless old man to a startling figure of painted features and white, sightless eyes, a figure not of waking but of sleep, with the strange haunting reality of dream.

She was shocked when he turned and, with the tottering steps of an old man, walked toward the lodge. He stooped through the entrance, reappearing in a moment with a painted bow and brightly beaded quiver of arrows. He strung the bow with difficulty and came back toward the tripod, singing now in a high nasal voice, turning his face from side to side in sightless searching.

When he found the tripod, he came toward Leah and touched her. "Granddaughter," he signed, "which way are the Wasichus?"

She pointed toward the soldier camp, still not guessing his intent; he caught the direction by feeling her hand.

The group of soldiers had stopped a little way out between the camp and where Leah stood. The old man turned toward them, shouting thinly, "Hoka hey, hoka hey," trying to run but only tottering along. He put the whistle in his mouth and blew it shrilly as he moved toward the astonished soldiers. A little way out he paused, put an arrow to the string, and shot. She saw the flight of the arrow, slow and curving over their heads, veering in the wind.

The soldiers scattered to both sides, shouting, leaving a trooper on horseback alone in the opening. The Indian again ran forward and halted, this time hitting the rearing horse. The arrow struck the hip, just puncturing the skin and flapping down against the flank. The horse exploded into bucking, throwing the trooper in a wide arc out and down at the end of the reins.

One of the others ran in behind the Indian with a drawn knife. When he drew the bow for another shot, the knife flashed behind him. She heard the snap of the cut string; the arrow fell to the ground, the bow leaped out of the old man's hand. He did not try to retrieve it but stood with arms folded, blowing defiantly on the whistle. He was surrounded by laughing, shouting soldiers, but he was not defeated. They were close, but none of them touched him; and she sensed a nervous restraint in their laughter.

The trooper with the horse was back in the saddle now, his face white with fright or anger. He unbuckled a coil of rope from the saddle and, forcing his way through the ring of soldiers, dropped a loop over the Indian's shoulders and turned the horse toward the lodge.

Leah ran forward and grabbed for the bridle, but the horse shied and broke past her at a gallop. The old man was jerked off his feet and dragged along on his back. He struck the ground hard; the whistle shrieked once with his expelled breath and was silent. Near the lodge the horse began plunging and the rider dropped the rope. She ran over to Walking Bear and found him struggling to get up. She loosened the rope and helped him to his feet, relieved to find him unhurt. She led him to the lodge, and when he touched the tripod, he sat down. She threw the blanket over his shoulders but he did not seem to notice.

He was singing again, oblivious to all around him, a death song, she knew. She left him then, sadness and wonder in her heart.

In the afternoon she was in the doctor's office when an officer rode in from the soldiers' camp.

"There's something wrong with your Indian," he told the doctor. "I couldn't see that he was hurt in that little skirmish this morning; but he's acting damn queer. You better have a look."

"There's nothing I can do. He's decided to die, that's all. But if he might have been hurt, I'll look at him."

Again they drove to the camp. Walking Bear was still sitting by the tripod; but before they touched him, Leah knew that he was dead. The doctor laid the body back on the ground and examined it briefly.

"Was he hurt?" the officer asked anxiously.

"I don't think so. He decided to die and did. It's something I'll never understand; but there it is."

"Do you think this could cause trouble with the Indians, supposing we can herd them back here? It was his own fault, but they might not think so. Maybe we could give him a military burial as a kind of gesture."

The doctor shrugged. "You can talk to the agent about that."

It was Martin who brought the coffin and prepared the body for burial. Leah had come with him to help, but there was nothing she could do. She stood watching, startled by the eagerness with which Martin approached the task. He began by wiping all the paint off the face and body, rubbing and rubbing at each wrinkle till the last trace was gone. He worked at it with a concentration and a visible tenderness that revolted her; she could not watch him any longer. She turned and walked away, standing with her back turned till she heard him place the lid on the coffin.

When she came back she found him standing in uncertainty, in his hands the whistle, the feathers, and the bird he had taken from the body. She took them from him, saying nothing, and put them back in the bundle on the tripod. She helped him lift the coffin onto the old buggy.

"The funeral will be in the morning," he told her. "A decent, Christian burial, heathen though he was."

She could see he was pleased with what he had done; and without knowing why, she resented him for it. She could hardly bring herself to ride with him.

It was late in the night when she awakened. Martin was asleep in the next room; she could hear his heavy breathing. She had been dreaming, she knew, though she could not remember the dream; but she was filled with a sense of incompleteness, of something left undone. Without hesitation, she began dressing; and it came to her what it was she had to do.

She left the house quietly and, in complete darkness, harnessed the horse, working patiently till she had all the straps untwisted and in place. She led him out of the yard and along the road toward the camp, able to see dimly after the darkness of the barn.

The moon was new—there was only starlight, a glow like frost in the sky; the wind was cold, fitful, making dry, papery sounds in the weeds along the road; yet oddly her impression was not of fear but of beauty. She was fully awake now, yet apart from herself as if she were still dreaming; she could not believe that this was herself, that she could have the courage to do what she was doing. And yet she was not really afraid, only intensely aware, moving effortlessly in beauty and strangeness.

She left the road and circled the soldiers' camp, coming up to the lodge from below. She found the old buggy and hitched the horse to it, moving quietly and without haste. She heard the sentries shout to each other startlingly close, yet she left the horse and, searching till she found the tripod, unhooked the bundle and put it in the buggy. She left then leading the horse slowly, the sound of the buggy tumultuous in the night. But she kept moving, expecting the shout of the sentry, anticipating a wild uproar. But there was nothing; and in a little while she was beyond hearing.

She crossed the creek west, following a narrow trail till she reached the hills, where she left it and climbed, leading the horse carefully around rocks and brush. It was slow, tortuous work; yet she kept on, finding an obstinate pleasure in the very difficulty. Stopping often to rest the horse, she found stones to block the wheels and take the weight off the traces. It was something she thought of herself; she could not remember having seen it done. After a long struggle she reached

he top, finding a patch of cedar next to an outcropping of
ock. She maneuvered the buggy carefully between and
topped, blocking the wheels before she unhitched.

She took the lid off the coffin and placed the medicine bun-
lle inside, remembering clearly the proud, painted figure of
he Indian, grateful that she could not see him now in the
larkness. She thought of repainting him, of redoing what
Martin had undone; but she knew she could not do it right.
t would mean nothing. Yet except for the darkness she might
ave tried.

She got down then, leaving the lid partly open, and stood
ooking down the hill the way she had come, seeing it as a
lark impassable jumble of stone and brush; she could hardly
elieve she had come through it. The scene was strange; but
s she stood the strangeness was gone; she was enveloped in
eace and a sense of completion. She could leave then.

## 58

here was a whiteness of cold over the badlands; high rip-
led clouds, red when the dance began, caught now a pale
lumination from the crescent moon low over the eastern
ills. A fine cold frost, a shining breath, descended slowly,
nixing with quiet, rising dust, giving it a faint shine and set-
ling unmelted on the figures of clay, the Silent Ones, invest-
ng them with a light as of life.

Turning Hawk stood within the circle, intensely aware of
he ring of dancers though he saw them but dimly, conscious
f the life of each person who moved across his vision: a liv-
ng hoop revolving, himself at the center, pulled and drawn as
y invisible strings. If he were to fall, the strings would break,
he figures fling outward into darkness. And though he stood
n solid earth, he felt unbalanced, uncertain.

Outside the circle he could see the strange Indians from
ine Ridge, Oglalas, who had come to persuade the people
o give up the dance and return to the agency. And though

he knew their hearts were good, he resented them and had talked against them. But still they waited.

Behind him in the circle he could hear Eagle Voice and the Blue Cloud chanting, drawing dancers from the circle, the first of the evening, to begin their visions. Some had fallen already and lay darkly against the frosty earth. The Blue Cloud was tireless and intense; the visions he led the dancers to were pleasant and of a past, familiar beauty. Since they had made this camp, he seemed to dominate with a strong spiritual power. To the west the butte sloped upward darkly, striped with frost that shone like clouds on darkened skies. Looking upward, Turning Hawk remembered the white buffalo, the white cow; saw the Blue Cloud on the yellow horse ascend the slope, gun held high; the white figure at the top, motionless for an instant and then gone as the gun fired. He shook his head, looking closely at the slope, almost expecting, so real was the memory, to see the horse and rider falling downward.

He could not bring himself to begin: the power he had been given over the dancers frightened and repelled him. It was not the same as that of Eagle Voice or the Blue Cloud he knew. Another spirit moved him, terrifying the dreamers giving them visions of horror and fear.

He would try it once more, hoping it had changed, that he could bring them to the road of light, not darkness. Reluctantly he moved outward toward the dancers, seeing dread move in the eyes of those passing before him. They did not blame him, he knew; the power was above himself and stronger. But they were afraid; they wanted only to see their friends and relatives who had gone before, to talk with them and see them happy in the old ways.

He approached slowly through the gleaming dust, delaying watching the dancers closely in the pallid light. The frost had melted on their hair and faces and glittered there like beads of glass or tears. He was drawn toward them, yet hurt by the fear in their eyes. He took up the song, moving with the dance; but it was a long time before he felt himself possessed by the power. Only a single dancer, a young man called Red Sleeve, had come under his hand when the pause was called for the waking of the dreamers. He waited, himself in dread till Eagle Voice touched Red Sleeve and he awakened to tell his vision.

"I stood in the dance circle but alone in darkness, looking

at the west where the color of red rose high like dust, believing I would see the dancers beyond death. But as I watched, the sky changed: it shone clear, not as dust but as water, still red but a deeper, darker color. It shone and glimmered as the surface of a pool, and I was above, looking down, seeing the faces of many people at the surface. They were far down and dim and yet I knew them as friends. I came nearer expecting to see my parents and all those who have gone before; but it was not so. The faces that looked up at me from the red water were the faces of the living, and strangely, my own face was among them.

"I fell in fear into the red pool, splashless, and it was not blood but dust rising above me, yet I was drowning still; and I awakened."

Seeing Turning Hawk standing over him, Red Sleeve was seized with a violent trembling; he rose and staggered away, moaning softly as he went. Turning Hawk also left, moving to a place among the dancers, knowing he would not enter the circle again as leader . . .

It was morning. Outside the lodge Turning Hawk could hear voices, the strange ones of the Indians from Pine Ridge speaking quietly and calmly; those of his own people, sharp and defiant. They were waiting for him, he knew, and yet he did not move.

Farther off, he could hear voices in mourning, the people of Drifting Crane, who had died in the dance. He had fallen early and at the end of the dance he was still unmoving. They had looked more closely and found his face white with unmelting frost. The mourners were moving away, their voices dying and lost in the cold air.

He went out then to talk and hear the arguments again. But he was impatient and angry; the arguments would be the same, he knew, and at the last, nothing would be settled.

"It is true," the strangers' leader, Black Pipe, said, "the white man is a thief and a liar; he has taken our land with big promises to pay and has paid us nothing. But his numbers are many. He has defeated us in war and we cannot fight again. But some few of his number speak for us. Perhaps these promises he will keep; his councilors are slow. In this there is a small hope of life. But to stay and starve or be shot down like dogs—there is no hope in this."

There was a moment of silence and Eagle Voice spoke.

"I have read a white man's newspaper that says, 'If the army would kill a thousand or so of the dancing Indians there would be no more trouble.' Perhaps they are rounding us up as they do their cattle, to make the shooting easier. I would rather die in the open chase like the buffalo than be corralled and slaughtered."

"It cannot be an open chase," Black Pipe said. "His soldiers surround us now. It is true they cannot follow us in the badlands. But starvation will drive us at last into his corrals; he has only to wait. So there is not even the choice of how we will die; only the hope that he will keep his promise."

The Blue Cloud spoke now, in signs. "We have the hope of the dance. The new earth will come and the white man be no more; until then we have the spirit clothing to protect us. No white man's bullet can pierce it."

"I cannot believe it," Black Pipe said. "We have guns among us. Is the shirt defense against these?"

Several answered in affirmative.

"Would any stand before these guns with only the shirt to protect him?"

He looked around the circle, but no one answered.

Eagle Voice translated the question in sign to the Blue Cloud, who immediately nodded. There was a moment of silent shock.

"If you kill him," Turning Hawk told the strangers fiercely, "you will only leave here wrapped in the red blanket."

"We would not shoot," Black Pipe hastened to assure him. "I only thought there might be some among you who would like to see this tested."

It was a break in the resistance, Turning Hawk could see, and he was still angry. But he could not bring himself to stop it. Only yesterday he would have driven them out of the camp for the suggestion. Now he only stood, immobilized by the feeling that this had happened before; that it was unavoidable now.

For a while there was excited argument. With detachment, he watched, only speaking to quiet the young men when it looked as if there might be a fight. In the end it was agreed on: four of the younger men with good rifles would shoot.

They moved off toward the lodge of Eagle Voice, the Blue Cloud leading. When he reached it, he disappeared inside and in a moment a small smoke emerged from the top and his clear voice rose in song above the sound of the people. The morning was incredibly bright. High thin clouds still hid the sky, a fine frost still fell. But the sunlight through the haze seemed multiplied. The earth was white with the thin powdery frost scarcely discernible to the feet and of a brightness that pained the eye.

The Blue Cloud reappeared, his face freshly painted, a small white bird form in his hair. Coming into the light he blinked his eyes several times as if in amazement, then moved off quietly, in his face a fierce joy. He crossed the camp circle swiftly, though he only walked. But the four young men following broke into a trot, never taking their eyes off him, as if they expected him to disappear.

Turning Hawk followed slowly, deeply involved, yet detached from the scene around him, his sight clouded and wavering.

Beyond the camp circle, among the Silent Ones, the Blue Cloud stopped, and for a moment, even in the brilliant morning light, Turning Hawk found it hard to see him. With the white shirt above, grey buckskin leggings below, and white bird in his hair, he was suddenly a part of the jumble of strange figures. Only his hair, the red of his face like a splash of blood, the blue figuring of the shirt marked his presence. He looked as old and weathered as the rocks.

Behind him a thin tapering spire of sandstone rose, topped by a wide slab of rock that balanced delicately on the point. How it stayed there Turning Hawk could not tell, but it seemed that a breath would send it crashing downward to crush the small figure below. He wanted to shout, to tell him to move, but he did not. The Blue Cloud stepped up onto a square, altar-shaped rock, and from seeming an old man a moment ago, he seemed now a child, small and of an open, eager demeanor.

All the people had gathered in a semicircle behind the four young men. They waited silently and expectantly, almost breathless; yet Turning Hawk sensed in them an anxiety, a hardly suppressed violence.

The Blue Cloud stood with his arms straight out from his body so that the wide shirt was extended on either side of him. From the distance he was square and flat, a figure carelessly drawn against a muddled background.

The young men raised their rifles together and fired.

Turning Hawk saw both sides of the shirt flick, heard the suddenly expelled breath of the people. The Blue Cloud staggered backward and stopped and stood as before; and for just an instant Turning Hawk thought he was unhurt. But his vision had cleared with the firing, and he saw the hole in the shirt.

The Blue Cloud's arms lowered slowly, and he collapsed behind the rock.

A single sound broke from the people, a violent cry of pain and anger. The four young men stood frozen, their guns half lowered. Turning Hawk felt the people turn toward the strangers; and for an instant their lives were in balance.

He turned and shouted, "Wait," and the moment passed. He went forward with Eagle Voice and found the Blue Cloud sitting behind the rock, his arm pressed against his side. Below it, his shirt was soaking blood. He looked at them with the hurt, uncomprehending eyes of an injured child.

The four young men carried him on a blanket to the lodge of Eagle Voice, and Turning Hawk left them, knowing somehow that the man would live. The strangers were leaving, having won their point. He let them go.

In the afternoon Turning Hawk gave the order to break camp. He was reluctant to go, yet he knew there was no other way. Almost a month had passed since they had fled the agency without their rations. The cattle, a few strays picked up on the way, were gone; a few bony horses and dogs were all that remained. All the people were hungry.

A cold wind had risen, filling the air with a thick, stinging mist of dust and snow, as resistant and suffocating as a current of water. It was a bitter, painful camp-breaking. The first drags were packed and ready to leave when a ragged band of Indians came in sight, moving slowly in the storm. They staggered in among the packed horses and stopped, exhausted, hardly able to speak. Turning Hawk knew them at once as Hunkpapas from Sitting Bull's camp on Grand River. They were starving; nearly all had frozen feet or hands. Among friends again, they gave way to weeping, and it was a long time before they told their story: Sitting Bull was dead, arrested and killed by the police. The band had scattered, pursued by soldiers, who were everywhere now.

Immediately the camp was in panic, the decision to move gone. Weeping, frightened women began unpacking their drags and, in the thick driving wind, pitching their lodges again. It would be better to go on, he knew; they could not hold out much longer. And yet he said nothing; his strength was gone. And in his heart he knew there was no choice to make, or any decision.

## ❧ 59 ❧

Westland rode with the officer beside the column of cavalry, the collar of his buffalo coat turned up around his face to keep off the stinging wind and sand. It was cold; dust and sand froze in the hair of the coat where his breath struck, giving it a gritty, wiry feel. It scratched his face like needles when he had to struggle with the horse to keep him facing the wind.

About midday, they struck the badlands beyond White River and halted in the lea of a high terraced butte to wait for the scouts. They dismounted and grained their horses and sat down in a line under the terrace, holding onto the hitching straps.

It was quiet, seeming almost warm and unexpectedly peaceful after the buffeting of the wind. Dust eddied in the air, standing out like a blown flag from the top of the terrace and curling down. Sand dropped steadily around them with the gentle sound of rain.

Below, the flat they had crossed was in stormy turmoil, dust taking the shape of the broken wind currents that dropped off the badlands. The butte above seemed to split the flow so that from either side it flowed inward, converging on the flat and surging back and forth, whirling and twisting. Lines formed on the right and left and moved out like waves or lines of marching soldiers; met and broke, showing for an instant the interference pattern of waves crossing, then scattering in little puffs that diffused in the distance to a wall of dust.

"By God, it's a hell of a day to be huntin' Injuns," the officer, a major, complained. "They got no more sense than animals, draggin' their families around in weather like this."

291

"Do you think they like it any better than you?" Westland asked.

The officer looked at him blankly. "What the hell they doin' it for then?"

"I don't know. Because they're afraid of the army, I suppose. Or, more likely, because they're starving. But as long as they're coming in by themselves why bother them?"

"Orders. I got orders to bring 'em in, that's why. If they give me the slip like they did old Summers, I'll catch hell, that's why. I thought you wanted to get in touch with 'em, too."

"If they come in, I'll see them anyway. I don't think they ought to be crowded any more. It's just a feeling I have, that's all."

"With feelings like that, you'd make one hell of a soldier. Well, all you got to do is tell 'em we don't intend to hurt 'em. And we don't. All they got to do is cut out this damn fool dancin' and everything is gonna be all right. The army may be rough on 'em, but at least we won't starve 'em like the agents and the Society of Indian Friends."

"Just keep them in stockades until they die off from natural causes the way Sheridan wanted to do?"

"I don't think you like the army, do you? Hell, it was the traders and buffalo hunters that ruined these Indians. The army just comes in and cleans up when a mess develops."

They did not have long to wait. The scouts came in from around the butte, Cheyennes dressed in cavalry uniforms. They had found the Indians, coming out of the badlands. If they held their present trail, they would cross the flat below.

"That's damned white of them," the Major said. "All we got to do is wait and they'll fall right into our laps. When the time comes, we'll mount up and head 'em off. Nothin' to it."

Waiting, Westland climbed the butte with the Major and from the point watched the Indians come down a small valley that opened out onto the flat. They were spread out a long way back on the trail, moving in little groups that appeared and disappeared in the currents of dust. There were no wagons or buggies, only packed horses and drags. Some of the Indians carried packs. There were even a few dog travoises, the overloaded animals huddling along at the heels of their owners, hardly ever appearing through the sheet of ground dust.

They came slowly, driven by the wind at their backs, bent over, heads bowed. One of their scouts passed close below the point of the butte, but he did not even look up. He was bowed over the horse, blanket pulled over his head, fluttering raggedly in the wind.

Westland had been here before, he remembered, had camped with the Indians in this little valley on the trip to the cattle hunt. The memory came clear: the white flat at the head of the valley, the painted, feathered Indians, the ceremony of the scouts. And, strangely, the memory was clearer than the scene he watched; it had the reality of waking, and this, dim and dust-darkened, the reality of dream.

He drew back behind the point, shaking his head, clenching his hands to quiet their trembling. But the feeling of dream persisted. He closed his eyes and for just an instant was astride a horse driving ponderously down, a wailing, like wind, in his ears. He opened his eyes, remembering the dream of the horse, and thrust it from his mind with a distaste that was almost nausea. He looked once more at the straggling Indians through the white dust that rolled and roped above them and turned away, tears in his eyes, the taste of the bitter dust in his throat.

For the moment he was sorry he had come—he could have waited at the agency. But the new agent—there was still another since he had left—had asked Westland to come with the troops, thinking his presence would reassure the Indians. He had heard also that this band was to be shipped to a military post instead of being returned to Arrow Creek. So he had come, anxious to see his friends again after the long absence —he had left Arrow Creek in May, spending most of the time since at Pine Ridge, though in the fall he had made another trip to Nevada. On Christmas Day, hearing there was a new agent, he had returned to Arrow Creek.

He might have known what to expect, he thought. It was the same at Pine Ridge, the ghost dancers moving reluctantly into the agency, driven by starvation and cold, in constant terror of the troops surrounding them. The most ardent of the dancers, those led by Crow Dog, Two Strike, Kicking Bear, and Short Bull, had already come out of the badlands and were camped near Pine Ridge. These that Westland now watched were among the last to come in.

The officer had already started back down the butte. Westland followed, catching up just as he gave the order to mount. The troops rode out at a gallop, in single column, drawing a long line of white and blue across the flow of the wind. When the last riders were clear of the butte, the line stopped and formed facing the Indians.

It was a while before the first Indians noticed the soldiers. And when they did, they only stopped, straightening their bodies from the bent, enduring posture, immobilized, as if all their strength were consumed in resisting the storm that pressed them onward. Groups from behind caught up, stopping beside the others, spreading to a wide, ragged spot on the flat. In a moment, over the wind's rush, Westland heard a sound of many voices in a sad, lost singing.

"What in hell is that?" the Major asked.

"Death songs."

"You mean they think we'll attack them?"

"What do you think?" Westland asked angrily. "It's your job, isn't it?"

"No, by God, not a poor, pitiful bunch of animals like that." The Major rode off in a huff to where the Cheyenne scouts waited, and in a moment these rode forward under a white flag.

The Indians surrendered quietly when they found they would not have to give up their guns.

"They still don't trust us," the Major said later. "They say all they have to eat is what they can hunt; as if they thought we'd starve them or shoot them down."

They moved on, the Indians scattering out along the trail as before but flanked now on either side by cavalry. Westland did not join them; he rode off to the side by himself, ashamed of his own comfort—the buffalo coat, the fat, strong horse—among the ragged, struggling Indians. From a distance he picked out Little Wound riding with a pack on the pinto horse Westland had given him. The animal was hardly recognizable, plodding with lowered head, tail and mane blown forward with the wind. Beside the pinto Blue Fawn walked, leading two horses with packs.

The band moved without words, the only sounds the grinding and chattering of the drags, horses' hoofs, and hardly audible, the crying of small children in their travois baskets. All, even the mounted soldiers, moved bowed over, enduring under the cold wind as under some universal grief, the darkness of dust moiling above them.

They traveled steadily, crossing White River and reaching

the forks of the trail in early evening. Some of the Indians tried to take the trail to Arrow Creek but the Major stopped them, giving no explanation but pointing west along the trail to Pine Ridge. The leaders moved on but a group of young men farther back in the column tried to leave the ranks and go along the wrong trail. They were immediately surrounded by troopers with rifles aimed.

There was sudden, explosive panic. Women screamed and, leaving their horses, ran off the trail, dragging crying children. The men caught the loose horses and moved off in another direction, not trying to fight but drawing the troops away from the women.

The Major rode back and forth frantically, shouting at his men not to shoot, trying to herd the Indians together again. Soldiers, trying to head off the running women, rode back and forth in front of them, waving their arms, shouting like cowboys. But the women ran blindly, even bumping head on against the horses.

Westland saw a woman with two children fall exhausted and crawl under a sagebrush. She hid the children under her robe and lay face down on the ground. In a moment the drifting sand and dust had colored her robe till she was hardly visible.

Beyond the men he saw Little Wound alone, riding off at a gallop, two troopers already in pursuit. The pony was fast and it took them a long stretch to catch up. And when they did, he only lit out in another direction. Westland could see the troopers pointing back toward the bunch, not knowing the boy was blind. He rode out at a gallop, seeing the men chasing the pony back, whipping it with their quirts. He cut in front of them and collided with one, jumping clear of the saddle as his horse went down. He got up, caught his horse and, without looking at the fallen trooper, turned and searched for Little Wound till he saw him among the Indians again.

The trooper had been stunned; he got up now swearing, looking at Westland as if he might jump him. Westland watched, saying nothing. He had hurt his shoulder in the fall and it was aching and throbbing; yet he felt elated, for an instant relieved. He waited with a kind of joy for the soldier; and was immediately ashamed of himself, seeing the futility and inconsequence of what he had done. He forced himself to smile at the soldier. "I'm sorry I upset you. I know the boy on the pinto; he's blind."

The soldier turned away and, for a moment, Westland thought he was ashamed. But, mounting, he gave Westland a look of contempt. "Damned Injun lover," he muttered and rode off.

The Indians were scattered out at least a quarter of a mile. He could see women disappearing into a gully parallel to the trail where the troops could not follow on horses. The men and boys were still together, quiet now.

The Major was rounding up his troops, shouting orders. In a little while he had them in formation again, lined out along the trail. He gave the order to ride and, surprisingly, continued, with all the troops, along the trail. Westland fell in with the last men and, looking back, saw one of the Cheyenne scouts talking to Turning Hawk.

The trail crossed Red Hail Creek to the right of where the women had gone, close to the gully where it joined the creek. Beyond, the troops turned off and, in a little flat, dismounted and began making camp.

Across the creek, Westland saw the Indians coming slowly along the trail. When they crossed, the women and children were with them again. They turned off and made camp between the soldiers and a ravine that came in from the west. Westland was unsaddling his horse when the Major joined him.

"I apologize, Major," he said. "There could have been trouble back there; I admire your restraint and understanding."

"Well, it worked, didn't it? I knew it would. Hell, they're like animals in a trap—scared to death. I don't know why but they are. They ain't logical at all."

"Is anyone logical about feeling? I think I'm as logical as anyone, but you know their feeling even infects me. Where's the logic in that?"

The officer shrugged, looking at Westland curiously, and went on about his work.

As darkness came, the wind died. But in the air the dust still drifted and swirled, sifting downward, muffling all sound like fog or snow. Around the camp, fires burned yellow and orange like little sunsets through the dust. The quiet was startling after the wind. In Westland's ears was still a rushing sound; his body still felt bowed under the invisible force.

was not a change, he felt, but a lull; it would begin again, suddenly and with renewed fury.

It was late when he went to the Indian camp, taking with him the bundle of presents he had brought from Nevada on his last trip, things given him by the Indian Messiah: small, elliptical cakes of red paint from the sacred mountain, magpie feathers, piñon nuts, a rabbitskin robe. He would be glad to see his friends again, he knew; and yet he moved reluctantly, feeling himself cast in an ambiguous role.

He passed the first lodges, seeing at the center of camp a fire around which a large group of Indians were gathered. As he approached the whole group rose and came forward to meet him. They gathered around him quietly, waiting for him to speak; but something in their attitude—an intense respectfulness, almost reverence—kept him silent.

One moved out of the group and approached him slowly, one arm outstretched, in his eyes an odd, hypnotic shining. He paused and Westland recognized him as the Arapaho who had been on the cattle hunt. His face was pale and he moved stiffly as if wounded. When his hand almost touched Westland's face, he began releasing his pent-up breath in short bursts, "Hu, hu, hu," swaying his body rhythmically.

Only then Westland realized that the Indians knew he had been again to see the Messiah, though he had told no one. He understood his own reluctance: he was a priest in their eyes; he could not change it now. The Arapaho touched his face lightly and dropped his arm. He moved unsteadily back among the Indians, looking as if he might faint.

Eagle Voice came forward and, grasping Westland's hand, looked into his eyes for a long time, as if to find some profound truth or reassurance.

"We are glad you have returned," he said finally, "white man though you are. We know you have been to the land of Our Father; take pity on us and give us word of Him."

Westland spoke briefly, pausing for Eagle Voice to interpret, trying to weigh the significance for them of his descriptions of the Messiah and the dances he had seen, but he could not. He watched himself as from a distance, seeing clearly the ambiguity of his position. But he was not amused. Their feeling touched him, giving to his role a meaning deeper than logic.

When he finished, Eagle Voice again took his hand and, facing the west, prayed silently, lips moving, tears standing in his eyes. Finished, he stepped back to a place in the crowd and another came forward to take Westland's hand and in the same manner pray. He stood quietly, holding his face impassive as the Indians prayed, understanding little of their prayers, only that, having seen the Messiah, he was, in their eyes, invested with grace.

A long time he stood, till the last Indian present had taken his hand and prayed, involved in their feelings till he was himself on the verge of tears. But it was not mystery he felt, or reverence, but a dark, profound grief.

When they had finished, he unwrapped the presents, producing first the bag of piñon nuts and holding them out. The Indians filed by him, each taking one, thanking him profusely.

He could stand it no longer. Blindly he put the rest of the presents into the hands of Eagle Voice and fled. And in the darkness between the two camps, he stood and wept.

## 🐉 60 🐉

Martin could not sleep; though he had ridden all the way from the agency with the reinforcements the Colonel had brought, arriving in the night cold and exhausted, the strangeness and a palpable tension in the air would not let him relax. After a brief interview with the Major who had just captured the Indians, the Colonel had gone to sleep immediately and breathed now in long even snores, a brassy, windy sound like horns in the distance.

They had arrived in moonlight, coming down from the hill above the little flat, and he had seen the camp clearly, though without detail or coloring, a delicately shaded drawing that hung now in the darkness above him. The sounds outside the tent he could place clearly on the picture—the relayed call of the sentries, moving like a point of light, encircling both the soldiers' camp and the ring of tepees near the ravine; he could even tell when the call passed through the ravine by the softened, slightly echoing sound, could follow it along the other side, then back again.

He could hear singing in the Indian camp, though there were no drums, only the low, repetitive strains of the Ghost Dance songs. On the picture, he saw the Indians as a circle around the dead tree from which the white flag drooped; in darkness the tree shone, lit by the singing.

From somewhere in the square of soldiers' tents a voice rose—he could not place it exactly. It seemed to float and move in the air like St. Elmo's fire. He felt that someone was singing in his sleep, a Christmas carol in a strange tongue. The children at the agency had sung it on Christmas three days before, but in English. He tried to remember the words but could not and lay back listening, little chills moving in his blood as the voice rose and fell, lonely and plaintive in the night. It faded till he could no longer hear it; and he lay wondering doubtfully if it had been real.

But the singing in the Indian camp continued, keeping him suspended between sleep and waking till almost morning. And when he sank at last in sleep, he was jerked upward violently by a bugle blowing reveille.

The Colonel had already gone; he was talking with someone outside the tent, and Martin, listening, could detect in his voice the same brassy tone of his snoring. He dressed quickly and stepped out into cold early light and found the Colonel surrounded by officers. Martin did not join them but stood apart, hearing bits of talk and laughter, knowing when their voices lowered now and then that they were aware of his presence. He was surprised by the appearance of the camp in daylight; it was ugly and unrelieved, the colors harsh against the dull monotones of the landscape: blue uniforms, wagons and ambulances blue with black wheels. The camp was in a small flat west of Red Hail Creek. South of the flat a ravine curved down out of the hills, ending at the creek below. Along it, beyond the circle of tepees, the ragged scrawny herd of Indian ponies grazed. North and west a low knoll rose and around its base the horses of the cavalry were picketed, sorrels, bays, greys, and blacks; fat, short-haired, and big compared to the Indian ponies. Troopers watered and fed their horses to a series of bugle calls, a stiff, mechanical ceremony.

Beyond the creek a few log cabins of a permanent Indian camp were scattered, windows and doors gone or broken, roofs caved; above them the low grey hills of winter rose toward the horizon.

The soldier camp was busy; fires sent up smoke in thin,

white stalks; bugles, shouting, horses nickering filled it with sound. But the Indian camp was quiet; a few Indians stood by their lodges staring at the soldiers.

The sun rose through mists, touching the lifeless hills, the smoky tepees of the Indians, the white tents with tones of flesh, a living color Martin had never seen before on the land, for an instant joining them. But as the sun rose, the color died and he could not credit even the memory.

He had a silent breakfast with the Colonel and a reporter. When they were finished, he stood with them outside while the Colonel took over the command from the Major who had captured the Indians the day before. To Martin's surprise, Westland was with the Major. When the Major had made his report, they stood talking informally.

"I don't think, sir," the Major said, "that we should try to disarm them now. When they're among the other Indians at the agency and have food, they'll give up their guns with no trouble. They're scared crazy now. They've been refused their rations and have nothing to eat except what they hunt."

"Major, how these Indians feel is none of my affair. My orders are to disarm them and take them to the railroad where they can be shipped to a military post till all this fuss is over. I intend to do just that—and no nonsense."

"Sir," the reporter asked, "do the Indians know of this order?"

"It's possible they do—I haven't kept it secret. What difference does it make?"

"They might decide to die," Westland said, "like the Cheyennes at Fort Robinson."

"You mean fight? That bunch of whipped dogs? You ought to be a reporter and write wild-west stories for the newspapers."

"It isn't a matter of defeat; if they believe they are being disarmed just to be starved or shot down, what do they have to lose?"

"That's nonsense; they can't believe that. After all, we're Christians here, not savages. What we're doing is for their own good, even if they don't know it. If we leave them armed, they might start trouble. In any case, there's no room for argument; I have my orders and I intend to carry them out."

The Colonel spoke with a finality that broke up the conversation. And though Martin did not especially like the man, he felt a reassurance in his certainty. He knew what he was doing; he had authority. And as he deployed his troops, Martin was even more impressed by his efficiency.

There was a flurry of bugling through the camp, officers shouting, troops saddling and mounting and forming in line. Two troops, black and sorrel, in column of twos, crossed the ravine and formed in extended order east of the Indian village, followed by the mounted Indian scouts, who formed nearer the ravine. A troop of greys moved to the north of the village near the creek. A bay troop lined up at the foot of the knoll on top of which the detachment of artillery had already set up four Hotchkiss machine guns. Two troops of dismounted men marched to the space between the two camps and formed a right angle, the point toward the Indian village, and stood at attention. All the movements were even and controlled with an impersonal, machine-like precision that frightened Martin at the same time that it reassured him.

The Indians had gathered silently under the white flag in the village, their faces dark and expressionless as they watched the maneuvers of the cavalry surrounding them. They were drawn together in a round compact group, touching each other as if for protection. Above the noise of the camp he thought he could hear a low moaning, a faraway sound of grief or an animal in pain, but he could not place its source. He could not even be sure he heard it.

When the troops were in place, the Colonel and several officers gathered in the space between the camps in front of the V formed by the dismounted troops. Martin and Westland were both back near the tents, though apart. The Colonel turned to Westland now and pointed to the knoll where the Hotchkiss guns were mounted.

"You can go up there with the Captain in charge," he said shortly. "You'll be safe there and out of the way. I can't have any sympathizers here encouraging them to argue."

Westland turned without answer toward the knoll; and Martin felt a quick satisfaction, as if he had somehow defeated a rival. But in a moment he followed part way up the hill, not wanting to be in the way himself.

An interpreter walked to where the Indians were gathered and returned with Turning Hawk, who carried a pipe, held up conspicuously. He coughed continually as he conferred with the Colonel, and his voice was so low that Martin could not hear it from where he stood. After talking with the Colonel, Turning Hawk went back alone to the village and returned with the men and boys. They all sat down, forming a crescent in the throat of the V made by the troops. Their blankets were drawn tight around them, their faces painted as if for the Ghost Dance.

The Colonel spoke, though Martin could not hear what he said. A group of Indians rose and went back to the village, returning after a tense interval with two guns. They put these on the ground and returned to their places in the crescent. The Colonel spoke to them angrily and, through his officers, ordered the troops up close to the seated Indians. The troops had been formed at right angles; but as they moved up, the lines bent to the shape of the crescent. They were so close they were almost touching, guns angled down at the Indians.

In the village, the moaning sound Martin had heard became a wailing of women. He saw them gathered under the soiled flag, their faces vivid with fear.

A detachment of troops moved to search the tepees, marching to the village in rectangular column, then spreading out around the circle. He saw the Indian men stir; the women drew closer together, except for a few who, on the approach of the troops, had run to their tepees. The soldiers, entering, sent them out again. Above the sound of the wailing he could hear the shrill voices of the protesting women. From some of the tepees he saw furniture flung—pots, blankets, even medicine bundles and tripods. He saw one soldier stoop to enter a lodge; a woman standing by the entrance kicked him behind and he sprawled inward. He emerged instantly and seized the woman by the hair and the two of them rolled on the ground. Some of the troopers came back carrying an assortment of guns which they stacked by the officers' tents.

There was a new sound now, a high shrill whistling that seemed to come from the seated Indians. From a horn of the crescent he saw a painted Indian rise and move in a circle, blowing a whistle; saw him stoop, then straighten, and above his head a puff of dust bloomed.

Some of the seated Indians were singing, not the songs he had heard in the night but low, tense, humming songs of uncertain melodies that he knew were death songs. He heard the Colonel's voice raised suddenly and harshly above the wailing and singing; but it did not reassure him now.

The painted Indian returned to his place in the crescent; at the same time one of the seated Indians made a quick,

rking movement. A feather of smoke stabbed toward the
fficers. And as the report reached Martin, fire and smoke
urted from the troopers' guns into the crescent of Indians;
e sound struck him with incredible violence.

The solid group of Indians was changed instantly to a tan-
ed, writhing mass, the living springing upward to throw off
eir blankets and rush with clubs and knives against the
ry guns, the flung arms and legs of the fallen clutching at
em as they passed over.

Martin could not move or cry out, and yet his hands and
ms jerked with the sound of the firing convulsively and
ithout volition. Above him the Hotchkiss guns burst into
und, and he thought the gunners had gone wild and were
ing into the melee of troops and Indians below; then he saw
e nearest tepees seized as by violent wind, cave, and catch
e; the mass of women and children under the white flag
umpled and scattered, as slowly as worms untangled from
knot, leaving at the center writhing, curling bodies that
emed to seek cover in the earth.

Shells streamed over him, a ceiling of angry flight; the
und of the firing brazen, bursting, beating his eardrums.
nd over the monstrous, mechanical noise, an animal sound,
screaming hardly audible but more terrible than the guns,
e agony of the wounded.

From the knoll on his right the bay troop swept downward,
bers drawn, toward the shattered group of women and chil-
en, who struggled with dream-like haste and slowness
rough the pony herd toward the ravine, leaving a trail of
llen that the guns caught. The troop struck the running
omen, sabers flashing in the sun; the fire of the cannon
oved back across the village, away from them, following a
nch of running ponies, dropping the ones behind, smash-
g them to earth with gigantic power.

The bay troop swept on, leaving a swath of fallen, turned
a blue and bay curve at the edge of the ravine, and gal-
ped single file along it.

The women still on their feet were running toward the
oopers now as if blind; behind them the wounded crawled,
me dragging limp or struggling children.

Martin was running now, not knowing what had started
m. His legs moved puppet-like; he was afraid, yet he could
t stop or change direction. He ran toward rattling rifle fire,
are dimly of a white-shirted Indian running ahead of him

303

pursued by a swarm of blue troops. He passed the hoarsely shouting Colonel, seeing beyond him the crescent of dead Indians, at its edge a few blue-coated troopers, dead. He passed a bleeding Indian writhing snake-like toward the pile of bodies under the flag.

His legs stopped then; and beside him a white-shirted Indian rose up. Part of his face was shot away; blood ran from his throat and his eyes were bloody; but he was singing. He staggered toward Martin, knife in hand, face fiery with blood and paint, and Martin waited breathless, heart-stopped, unable to defend himself. The Indian was thrust forward suddenly, struck from behind; in the same instant Martin was struck, flung to earth. He tried to stand, feeling no pain, but his legs would not move. Something struck him again as he lay, flashing fire over him, and he lay in silence. But for a little while there was light enough for him to see.

## � 61 🌿

Turning Hawk had been sitting in the council crescent, involved wholly in the wailing of the women, the rising death songs of the men. Behind and on both sides the soldiers closed in a curve like a drawn bow, the metal of the guns cold and glittering. A searcher lifted the robe of Wolf Head, a single rifle fired, and a soldier chief screamed, hit.

Instantly the bow of guns fired.

Turning Hawk, hit in the first volley, sprang up, one arm hanging useless, and turned toward the village, facing a soldier who fired wildly as fast as he could work the lever of his gun. Turning Hawk rushed the soldier, seeing, beyond, the women crumpling under the fire of the cannons. Bullets ripped at him, almost throwing him to earth, but he kept moving and saw doubt and fear whiten in the soldier's face. The gun aimed at his chest and he leaped aside, but it did not fire. He struck with his knife, and the soldier fell, tearing the knife from his hand and he ran on weaponless, thinking only of his daughter and Little Wound. A bullet struck him from behind

304

ind, tearing through his side and throwing him to earth; he
vanted to stop, to lie still. His eyes blurred, and yet he
thought he saw a child struggle up from the bodies under the
flag. He tried to stand but he could not; his legs were numb.

But far off, through air as red as blood, he saw the child
till struggling. He forced himself ahead, bending and straight-
ning his body, worm-like, pain searing his chest with each
move, blood in his throat hot and strangling. Something
truck his back, drawing across it a line of fire; dimly he saw
. soldier move over him and on, a long knife flashing from
is hand. He turned his face to the earth and moved on,
ending, straightening, keeping in vision the bodies under the
lag, a child rising in the fire of the cannon.

A long time later his one remaining hand touched flesh; he
aised his head and dimly saw the bodies of the women, one,
with wild lifeless eyes, holding the severed hand of a child.
Among the bodies he saw the familiar beaded blanket of Blue
Fawn, and after a long time of struggle at the edge of dark-
ess, reached it and found her dead. His heart longed for the
arkness, yet he could not die until he had found the boy.

He tried to move again, but could not; the strength of his
ody was gone. Only his arm would move, and with it he
earched as far as he could reach. Under his daughter's robe
e felt a movement: a small arm reached and drew back. Joy
lled him, and he found the strength to move, to roll over till
e child was between himself and the body of the mother.
e worked his hand under the robe, finding the child held by
e weight of her arm and shoulder, wet in spots with blood.
e felt carefully over the struggling young body and, finding
> wound, caught the small hand and held it, quieting the
>y's panic with the last of his strength. And when the strug-
es stopped and the hand touched his in attention, he made
e pushing sign for wait, again and again and again, as he
nk nightward at the world's edge.

Little Wound had been standing with his mother at the center of camp, surrounded by women, enclosed in subtle, female odor. But he was not comforted. Above it the odor of fear was pervasive and strong. He wanted to escape its suffocation but could not—his mother held him, fingers digging sharply into his shoulder. He touched her hand to remind her to loosen it, but when she ignored him, he lifted her fingers one by one and pushed her hand down. It hung stiffly at her side, fingers still curved.

The fear grew suddenly. He touched her face with finger tips, finding her lips parted, feeling a sound escaping that was neither crying nor singing but a strangling as if her breath were constricted by hands at her throat.

A rifle shot crashed, then a volley rapid as a ripping of canvas. His mother stiffened, screaming, and seized his arm with unbelievable strength, lifting him off the ground. In the same instant something struck the ground near him in a quick succession of explosive blows, stinging him with rocks and sand, each one striking closer, releasing a dusty, powder smell. One of the women touching him was struck and flung violently away. The explosions softened, muffled by her flesh, flinging in the air a smell of blood.

His mother was hit and thrown backward, but she did not let go. He was flung to earth, crushed breathless by her weight as she fell above him. He struggled to escape, then stopped; took all his strength just to breathe. He could not waste fighting. He felt the shells walking with heavy impact on the earth, softening sporadically as they struck flesh. One struck the earth by his head and he stiffened, expecting the searing metal in his body; instead he felt his mother jerk again and relax shuddering as the metal feet walked on.

Blood drenched his neck and the side of his face with her stifling odor and he thought he would drown. In panic he struggled snake-like from under the main weight of her body and stopped, breathing free with only her arm and shoulder across his body at the waist. He rested and struggled again but he could not escape; besides the weight of her arm on his back, her body lay on his blanket, holding him fast. He struggled until he was exhausted, then lay sobbing in a terror of restraint, the odor of death heavy in the unmoving air.

He felt the heavy shells striding far off toward the ravine; rifle fire still chattered, seeming light and harmless after the cannon; it chattered from the soldiers' camp, then nearer and all around him, going on in the distance. He felt the horse herd stampede through the village, the pounding of the big shells following them like a runner.

Smoke was in the air—canvas burning, mixing with the odor of metal and blood and death. The big shells walked near again, and again he surrendered to panic. He was still struggling when a hand touched him—he knew it instantly as his grandfather's even though the terror still held him. The hand moved over him, finally catching his hand and holding it quiet.

He stopped struggling then, the fear gone, withdrawing his hand and placing it above his grandfather's, waiting for a sign. The hand moved up, dropping in the pushing sign for wait, repeating and repeating, each time more weakly, ending finally in a jerky meaningless spasm.

He drew his hand away in horror and lay frozen for a long time. When he touched the hand again, questioningly, it was cold and lifeless.

But he did not struggle any more; firing, not heavy now, still shook the earth, and he was afraid. But a power had been given him to resist it. He lay waiting, quiet and determined. He would not give himself easily to death.

🏶 63 🏶

Westland had stood on the hill behind the guns, looking down on the two camps, his vision dimmed as though he had over-exerted. He could see only the groups of Indians and soldiers and no individuals; they were far away and blurred. His eyes were watering so that he had to keep dabbing at them with his handkerchief, and there was an aching tightness in his throat.

He wanted to leave, to walk on down the far side of the hill and shut it all from sight. No one would stop him, he knew. And yet he felt restrained, imprisoned on the hill with the blue-coated soldiers, the glittering, polished guns.

He was feeling this when the wailing began, an eerie, nightmare sound toward which, for an instant, he seemed to fall headlong. Then the sound of rifle fire struck him, clearing his vision. He saw the troopers fire into the crescent of seated Indians, the knives of flame from the gun barrels pointing inward, the smoke white and spreading. The Indians still alive sprang up, revealed in white ghost shirts, rushing forward in smoke to impale themselves on knives of fire.

Near him the machine guns burst into firing, the sound vibrating blows against his body. The one in front of him danced violently, the barrels turning and glinting in the sun. Beyond he saw the shells of all four guns curve down, converging, seeing only then that they were dropping into the huddle of women and children under the flag. These were already scattering, leaving behind a thinning line of dead and wounded. The leaders ran toward the horse herd and his gaze, following, seemed to draw the shells after it; the very women he watched were slammed to earth as if violated by his glance.

He saw the charge of the bay troop cut the line and turn, a red and blue sickle; saw the horse herd stampede through the village, the shells again following his gaze, dropping the running animals violently to earth. He turned wildly to the officer to get him to stop it and found the man wild-eyed, covering him with a pistol. He stiffened, expecting a bullet, but the officer looked away toward one of the gunners. A gun had jammed, and the officer ran over and stood yelling at the gunner, waving his pistol. The gunner worked feverishly, burning his hands every few seconds as he touched the gun barrels.

A few of the women had reached the ravine; Westland could follow their progress by the bunches of troopers riding along both sides, shooting down.

The officer left the jammed gun and ran to one of the others, shouting. In a moment one of the crew brought up a mule and the gun was loaded. The officer ran down toward a rise where the ravine curved; the crew followed and set up

308

the gun to sweep the ravine where the women would have to pass.

The other guns and the rifles below were stopping, and above the ringing of his ears Westland could hear the wild, animal screaming of the wounded. He went down then, moving in a haze, still unbelieving. Something touched his side like a hand clutching and he turned and looked. But there was no one near. He went on down and found most of the soldiers gathering at camp, though far up the ravine he could still hear yelling and shooting. Some of the officers were working with the wounded troopers; the rest were trying to bring order among the men. But these were having little success; a mass of soldiers had gathered beside the wounded, and no amount of shouting would move them.

Westland pushed through the group and found the surgeon moving hurriedly among the wounded. Beyond, he saw the shape of the council crescent formed by the bodies of the dead. There were no living there. At the tips of the crescent, directly across from each other, a few dead troopers lay.

Dead Indians in ghost shirts marked a wide path through the village, where smoke from the burning lodges hung low to earth, drifting off across the ravine toward the hills.

He moved among the dead Indians searching for Little Wound, steeling himself against what he might find. But neither Little Wound nor Turning Hawk was in the crescent. He walked toward the village and was stopped in a moment by a wild commotion among the soldiers. They were scattering in all directions, making no outcry but with such desperate, terrified faces that his own heart constricted. A line of them surged over the wounded, some tripping and falling, causing a fearful moaning and screaming.

An old woman had appeared quietly among the men. She moved now with startling agility, hands stretched forward as in blindman's buff, trying to touch someone. She was faceless; part of her lower jaw was shot away and there was a wide gash across her forehead. Her eye sockets were pools of clotted blood. She had no blanket and the white ghost shirt was a spattered, figureless red. She continued to follow the soldiers, holding out crimson arms and hands, making strange gurgling sounds in her throat. And the soldiers scattered before her, white-faced and silent. One tried to shoot her but another, without a word, knocked the gun out of his hands. The surgeon moved toward her, but retreated, turning again to the wounded troopers, glancing nervously at the woman as she circled.

Westland went back then and intercepted her. Coming near, he spoke to her in Sioux, but she did not seem to hear and kept up the gurgling sounds, continuing to search. He stepped in front of her and held out his hands, steeling himself not to flinch at her wet touch.

When she felt his hands, she stopped and was silent except for the liquid snoring of her breath. She examined his hands carefully, her fingers leaving little prints like the tracks of animals. She came closer, holding her face out as if to see through the clotted blood, and touched his cheeks lightly and tenderly with her fingers. He remembered her then—mother of Eagle Voice. She stepped back, making a sign as if writing in a notebook, and he knew she had recognized him.

"Grandson," she signed, hands a blur of red, "where are my relatives?"

Involuntarily he stepped backward, but she moved with him, touching his hands, waiting for an answer. He looked wildly around at the white-faced, staring soldiers and found no help, only a uniform look of repulsion and fear.

He made the sign slowly and painfully, "Grandmother, gone under, asleep."

She drew away from him with a drowning cry that became a shrill wailing as her throat cleared, and moved off unsteadily toward the smoking village. The ring of soldiers parted widely for her to pass.

The surgeon and the Colonel came forward.

"Did you actually communicate with her?" the Colonel asked.

"Yes. She asked after her people."

He started to move away but the surgeon caught his arm. Reaching forward with a wad of cotton, he tried to wipe the blood from Westland's face. But he jerked away, suddenly angry—and as suddenly calm—and went again toward the Indian village. The ring of soldiers opened silently before him.

The Indian scouts were scattered out along the way the women had gone, standing in little groups, and he knew without seeing that they were guarding a few wounded women and children from the troopers who still hunted along the ravine.

He went toward them, searching among the dead for Little Wound. With no surprise he found Martin lying beside the shattered body of Eagle Voice. The arm of the dead Indian lay across Martin in a grotesquely affectionate way; he saw only then the knife buried in Martin's chest and knew he was dead.

At the edge of the circle of dead under the flag he found Turning Hawk and Blue Fawn, but there was no sign of Little Wound. He went on then hurriedly, unable to search longer among the dead. He approached all the little groups of scouts, looking at the few children they guarded and moving on; none of them was Little Wound.

He went back and, after some argument with the Colonel, was given a wagon and assigned two troopers to gather up the wounded Indians. He filled the bottom of the wagon box with hay and, taking the lines from the trooper, drove slowly among the dead to the first group of scouts.

❦ 64 ❦

Little Wound lay suppressing the urge to struggle. The body of his mother grew cold and stiffened, the odor of blood faded till he could hardly detect it. The firing of the guns stopped and he felt horses and a wagon pass near him, knowing by the heavy, battering hoofs that they were soldiers' horses. Later the wagon passed again, followed by a group of riders far off.

He lay a long time, feeling no vibrations in the earth; still he knew he had to wait longer. His muscles were jerking, rebelling at the restraint of the cold arm across him; but he would not release himself again to panic. It was too soon; soldiers might still be near.

He remembered the ball of beeswax in the pouch at his waist, and his muscles stopped jerking. Joy rose in his heart and, with patience and care, he worked his hand downward, finding the pouch pressed under him. After a struggle he worked it free and drew out the wax.

311

The air under the blanket filled with a sweet, grassy odor that grew stronger as the wax warmed in his hands, reminding him of spring rain and the flutter of wings at finger tips; and, in the same mood, the white woman who had given him the wax.

He kneaded it a long time, attempting nothing, but with his fingers catching the random forms from the changing wax, his mind creating in a way that was like dreaming: a buffalo became a turtle; the turtle, a sweat lodge; the sweat lodge, the whole world, earth flat under a great half-sphere of sky, himself and all living things within it as the turtle within its shell. And, in vision, figures arranged themselves in the circle: animals, trees, a hoop of lodges and, at last, the people; his perception was a hand moving in space, knowing with joy the textures and shapes of all. But as the hand moved, a fear, a breath of chill touched him.

He held tight to the vision. But it changed subtly to the memory of a dream; the circle became a field of light on a yellow plain, far off and dim; and in the field was a hoop of lodges and all the people. Then it was gone, the light receding, growing smaller like the end of a tunnel into which he was drawn swiftly and irrevocably.

Momentarily he was lost in terror, finding himself again as his hands worked with frantic effort on the wax, releasing new odor that calmed him like the touch of hands. He made a sweat lodge, trying to shape the vision as it had been. But he could not. The trees and the animals—he could make these—but not the circle of lodges or the people. He was alone.

He let the thought come over him slowly like icy water filling a pool. But he did not give way to terror again. And after a time he was again lifted, placed under the half-sphere of sky with the animals and the trees. And the earth was a hand holding him. He squeezed the wax into a ball and returned it to the pouch, aware that the air had turned cold. He could feel a wind tugging the blankets that covered him; almost all odor had gone.

Without struggling to free himself, he considered what he would do. It was night, he knew. He had felt no vibration for a long time, so he knew there were no soldiers near. He would have to free himself from the cold arm soon or he would freeze.

He lifted experimentally on the arm, bunching the muscle

of his back under it, and found that he stirred the whole body of his mother. If he could free the blanket, he thought, he could squirm from under the arm.

He remembered his knife and, in a burst of excitement, drew it from his belt and began cutting the blanket where it passed under the body. It took him a long time; the space was cramped, and where his shoulder was pressed against his mother he could not reach with the knife. But when he had cut all he could reach, he found that by straining outward with all his might, he could tear the rest.

When the blanket came free, he tried to move downward; but still the cold arm held him, catching under his shoulder so he could go no farther. He moved back to his first position and tried to go forward, but another body blocked his way. He lay quiet, thinking, then worked back down till his back muscles were again under the arm and, bunching them strongly, felt the arm raise a little. He pulled his elbows close to his chest for leverage, and gradually and painfully worked his knees up under him. The pressure on his back was almost more than he could stand; but he kept working, feeling the arm raise till his knees were all the way under him. His face was pressed against the frozen ground, his neck helping to support the weight on his back.

He moved backward slowly, scratching his face on the ground. But the weight slid down his back and along his shoulders. And at the last moment he jerked backward with all his strength so the arm would not catch his head, and was free.

His mother's beaded robe still covered him; he crawled from under it and stood up, a wind, cold and laden with snow, striking his bruised face, almost taking away his breath. He wrapped himself in the beaded robe and began exploring, moving carefully, keeping his direction by the angle of the wind. He found the spot where his mother's lodge had stood, but there was nothing; only a few poles still stood, burned almost to breaking. Bits of charcoal came away in his hands. Beneath the poles he walked among burned remnants of his mother's furniture, exploring with his feet.

He went around the circle, finding all the lodges down, all burned or partly burned. In some were bodies he did not examine. Coming back to his mother's lodge, he dug among the snow and ashes, finding an unburned parfleche with some dried meat. He took this and found his way back to the

313

place under the flag. He left the meat by the bodies of his mother and grandfather and began searching—for what, he could not tell. But even with a blizzard beginning and a shelter yet to make, he had to know what was around him.

There was snow on the ground, but only around the projecting rocks and the bodies did it have depth; in the lee of these it formed tapering drifts that came over the tops of his moccasins. But they helped him find the bodies of the dead.

All the way to the ravine he searched, hands reaching to touch some living animal or person. The wind pushed at his back, clutching and tearing like unfriendly fingers; he was afraid and yet he did not stop. He went along the ravine till there were no more bodies and stood at its edge, chilled; then, as if awakening, he came back, following the line of bodies to the flag. Here he began gathering blankets for a shelter. He did not like to take them from the dead; and yet he knew that the women, if living, would give them freely.

He found a bundle of blankets and, unrolling it, felt something move and drop softly to the ground. He bent to touch it and was startled to feel warm living flesh; a tiny hand closed tightly on his finger and would not let go.

A feeling of joy and terror filled him; for an instant he wanted to jerk free and run, but he held himself quiet. The hand was pulling gently on his finger; he released the tension of his arm slowly and a small mouth closed warmly on his finger and sucked hungrily. And the fear was gone.

He examined the child briefly—a girl, he found, by the cradleboard and clothing; he wrapped her again quickly though she protested vigorously. Carrying her to the parfleche, he left her while he brought more blankets and searched for sticks to make a frame. He searched for a long time, finding nothing but two rifles among the bodies of the dead at the edge of the soldier camp. He brought these back, not knowing yet how he could use them.

He was cold; his face and feet were numb. And when he thought of the baby, desperation filled him. He thought of taking her and searching the ravine for some cave for shelter. But he could not bring himself to leave the spot. He thought of lying down where he had lain before and covering himself and the baby with all the blankets he had brought. But he was afraid he might sleep and not awaken.

He explored the spot with his feet and found it partly

314

filled with snow. His foot touched his mother's arm, then the arm of his grandfather, both extended nearly across the little space. He lifted his grandfather's hand, raising it high, turning the body on its side. It stayed that way, the hand reaching stiffly as high as his head, fingers spread.

He knew then what he would do; and after a struggle, lifted his mother's arm also, moving the body till the hand was directly across from his grandfather's and extending upward. He tilted the two hands inward till they joined, the stiff, outspread fingers interlocking, making a triangle, the beginning of a lodge.

He leaned the two rifles from the other sides, butts down, tips against the angle of the fingers. The beginning gave him new strength and he fought the wind back to the soldier camp, where he found more guns. He brought these back and leaned them in the spaces between the arms and the other guns, completing the frame. He gathered a pile of stones, then began covering the frame with blankets, using the stones to hold them at the bottom, impaling the top edges on the stiff fingers. He put on all the blankets he could find, interweaving the edges, saving only the one he wore and the ones the baby was wrapped in. Finished, he wound the whole thing with a rope he had found at the soldier camp.

For entrance, he moved a stone and raised the blankets. He put the parfleche in first, then the baby, pushing her ahead of him carefully, finally crawling in himself and replacing the stone.

It was a small lodge; the blankets sagged inward. But in the center he could sit upright. And after the wind, it was warm and quiet. He unwrapped the baby and leaned her cradleboard against his knee, covering her again but leaving her hands and face free. She did not cry but seized his finger again to suck.

With his free hand he opened the parfleche, brought out a piece of dried meat, and began to eat. But the first bite he chewed fine and gave to the baby; she sucked the food happily from his lips.

In the warming air the odor of the child grew, a springtime smell, not yet a person odor, reminding him of grass and the sweet, rich wax. He touched the floor of the lodge and found the snow already melting. The damp earth was giving off a faint, female smell.

He was warm and at peace.

315

## ❧ 65 ❧

The last of the wounded women had been carried into the church; the wagon was gone. Leah stood for a moment outside, gathering her courage, the sting of the frosty air in her lungs oddly pleasant and comforting.

The sky was cold and clear, the stars bright. There was no moon, yet there was a lightness that was more than stars, a faint, ethereal sky shine, glowing over dark hills. Somewhere in the distance a freighter's team bells rang with slow rhythm, a minor chord that brought tears to her eyes, becoming for an instant, with the cold and the night, the atmosphere of her past.

With an effort she moved to the door and opened it, spilling a flood of yellow lamplight into the darkness. She stepped inside, released, closing the door firmly behind her. She was startled by the look of the chapel, though she herself had helped change it. The pews were gone and the floor along the wall was covered with hay. On this were beds of blankets on which the wounded women lay while the doctor moved among them. On arrival they had been numb with terror, as if they expected still to be killed. But once inside they had changed gradually. And in a way she could not analyze, the chapel also had changed, becoming Indian, a pagan sanctuary: the green hay with its sweet earthen odor, perhaps (she knew it now as an Indian smell); pungent wreaths of cedar in the windows; the Christmas tree that still stood, decorated with popcorn and shining strings of rose hips, hawks' bells, and bright bits of glass, itself cedar, to the Indians sacred as a symbol of endless life; and most of all, radiating from the center of the ceiling, a sunburst of yellow streamers—these things she could see and understand; yet they had been here before.

But it was Martin, she knew suddenly, that in the past the chapel had embodied; yet now, even though he had helped with the decorations, there was no sign, no vestige of his presence left, as if dying he had taken with him all his past. Of his strange Biblical fierceness, nothing remained. She was startled by the insight, seeing for an instant her heart as the chapel, emptied now of the past and all its terrors and Martin himself become a figure of a dream lived long ago.

The women, silent when they were brought in, were wailing and moaning in both relief and pain. She moved to help, affected deeply by the crying but thinking it was not as bad as the silent terror had been. Only the women with babies were quiet, unmindful of their own suffering.

There were four babies, all of whose mothers were badly wounded; but only after much reassurance would the women give them to Leah to care for while their own wounds were treated. One by one she washed them and wrapped them in warm blankets, placing them finally near the fire where their mothers could see them.

As she worked, Westland came back from returning the army wagon in which he had brought the women. He came into the chapel and stood beside her trying clumsily to help. She hardly recognized him now in the light; his face was smudged, his clothing covered with dried blood. His eyes were bloodshot and feverish, their expression tense, but his face looked numb.

"You'd better get some rest," she told him. "I'd like to help you, but I can't now."

She was amazed at what she had said, hardly knowing herself what she meant by it. He did not understand her but went on staring at her with blank expression. She pushed him gently toward the stove and he moved away without words as if walking in his sleep.

She had just finished with the babies when the door opened and a blue-coated officer in a high priest-like collar came in—a doctor, she knew, by the green silk sash he wore.

Instantly at the sight of the officer the women were screaming and struggling. One, whose baby Leah had put by the stove, crawled toward it, though her legs were both shot through. Reaching her child, she covered it with her body as though to shield it.

Leah ran to the stove and, sweeping all three of the other babies into her arms, carried them back to their mothers. The officer retreated, beckoning to Leah as he closed the door. She followed resentfully and found him waiting on the steps.

"I came to help," he told her, "but I see there's nothing

317

I can do. Maybe I couldn't stand it anyway—wounded women and children are outside my experience."

He gave her some bottles of beef extract he had brought for the babies and turned to go, looking pale and weak, as if he might faint; and the resentment she had felt for him before faded.

Leah went back to the women and children then. And after a long time she noticed Westland again. He was standing by the stove looking like a sleepwalker. He had taken off his coat and for the first time she saw that his shirt was covered with blood on one side below the waist; with a shock she saw there was a hole in the shirt above the blood. She went over to him, but he did not see her even when she spoke; she touched him quickly, chill moving in all of her body. He started like one awakening.

"You're hurt," she said accusingly. "Why didn't you say so?"

He shook his head. "I'm not hurt."

She pointed to his shirt and he glanced down.

"No. It's someone else's. I helped with the wounded, you know."

"It's from the inside, and there's a hole. You don't believe it yourself, do you? I thought you were just being heroic."

"Not me. I faint if I'm scratched."

He smiled, looking at her for the first time, almost fiercely, his eyes shifting their focus as if his gaze entered her, and her breath caught tightly in her throat and held. With an effort she turned from him and brought the doctor, watching as he undressed to the waist. There was a small hole in the left side of his chest and a red line running around the lower ribs.

"I wasn't even in it," he said with surprise. "I was way up on a hill with the artillery."

"It's happened before," the doctor told him. "A spent bullet; followed the rib around." He traced the red line with his finger, stopping over the muscles of the back. "I can feel it under the skin. It'll come out easy. Do you want morphine?"

"No. I haven't felt it yet. I must be anesthetized already."

"I'll give you a shot anyway. You'll sleep better."

He took the bullet out and bandaged the wound.

Leah helped Westland dress and led him like a somnolent

318

child to a bed of hay. She had to push him gently to make him lie down. He slept instantly and she covered him with a blanket, hurrying in an odd breathlessness. Later the doctor also slept, and she was left alone to watch over all the wounded.

But she was not disturbed. She knew the doctor had done what he could. All the women, even those she knew would die, were resting, momentarily free from pain. Only the babies were awake and stirring. She heated the beef extract with water and fed them, feeling such tenderness for them that her breasts tingled as if she might give them milk.

The woman who had crawled to her child when the soldiers came had moved over near the tree; Leah had covered her and made a bed of hay beside her for the child. She was nursing it now, a full breast as large as the baby's head bared in the yellow lamplight. She was singing softly and the child, eyes closed, sucked lazily, his small brown hand walking on his mother's skin. Above her the tree rose green and living, alight with jeweled rose hips and bright glass fruit. In the air, over the smell of blood and death, was the summery odor of hay, of cedar, of the women, a live earthen incense.

Leah was tired, and yet she had no need of sleep. Within her was a welling, a feeling not so much of strength as of capaciousness and a sense of the beauty she knew over all the horror of the night.

The woman under the tree stopped singing and for an instant their eyes met above the baby. There were tears in her eyes and in Leah's, and between them such a wave of understanding, of woman strength, that suddenly there was no death or terror in all the world.

The woman looked away but Leah still watched; and only after a long time did she notice that her own arms were crossed over her breast as if holding a baby: sign language for love.

In the afternoon Westland rode down out of the hills an
saw from a distance across Red Hail Creek the knoll, t
ravine and, in the little flat, the dark skeletons of th
burned lodges. Where the cavalry camp had been he cou
see nothing. Snow whitened the ground in curving pattern
swept clear of the high spots, drifted in delicate ridges
the low. After three days the blizzard had stopped, and
burial detail had been sent out from Arrow Creek. He cou
see the soldiers between the ravine and the burned lodg
working at a trench; dark earth lay in a long heap at th
side and he could see dirt from many shovels flying up an
out, curving and spreading. He crossed the creek and sa
the ridges made by the bodies of the dead Indians, snov
drifts marking their places, white monuments varied an
fitting.

On the butte southwest, beyond the soldiers, Indians fro
other bands had gathered, sitting their ragged ponies
quietly as statues, looking down.

Beyond the trench Westland saw a wagon moving alor
the ravine, two soldiers beside it loading the dead. As
approached the campsite, another wagon pulled away fro
the trench and came toward him, stopping where the cou
cil had been held. Two of the three soldiers got out an
began loading the bodies, feet breaking the carved lines
the drifts, darkening the snow. Some of the bodies we
frozen to the ground and one of the soldiers brought a crov
bar from the wagon to pry them loose.

Westland stopped his horse and from where he sat
could hear the bodies come loose with brittle, tearir
sounds. The doctor and Leah, following in the buggy, pulle
up and the three of them watched in silence. The soldie
talked as they worked and he could hear bits of their co
versation.

"If they were Christian people, it'd be a job I couldn't do
one said. "I'm kind of a softy myself, got a weak stomach

Alone, he threw the body of a boy into the wagon; it struck with jarring wooden sound on the floor, with arms and legs outstretched. The soldier in the wagon moved it several times before he was satisfied.

"They don't stack worth a damn," he commented. "They ought to be limbed; this way it's gonna take more than one load."

Another wagon came from the trench, driving among the skeleton lodges of the Indian village, stopping where the women had fallen under the flag. Westland watched them begin loading, aware that there was something different in the huddle of bodies since he had seen them last. At the edge, a small conical shape of blankets rose above them, ragged and partly covered with snow, but a suggestion of order in the confusion of death.

One of the soldiers seized the legs of a body beside the one, lifted, and it broke loose suddenly. But an arm was entangled in the blankets. The soldier tugged and swore and finally it came loose, dragging some of the blankets off the one. Westland watched the two soldiers load the body, and as the dark, frost-grained face was turned toward him, he saw that it was Turning Hawk. Looking back at the tangle of blankets he saw movement under them and, as he watched, little Wound emerged, springing to his feet and drawing his knife.

The soldiers, returning, stopped in amazement in front of the boy; and he was aware of their presence. As the soldiers stepped forward, Westland rode toward them, seeing the boy strike swiftly with the knife, slashing one soldier's coat sleeve. The man stepped backward, swearing.

"The little bastard's fierce—watch that knife."

Westland had already dismounted and was running toward them, putting himself in front of the soldiers. But Little Wound did not recognize him. He was striking all around him with the knife, face frightened but determined.

"We'll both jump him," one of the soldiers said.

But Westland turned on them fiercely. "If you touch him, I'll kill you."

The two drew back, one reaching for his pistol. Then they both looked away and Westland saw Leah running toward him from the buggy. She approached Little Wound, moving in a curve to the windward side, waiting for him to catch her odor, Westland knew.

Instantly the boy's face softened. The hand holding the knife dropped to his side; the other reached out tentatively in the questioning sign.

In Leah's face Westland could see the desire to take the child in her arms. But she did not. Instead she spoke to him in sign. He dropped the knife and his hands followed lightly.

"In my heart is daylight; clouds rise."

He followed her hands, and signed, "Will the long knife kill me?"

"No. With me you are safe." She ended with arms crossed pressed to her breast.

The boy's face relaxed, assuming a subtle shining as if reflecting the light of Leah's face. He swayed slightly and she dropped to her knees, drawing him into her arms.

Westland approached carefully, not knowing he wept till as he bent over them, tears fell warm on the back of his hand. Little Wound drew back and touched him in recognition, then turned and, dropping to his hands and knees, burrowed under the blankets, emerging in a moment with a wrapped bundle. He stood with it carefully and folded back a blanket, revealing a small, dark face with sleep-heavy eyes. A tiny hand reached out and seized his finger and drew it toward sucking lips. He gave the child to Leah and stood close to her, hands held near her face as if warming them at a fire; and though she held the baby with both hands, he was included in her embrace.

One of the soldiers had pulled the rest of the blanket off the cone, revealing a woman's arm outstretched, fingers spread. Westland knew, without seeing the face under the snow, that it was Blue Fawn.

A soldier came from the trench to call the doctor—another wagon had brought in some wounded women who had survived the storm. The doctor took his bag of medicines from the buggy and went with the soldier.

"You can get some wood and build a fire," Leah said. "They must be starved. I have some food in the buggy."

Westland rode to the ravine, made a bundle of wood, and dragged it back with his rope.

She was sitting in the buggy when he returned, wrapped in a blanket with the baby; Little Wound sat beside her. She was looking down at the baby, face soft, lips parted; and riding close, he saw her breast bared, the baby sucking with visible content. She looked up at him not with embarrassment but warmth and pride. Her eyes were alight and dreaming, far-focused; and yet they saw him and gave him warmth. He moved slowly and in wonder, building a fire.

Both children were fed, the baby changed and wrapped warmly, still in her cradleboard. Westland put them all in the buggy and, tying his horse behind, drove to the trench to find the doctor. Leaving the buggy at a distance, he found the doctor working with two Indian women, both with small children. He had put them in a wagon near the trench and was dressing their wounds and frozen limbs.

The last of the dead Indians were being unloaded at the end of the trench, then passed on by soldiers to two others below, who stacked them crosswise in the trench.

Westland watched these, one a tall, loose-jointed man with a morose face, the other young with mincing, affected manner. The tall one helped move the bodies with distaste, leaving them where they fell, making no attempt to arrange them in the space. The other was doing most of the work, sometimes moving heavy bodies alone in order to give some touch of order to the confusion. But when the last body had been dropped in, there was still room at the end of the trench; there had been no need of all his care.

The tall one climbed the end of the trench, scrambling up with the help of a friend. The other climbed the sloping hill of bodies, clowning a little. At the top he tried to jump out without using his hands, but a body rolled under his foot. He fell and for a moment was wedged tightly in the side of the trench, held immovably by dead limbs. His face lost its smile and for an instant was caught in a screaming expression, though no sound came. A soldier above him began shoveling dirt on him playfully. The man screamed then in such terror that all the soldiers around dropped their shovels and rushed for their guns. Finding them they looked around fearfully as if expecting an attack.

The soldier who had thrown the dirt reached down and hauled the yelling man out of the trench, slapping his face roughly when he was on his feet. The man stopped yelling and grinned sheepishly. And for an instant there was silence.

From far off on the buttes Westland heard singing, strange mourning sounds that rose and fell, floating overhead like flights of birds. An officer spoke harshly and too loud; the soldiers recovered their shovels and, with desperate haste, began covering the grave.

Westland turned to the doctor and waited. He could see Leah still seated in the buggy, completely engrossed, not looking at the burial. He wanted to return to her and leave. It was not a desire to turn his back on the scene but an intense awareness of life, drawing him into the future. But he waited.

The soldiers finished and loaded their tools. And as they climbed out into the wagons, an old Indian, an army scout, stepped close to the giant grave and, throwing off his blanket and wide hat, stood almost naked in the cold. He held his arms out rigidly like one in a trance and prayed in his own tongue.

"Earth, Grandmother, these your children return to you, as all that are born and live, having but one mother who endures, return. Receive them with tenderness and give them peace—peace above and below and around, still and everliving as the roots of grass and the green trees; quiet, a mother's gift.

"Grandmother, yours are all the beings that have lived and will live; help us, the living, to be to them as relatives.

"Grandmother, have pity on all these your children."

Again, in the silence, thin falls of sound descended from the buttes, sad and winged. Again the officer spoke and the rest of the sodiers climbed into the wagons and departed, one staying with the wagon in which the doctor tended the wounded women.

For the first time, the doctor noticed Westland and looked around till he saw Leah.

"Take the buggy," he said, "and leave me your horse. I'll ride back in this." He extended his hand, gravely. Westland shook it and, without a word, left.

He took the trail to Arrow Creek, but slowly. Where the trail ascended, he pulled off and drove to the top of a windswept rise to look back for the last time.

It was evening now. The sky was clear of cloud; the sun sank and the whole western sky burned red and shining. From the buttes he saw a line of mounted Indians moving down. The flat was quiet; nothing moved. The grave was black against the snow-powdered earth, corners sharp and square. Around it curved a wide path of tracked and muddied snow. The circle of skeleton lodges was barely visible, broken in places where even the poles had burned. For an instant the voice of Turning Hawk came to him, "All that lives is round: the body of a man, the stem of a plant. The sun and the sky, the earth and the moon are round as a shield. A circle bounds the edge of the world where the four winds travel and is the shape of the whirlwind. The day and the night and the moon circle in the sky; the seasons of life and death follow. It is a symbol of life and the world and time."

The Indians reached the flat and gathered around the grave, forming a broken ring, and he could hear faintly the sounds of their mourning.

He gave the lines to Little Wound and climbed out of the buggy and, facing the Indians, held his hands outstretched, in his heart not words but a silent praying. He stayed till the moment passed and turning found Leah beside him. In the buggy with the sleeping baby, Little Wound sat, serene and knowing.

East, the frozen land warmed in a red light. From between two hills round and female as breasts, a stream flowed, black against white, tinged with red from the evening sky, luminous, alive. Leah was looking up at him, on her face the same living light that was on the earth. His breath was forced out of him violently, held by her beauty; his vision blurred till she seemed to merge with the earth, the far-curving breasted hills. He was drawn toward her and within her, joined and lifted, carried in a swift flowing, a river, a wind, death like the past falling away.

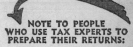